Your Life
WILL HAVE YOU
Back
ELLY MAGDALUYO

For my grandpa
who supported whatever I pursued;
be it writing, reading, music,
or shingling a roof with him.
You are deeply missed.

Your Life

WILL HAVE YOU

Back

Chapter 1

Somewhere in Minnesota

I walked down the side of the county road; one foot in front of the other, for almost two thousand miles. I'd left Oregon nearly four months ago, and it was now almost summer. I wasn't some crazy drifter; one day, I went for a walk to clear my head and didn't stop. I had just enough money on me to get the things I needed, but I was going to have to find a job soon. If I wasn't careful with the money I had left, I wouldn't be able to get a place to live.

I watched as my worn-down shoes touched the poorly paved road, staying to the right of the faded white line—as much as I could without falling off the unguarded edge. Tall trees towered above, casting shadows on the road. I looked up to see the trees with their leaves tussling in the quiet air, while small pieces of light pushed through the gaps. There was a small drop off on the side of the road with a creek that rolled over jagged rocks. The water was clear and sparkled as little pieces of sunlight glinted off the surface.

"Do you need a ride into town?"

I jumped with a gasp and looked toward the sound of the voice. I hadn't been paying attention. A pickup drove slowly next to me as I walked. The light blue paint was faded, and the white-wall tires were worn. It was an old Ford from the seventies and the man inside was probably in his thirties. He had dark gold hair and green eyes under a slightly fur-rowed brow. He didn't appear to be some creepy pervert like the hundred other guys that'd stopped me, but that didn't mean he wasn't.

I shook my head and mentally braced myself to run. "No thanks," I answered just loudly enough to be heard.

I'd jump down to the creek and go through the trees if I had to. By the time he got out of the truck, I'd have a good lead. My legs were well prepared after the stretch of miles I'd traveled, so I had an advantage.

"You realize town is about twenty miles from here, right?" His eyes narrowed.

I nodded. One more step back and I wouldn't have to jump into the creek, I'd fall and bust my tailbone on a rock.

"You can ride in the back if it makes you feel better." His voice was quieter than it had been before. Smoother. "As long as you're not allergic to dogs."

I looked in the bed of the old pickup; it was scratched and dented from years of use. There was a gray and tan spot-ted Australian Shepherd that sat happily as he sniffed the air. He looked friendly, and I could always jump out of the bed of the truck if something didn't feel right... and I *was* tired.

I nodded. "Thanks."

The guy waited for me to hop in the back and sit down

before he started down the road. The dog hardly cared I was there, it just panted happily. After a few minutes, it moved closer and laid its head on my lap. It was the softest dog I'd ever felt. I stroked its ear and watched as the countryside morphed into a charming small town. We passed a sign that read, "Welcome to Red Wing". I remembered seeing it on a map at a gas station early this morning. It was the last town before Wisconsin, and my plan had been to walk up the Mississippi River to the St. Croix River, all the way up to Stillwater.

I watched the town go by, with old brick buildings that looked like they belonged to a Western movie. The people seemed active. They just meandered around, something I hadn't seen much of anywhere else. I watched as two old men sat on a bench in front of the post office, just talking to one another. There were teenage girls with smiles on their faces as they walked down the sidewalk of the main street. It was nicer than I'd expected. Most of the smaller towns in Minnesota had been either industrial, or out-right dumpy.

We pulled in the parking lot of a hardware store and I hopped out of the back of the truck. The dog stood with its front paws on the side of the bed and whimpered while he shook his butt. Poor thing didn't have a tail, so I imagine he felt he had to compensate by wagging his entire hindquarters.

"Thanks for the ride," I said quietly to the man as he got out of the truck.

He nodded.

I walked toward the main street and looked both ways down the open road, preparing to cross.

"Hey, what's your name?" the man called after me.

I stopped and turned around, holding my hand up to block the sun. "Holly."

"It was nice to meet you, Holly." His voice was different—like we'd had a long and pleasant conversation. I wondered why that was.

I gave a small, shy wave out of politeness and turned around.

I walked to the nearest café and sat down in a booth. Everyone stared at me, so I looked down at the menu and waited for the waitress to approach. My face didn't seem to be plastered on the news on this side of the country, but I still needed to be careful.

"You look like you haven't eaten in days, Hun. What can I get you?" The waitress pulled one of three pens from her hair as she stood at the side of the table. She was older with a loose bun behind her head.

I looked at the clock. It was just before eleven.

"The lumberjack breakfast," I answered quietly as I put the menu back in the holder.

"Anything to drink with that?"

I shook my head. "Just water."

"I'll get you some coffee too." She smiled, then walked back toward the counter.

I picked up the newspaper on the edge of the table and pulled it apart to find the job ads. I needed to find more money, and I needed something that wouldn't require me to fill out any paperwork. I didn't want to be found.

As I sat there reading through the help-wanted ads, the bell on the door jingled and in walked the man who had given me a ride into town. I hid my face behind the paper.

"Good morning, Noah. Coffee?" the waitress asked

sweetly.

"Yep." His voice was different again. Happier. Why did he sound so different every time he spoke?

I stole a glance over the paper to find him standing in front of me.

"Can I join you?" he asked politely.

I directed my hand to the empty booth in front of me and folded the paper. What did he want with me?

"Here you go, Hun." The waitress placed a cup of coffee in front of me, then the man named Noah. "I have some great peaches to go with your pancakes this morning."

Noah smiled at the waitress. "Sounds good." His voice was slightly different again and his smile was tight. It looked... uncomfortable.

"Is this your friend?" she asked him as she looked at me.

Noah looked at me for just a second and smiled. "Yeah, this is Holly. Holly, this is Janine, the best cook in Red Wing." He had this look like he was unsure of me somehow.

I looked away from Noah and gave an embarrassed smile toward the waitress. "Nice to meet you."

"You too, Hun. Your breakfast should be up in just a minute." Janine smiled at me again and went back to pour coffee for the older guys that sat alone along a long counter by the kitchen.

"Are you looking for a job?" Noah asked, pulling my attention away from Janine.

I looked at him and down at the paper in front of me. I flipped it over and nodded as I found somewhere else to look.

"Well, I could use some help. If you're not afraid of hard labor, I can pay a hundred dollars a day." Noah's voice was different again. It was stern and short.

I looked at him and tried to figure out what his game was. I wanted to say no to his offer, but I needed the money. If I could find some place cheap to stay and save, I could find somewhere more permanent to live. I couldn't keep walking forever.

I nodded.

"What's your last name, Holly?" His voice was hard again.

"Bennett." I spoke quietly. I'd been so isolated over the last four months, I wasn't sure how well my vocal cords worked at times.

"Holly Bennett." A smile flashed over his face. His teeth were ridiculously perfect and white.

I frowned and raised an eyebrow. Did he know his mood changed every three seconds?

"I'm Noah Jackson."

I tried to give a small smile.

"Where are you from?" His appearance stayed lighter, but his voice was a little flat again.

"Oregon."

He looked surprised for a second. "That's pretty far. What are you doing *here*?"

I shrugged and looked for Janine. I was starving, and maybe if Noah was eating, he'd stop asking so many questions.

"Do you have family here or something?"

My eyes set on Noah quickly, and I felt a ball of rage and panic in my chest. I took a deep breath and pushed it back down before answering with a quick, "No." I looked away from him and fidgeted with my hands.

"I didn't mean to upset you," he said quietly. "I'm sorry."

I took in a deep breath and sat a little straighter as our food came. "I don't like personal questions."

Janine sat our plates in front of us.

"You're in Minnesota. Everybody's full of them." Noah began cutting at his stack of pancakes. "I assume you don't have a place to stay?"

I shook my head and scooped a fork full of hash browns into my mouth. I was so hungry I didn't care if I looked like a starved dog feeding on a fleshy carcass.

"Well, I have an apartment over my garage. It's small, but it's better than nothing." His voice was almost harsh again.

I looked at Noah again. "Why are you trying to help me?"

He stopped eating and looked at me for a moment. "Because you look like you need it." He raised an eyebrow while his eyes seemed to focus on my disheveled appearance.

I frowned and looked down at my plate. I started eating again and tried not to take his words and scrutinizing look as a personal attack.

......

"I'll have to bring you some sheets for the bed and a towel or two. There's no washer and dryer up there, you'll have to wash your clothes in the house. If you go through the basement door there," he pointed to the house, "there's a laundry room to the left. Feel free to use it when you want, except Saturday mornings, I do my laundry then."

I nodded as I looked at the house. It was old and smaller—one level with a walk-in basement—set in a small hill that leveled out at the back of the house. The outside was dark blue, and there were spots of missing paint. The flower beds all around the house were filled with weeds and broken lawn ornaments.

"I'm fixing it up," he said when he noticed I was staring. "That's what I need help with."

I nodded again. "What do you want me to start on?"

He shook his head. "You can start tomorrow. Today, you can get settled in and sleep."

I felt relieved. I was prepared to work, but exhausted.

"You can go up, I'll bring you some sheets and towels." He nodded toward the apartment over the garage. There was no friendliness in his voice.

I nodded and started walking toward the stairs at the side of the detached garage. The steps were old and severely sun rotted. I was a little afraid the boards might break under my step, but they held.

The plain white door with a single window opened into a small kitchen area. To the right was a small window with faded yellow curtains that were pinned back at the center. The kitchen was a bare white and looked like it was from the early sixties. I kind of liked it. The fridge was the rounded type, showing its age with small patches of rust under the paint. Steril white painted cabinets with silver knobs lined the walls. The lower ones had white vinyl countertops, with little flecks of gold, making a U shape in the small area. There was another window over the kitchen sink looking out to the back of the property.

To my left, against the same wall as the door, was a small two-seater table that had the same vinyl as the countertops. I walked past the table through the doorway between the kitchen and the living room. A single couch sat in the empty room with white walls. There was a large window that looked out toward the road and on the left was another doorway into a very small hallway that went to the bedroom and bathroom.

I sat down on the bare mattress in the bedroom. The walls were plain and white like the rest of the place, with matching yellow curtains on the three sets of windows. Sunlight poured into the small room, making it almost blinding. I set my bag down on the bed next to me and started pulling out my clothes. None of them had been washed in a while. There hadn't been a town big enough to have a laundromat. I'd have to buy some new stuff as soon as Noah went into town next. I only had four sets of clothing I'd bought after I'd crossed the state line into Montana, along with the small bag I'd used to carry them.

When I left Oregon, I didn't take anything with me because I wasn't *planning* on leaving. I just maxed out every credit-card I had at the ATM and pulled what I could out of my bank account before I left town. After that, I tried to spend as little money as possible. I would find a cheap motel once a week to clean up and sleep. The rest of the week, I just slept outside or in a non-conspicuous place, like a library or a bus station. A hundred dollars would usually last me a week and a half.

Noah knocked at the door and I stood up to walk to the kitchen. He opened the door with an arm full of linens.

"Here's some bedding and towels for you. Did you want me to take some clothes into the house to wash?"

I shook my head. "I can do it."

Noah nodded. "Well... dinner is at six-thirty. It's Tuesday, so it's beef stew."

I nodded. "Thank you."

He nodded, looking me over like he was sad about something, then turned to leave. The only reason I'd remotely considered his offer was because of the way people in the diner seemed to interact with him. Janine, different guys at the breakfast bar, they all appeared to have some kind of adoration or deep respect for him.

......

I carried three of my four sets of clothing into the house to wash them. As I waited for them to finish, I made up the bed and put away the very few things I had. I read a book I'd stolen from one of the libraries in South Dakota while I waited for my clothes to dry. When I had something dry and clean to change into, I went in the bathroom to take a shower.

As I undid the disheveled French braid from my hair, I thought about Noah. He was such a strange person. He was extremely handsome, well kept, but there was something about him. I felt like he wanted to be a kind and happy person, but he would force himself to stop. His mood changed with nearly every sentence he spoke. I could see he had very set routines, but they seemed more like a form of torture to him than a practice of stability. Janine had expected him to come into the restaurant, he washed his clothes on Saturday mornings, and dinner was at six-thirty. I wondered what made him that way; it was unusual for someone so young to have such a set routine.

After I took a shower and changed into clean clothes, I laid down to sleep for a while. There was an alarm clock on the nightstand next to the bed. I set it for six-twenty. I had a feeling Noah would be upset if I was late for dinner. I probably should've been a little worried I didn't know him, but I could travel north like I'd planned if it didn't work out.

······

When I walked into the house, everything was spotless. I hadn't expected it since the basement was a disaster. The dog, whose name was Gifford, hopped up in tiny jumps—happily—as I came inside. He panted, and his bun-tail wiggled as he waited for me to pet him. I reached down and scratched his ear.

"Gif, go lay down," Noah sighed as he walked back toward the dining room.

I followed him and looked around. There were French doors that opened to the back deck. The dining room walls were covered in dark, ugly wood panels. There were some decorations on the walls, but they looked like they had been there for a long time. An old table sat in the middle of the room with place mats that looked like they'd run their course.

"Do you want to eat outside on the deck, or in here?" Noah asked with a light smile. Somehow, he looked more tired than I still felt. He hadn't appeared that way earlier.

I tried to give a returning smile. "Either one is fine."

"It's nice outside. Would you mind taking the plates and silverware, there," he nodded at the end of the breakfast bar, "and setting the table outside?"

I nodded and walked over to pick up the dishes. As I set the table outside, Gifford watched me from the doorway. I'd never seen a dog smile, but *he* was.

"Do you like watermelon?" Noah called from inside.

Was that even a question? "Who doesn't?"

"You never know." Noah walked outside with a plate of cut watermelon and a smile. "There's some bread in there, would you mind bringing it out?"

I walked in the house and grabbed the bread that sat on a plate all cut up. "Did you make this?" I asked, noticing the homemade shape.

"Yeah. I don't buy much from the store. I have a large garden out on the corner of the property, and I buy my meat from a friend up the road that has a farm."

I smiled and let out a small laugh. "I don't think I know how to make anything I can't stick in the microwave."

"We'll have to fix that, I guess." Noah smiled at me. This smile was different than the others. It was genuinely kind. He walked inside and came back out with the beef stew. "Well, that's it. Let's eat." Noah pulled out the chair nearest the house and sat down.

I sat across the table and poured myself a glass of water.

"What did you do for work in Oregon?" His voice remained kind and light.

"Um... I was serving my residency at a hospital." I looked down at my plate.

"So, it's Doctor Holly Bennett?"

With a pressed smile, I nodded.

"I know guys are never supposed to ask, but you don't look old enough. How old are you?"

I laughed quietly. "I get that a lot. I'll be thirty-two in July. And you?"

"Thirty-four. How long do you have left of your residency?"

"A long time," I sighed. "Four years in and about four more to go."

"Is there a particular branch of medicine that you're looking into?"

I nodded. "I'm in neurosurgery."

"Wow... That's pretty impressive." He handed me a small plate with butter on it.

I nodded. "What about you?" I looked at Noah.

"I used to build houses." His voice changed a little. It wasn't any less friendly, it was just a little sadder.

"Why'd you stop?"

Noah looked at me for a second like he was deciding whether or not he was going to tell me. "Well," he took in a deep breath and leaned back slightly, seeming ready for a long-winded answer, "I made a lot of money at it, I guess... but, I just stopped."

He didn't want to talk about it, just like I didn't want to talk about me.

"I bet they were beautiful houses," I said as a sign of surrender.

Noah smiled. "Yeah. I'm pretty proud of them. Did you always live in Oregon?"

"No." I shook my head and picked up my spoon. "Growing up, I lived in Northern California with my dad and brother. My dad was a doctor too, so I didn't see a whole lot of him until I was older and could understand the basics of surgery. He was a great man, though." I smiled at the memory of my dad.

"And your mom?"

I shrugged. "She's out there somewhere, I guess, but I've never met her."

"That must have been tough." Noah picked up a piece of watermelon.

"Not really. My dad was pretty great, so I didn't think about it too much. What about your parents?"

"They live North of here in Duluth. My dad is a retired college professor of about three years, so he and my mom moved up North. I don't know. They're good people. They've always loved the hell out of me and my brothers." He shrugged. "Can't complain."

"So, you've lived here your whole life?"

Noah nodded. "Yep. I was in the Marines for a little while, but other than that, I've been here."

The Marines. That explained a lot.

"Where were you stationed?"

"I was in California for a little while, then Texas."

"My brother thought about going into the military, but he decided he was too much of a wimp."

Noah let out a small, but easy laugh. "It's not always for the faint of heart."

······

After dinner last night, I went back up over the garage. Noah had been nice to talk to. It was the most human interaction I'd had in months. I'd helped him clean up and talked with him over a cup of coffee afterwards. Before I left the house, he told me what time we were going to get started and what I'd be doing. My first task was to paint the house. It was going to be the same dark blue, with a white trim. He was going to install new windows, shutters, hang new gutters, put down new shingles, and add a front porch.

At exactly noon, Noah and I stopped working and had lunch. After that, Noah wanted to go into town and get some different nails and a couple of other things. I asked if I could come so I could get some stuff of my own. He dropped me off on Main Street while he went to get what he needed. I hurried and shopped for some clothes and a few other things, then found a pay phone.

I waited for the ringing to break, and it did.

"Holly?" My brother's voice was panicked.

"Yeah... It's me." I hadn't talked to him since the day before I left Oregon.

"Thank god! Where are you? Are you okay?" Brad's voice was only relieved for a moment, before he wound himself up again.

"I'm fine."

"Everyone has been looking for you. The *police* have been looking for you."

"Tell them to *stop* looking," I snapped lowly as I looked around to make sure no one was watching me.

"Where are you? You've been gone four months."

"It doesn't matter where I am, I'm not coming home."

"Greg is really busted up Holl, what am I supposed to tell *him*?"

"You tell him nothing. And if you do, you tell him to move on." My voice was angry and bitter. Tears pricked at my eyes. "I have to go."

"No! Holly, wait! Just tell me where you are. I promise, I won't tell anyone."

"Goodbye, Brad." I hesitated, but hung up the phone. I loved him and I didn't want him to sit there worried for the rest of his life. I couldn't tell him what had happened... and I couldn't go back.

I sat down on a bench nearby, trying to reel in my broken heart, and waited for Noah. It was less than five minutes before he pulled up.

"Did you find what you were looking for?" he asked when I got in the truck.

I nodded.

When we got back to the house, I returned to painting without a word. Noah went back to what he was doing until it was time for dinner.

"Are you ready to eat?" Noah asked from the ground below me.

I nodded and climbed down the ladder. I followed him into the house. He'd already set the table. I went into the bathroom to wash the paint off my hands, and as I came out, I saw a picture on the wall of Noah and a blonde woman. They looked happy. She had shoulder length blonde hair and bright blue eyes. She stood on a good-sized rock next to Noah, and she was still an inch or two shorter than him.

"Are you coming?" Noah asked as he walked into the hallway.

"Who's this?" I asked with a smile.

His face turned somber. "My wife." He walked away.

I bit my lip. I knew better than to ask...

I walked into the dining room and sat down at the table with Noah. He didn't say a word, just scooped a large piece of lasagna onto my plate.

"I should have grabbed a bottle of wine in town. This would go perfect," I said, trying to break the silence.

"I don't drink." His voice was straight and the hardness was back.

I looked down at my plate and finished my food without another word. I helped clean up after dinner and went up to the garage. I sat on my bed, cutting tags off the clothes I'd bought. I became a little irritated that Noah had been so rude. How was I supposed to know that was his wife? And I didn't even know who or where she was. Were they separated? Divorced? Was she dead? Did she just pick up and leave like me? He acted as though I had personally attacked him with a simple question.

Chapter 2

The next morning, there was a note on my table along with a covered plate of food. Noah was going to be gone all day, but I could help myself to anything I needed in the house. He said I could take the day off as long as I took care of Gif. He hadn't mentioned anything about him leaving yesterday. Was this because I'd said something about his wife? And what did he expect me to do all day? Stare at the white walls of my bedroom? Go for a walk?

I ate the breakfast Noah left and went outside to get started. All day, I stewed as I painted. It didn't matter to me what happened to his wife; it wasn't an excuse to be rude. I had my secrets too, but I wasn't rude when they came up. The more I thought about it, the angrier I got. I finished the house around six, and half expected Noah would come home for dinner, but he didn't. I looked in his fridge. There was nothing that didn't require an hour of preparation. Who didn't keep a few frozen pizzas for a rainy day?

I went up to the apartment and sat with a book while I waited for Noah to come home. He was *going* to face me. I didn't need any details about his wife, but he should know he was rude.

......

I must have fallen asleep for a while because I nearly jumped out of my skin when Noah knocked on the door. I got up from the couch and walked to the back door.

"Can I come in?" he asked quietly, looking worn down.

I nodded and stepped away from the door to let him in. He walked into the living room and sat on the couch while I followed and sat on the floor under the big window across the room.

Noah leaned forward and sat with his elbows on his knees. "I'm sorry about yesterday."

I sat quietly.

"My wife, Kate, died two years ago. A drunk driving accident... I was the drunk..." His face stayed in a hardened expression.

I had struck two chords last night. "I'm sorry," I whispered quietly.

Noah shook his head. "You didn't know." He sounded slightly irritated that he had to remind me.

"No... but you've been polite enough to not ask questions about me, I should have extended the same courtesy." I fidgeted with the carpet in front of me.

Noah shrugged. "You don't owe me any explanations..."

We sat in a room full of silence for a moment.

"I went out for a walk..." My voice was quiet as I continued to pick at the carpet in front of me. "Before I knew it,

I was at the county line, then the state line... and I just kept walking."

"You walked from Oregon to here?" Noah looked at me with raised eyebrows. He also appeared to be questioning my sanity.

I gave a quiet laugh and nodded at the floor. "Yeah."

"Are you going back?" His voice changed. *Again.*

"No... I don't know what I'm gonna do, but I don't wanna go back." I continued to pick at the carpet.

"Well, you're welcome to stay here as long as you want."

I looked up at him. The corner of his mouth pulled back in a sympathetic type of smile.

I tried to return the smile and nodded nervously. "Thank you."

Noah took in a deep breath and looked around. "And since you're staying here, maybe we should fix this place up. Find something more than a couch for you to sit on." His smile held as he spoke. "Have you eaten?" He stood up from the couch.

I laughed timidly and looked at the floor. "I told you, I can't cook." I looked up at him, feeling nervous and insignificant as I stood.

Noah laughed. "Then come with me. I'll make something." He nodded his head toward the door for me to follow him.

I grabbed my shoes from inside my bedroom and followed Noah out.

"I think we need to work on these stairs tomorrow. I didn't realize how bad they're getting," Noah said as he walked down. "And I saw you finished the house. You didn't have to do that. You could have taken the day off."

"It was that, or go for a walk."

Noah chuckled quietly. "I guess you've done enough of that."

We walked through the dark, up to his front door. Gif started dancing and doing his little baby jumps when we went inside. Noah gave him a pet and Gif came to me for another.

"What would you like?" Noah asked from the kitchen. "I can make a couple of pancakes and some eggs, or French toast, or make some grilled cheese."

I walked into the dining room, then the kitchen. "It doesn't matter to me. I'll eat anything."

"I'll show you how to make French toast, then you won't starve the next time I'm not here." He looked at me mockingly.

"Poke fun all you want. I can't cook." I stood nervously at the end of the breakfast bar.

"You said your dad wasn't home much? What did you do then?"

"We had a live-in nanny. Lupita…"

Noah shook his head. "And she didn't teach you anything?"

I shook my head with an embarrassed smile. "Spanish?" I held up my shoulders. "I was kind of a nerd. I kept to my books and watched videos of my dad's surgeries."

Noah raised an eyebrow and shook his head as he pulled out a pan. "Time to learn." His tone suggested irritation, but his expression didn't match.

He instructed me the whole way through making French toast. When we were done eating, we sat outside on the back deck with a cup of coffee. Gif sat on the bench swing between us. Noah asked me questions about all the schooling I'd done to become a doctor, then we talked about my dissertation. Mine had been about neuro pathways when a personexperienced different sensations. He asked different questions and listened as I gave explanations. We talked until the sky started to lighten from the morning sun.

"I think we should go to bed and try to salvage the rest of a day." Noah smiled a little as he looked up at the fading darkness.

"You can. I've had so much coffee I won't be able to sleep for a month." I held out my hand to watch it shake.

"You should still probably try to sleep. I imagine you're still catching up after all the walking."

I shook my head. "I didn't really have a normal sleep schedule before. Serving a residency is worse than walking halfway across the country."

"Okay, well... if it's all the same to you, I'm gonna turn in." His irritated tone was followed by an eye-roll, "It was a rough day before I came home." Noah stood up and stretched.

"Where did you go?" I looked up at him.

"I went to see Kate." Noah reached down for my coffee cup and walked inside.

I stood up and walked inside with Gif at my heels. "Well... I'll see you later. Thanks for the food and the talk." I gave a kind smile and turned toward the front door.

"Hey, Holly?"

I turned around.

"I don't know what you're running from, and I know it's unsolicited advice... but running doesn't fix anything. Whatever you're running from... it comes back."

I bit my lip and nodded. "Goodnight." I forced a small

smile and went out the door.

······

Noah woke up around noon and got started on building new stairs up to my little apartment while I pulled weeds out of the garden bed. I'd never done it before, but somehow it was therapeutic. After I had all the weeds pulled out, I carried bags of fresh soil to each bed and put down new dirt. As I spread the dirt around in the bed nearest to the garage, my hand caught on something and sliced my palm open. I cursed and pulled my hand out of the dirt. The moment I lifted my hand to look, a line of blood ran down my wrist, soaking into the sleeve of my shirt. I stood up to go inside to my apartment, but Noah pulled the old stairs down as I walked over. He looked at me with a satisfied smile until he saw the blood coming from my hand.

"What'd you do?" He walked toward me with a combination of wide eyes and a frown.

"It's just a cut. Do you have a towel or something? And some super glue?"

"That's more than a cut. Let me see." Noah held out his hand.

"I'm fine, really. I just need a clean rag or something."

Noah pulled out a handkerchief from his pocket and wrapped it around my hand. He pulled my sleeve up, showing a deep red scar. I quickly pulled my hand back and yanked my sleeve down.

"What happened to your arm?" Noah asked as he frowned.

"Nothing. Do you have any super glue? I need to close this cut so I can get back to work." I ignored his concern.

"Yeah..." He walked into the garage.

I walked over to the water spigot on the side of the house to rinse my hand and the sleeve of my shirt.

"Here." Noah held out a tube of superglue after I had finished cleaning my hand.

I looked up at him. "Can you glue it while I hold it shut?" My voice was quiet. I knew I'd been rude, but if I apologized, he might start asking questions.

Noah took my hand and pinched the cut together while he drew a line of glue across my palm. His eyebrows were pulled together and he looked angry.

"What did you cut yourself on?" he asked when I looked up at him. He seemed taller standing so close.

"I don't know. It was under the dirt in the flower bed."

He ran his finger over the dried glue on my hand. I carefully pulled my hand away, feeling slightly uncomfortable with the amount of attention he seemed to be paying.

"You should probably wear gloves. There's a pair in the garage in the cabinet beside the door." Noah looked at me with a hard line across his forehead.

I didn't know if his awkwardness was a result of mine, or the other way around. We were two people who didn't know how to be around other people.

"The glue should hold," I said, taking a step back. He was standing too close to me and it was making me uncomfortable.

Noah nodded.

I walked back to the flower bed and carefully dug around with a shovel to find what had cut my hand. I pulled up a broken beer bottle. I looked back at Noah who was focused on cutting a piece of wood. Was this bottle from his drinking days? I couldn't even picture him with a drink in his hand. He was a rigid person, and I couldn't see him allowing himself a moment to relax.

I carefully buried the broken bottle in one of the bags of weeds and continued pouring fresh soil into the rest of the flower beds. The fact that Noah had seen the scar on my arm bothered me. I wore long sleeves so no one would ever see or ask. It was more than the lower part of my arm that was covered in scars. They extended all the way up to my shoulder with a few on my back and side. I hoped someday I would be able to have them removed and not be forced to wear long sleeves in the dead of summer.

"Are you ready to stop for dinner?" Noah asked from behind me.

I jumped, not having heard him walk up. I grabbed my chest as my heart pounded.

"Didn't you hear me come over?" Noah laughed wryly.

"No." I whispered as I looked down at the flowers I'd just planted.

"Are you okay?" His voice turned concerned again.

I wiped my arm across my forehead to push the flyaways from my braid away from my face. "I just need sleep."

"Gif! Get out of there!" Noah yelled quickly.

I jumped again.

"Why are you so jumpy?" Noah asked as he extended a hand to me.

I stood up and brushed the dirt off my knees. "I think I'm gonna pass on dinner. I need sleep." I couldn't handle the thoughts in my head.

"I haven't finished the stairs yet. I was gonna come back out after dinner."

I looked back at the garage. There were no stairs. *Dammit...*

"Just have dinner and you can nap on the couch or something while I finish the stairs."

I looked around, feeling trapped. I just wanted to go up and be alone.

"Are you sure you're okay?"

"Please don't ask me that," I said quietly as Gif ran up and leaned his head against the side of my leg.

Noah looked down at Gif, nodded, and waited for me to walk around the house with him. I went into the bathroom to wash up and tears came to my eyes as I scrubbed at my hands.

"Holly?" Noah knocked on the door softly.

I wiped the tears from my face and looked in the mirror. "I'll be out in just a second," I said quietly as I tried to hold my voice steady.

I could hear the floorboards creak as Noah walked back toward the living room. I hung my head and turned the sink back on to splash cold water on my face. After I dried my face, I walked out and sat at the table. Noah didn't say anything, he just filled his plate with food, and we ate in silence.

••••••

"Holly?"

I gasped and shot up from the couch in a defensive position. My breathing was fast and labored while I looked around to figure out where I was. My heart pounded and I held onto my chest. Noah took a step back, startled by my response.

"I didn't mean to scare you. I was just waking you up to let you know I finished the stairs." His voice was quiet.

I swallowed hard and forced myself to be calm. "I had a bad dream," I said as I shook my head and stood up from the couch. Gifford followed me to the door, whining. I quickly walked out to the garage, went upstairs, took a shower, went into my bedroom, and barricaded the door. Nobody knew where I was, but I still didn't feel safe.

••••••

"Holly? I need to go into town for some bolts, did you wanna come?" Noah knocked on my bedroom door.

I shot up out of bed. I had overslept and my door was still barricaded.

"Holly?" Noah knocked again when he didn't get a response.

"Just a second," I said quickly as I pulled the nightstands off the dresser. I set it down as quickly and quietly as I could, then shoved the dresser back to its place.

"Are you okay?" Noah asked after the racket I made moving the dresser back.

I quickly grabbed my robe. "Yeah. Sorry. I was just rearranging the room," I panted as I opened the door.

"It's exactly the same as it was before." Noah raised an eyebrow as he peered into the room.

"Uh..." I looked behind me trying to think of a quick lie. "Yeah, I moved it back. I didn't like it."

Noah looked at the room for a second, then me. "Did you want to go into town with me and we'll grab some breakfast while we're there?" He knew I was lying, but was polite enough to not say anything.

"Sure. I'll be out in just a second."

Noah nodded and turned around. I shut the door and let out a quiet huff. My heart was still trying to crack my ribs

34

from the inside.

"So, I was thinking we could put wood floors in here. I think it would look nice, and it's better than carpet." Noah's voice carried from the living room.

"Wood floors are nice," I said as I pulled on a pair of jeans.

"We can take a look while we're in town... And I figured we can look at some furniture while we're there."

I pulled a shirt over my head. "I'm fine with just the couch. It's only me up here."

"The kitchen table is older than I am. My parents bought it from a second-hand store when they were first married."

"I never use the table. I always eat at your house." I buttoned up my plaid shirt and walked out into the living room.

"We'll see what we find when we go into town. Are you ready?" Noah looked at me.

I nodded as I braided my hair.

"You have a tag on your sleeve." He stepped forward awkwardly and yanked it off.

"Thanks." I walked forward and followed him out the door to the truck.

When we got into town, we stopped at a discount furniture store. I tried to convince Noah I didn't need anything more, but he wouldn't take no for an answer, so I picked out a few things. I got a new couch, a rocking chair, and a coffee table. I convinced him the kitchen table was fine, and insisted I pay half the cost for everything else. I didn't like the thought of him spending money on me when I wasn't even sure if I was going to stay. The plan had been just to make some money, then find somewhere to live.

......

Two days later, I raked the lawn of leaves that had been sitting since the previous fall. Noah was re-shingling the roof on the house.

"Holly, come up here and help me." Noah yelled from the roof after a few hours.

I set my rake against a tree. As I walked up toward the house, I noticed the tall clouds rolling in. I climbed up the ladder to the roof and walked over to Noah who was on his knees tacking a shingle down.

"Have you ever used a nail gun before?" His voice sounded frustrated.

I shook my head.

"Of course not," he snapped quietly to himself as he stood up. He grabbed the nail gun and held it up. "This is exactly like a gun, always assume it's loaded and ready to fire. Don't point it at yourself or others. Got it?" He spoke to me as if I were a child.

I nodded and frowned when he looked away from me. *Jerk.*

"There's a storm coming in. I need you to help me finish this before it starts raining." He picked up a shingle sheet. "See this line here? Line it up straight with the other shingles." He dropped the shingle down and adjusted it. "Then nail it down." He slammed the nail gun down five times, popping nails down across the near center of the sheet. "Let me see you do one."

I grabbed a sheet and laid it down, making sure I'd lined it up perfectly.

"Here." Noah handed me the nail gun, his tone bitter.

I took the gun nervously and set it against the roof. I closed my eyes as I squeezed the trigger until it made a loud pop.

"Oh, good grief. It's not gonna kill you." He got down on his knees next to me. "Here, look." He wrapped his hand around mine on the nail gun and started popping nails down along the shingle. "Now, work fast. Those clouds aren't gonna hold up long." He stood up and walked to the other side of the roof.

I watched him walk away, feeling a little angry at how he was talking to me. The other day he'd been nice, but yesterday and today he was almost mean. I didn't understand what I'd done to him.

I looked down and started working on the roof. I got used to the jolt of the nail gun and started moving faster with every shingle I laid. It started sprinkling as I worked on the last row at the peak of the roof. Noah went along behind me, nailing down a cap over the peak. When it was done, I helped carry the tools off the roof.

"Go put this stuff away, and we'll stop for lunch. I have some stuff in the house that needs to get taken care of until it stops raining." Noah's tone was abrasive.

I nodded and grabbed an arm full of tools while Noah went inside. I looked around as the air went still and the clouds grumbled angrily. The air felt strange, like there was an abnormal amount of electricity. As I was walking to the garage with the last of the tools, I heard an odd sound behind me and the wind picked up heavily, nearly knocking me over. I hurried into the garage and watched as it down-poured so hard that the ground was instantly covered with puddles of water. Little white balls of hail started cracking down, some of them were the size of peas, and others were more like golf balls. My poor flowers...

Chapter 3

A Couple Weeks Later

I walked down the path toward the several acres that Noah owned northeast of the garage. We were going to fence off one square acre of land and build a large workshop in a clearing hidden in the trees. I didn't know what he was building the shop for, but it wasn't my business, so I didn't ask. He didn't leave much time for talking anyway. During the days, we worked hard, paused for lunch, and worked until dinner. Over dinner, we would sit quietly, I'd help him clean up after, then go up to my apartment to work on the floors.

I walked up to where Noah was already working.

"You're late," Noah said as he dropped an arm full of wooden posts that'd come from the back of his pickup.

"I'm sorry," I mumbled quietly.

His face was tense as he looked up. "I've already got a few post holes started. I'll show you how to do one and you can get started."

I nodded and looked down at the ground. The look on his face made me nervous. He looked at me like he hated that I existed.

"Come on," he said with irritation as he grabbed a sledgehammer.

I grabbed a post and carried it while I followed Noah.

"I know I haven't been here that long, but I wanted to ask if it'd be okay if I had Monday off. If not, it's okay." My voice was quiet.

"Monday's fine." Noah took the post from me and stuck it in the ground.

"I'll be gone for the weekend."

Noah nodded as he grabbed the sledgehammer. "What are you doing?" He raised the sledgehammer and cracked it down on top of the post.

"Um... I'm gonna go to a town called Stillwater. It's east of Minneapolis."

"I know where it is. What's there?" Noah turned and looked at me with a hard stare.

I looked down at the grass in front of me. "My mother, I think."

"Thought you didn't know where she was?" Noah's voice was softer.

I nodded. "I hired someone to find her for me before I left Oregon... He said they had a lead at a flower shop in Stillwater... I figure it couldn't be too hard for me to find out."

"You walked all the way to Minnesota on a possibility?" Noah's voice changed, and I looked up to find a mocking smile on his face.

I let out a quiet huff and nodded. My gaze fell back to the grass.

"Well, I have some cousins up that way I wouldn't mind seeing. I can drive you, if you want."

I shook my head. "I don't wanna bother you."

"If it bothered me, I wouldn't offer." He raised the sledgehammer up and cracked it down on top of the post again. "It'd be nice to take a break for the weekend." Noah's voice was lighter. He sounded more like the person who had come up to my apartment a couple weeks ago.

I nodded. "Okay."

Noah nodded once and pushed against the side of the post to see if it was stable.

......

On Saturday morning, Noah drove me to Stillwater, which seemed like a drive that took forever because we didn't talk. His bad mood had continued through the week, and though he seemed alright today, I didn't trust it. His mood swings made me nervous, so I stayed quiet and out of his way.

Noah pulled into the parking lot of a small motel. It was a little more run-down than the pictures online showed, but I didn't care.

"Here's my number if you need something. And I'll meet you here on Monday around three." Noah handed me a piece of paper.

I nodded. "Thanks."

"I hope you find her." He gave me a kind and hopeful look. He was wearing a dark burgundy colored t-shirt that made his green eyes even more vibrant than usual.

I gave a small smile. "Me too. Have fun with your cousins."

He nodded. "I haven't seen them since my aunt passed away. It'll be interesting."

I gave a polite smile. "I'll see you Monday."

He nodded again.

I shut the door and grabbed my bag out of the back of the truck.

"Hey Holly?" Noah called when I started toward the office of the motel.

I turned and looked at him.

"I meant what I said. Call me if you need anything." His voice had a slight inflection, like he was nervous. I didn't understand how that could be, or why he would care.

I nodded. "I will."

He gave me a nod and I turned and walked into the office. I'd already called to see if they would take cash. I'd found that giving a sob story about an ex-boyfriend beating the hell out of me usually did the trick. I didn't want to ask Noah for his credit card. He'd never had a problem with it because I always gave him the cash beforehand, but I still didn't like asking.

I checked in at the front desk and went up to my room to change my clothes into something a little nicer than jeans and a plaid shirt. I didn't want to meet my mom looking like a lumberjack, so I wore a pair of white capris and a navy-blue blouse that was made with a chiffon-like material. The color was dark enough that my scars wouldn't be visible, and thin enough that I wouldn't look like a crazy person bundled up for winter. I let my hair down and tossed it with some hair spray. I hadn't done my hair in months. It'd been just as long since I'd done my makeup.

I walked around town for a little bit before going to the flower shop where my mother was supposed to be. My stomach twisted in knots, which seemed silly. I wasn't walking in there to ask her for anything, I just wanted to meet her.

I took a deep breath, reached for the door handle and walked in. The inside of the store didn't feel like I was really inside, just between buildings maybe. There were large skylight windows that made up the ceiling of the store; and vines that grew up all four walls. Antiques hung from the near invisible bricks while the vines grew around them, making them a part of the wall. Little misters hissed from under the vines, making the air muggy.

"Can I help you find something?" a woman asked as she set a vase of flowers on a stand near the front counter. I looked at her carefully, hoping I would recognize her from the pictures I'd seen of my mother, but there was nothing that stood out.

"Do you have any peonies?" I asked quietly. I didn't know what else to say. This lady couldn't be my mother. Her facial features were too rounded. My father had always told me I looked identical to my mother, and I had more prominent cheekbones than the woman standing in front of me. I also had my mother's dark brown doe-eyes, and this lady's were gray.

"You know, I don't. But I can order some if you'd like. Is it for a special occasion?" She smiled at me kindly.

"No." I shook my head. "That's okay."

"Bev, do you know what the hell I did with my glasses?" A lady walked from the back looking down at the tables behind the counter.

My nerves shook me and my palms started to sweat.

"They're on your head." The woman in front of me answered flatly.

"Right. Of course they are," the other lady grumbled as

she reached up.

"Are you Clara Hindsley?" I asked before my brain could stop me.

"Who wants to know?" The lady looked up through her glasses with a scowl. She looked at me for a moment and cursed under her breath. "Bev, I'm gonna go to lunch." The woman looked at me as she spoke.

"Okay. Are you coming back?" Bev asked.

"It's my store. Who cares? That's what I pay *you* for." My mother continued to stare at me.

"Alright then. I'll just be here." Bev walked behind the counter.

"There's a coffee shop on the corner, I'll meet you there in just a minute," my mother said in a short tone to me as she pointed in the direction of the coffee shop.

I nodded and turned around. My hands shook so badly I could hardly open the door. It felt like the ground was shaking as I walked to the coffee shop and sat down at one of the tables outside. I sat so my back was facing the direction of the flower shop because I didn't want the temptation of staring at the mother I'd never had. I also didn't want to see her run from me either. Ignorance was okay.

"Can I get you something to drink?" a girl asked as she approached my table.

"A cup of tea," I nodded, but my voice gave out. My nerves were more than I could handle.

"Any particular kind? Black, green? We have a really good jasmine."

"Any kind is fine," I said quickly. I wanted her to leave.

"Clara. It's good to see you. Coffee?" the girl said as she looked behind me.

"Do I ever get anything else?" Clara's voice was rough, and she gave a scoffing look.

My mother walked around the side of the table and sat down in front of me. The girl walked inside and I looked down as I pressed my hands together to keep them still.

"So, how'd you find me?" my mother asked with a snap.

"There's only two other Clara Hindsley's in the country and they weren't it." I looked nervously out at the street, then back at her.

"Well... that makes sense, I guess..." Her voice was less abrasive. She looked me up and down, her jaw set like she was unsure of me. Clara looked very different from the picture I'd seen years ago. Her face was much older, and I could tell her hair had been dyed its red color. She had cold and dark eyes, not so much like mine anymore. "So, what do you want?" she asked when I didn't say anything. "Money? A family reunion? What?"

I looked down at the table and shook my head. "I just wanted to meet you. I don't want anything."

I could feel her stare cutting through me.

"Well, how's your father? Still cutting into people's heads and parading around like a god?"

I shook my head. "He passed away about four years ago." I looked at my mother again. I probably looked as cowardly as I felt, and I had no reason to feel that way.

Clara stared at me for a second. "Hm... What about your brother?"

"He lives in Portland, Oregon. He's a lawyer—a partner at a law firm." I started to feel a little more comfortable as I spoke. Brad was a topic I could easily converse about.

She laughed. "He always was an argumentative little

shit. It's fitting he'd grow up and suck the life out of people." Clara dug around in her purse and pulled out a pack of cigarettes. "How old is he now? Thirty-five?"

"Thirty-seven," I corrected politely.

"So that makes you, what, thirty-two next month?" She spoke with a cigarette between her lips as she lit it and swatted away the lingering smoke.

I nodded.

"And what are *you* doing with your life, besides being anorexic? Haven't you heard that not eating will kill you?" Clara's voice was raspy. I could tell she'd been smoking for years.

"I'm a doctor."

"Good grief..." She rolled her eyes and shook her head. "Another god-complex."

"Here's your tea... and your coffee," the waitress said as she set down our drinks. "You know, you two look alike," the girl smiled.

"Get lost, Honey," Clara said as she waved her hand dismissively at the waitress. "So, what do you want to know?" Clara asked when the waitress walked away.

"Nothing. I just wanted to meet you."

"Well," Clara poured some liquor from a flask into her coffee, "I'll be honest with you. I stayed away for a reason. I hated your father, and more than that, I hated kids."

"I'm not a kid anymore."

"No, you're not, but you don't seem to have respect for people who don't want to be found." Clara looked at me with hard eyes.

"I don't want to be found either."

"Well, good... then you can imagine my disappointment." Clara put the cigarette to her lips and took in a long drag.

I looked down. I didn't know what to say. I had a mind full of questions and they'd gone dead the minute I saw her.

"I couldn't have known you didn't want to be found." I looked at her again, reminding myself I had to.

"It's not rocket science, Girly. I haven't been around for damn near thirty-two years."

I looked at Clara, her snide tone pissed me off. "My dad was a smart man, he always told me to count my blessings."

Clara laughed and put out her cigarette as she stood up. She threw a ten on the table. "Here. Call it child support. Keep the change for college expenses." She continued to laugh and walk away.

I sat rigid in my place. If I got up, there was a chance I'd do or say something I'd regret. What kind of a person would be so cruel? And how in the world did my father love her as much as he did? He'd always spoken fondly of her. Brad didn't, but I expected it was just because he'd been hurt by the abandonment he felt.

·······

I sat in my hotel room the rest of the day and read a book I'd picked up from one of the stores downtown. I felt like I was walking the country again and it was wreaking havoc on my nerves. I went to bed early, but every little noise kept waking me. I finally got to sleep for more than an hour, but someone knocked on the door. It was easy to assume it was either Noah or my mother, but I still opened the door carefully, ready to shove it closed if necessary. My blood pricked and my brain fell into a mix of confusion. I couldn't be looking at a ghost... unless maybe I had a brain tumor, but it was unlikely.

"Hi, Holly," a man identical to my father said with a nervous expression.

I swallowed hard, trying to figure out what the hell was going on. Was I dreaming?

"You haven't seen me since you were a baby, but I'm Garrett, Fran's brother. Can we talk?" He looked hopeful, sad, and nervous at the same time.

I started to shake my head but didn't. "My dad didn't have a brother."

He nodded. "He did, but I doubt anyone told you... Brad would remember me."

There had to be some kind of connection. He looked exactly like my dad, knew names he wouldn't otherwise know, and seemed very sure about all of it.

"Clara doesn't know I'm here. She told me about your exchange with her earlier, and I'm sorry about that. She was trying to protect *me*."

"There were no pictures of you in my grandparents' house," I said calmly, wondering what he'd have to say to that.

He shook his head. "No, and I'm the reason they didn't keep pictures of *you* either."

There was no way he could've known that if he was some kind of fake. Even my mother wouldn't have known that. Brad was probably the only person alive who'd have information like that.

"Let me get a sweater and I'll come out," I said quietly.

Garrett nodded. "I'll wait."

I closed the door, grabbed a sweater, then took a few deep breaths. My body was vibrating with fear, but I didn't have a real reason for it.

"Sorry, I'd invite you in, but I'm here with a friend and he's sleeping," I lied as I came out and closed the door behind me. Maybe if Garrett thought there was someone with me, I was a little safer.

He nodded once. "I'm sorry to intrude, but I've waited a very long time to see you and talk to you."

"If my grandparents and dad x-ed you out of the family, you must've done something serious." I stood against the railing across from my door. Garrett was sitting in one of the two plastic chairs beside it.

He nodded. "Yeah... Um... Before I tell you, I want you to know I'm not here to turn your life upside down, or because I expect anything from you." He took in a breath looking me over with nervousness in his eyes. "You're my daughter."

My eyebrows raised. There was no way.

"Your mom and I were having an affair for three years before you were born. I was really messed up on pills, and you were a result of the affair. Your dad knew, and I was there when you were born, and I saw you... I knew I couldn't be a dad... not a good one anyway. And Fran... it didn't matter to him. He loved you, so... he put his name on the birth certificate and raised you as his own." Garret looked beside his leg, grabbed a yellow envelope, and handed it to me. "He sent me letters every year, telling me of your accomplishments, the things you were interested in, and sent pictures."

I felt like I was either going to cry or puke. Looking at Garret was too hard and I needed some kind of proof, so I opened the envelope. There were a bunch of letters and pictures. Tears welled in my eyes as I looked at my dad's handwriting; hearing his voice in my head as I read a few lines of the first letter was easy because Garrett sounded just like him.

"Holly... giving you up was the best and hardest thing I've ever done. It was best for *you*. I was so messed up, in so many different ways. It wasn't just the pills... I knew you'd be better off with Fran..."

"Why didn't I know this?" I looked at him, trying with everything in me not to burst into tears. "And why now?"

"You didn't know because that was the agreement I made with Fran... He would take you and raise you as his own, but I was never allowed to see you or be in the picture in any way..." Garrett rubbed his hands together as he looked down at them. "Your mother left with me. She and I are together, but not... I live in Rochester and work at the Mayo Clinic as a cardio surgeon, and she lives here and has her flower shop..." He looked at me. "Bev told me you were here, and I had to see you. I've missed you your entire life and regretted... not being able to be your father. I know I can't do that now, and I have no right, but I just wanted to meet you... If you want nothing to do with me, I understand, but I just wanted to meet you and... come clean."

"Um..." I looked down at the wad of letters in my hands, pressing my lips together, trying to find words. My brain was so broken and muddled that I didn't know what to do. I rubbed my forehead and looked out toward the pool below. The thoughts in my head were raging, but also incoherent. I was so damn hurt I didn't know what to do with it. "I don't know what to say right now. You're just kind of dropping this on me, and..."

"I know, I'm sorry, and I don't expect you to say or do anything. I just wanted to meet you."

I nodded. "I know something about that... I just wanted to meet my mother, but she dropped ten bucks on the table to pay for coffee and called it child support."

Garrett shook his head with an eyeroll. "That's Clara. I'm sorry about that. She didn't want you to find out about me, or vice versa. I found out because Bev, her employee, slipped up without knowing better, then I confronted Clara."

"Why...? Why didn't she want me to find out about you?"

"Because I'll choose *you*... Clara's the selfish kind. What's hers is hers and no one else's."

I shook my head and wiped a tear out of the corner of my eye. "I'm an adult. There's nothing to choose, and it sounds like you made your choice a long time ago."

The corner of his mouth pulled back in a sort of disappointed pout. "I did what was best for *you*... I was sleeping in my car when you were born."

I shook my head. "Human babies have a forty week gestation period, I don't imagine I was an exception. Clara's a fairly slight woman and it was her second kid, I can't imagine you didn't know before I was born, meaning you had time to change your situation and didn't." I handed the letters back to him. "My dad is Francis Bennett, and if he didn't want you around, he probably had a good reason. He might be gone, and he may have lied to me, but I still trust him. Thank you for choosing better for me, but I can't take this on. I have wildly bigger problems right now, and I just can't with this. Have a good night." I went to the door, unlocked it, and slipped inside quietly. My heart felt like it was physically being torn to shreds in my chest and I had to stand there for a second just to reel from the pain. Coming to find Clara had obviously been a horrible mistake all on its own, but this... I couldn't handle.

I walked over to the phone and dialed Noah's number.

"Hello?" Noah had a residual laugh that wasn't meant for me.

"I'm sorry. You sound busy. I shouldn't have called."

"I'm not busy. What's up?" His voice was lighter than I'd ever heard, almost like we were friends and he was happy to hear from me.

"Nothing. I shouldn't have called. I'm sorry."

"I told you to call if you needed something. What do you need?" He sounded like he was forcing himself to be patient with me.

My mouth gaped for words, but nothing came out. I was too upset and the screaming in my head was becoming overbearing.

"Are you okay?" Another tone, this one more concerned.

"Can we go home?"

"Sure. I'll be there in a half hour, is that alright?" There was no pause or hesitation in his answer.

"Yeah."

"What room are you in?"

"Fourteen."

"I'll see you in thirty minutes."

I nodded even though he couldn't see. "Okay." I hung up the phone and took another quick shower to clean myself of the filth I felt.

⋯⋯

I damn near screamed bloody murder when Noah knocked on the door because I was so distracted with my raging thoughts.

"No wonder you want to leave. Good grief." Noah frowned with disgust, looking next door where a bunch of yelling and banging was coming from.

I nodded.

A loud crash against the wall made me jump. I covered my mouth and closed my eyes as my heart pounded harder and my cheeks burned.

"Come on. Let's head out of here." Noah took my bag from my hand.

I nodded and forced my eyes open, feeling like I might throw up. He let me step out first, putting himself between me and the neighboring room. I walked along the railing toward the stairs.

"Larry! You get back in here and clean this up!" A woman screamed just before a tattooed kid blew past Noah, shoulder checking me as he bolted for the stairs.

Noah wrapped a quick arm around the top of my shoulders from behind, to keep me from falling. "Hey!" He barked loudly. "Have some damn respect!"

I was frozen. I felt like a crazy person with shouting voices in my head I couldn't quiet.

"Are you alright?" Noah rubbed my shoulder.

I forced myself to nod, grateful that he couldn't see my face.

"Come on." He dropped his arm.

I walked to the truck and got in quickly. I made a point to keep my eyes out the window next to me so he wouldn't see the occasional tear that slipped.

....

Noah didn't say anything until we were parked in the driveway. "I take it things didn't work out with your mom?"

53

I nodded and grabbed at the door handle to get out. Noah got out, grabbed my bag, and carried it up the steps to my apartment behind me.

"I'm gonna make us something to eat. Unpack and come inside when you're ready." Noah's voice was kind as we stood outside my door.

I nodded and reached out to take my duffle bag from him. He went back to the house. I went inside my apartment, put away my stuff, and sat down on my bed for a moment. The heartbreak that'd been caused three hours ago was still aching. Then there was the surge of fear because of the fighting people next door. It had hit me harder than it should have. I closed my eyes and took several deep breaths. I wasn't that person. I'd left everything behind. I had to be okay now…

I stood up after a few minutes and walked over to the house. Gif jumped up happily when I walked in. I pet his ear and walked into the dining room.

"Can I help with something?" I asked quietly.

"Nah, just waiting on the oven."

I nodded and sat down at the breakfast bar.

"I made a pizza. I took you up on your advice of keeping one in the freezer." Noah gave a mocking smile.

I forced a smile at him, then looked down at the counter in front of me. A silence fell over the room and Noah stared at me. I pretended not to notice and kept my gaze at the counter. The oven timer went off and Noah turned around to pull the pizza out.

"I'm not gonna be around much tomorrow. My friend's kids is getting baptized, so I'll be home for an hour after church, then they're having a party afterwards." He set the pizza on top of the stove and started cutting it.

"Okay." My voice was quiet. I watched as he pulled two plates out and put a couple slices on each.

"You can come with if you want. It's better than sitting around here all day." Noah turned with a plate in his hand and set it in front of me.

"No, I'm gonna finish the flooring in my apartment." I picked up the plate and slid off the bar stool to follow Noah outside to the bench swing.

"Don't worry about it. It can wait until Monday." Noah sat down in his spot on the left side of the swing.

I sat down and set my plate in my lap. "I wanna keep myself busy."

"Suit yourself," Noah shrugged.

I took a bite of the pizza and forced myself to chew and swallow. I wasn't hungry, but the word 'anorexic' was stuck in my head from earlier.

"So did she recognize you when she saw you, or did you have to tell her who you were?"

I looked at Noah. "No, she recognized me. I asked if she was Clara Hindsley, and when she looked up, she knew exactly who I was."

"What did she say?"

"A four letter word."

Noah laughed a little. "Seriously?"

I raised an eyebrow and nodded as I looked at the plate in front of me.

"How old were you when she left?"

"Two days." I looked at Noah.

He frowned for a second and shook his head. "I don't understand how a parent could do that... just walk out."

I shrugged. "It doesn't matter... It's done." I took another bite of my pizza.

"I'm sorry it didn't work out for you."

I shook my head. "Nothing changes."

We were quiet for a few minutes as we ate.

"Why did you want to find her? Besides obvious reasons."

I looked out at the darkness of the back yard. There was only light from the windows behind us. I couldn't tell him the truth, that I wanted a place to hide. Where better than with the woman who had been hiding my whole life?

I bit my lip. "I thought it would be nice to have one piece of my family... I can't talk to my brother, and my dad is gone..." I looked at Noah who was watching me carefully. I stood up and reached my hand out to take his plate. "Did you want another piece?"

"No. I'm good." He handed me his plate. "Thanks."

I walked into the kitchen and washed the plates quickly. I wanted to get away from the prying questions that made me uncomfortable. They made me think about why I missed my dad so much. If he were alive, I'd be in California with him, instead of here with a random stranger. And I wouldn't feel so terrified either. Where Garrett was concerned, I was pretending I didn't know what he told me. Francis Bennet was my father...

"I was gonna watch a movie, did you want to join me?"

I jumped at the first sound of Noah's voice and dropped the plate that was in my hand. It broke as it crashed down into the porcelain coated sink. I closed my eyes and tried to make my heart stop pounding. It was making me dizzy. Noah grabbed my hand out of the sink and looked at it to check for any cuts.

"I'm fine," I said as I looked down at my hands that dripped with water.

"You have *got* to be the jumpiest person I've ever met." He shut the water off.

"I'm sorry about the plate. I'll pay for it."

Noah looked at me like I was crazy as he pulled out the large pieces of broken plate from the sink. "It's a *plate*."

I wiped my hands off on a towel. "I should go."

"You don't wanna watch a movie?"

I shook my head. "No. I need to go to bed. Thank you for everything today. I'll see you tomorrow—or Monday, I don't know." I turned and walked away as quickly as I could without running.

I needed to breathe and the only place I felt like I could do that was in my little apartment.

Chapter 4

July 4th, Four Weeks Later

Noah and I didn't talk to each other much after he had taken me to Stillwater. He'd tried to be nicer for a few days after that, but went back to his abrasive mannerisms. I just kept working and not talking. Yesterday though, he had been especially grouchy. Nothing I did was right. Eventually, he had me carry cinder blocks from one end of the property to the other because it was fool proof. I didn't complain, I just did what he was paying me to do.

I didn't want to create close ties with Noah anyway. We both had skeletons in our closets. He was helping me with a job and a place to live, and I was helping him with fixing up his property. It worked for both of us. I would get up in the morning and work all day, then go up to my space above the garage. He rarely bothered me there. He'd only come inside to help me carry pieces of furniture in. Otherwise, he'd stay in his house and I'd stay in mine.

••••••

Noah stood in the late morning sunshine when I opened the front door of my apartment.

"I'm gonna meet up with a few friends. We're gonna go hang out at the lake and watch the fireworks later. You wanna come?" Noah asked with a lightness on his face.

I'd barely woken up and the sun was still too bright for me. "You have friends?" I raised my eyebrows in surprise. I realized it was a rude response without a smile, so I pulled the corner of my mouth up.

Noah smiled and shook his head with a huff before looking at me with a waiting expression.

I shook my head. "I think I'm gonna hold down the fort with Gif."

"Come with." Noah shrugged. "If you don't like my friends, then we can find something else to do."

I opened my mouth to say no, but his face was so hopeful. "Okay."

Noah gave me a small smile and looked down at his watch. "Can you be ready in thirty minutes?" He looked back at me.

I nodded.

Noah walked down the stairs with the sun glinting off of his sandy blond hair. I closed the door and went to my room to change out of my pajamas. I pulled on a pair of shorts and a thin white linen blouse, combed the braid from my hair, and went into the bathroom to brush my teeth. It was a little nerve-racking to think about meeting his friends. I wasn't actually convinced he had any since no one had ever come over and he didn't go out, except to the store.

I brushed my hair and looked in the mirror. My face

was less sunken than a month ago because my cheek bones no longer looked like they were going to cut through my skin. It felt like it'd been forever since I looked in the mirror. My brown hair fell down in soft waves to the top of my waistline. I was pretty sure my hair was going to have a permanent kink from wearing it in a braid every day for nearly five months. The dimples in my cheeks made me seem friendlier than I felt.

I walked away from the mirror and grabbed my sandals from the closet. After that, I poured myself a bowl of cereal and watched the clock as it neared the half hour. The sunshine outside was warm as I waited at the truck. Noah wasn't outside, which was strange. When he said a half hour, he meant it.

Gif ran around from the back of the house toward me. Noah walked around the side of the house with a rope in his hand.

"What's that for?" I asked as he walked toward the truck.

"My friend needs it for his boat." Noah threw the rope in the back of the truck and got in.

I got in and he pulled out of the driveway. Noah kept looking at me and I pretended not to notice until he didn't stop.

"You keep staring at me," I pointed out with an impish smile.

"Your hair is down." He looked at me again.

I looked at him for a moment, unsure if there was a point to his statement.

"It looks nice." He gave a small smile.

I looked forward. He'd never complimented me before.

I didn't know what that meant... or why he seemed to have a happy bug up his butt. He'd been such an ass yesterday that I'd honestly contemplated packing up my stuff, flipping him the bird, and walking to whatever destination was next.

"'Thanks, Noah. That's so nice of you to say.' 'You're welcome, Holly.'" Noah created a conversation mockingly and smiled at me.

I bit my lip nervously. "Thank you." I didn't look at him.

"You're welcome." He looked at me again. "What are those bracelets for?" Noah looked down at my wrist.

I looked at the brown string of leather wrapped around my wrist. The word *Strength,* and an infinity symbol were made of brass and tied into the leather strand.

"Infinite strength," I answered as I repositioned the bracelet. I hadn't taken it off since I bought it in Idaho.

"Is that like something you live by or...?"

"Trying to." My voice was quiet.

......

We sat in silence the rest of the way to the lake. A group of six people smiled and walked up to us as we parked.

"Noah!" One of the girls smiled brightly. She had bleach blonde hair and perfect white teeth. She wasn't wearing much, which made me uncomfortable. She wore tiny jean shorts and a bright red bikini top that was a little too small for her bust size.

"Hey Terri, where's Jess?" Noah asked as he walked up to her to give her a hug.

"He had to work," she answered as she held her beer away and hugged Noah. She turned to me. "You must be Holly. I'm Terri." She reached out her hand to me with a smile.

"Nice to meet you." I shook her hand, forcing a polite

smile.

"Come on, I'll introduce you to everyone." Terri nodded her head toward the group. "Chris, say hi, this is Holly, she's with Noah," Terri yelled.

"No, I'm not—" I quickly tried to correct her.

"Relax, Honey. You're with friends." Terri smiled at me. "That's Bridgett, and Carrie." She pointed to the two other girls that were also in shorts and bikini tops that didn't fit. "And that's Dallas and Johnny. Dallas is married to Bridgett, Carrie and Chris are married, and I'm just complicated." Terri raised her eyebrows and smiled at me. "Do you wanna beer?"

I looked at Noah who was standing behind Terri now. "No thanks," I said quietly.

"Suit yourself. I'm gonna grab another." Terri shrugged and walked toward the boat.

"You can have a beer if you want. I don't care." Noah gave a crooked smile. "These guys drink their faces off, but they're good people."

I shook my head. "I'm okay."

"Come on you guys! I want to get out on the water!" Terri yelled from the boat.

Noah followed me and offered an arm as I stepped over the side. I half expected him to just let me fall on my face, especially after yesterday.

"Here, drink up, girl." Chris handed me a beer and walked to the back of the boat.

I stared at the beer in my hand.

Noah laughed. "It's not going to kill you. It's a beer."

I looked up at him feeling confused. Who was this guy? Noah was always uptight and serious, now suddenly he was happy and carefree?

"Holly, come over here," Terri waved from the front of the boat.

"Go talk with the girls. They're nice." Noah nodded toward them with a smile while looking at me.

"Come on." Terri grabbed my arm and pulled me over toward Carrie and Bridgett.

I sat down on the padded bench with my beer and took a drink.

"So, Noah says you're a doctor? That's crazy." Terri's eyes were bright with fascination.

"Yeah." I gave a shy laugh.

"So, do you cut people up and stuff?" Carrie asked as she rubbed tanning lotion on her legs.

"God, she's not a butcher, Care," Bridgett said as she threw out her towel over the bench.

"Something like that," I answered. I felt awkward because these girls were bubbly—like fifteen-year-olds. They made me feel old, though they were probably the same age as me.

"You're from Oregon? What's that like?" Terri asked.

I shrugged. "It's nice. Kind of like here. Green, a lot of trees, it just rains more."

"I love rain," Bridgett said with a smile as she laid back to tan, "but I also love the sun."

The girls peppered me with questions, but none of them were very personal, so it didn't bother me. The guys stood at the back of the boat and blasted Creedence Clearwater Revival. I'd never seen Noah laugh or smile so much. It was odd. I kept stealing glances every now and then because I liked watching him, he never looked happy. Today he looked like a different person.

"So, what's it like living with Noah?" Terri asked quietly, pulling my attention away.

"I wouldn't know. I live above the garage." I smiled a little. What kind of a question was that?

"Still. He's like the sweetest person ever. You're so lucky." Terri stole a glance in Noah's direction.

I frowned a little as I smiled. Noah was mostly an ass. Was he just different around his friends? "We're not together. I just live above the garage." I shook my head.

"Not anymore, Sweetie," Bridgett said, lifting her sunglasses to look at me. "He brought you to meet *us*." Her full lips pulled up in a smile. She glanced over at the boys, lowered her glasses, and readjusted her boobs to look perkier. Any *more* and they'd bust her top...

I looked at Noah, feeling a little mortified. He looked at me and smiled.

"Oh my gosh. You're so cute. No wonder he likes you so much." Terri put her hand on mine. "Doesn't she remind you of Kate?" Terri asked Bridgett.

"Yeah. She's quiet," Carrie responded from her statue-like position. Her short blonde bob didn't seem to move despite the wind and the fact that she was laying back. She had a small pointed nose and lips that weren't quite as full as Bridgett's, but had the same bright shade of red lipstick.

"You know he was married before, right?" Terri asked quietly.

I nodded.

"Did he tell you what happened?" Terri's eyes were honest.

"You better not let Noah hear you, Terri. He'll flip shit,"

Carrie warned.

"Well, Noah used to drink a lot. He was kind of a party boy in high school. Anyway, we had a party for their five-year anniversary. She told him she was pregnant, and he was like, *way* happy. Anyway, he bought shots for everyone, had a few too many, and they drove home. It wasn't even his fault, a semi blew a stop sign and the road was wet, he couldn't stop in time."

I looked out at the water. I could feel the sympathetic look on my face, and if I looked at Noah, he'd know what Terri just told me.

"He hasn't drank since... or smiled until you came around. My sister said he came into town two weeks ago and he was smiling and saying hi to people. He hasn't done that in forever."

I looked at Terri. She thought *I* was the reason he was smiling? I was pretty sure that it was the opposite.

"Honey, he hasn't smiled like this since Kate was around," Terri said as if I hadn't understood her the first time.

"That's the truth," Bridgett said as she rolled over onto her stomach. "He was kind of an ass there for a while."

I smiled to myself and tried not to laugh. "I'm sure it has nothing to do with me." I took a drink of my beer to hide my smile.

"Hold on girls. We're gonna open'er up," Dallas yelled over the music.

......

Dallas drove around the open lake going so fast I felt slightly uncomfortable. I'd only ever been on a boat in the ocean where it was open and there were only waves to crash into. Dallas drove like someone's life was on the line, took hard turns, and caused large wakes in the water. Once he had the need for speed out of his system, he stopped in the middle of the lake and the girls jumped in the water.

"Come on," Noah said with a smile as he pulled his shirt off, then reached his hand out to me.

I looked at the other guys who were jumping off the back of the boat.

"I'm okay here." I looked at Noah and forced a smile.

"Come on. I promise, nothing bad will happen if you have fun." He smiled and continued to hold out his hand to me.

I took a second to decide, then took his hand. "You're strange sometimes," I mumbled as I stood up on the bench on the side of the boat with him.

"Because *you're* normal?" He laughed and gripped my hand tightly. "Three."

Noah and I jumped off the side of the boat and splashed into the water.

"Holly. Grab a floaty!" Carrie said as she threw a floaty off the boat toward me. "The guys are gonna go wakeboarding."

I pulled the floaty toward me and hung off the side.

"Who opened their big mouth?" Noah asked quietly.

"What?" I looked at Noah.

He hung off the side of the floaty with me. "You keep giving me that look that everyone gives me. So, which one of the girls opened their big mouth?" His face was still light and didn't look angry.

"Nobody's said anything." I didn't look at him. "Terri just wanted to know if she was going to die of cancer for being out in the sun so much." I shot him a smile.

"So, Terri blabbed?"

"I didn't say that." I shook my head and watched as everyone splashed around in the water. "Nobody told me anything I didn't already know. Except that you're acting strange, which I also knew."

"Hm." Noah made a little huff. "Strange? *They* said I was acting strange?" he asked with skepticism.

I looked at Noah who was suppressing a smile.

"No, *I* think you're acting strange, *they* confirmed it." I smiled a little.

"I think *they* think I'm acting normal. And why is being happy strange?"

"You're happy?"

"I asked you first."

"It's strange for you." I looked back at everyone as they laughed and pretended to be offended at the other for splashing them.

"Well, I'm beginning to think it's *nonexistent* for you."

I shook my head. "It's not nonexistent..." I took in a deep breath and let it out before I looked at him again. "Just waiting for it to come back."

"That's depressing," Noah laughed. "Go float with the girls. I'm gonna trash these guys at wakeboarding." Noah swam to the back of the boat.

I got up on the floaty and watched the sky for a long while. Carrie, Bridgett, and Terri went on about something, but I didn't pay attention. I wondered what it must have been like for Noah to lose his wife. I'd never loved someone like that. My ex was the closest I had ever come to love, and that wasn't love.

"You look like you need another beer," Bridgett said

as she tossed a can at me. "Come here. Give me your hand." Bridgett reached out her hand to me. I grabbed it and she pulled herself closer and looped her arm through mine so we would float side by side.

"So, what's your story?" she asked.

"Don't have one."

Bridgett lifted her head and pulled up her sunglasses to look at me. "Well that's crap... I'm a therapist, Honey. I can see there's something wrong from a mile away." She laid back down with her face to the sky.

"I'd rather not talk about it." I tried to keep my voice polite. I didn't want to be rude and give Noah a reason to pitch a fit at me.

"Oh, don't worry, Gidget and Big-Mouth are over there gossiping about who knows what." Bridgett gave a dismissive wave toward the other two girls. "Tell me your story. I know it's a good one. I saw that long scar on your side when you jumped in the water with Noah."

I swallowed hard.

"Take a nice big drink of beer and tell me what happened." Bridgett turned her head toward me.

I shrugged. "I'm sorry. It's kind of private."

"Well, if you ever want to talk about it, come find me." Bridgett patted my arm. "And don't worry. I won't tell anyone." She gave a crooked smile. She was strangely pretty. She had a bulb-nose that looked pointed at different angles, and full lips that made her look like she was always pursing them. She sounded like an airhead when she spoke, but I could tell she wasn't.

Bridgett laid back again. "I think you and Noah will be good for each other."

"I just work for him."

"Keep telling yourself that. I may have my sunglasses on, but I see the way he looks at you. He's looking at you right now."

I looked down to see the boat pull up near us. Noah was looking at Bridgett and I with a smile.

"You girls ready to eat?" Dallas yelled from the boat.

"It's about time! I'm starving," Bridgett snapped as she sat up. She slid off of her floaty and swam to the boat. Carrie and Terri followed suit, so I did too.

Noah reached his hand down to me. "Did you have fun?" he asked as he pulled me up.

I shrugged and gave a shy smile. Bridgett handed me a towel as she shook her hair out.

We pulled up to a shallow part of the water and the boys jumped out to push the front of the boat onto the bank. They helped each of the girls out of the boat because it was just a little too far to jump and not hurt their knees. Noah reached his hands up and held the top of my hips as he helped me down. His seemingly normal gestures kept baffling me.

"Are you okay?" he asked quietly as he let go of me.

I gave a fake smile and nodded as I started to walk toward the grassy hill where everyone else was.

"Hey." Noah took my wrist to stop me.

I looked at my wrist in his hand as my heart pounded. He let go when he saw the look on my face.

"I'm okay," I nodded. My cheeks burned from the embarrassment and fear.

Noah looked at me for a moment then nodded. "Okay."

We walked up to the others and helped make food. After we were done eating, Chris pulled out a guitar and started strumming as the sun began to set. Terri's boyfriend, Jess, showed up and they couldn't keep their hands off of each other.

••••••

"When are we gonna go see the fireworks?" Carrie whined after we were all done eating.

"They don't start until ten," Noah said as he walked over to throw his plate away. "It's only eight-thirty, but Holly and I are gonna go and hold down a spot for everyone at the park."

"You guys wanna ride back to the dock?" Dallas asked with a mouthful of food.

"No. It's not that far. We'll walk."

I stood up. "See you guys there."

"Bye you two," Terri crooned with an implicative tone.

"Play along," Noah whispered as he took my hand and pulled me away.

The girls whooped and hollered as we walked away. I shook my head and took my hand back when we walked over the hill and out of sight.

"Have fun sometimes. It's not that bad." Noah laughed.

What?

He looked at me when he realized that I was staring at him. "It's hard sometimes, but there's worse things."

"Where is this sudden optimism coming from?" I asked, shaking my head.

"I had a realization last night."

"That you're bipolar?" I raised an eyebrow. There was no sense in faking smiles *now*, he'd return to being an ass tomorrow.

"No. That I've been pretty bitter... Not that I don't have

71

a reason, but I realized I still have another fifty or sixty years left. I can walk around angry every day, or I can try to be happy." Noah looked at me. "So, the question is, what about you? Are you gonna learn to be happy, or are you gonna just... survive?"

I looked at Noah and felt angry, but not necessarily at him. I looked forward and kept walking.

"Do you have a scar down your right side? Chris said he thought he saw one when we jumped in the lake."

I stopped and looked at Noah. He *had* to know better than to ask about my scars. I walked faster. I was going to walk right through the tears that threatened my eyes, just like I did last time.

"I told you it's gonna catch up," Noah said from behind me.

I whipped around. "Because of you! I didn't *want* to jump in the water, I didn't *want* to sit there while Bridgett pried at me, and I *don't* want to have this conversation with you. I'm glad you feel better—I really am—but just because you're on cloud nine, doesn't mean *anyone else* is."

Noah looked at me with shock for a moment, then his normal frown set in. "It's a choice, Holly. You either make the choice, or you don't."

"I'd really like for you to take me home." I looked off toward the trees, unable to look at him.

Noah drew in a deep breath and let it out in a huff. "Just stay. I won't bother you about it again... You have my word."

I swallowed hard, trying to push the tennis ball in my throat down.

Noah walked up and stopped in front of me. "I'm sorry." His voice was quiet against the wind from the lake.

"Maybe you're not ready to put the past behind you, and I know better than to push... I'm sorry." Noah reached up and touched the top of my cheek bone with his thumb to catch a defiant tear on my cheek. His touch sent a wave of electricity through my body.

I turned and crossed my arms around my stomach and walked toward the truck. I'd be lying if I said I hadn't thought about Noah and I, but the more I thought about it, the more I knew it was a terrible idea. I didn't walk away from my life in Oregon to find someone else to torture me. I left to be by myself. I had a habit of picking the wrong people, I wasn't about to do it again.

......

We drove to the park and found a place to sit. There was a live band playing in the gazebo entertaining everyone as they waited for the fireworks. Noah's group of friends showed up about fifteen minutes before the fireworks started. After, everyone wanted to go dance to the music near the gazebo.

"Come on you two, it's time to dance." Carrie said as she grabbed our hands and pulled us off of the park bench toward the grass where everyone else was dancing. "Put this hand here," she said, putting my hand on Noah's shoulder. "And you put this hand here." She pulled Noah's hand against my waist. She ducked under our arms. "And hold hands like this." She pulled our hands together. "Now stand closer and dance." She pushed me closer to Noah.

"Do you wanna dance?" Noah laughed as Carrie walked away to dance with Chris.

I laughed and we started to dance slowly. All the trees around us were hung with small light bulbs on a rope line;

the lights gave a soft glow to the grass below us. People all over the park danced in small circles with someone. I looked at Bridgett and Dallas. They smiled at each other as they danced and talked. Carrie held on tightly to Chris and had her eyes closed. Terri gave me two thumbs up and a grin behind Jess' back. I laughed and shook my head.

"What?" Noah looked down at me.

"Terri." I shook my head. "She has ideas, and she's pushy."

Noah laughed quietly. "She's always been that way."

"And you didn't help with your little hand holding gag."

"Or, I wanted to hold your hand." Noah suppressed his smile as he looked out at the crowd of people. He looked back at me lightly.

I narrowed my eyes at him. "You've put something in their heads, and that means there's expectations." I raised an eyebrow.

Noah let out a sigh and pulled me closer. "Breathe. You think too much."

I couldn't let the muscles in my back or shoulders relax. I was trying not to be so rigid, but it was in vain. He had a weird sense of humor about things, and I didn't know if he was kidding or serious. The fact that he appeared so comfortable near me made me squirm. I hated when he was a dick, but I didn't want him thinking dancing and holding my hand was okay either.

"You're turning purple," Noah whispered.

I took in a breath and let it out. His shirt smelled like sunscreen and lake water. I focused on the scent and put everything else from my mind. My brain was shouting at me to run like hell, but it was also telling me I couldn't. Noah might hate me, but I knew for a fact I was safer where I was than anywhere else. Noah was also about six-foot-four, burly, didn't take shit from anyone, and that would give someone pause if anyone found me.

Chapter 5

When we got home, Gif danced around in the dark waiting for us to pet him. Noah looked up at the moon. It was so bright it lit the property where there weren't trees.

"Thank you for inviting me today," I said quietly as we leaned against the front of the truck, staring at the moon. Gif nudged my hand with his nose, so I stroked his soft fur.

Noah looked at me with a small smile on his eyes. "Did you have fun?"

I nodded.

"I told you nothing bad would happen." Noah's smile grew.

"My legs are sunburnt." I held a straight face and looked back at the moon.

Noah made a smirking sound that turned into both of us laughing.

"I think I need to go to bed." I shook my head and wiped

my hands over my cheeks.

"Wait." Noah caught my arm gently and pulled me to face him.

I stood there in a state of suspended animation. His face looked so kind, and the way his hair was swept to the side made it even more so. He brushed the hair away from my face and our eyes caught. Even when he was angry and stomping around, he had beautiful green eyes I couldn't help but notice.

My brain didn't register how the kiss happened, but I knew it wasn't me that instigated it. One of his hands gripped my waist and he held me close as our lips touched. I wrapped my arms around his neck. I knew better than to do what I was doing, but a kiss had never made me feel... so stunned. It was radiating through me...

His thumb rubbed over the start of the scar on my side, with my thin shirt between. It made my better sense come back. I walked away quickly, went up to my apartment, closed the door behind me, and leaned against it. My legs felt weak and the bubbly feeling of adrenaline turned to spiking nails of fear and unease.

"What are you *thinking*?" I scolded out loud.

I pushed off the door and paced the kitchen for a minute before I went in my bedroom. Out the window, Noah was still sitting on the front of his truck. I sat down on my bed and tried to straighten out my thoughts... Nope.

I stood up and walked back outside. Noah watched me apathetically as I marched toward him.

"Why would you do that?" I snapped harshly. "We had a good thing and you just made it complicated. I was just some messed up person you found on the side of the road, and you were someone who needed help fixing the house." I directed my hand from the road to the house as I spoke. "Now you've made it complicated." I dropped the hand that was directed at him. "Are we just gonna get back to work tomorrow and pretend like this didn't happen? Is this you trying to screw with my head? Being nice one minute and a dick the next?" I stayed where I was as I verbalized every thought in my head. "I live above your garage. You pay me every week for the work I do here... You don't even know me. You have no idea why I'm here. Do you realize that? How you have no idea who I am? I could be some felon who escaped prison and lied to you about everything."

His arms were crossed in front of him while he wore an amused smile.

"Great, so this *is* a game to you." I shook my head, looking at him with disgust.

He shook his head with the same smile. "No. You're funny when you're mad. I'm not trying to screw with you."

I shook my head with more irritation and disgust, and swallowed to dislodge the knot in my throat.

Noah's smile faded and he tilted his head slightly as he appeared apathetic again. "You're Holly Bennett from Portland, Oregon. Today is your birthday—happy birthday, by the way. You graduated from San Francisco University High School at the age of fifteen, then went on to Berkeley for your bachelors, masters, and doctorate. Your father, Francis Bennett, was considered to be a world-renowned brain surgeon, who was killed by a virus he contracted from a patient. Your brother's name is Brad. He lives in Portland and is currently a divorce attorney. He posts your picture online once a week with a description of you, and a number to contact if you're spotted. And Greg—who looks like a dick by the way—would be the boyfriend you walked out on. He'd like you to call him because he's devastated about 'what happened'. You have one outstanding parking ticket in Eugene, Oregon." He narrowed his eyes. "Hardly criminal. The internet is a big place." Noah kept his arms crossed with musing smile on his face.

"None of that means you know who I am. And Greg *is* a dick. That's what no one knows. He's a manipulative and abusive *asshole*. He's also my brother's best friend. The brother who is pissed at me for getting kicked out of my residency program because his best friend took a knife to my side." I lifted the side of my shirt and showed the fourteen-inch vertical scar.

Noah's expression changed with a slight frown.

"Yeah. Exactly!" I gestured at his expression. "Did you know I'm *that* girl…? The one who perpetually lets her boyfriend beat the hell out of her?" I pulled up the sleeve of my shirt. "This is from being thrown through the back door of *my own house*. Took me a few hours to dig the glass out of my arm. I missed a few pieces, so they still surface once in a while." I pulled at the neck of my shirt over to show the scar under my collarbone. "This one is from a rock. Cracked my collar bone, but it was okay because my brother was really happy I didn't die in the car accident I staged to cover it up. Did you research my brother too? Did you find out that he illegally forged documents on a case, and Greg—who employs my brother—cleaned it up nice and pretty so Brad wouldn't go to jail? No, probably not, because none of those things are posted on the damn internet."

Noah watched me carefully, unmoving.

"I went for a walk and I didn't stop. And then you came

along and offered me a place where I could just work and be okay…" I got quieter as I tried to fight the lump strangling my voice. "You're kind of an ass, but it's nice because lines don't get blurred. I work for you, and I live here without any attachments… Now you've taken that away…" I pushed my hand against my chest like I could push the panic down.

"Come on." Noah held his hand out to me.

"No." I put my hand behind my back.

Noah pushed off the truck and walked toward me. He took my hand and towed me behind him into the basement of the house. We stood in front of the gun safe and he pulled the keys from his pocket to unlock it.

"Pick one." Noah pointed at the guns inside once the door was open.

"I don't know the first thing about guns. The closest I've been is pulling a bullet out of somebody's chest." That wasn't entirely true, but I'd still never shot a gun before.

"Just pick one." He nodded at the safe.

I looked at him. I wasn't going to pick one. Noah pulled a large gun out and another small one. He grabbed two boxes of ammo, two earmuffs, shut the safe, and grabbed my hand again.

"What are you doing?" I asked as he towed me outside and around to the backyard.

"Stand right here." Noah pulled me closer to him after he stopped. "Now take this." He held out the bigger gun to me.

"I don't—" Noah shoved the gun into my hand before I could protest.

He opened the box of ammo and pulled out a few bullets. He set the box down and took the gun back to load it.

"Here. Aim at that tree and start shooting." He carefully handed the gun to me and pointed at the tree that he wanted me to shoot at.

"I can't shoot a gun." I shook my head. Was he nuts?

Noah put earmuffs on me. "Can't and won't have different definitions." He stepped behind me and held the gun up against my shoulder. "Here. Put one hand here to stabilize and aim, and your other hand right here. Don't put your finger on the trigger until you're ready to shoot," he said as he pulled my hand up to hold the gun. "Put this arm down." He pushed on my elbow gently. "Spread your feet a little more."

I looked down and readjusted my stance.

He touched my arm to lower it again. "Now use the sights to aim at the tree." Noah kept his arms around me as he helped me hold the gun up. It was heavier than it looked. "Are you ready to shoot?"

I nodded. I was a little terrified, but he wasn't going to let me chicken out.

"That tree is everything you're mad at. Shoot it." His voice was abrasive.

I took a second, focusing my panic and anger at the tree. I pulled the trigger and the gun shoved back into my shoulder. Noah pulled on a metal lever and a bullet casing popped out of the gun.

"Again." He said quickly.

I focused on the tree and pulled the trigger. Noah pulled the lever and told me to shoot again. This time, I watched the bright blast from the end of the barrel when I pulled the trigger.

"Good." Noah took the gun from me. "Now try this one. It doesn't require as much effort." He grabbed the smaller gun off the back deck. He cocked it back and handed it to me. "This has seventeen rounds, keep shooting until it's gone."

I took the gun nervously.

"Focus. That tree is Greg."

I shot the gun at the tree and actually hit it this time. Once the first round was out, I shot a second and a third. I kept shooting but felt bad for the tree. Noah took the gun from me when it was empty and popped out the empty clip. He shoved in a new one and handed me the gun.

I looked at him, feeling unsure.

"Keep shooting." He nodded at the tree as he started loading bullets into the empty clip. "I know you haven't gotten it all out yet. Keep shooting the tree until you feel better." He looked down and continued putting bullets in the other clip.

I aimed at the tree and fired a round.

"No. Stop. You're doing it wrong." Noah put a hand on my arm.

I carefully handed him the gun. He flipped a switch on the side and the hammer went down, but the gun didn't go off. He set it down on the deck and turned me to face him.

"Close your eyes."

"What?" I laughed dryly.

"Just do it."

I closed my eyes with a huff.

"How did it feel when he hit you?" Noah asked.

"It hurt." I shook my head and shrugged. How did he want me to answer that?

"Not the physical pain... how did *you* feel?"

I shook my head. Wasn't it obvious what a person would feel in that situation? What did he want to hear?

Noah grabbed the tops of my arms quickly, squeezing harder than necessary. "How did it feel?" he yelled.

My eyes flashed open as the panic in my chest rose.

"There." Noah pointed at my face. "Shoot that feeling." He handed me the gun and turned me to face the tree.

I fired the gun feeling like the trigger was too slow to match my rage. I kept pulling the trigger until the gun was empty. He pushed a button to drop the empty clip and put the half-full one in.

"Push this down to release the slide and shoot." Noah touched a small lever on the side.

I pushed it down and started shooting again until the bullets were gone. I dropped the empty gun to my side and pulled off the earmuffs as I stared at the tree with tears hanging in my eyes. Noah carefully took the empty gun from my hand.

"Can I have the bigger gun back?" I whispered, continuing to stare at the tree.

"Knock yourself out."

I turned to pick it up from the deck, put my earmuffs back on, and blasted a nasty hole into the tree. I pulled the metal lever the way Noah had, to release the shell, and blasted it again. Noah took it to put more bullets in after the third one and gave it back. I kept going until my shoulder felt like it was permanently damaged.

"Better?" Noah asked when I handed him the gun.

I took a second to decide. "I'm hungry," I laughed as I stared at the half naked tree. I looked at him and tried to hold onto the smile.

Noah reached down and grabbed my hand. He looked at the bracelet for a second and turned my wrist over. He undid the clasp and unwrapped the long strand of leather from my arm.

"What are you doing?" I asked as I frowned in confusion.

"I'm taking it."

"Why?"

Noah wrapped it up in his hand. "I'll give it back eventually."

"How about giving it back now?" I felt bugged.

"You've been using it as a tool to keep everything in. That's not what it should mean." Noah started walking around the side of the house with the guns I'd used. "Everyone thinks I'm an ass, but I'm okay with it. My anger isn't staying in."

"I'm not angry. I'm moving on." I walked after him.

"Then you suck at it... And you *are* angry, you just haven't figured it out yet." He opened the glass door to the basement. "Just like you have to figure out happiness is a choice."

"It's not black and white. You can't just choose to be happy."

"You're right. It's not black and white. You have to fight for it. It's probably easier to be lazy and give up." He put the guns in the safe and turned to me. "What have you been fighting for since you came here?"

I looked at Noah. "To keep my head above water."

"What water?" He spread his arms, directing in both directions. "You're here. Away from everyone and everything. You walked across thousands of miles of dry land to get here. What the hell are you fighting?" His tone suggested that I'd said something preposterous. He watched me with raised eyebrows as he waited for an answer.

I wasn't fighting for anything. I'd been struggling against a tide that was no longer there, but still felt like I had to struggle.

"Nothing," I answered quietly.

"There's a world at your feet... Be happy *in* it, or be miserable *with* it." Noah directed his hand toward the stairs.

I walked up the stairs and into the dining room. He made me feel like a child being lectured by their parent, but he was right.

"Do you want a grilled cheese?" Noah asked as he walked into the kitchen.

I nodded and sat down on the bar stool at the breakfast bar.

"You thought of all of this last night?" I asked quietly, pulling back the conversation from the lake.

"Along those lines." Noah opened the fridge and pulled out a glass pan with foil on it. "I was up half the night making these." He pulled the foil off the glass pan to show several cupcakes and set it on the counter in front of me. "It's a little late now, but happy birthday."

"You made these for me?" I asked with a smile as I pulled one out.

Noah leaned over the counter on his elbows and nodded. There was a small smile on his face.

"Thank you." I looked at the chocolate cupcake and smiled. "I don't think I've ever had cupcakes that didn't come from a store." I looked at him.

Noah pushed off the counter and shook his head. "You've *got* to stop saying depressing things." He bent down to pull out a frying pan from the cabinet and set it on the stove.

"I meant it as a compliment. Thank you for making me cupcakes." I set the cupcake down on the counter and reached back to braid my hair.

"You're welcome." Noah turned to grab a loaf of bread. "What are you doing?"

"Braiding my hair?" I paused, raising an eyebrow.

"I like it down."

"It's in my face, and I look like a shaggy dog."

"You don't." Noah's voice was low. "You look nice."

......

Noah made grilled cheese and we sat outside on the bench swing as we ate them.

"Tomorrow, we're gonna clear out those trees back there," Noah said looking out at the backyard.

"Why?" I asked as I put the last bite of grilled cheese in my mouth.

"I'm gonna build a house."

I looked at Noah like he was crazy. "Just like that? You're gonna build a house...? What about *this* house?"

"I'll sell it and have it hauled off the property when I'm done building the other one." His tone was so simplistic. It was like he was talking about moving a stack of papers.

"You know, I think there's a nice funny farm in town." I raised an eyebrow and pointed in the direction of town with my thumb.

"I'm not crazy. This house is more work than it's worth to me, I don't want to be here anymore, and I've been holding on to it for too long."

I continued to look at him wryly.

"I haven't slept in my own bedroom since Kate died. I just closed the door and left everything untouched." He looked out into the trees. "I still haven't gone in there."

"Maybe it's time."

Noah looked at me.

"You made me shoot a gun and you took my bracelet." I held my hand out, ready to lead him into the house. "I know you're an insomniac like me; we can pack everything up so you don't have to worry about it anymore."

Noah took my hand. "Maybe tomorrow." His thumb rubbed once over the back of my hand.

......

The next day, Noah taught me how to use a chainsaw and we cut down trees in the backyard. I'd cut one down, cut the branches off, and cut the center of the tree into pieces. Noah would load the logs into the back of the truck and unload them behind the garage for firewood. He bundled the branches and hauled them to the front yard to take to the dump another day. Together we cleared about twelve large trees and a bunch of little ones.

I didn't like the idea of him building a new house to get rid of the old one, but I somehow understood. There wouldn't be a day he wouldn't look at his house and think of Kate. On some level, it would be like going back to my house in Oregon and pretending like nothing had ever happened. The very thought made me want to fly home just to set my house on fire. I was comparing apples to oranges, but they were still fruit.

Chapter 6

A Month Later

Things between Noah and I were more normal than I'd expected. It wasn't like the kiss had never happened, because we were different around each other, but it wasn't a bad thing. Noah would talk my ear off when we weren't working instead of sitting in silence like before. His obsessive habits started to loosen and his responses didn't feel like a backhand to the face. He just enjoyed the day. Every now and then, he would do something spontaneous like throw a pinecone in my direction or crack a joke. We worked long days, but they were fun.

When I wasn't working with Noah, I worked on making my little apartment nicer. I had enough money to buy some more furniture, decorations, and some paint for the walls. Noah had offered to help, but I refused. I needed something that was mine. I think he was happy I was starting to feel at home. For him, it meant that I was planning to stay.

"What are you doing tomorrow?" Noah asked as he stabbed at his salad.

We were outside on the deck having dinner.

"Same thing I do every Saturday, I guess..." *Nothing*. I looked at Noah.

"I have something I have to do early in the morning, but I was wondering if you'd want to spend the day with me after that?" He looked at his plate and nervously pushed around a crouton with his fork.

"Are you asking me out on a date?" I raised an eyebrow.

Noah looked up and it was the first time I'd ever seen him appear shy or mildly embarrassed. "Sort of..."

I nodded. "Okay." I gave a small smile.

"I should be home around nine."

"I'll be ready by nine then. What are you planning?"

"To bring you to one of the houses I built. The guy called me yesterday. They had some hail damage from the storm a few days ago and he needs a few things fixed. I need to get a few pictures and figure out what I need. He doesn't trust anyone else to do the repairs and I think you'll like the house."

"Sounds like fun. Where's it at?"

"About an hour and a half from here, outside of the cities."

I nodded.

......

The next morning, I woke up around eight to take a shower, dried my hair and put it in a braid, like usual. I pulled on a pair of white shorts and a denim top, then rolled the sleeves halfway up my forearms. Only one of my scars showed so it didn't look overly conspicuous. My hair had taken too long to dry, so I hurried as I brushed my teeth because I was running late.

"Holly?" Noah called through the small apartment.

"I know, I'm late. I'm sorry!" I yelled as I hurried into my bedroom to find a pair of sandals at the bottom of my closet.

"You're not late. I'm early," he said calmly as he stood in the doorway of my room. "It looks nice in here." He looked around the room.

I looked up from the floor as I put my sandals on. I had painted the walls a light sea blue. The curtains were white, hung high, and draped down to the floor to make the windows look bigger. I'd bought a headboard, new bedding and pillows, added an accent chair to the corner, painted the dresser and nightstands an off-white, hung a few decorations on the wall, and added a couple of off-white shag rugs over the dark wood floor.

"It looks like a beach house."

"That's what I was going for." I smiled as I stood up.

Noah looked at me and gave a small smile. "You look nice too."

I rolled my eyes and grabbed my purse. "Thanks." I attempted to walk past him, but he gripped the doorway and blocked me.

I took a step back and raised my eyebrows. "Yes?"

"You look nice," he repeated with a smile.

I let out a sighing huff and shook my head. "Thanks, and I heard you the first time."

Noah pressed his lips together in a tight line and shook his head. "You rolled your eyes the first time and got huffy the second. Take a damn compliment. You look nice."

I took in a deep breath and held it for a second.

"Are you getting ready to jump in a lake?" he laughed.

"I'm trying to 'take a damn compliment'... Nope." I let out my breath. "Can't do it." I ducked quickly under his arm.

Noah turned and caught me around the waist before I could get a step into the living room. "Scared fish." He moved in front of me and carefully pinned me in the doorway with a smile.

I looked up at him and tried to ignore that my heart was jack hammering with fear. He was far bigger than Greg and could stop me from moving without so much as a struggle on his part. Noah would be angry if he knew *that* was the thought in my head, so I worked on keeping a poker face as I looked up at him.

He smiled, pulling the ponytail holder from the end of my braid.

When I looked over into my room to watch Noah snap the band onto my bed, he gently pushed my chin up and kissed me. An explosion of bubbly adrenaline went from my stomach to my outer limbs and I relaxed against the doorway. His thumb feathered over my cheek and he broke the kiss.

"You look nice," he whispered and kissed me again, but it was shorter.

"Thank you."

He smiled and moved back just enough to look at me. "Are you gonna yell at me again?"

"I'm too curious to see the house you built."

He chuckled and dropped his hand from the doorway. "Come on then."

I followed him out the door and down the stairs.

We drove down the country road in the opposite direction of town. The sun fell on the road in patches through the leaved trees. The air smelled like the creek water and moss. I held my hand out the window to feel the soft wind between my fingers.

"You look happy," Noah said quietly. He looked at me with a smile.

I could feel the smile on my face. "I love it here... The mosquitoes are miserable, but it's beautiful, and the way the sun shines... I don't know. It just feels good."

Noah smiled.

......

We drove down a long road and came to a massive gate. Noah pulled up to the keypad and entered a code.

"Close your eyes."

I looked at Noah. "No way."

"I'm serious. It will be worth it. Close your eyes."

I closed my eyes as he pulled through the gate. The house couldn't be seen from the road because of a thick forest. I wasn't sure what to expect, because my expectations had already been thrown by the large gate at the front of the house. I'd expected a slightly nicer than average house, but the elegance of the front gate suggested different.

"Can I look now?" I asked when he turned the truck off.

"No, and don't peek."

"I'm not peeking."

I listened as he got out of the truck and walked around. He opened the door and guided me out. He put his hands over mine to cover my eyes.

"Are you ready?"

I nodded. He dropped his hands and I opened my eyes. My smile fell.

"It's modeled after Norwegian Stave church architecture," he said quietly. I could hear the smile in his voice, but I was too focused on the house to look at him.

The house looked about three stories tall with sharp A-frames that had wood shingles down the sides. All the windows were elongated-diamond shaped glass panes, and surrounded with a lighter colored wood. On the third level up, at the edge of the A-frames, were four Norwegian horse heads that pointed with their noses toward the sky. It wasn't a house... I didn't have words for what it was, but it wasn't a house.

"Come on," Noah took my hand.

"Noah!" a man said as he came outside.

I looked to the right side of the house near the front door. The outside entrance to the house was tucked back around a corner, and tall trees made it appear private but welcoming. Above the front door was an impossibly large window with the same diamond stained-glass pattern.

"Lars, how are you?" Noah stepped forward and shook the man's hand.

I pulled my attention back to the man in front of us. He was probably in his early seventies with white hair, a stubble beard, and gold rimmed glasses. He was slight of frame but appeared confident and kind.

"I'm very well, thank you. Who's this gal you've brought with you?" The man smiled at me. He had a thick Norwegian accent which explained the nationality of the architecture.

"This is Holly. Holly, this is Lars."

"Nice to meet you." I extended my hand and smiled politely.

He took my hand in both of his with a big smile. "Wonderful to meet you, Holly. Welcome." Lars waved for us to follow him. "Come around to the back."

We walked around the house and I couldn't quit staring. I felt like I could look at the house forever and I would never be able to memorize all the intricate woodwork. There were pieces of wood that hung down from the inside of the A-frames that looked like wooden doilies. I'd never seen something so beautiful.

"Around here you can see some of the woods are broken," Lars said as he pointed to a group of shingles. "And there on the side, I've a leak into the house. We can go inside so you can look." Lars walked up the stone pathway to a set of stairs. I imagined he used an odd choice of words because of the language barrier.

I followed them and looked at the stained-glass windows that formed a large cathedral arch. The back of the house looked completely different around the base. It still had all of the woodwork, and the top two stories were the same, but everything focused around the cathedral-like windows. I glanced behind me and noticed there was a private lake that the windows looked out to.

When we walked inside, I could have cried. It looked like a church instead of a house. The beams that drew up to the ceiling had shallow notches—about three inches long—along the edges, making it more decorative than a plain beam. Every doorway had wood panels with intricate Norwegian carvings.

"What do you think, Holly?" Lars asked with a smile as he pulled his attention away from Noah.

"I've never seen anything like it." I looked up at the ceilings in awe.

"I asked Noah to build me a church I could live in. All of these carvings are done by hand, by different Norwegian craftsmen." He pointed around the house.

Lars gave me a tour of the three-story mansion, and every room was its own piece of art. I had no words. I just stood speechless and looked around as if I'd been blind my whole life. I'd been to different parts of the world with my dad and brother, but Noah's beautiful work put every old structure I'd seen to shame. The house was so grand it was comparable to any famed historic mansion.

......

"So what'd you think?" Noah asked as we pulled out of the gate.

I shook my head. "*Now* I want to yell at you."

He laughed. "Why?"

"Because you can build something like *that*... and you're just—" I couldn't finish my sentence. "You have a gift and you're not using it. That is the most beautiful house I have *ever* seen... You're wasting your time fixing up your hopeless yard when you could be building pieces of history. You were on the front cover of a prestigious magazine because of your amazing talent... and now you're hiding in your backyard. I can't understand it... How could you just stop?" I shook my head and looked at Noah.

"First of all, do you know how much it costs to build something like that? Not many people have the kind of money he has. That house cost him about seven million in materials alone—and I'm not talking about the decorative stuff from Norway. Secondly, I haven't stopped... I'm just on hold for a while. Something like that takes inspiration, and I haven't been inspired."

"Find some inspiration then." I shook my head. "Find someone who has the money..."

"And how'd you know I was in a magazine?"

"Lars had a copy hanging on the wall in his study."

"Well, I'm glad you like it so much." Noah smiled as we drove down the road. "Are you ready to find some food?"

I nodded.

·······

After we were done eating, we drove for two hours to Duluth. Noah pulled up to a house that was tucked into a small forest of trees and gardens. The house was a light blue with large river stones lining the bottom. It looked like a country home met a cottage.

"Well, this is my parent's house."

"Parents?" I looked at Noah.

"Yeah... They said if I didn't bring you to meet them, they'd come to us. Believe me, this is the better option. We can leave when we want to."

I looked at the house and swallowed hard.

Noah laughed. "I'm not feeding you to the lions. It's just my parents. They're nice. Come on." Noah got out of the truck and walked around to me. He opened the door and reached his hand out to me. "The only person you have to watch out for is my brother Moses. He likes to crack jokes wherever he can. Gabe usually has a stick up his ass, so he probably won't say anything to you. My mom, Linna, will squish your face a thousand times and smile at you, and my dad's quiet. He's always got his nose in a book. You'll be lucky if he says hi."

I looked at the house nervously as I rolled down the sleeves of my shirt. Noah stopped me when he noticed.

"Relax. No one will pay attention." He let go of my hand and rolled my sleeves back to the way they were before. "You have nothing to worry about." Noah took my hand again and walked up to the door.

"Mom?" Noah called when we walked inside.

There was a large window above the front door that casted light into the entryway. The floors were all dark wood with white trim along the edges of the light-colored walls. Straight ahead was a long hallway with a large staircase to the side. To the right was a formal living room with a grand piano, and a well-used cello that sat in the sunshine from the wide windows. To the left was a dining room that had windows overlooking a garden on the side of the house. It was a very open and inviting home, and it smelled lightly of Irises.

"It's a little less ambitious than the house you saw earlier, but this one is my favorite."

I looked up at Noah. "You built this?"

"You didn't think my parents would just settle for some prefabbed box when their son has a knack for building, did you?"

"You're gloating," I said as I looked around.

"Maybe." He laughed quietly.

"Oh, you're here!" Noah's mom said excitedly as she held her arms open. I thought she was going to hug Noah first, but she went straight for me. "Look at you, you're so beautiful." She patted my back as she hugged me. She pulled away quickly and squished my face in her hands. "Oh, just look at those beautiful eyes and those sweet dimples." She smiled at me, then kissed my cheek.

Could she even see my dimples through her hands?

She had a kind smile and pure hazel eyes. She looked so

different from Noah. Her hair was a dark natural brown with a hue of red, wisped just perfectly to the side. She had a round button nose and thin lips.

"Mom, don't overwhelm her," Noah said quietly.

"Oh, you hush," she said as she let go of my face to hug Noah and kiss his cheek. "You look good, Honey. How are you?" Linna held his face in her hands with a brilliant smile.

"Same as always," he sighed. "Where's dad?"

"He's in his study, let's go say hi." Linna walked down the hallway, Noah and I followed. "Thomas, Honey. Noah's here with Holly."

"Who?"

"Holly. Remember I told you Noah had a new friend?" Linna turned through a set of glass French doors into a small room that had a two-story ceiling with windows all around the top. There was a small spiral staircase in the back corner of the room that went up to a catwalk with a telescope.

"Oh, yeah."

I looked down from the ceiling at Noah's father who looked exactly like Noah but older, with faded gray hair. I could see by the muscles in his face that he'd previously suffered a stroke, but no one else would have noticed.

"Hello, Sweetheart, it's nice to meet you." He walked around his desk and hugged me. His voice was rough but calm. There was no abundance of excitement like Noah's mom.

"You as well." I gave him a kind smile before I gently hugged him.

"Son, how are you?" Thomas nodded at Noah.

"Been busy working to start the new house." Noah's voice was different as he spoke to his father. I looked up at him to watch the expressions on his face. He wore a stone-hard look like he might have been angry. I looked at Thomas to check his expression, but he seemed oblivious.

"It's about time. That cat-box you live in isn't a home." Thomas walked back around and sat behind his desk.

"Come on Honey, let's go into the kitchen. I made some fresh cookies just for you. I want you to have some before your brothers show up." Linna pulled at Noah's arm.

Noah was giving his dad a hard glare. Thomas kept his head down in a book, completely unaware. Noah turned and we walked straight through the hallway and into the brightly lit kitchen. It was painted a cheerful yellow with windows between the cupboards and countertops.

"Have a seat. Do you want some tea or coffee?" Linna asked as she walked over to the counter to grab a square container filled with cookies.

"Coffee is fine for me." Noah sat down at the kitchen island.

I looked back across the hallway at Noah's father. I didn't think he meant to be rude. I could see from the books on his desk and certain mannerisms that he was incredibly intelligent and had to try very hard to be an acceptable level of normal. All his responses seemed detached.

"Holly?" Linna asked, drawing my attention away.

"Coffee is fine. Thank you." I sat down at the kitchen island.

"So, Noah tells me you're a doctor. I was a nurse practitioner for fifteen years." Linna pulled a pot from the coffee maker and poured three cups.

Noah pushed the container of chocolate chip cookies toward me.

"How was that?" I asked with a kind smile.

"It was hell. I always came home with something contagious." She smiled. "How do you like Minnesota so far?"

"It's nice. I like the weather a little better."

Linna set two cups of coffee down in front of Noah and I. "It's nice in the summer, but just wait until winter comes and it feels like it never ends."

"Where is she? This new girl that calls herself Holly?" A voice came from the dining room.

Linna turned her head toward the doorway of the dining room. My gaze followed.

"Moses, I thought you weren't coming for a while." Linna smiled, turning her body to face him.

"Noah has a new girl, so I called into work and told them I died in a car accident yesterday."

"Oh." Linna frowned and waved her hand dismissively before stretching up to hug Moses with a smile. He was tall and skinny, wearing red nerdy glasses. His hair was a dark mop of floppy curls. Moses looked more like Linna, but still had a few of Thomas' features, like the strong jaw line. Noah had it too.

"Mom. Don't embarrass me. I have to do it for myself," Moses whined as he let go of Linna. "You must be Moses, I'm Holly." Moses bent over in a quick bow and held his hand out to me.

I laughed quietly and shook his hand.

"It's a great pleasure," Moses said before he kissed my hand.

"Act normal for once," Noah snapped.

"Sorry, Miss Holly, my little brother is in great need of harassment. If he doesn't get it, he might become cheerful, and nobody wants that. Have you ever seen a gremlin smile?" Moses' face pulled up into a terrifying smile as he bared his teeth like a vampire. His eyebrows made a gruesome V shape.

"Stop it!" Linna smacked Moses' arm gently with a disapproving click of her tongue.

Moses laughed and I laughed quietly to myself.

"She's cute little bro, where'd you find her?" Moses asked as he walked behind us to the cabinet for a glass.

"When is Gabe coming?" Noah asked Linna, ignoring Moses.

"I'm already here. Somebody decided to take up the whole driveway with his rattle can of a car."

Gabe walked in from the dining room. He looked more like Moses, but his hair was straight and brown. He had a thick beard and Noah's familiar hard frown. His expression was rigid as he walked into the room. He wore a fitted suit with a dark silver tie that was perfectly tucked into his jacket. Based on appearance, I pegged him for more of a perfectionist than Noah.

"Gabe, Honey, this is Noah's friend Holly," Linna said kindly. Her demeanor toward him was different than Noah or Moses. She was careful.

"Hello." He extended his hand without a smile. His voice was flat.

"Nice to meet you." I gave a shy smile and shook his hand.

"How'd the hearing go yesterday?" Linna asked as Gabe walked over for a glass of water.

"Stupid judge didn't know what he was doing, but we got what we wanted. I just got done with a meeting with the clients. They didn't want to wait until Monday."

I watched Gabe carefully, there was something dark about his personality. He looked angry and stressed. Gabe's demeanor was somewhat like Noah's the day before the lake.

"Gabe is a lawyer," Linna told me proudly with a smile.

I smiled at Gabe politely. "What type of law do you practice?" Maybe if I was kind he would ease up.

"Land rights and zoning." He didn't look at me as he answered my question.

"My brother is a divorce attorney mostly, but he settles some land disputes on the side."

"Divorce attorneys aren't lawyers, their scumbags."

"Hey!" Noah's voice was short and sharp.

"That's what I tell my brother." I gave a small smile, trying to defuse the situation quickly.

Gabe smiled and laughed quietly as he chewed on an ice cube. I had a smile of satisfaction from being acknowledged by more than a straight face. I looked at Noah who was staring with a hard glare at Gabe.

"What do you do?" Gabe looked at me.

"She's a doctor," Linna answered proudly.

Gabe laughed quietly. "That's more schooling than I wanted to do." Gabe walked over closer to me and started talking to me about my medical schooling and different surgeries I'd done. Noah talked with his mom and Moses while Thomas sat in his study as if the world didn't exist.

Linna asked Moses and Noah to go outside and help her move a trellis, Gabe had to take a call, and that left me in the kitchen. Instead of going outside to find Noah, I went in to talk to Noah's father. I stood in front of the desk and looked at the book he was reading.

"'The devil hunts man, just as man hunts food,'" I quoted quietly.

Thomas looked up and set his book down. "You've read this?"

I gave a kind smile with a nod.

"It's a terrible book." He looked at it in disgust, shaking his head.

I laughed a little. "Then why are you reading it? You have all of these books." I turned to the shelves of books on the right side of the room.

"Because I believe every book contains a piece of knowledge I don't have." Thomas stood from his chair and watched as I looked over his collection. He seemed a little nervous, like he didn't know what he should be doing.

I smiled. "That's a beautiful way to view it." I reached forward and touched the spine of a book that looked older than both of us combined. "Where did you get all of these old prints?"

"Most of them Moses finds for me, he works at the library when he's not teaching, and the rest were gifts from students who knew I collected." Thomas sounded like Noah for a moment.

I smiled and turned around. "What did you teach?"

"Physics and astronomy." He directed his hand up to the telescope above us.

I looked up. "I bet you've seen some beautiful things." I looked at Thomas again.

"I have," he nodded. He gave me the same smile that Noah gave me every now and then, like he appreciated my company. "Tell me something..." he directed his hand for me to sit in the chair at the front of his desk before he sat down. "What's piqued your interest in my son?"

I smiled shyly and moved to sit down. "I think you've misunderstood... Noah and I aren't—" I struggled to think of an appropriate word. "We're just friends."

Thomas took in a deep breath with a hard look on his face. "You've seen my collection of books here." He directed his hand to the shelves of books.

I nodded, unsure if his words were a question or a statement.

"I've read many a great love story. Love stories that have been made famous, and stories that are as quiet as the heart's whisper. The way my son looks at you, the way you look at him... I see what's there..." He sat back in his chair. "I assume that you've been told about Kate?"

I nodded.

"Kate was a beautiful young lady, much like yourself. She was very well loved in this family, but never once did my son look at her the way he looks at you. I don't mean to imply he didn't love her, of course." He held up his hand as if I were about to interrupt him. "I believe he loved her a great deal, but he never looked at her so fondly. So, I ask again, what's piqued your interest in my son?" He leaned forward and folded his hands together as he waited for my answer.

I thought for a moment, feeling intimidated by his embellishment of words. "If I had an answer, I'd give it to you," I said kindly. "I'm still trying to find out for myself. Whatever it is, it's new and foreign. Right now, it's unexplainable moments."

Thomas looked behind me with eyes that were full of thought.

"Are you okay?" I asked.

"Shh." He held up his hand and stood abruptly. "I've

got it!" He quickly hurried out of the room.

I felt confused and walked out into the hallway. Thomas was humming loudly as he walked down the long hallway.

"Are you okay?" I asked again.

Thomas started humming louder. I didn't know what that meant. I turned to the back door and stepped outside. Noah smiled at me.

"I think I broke your dad." I pointed behind me with a nervous wince.

Noah's face changed, and so did Linna's and Moses'. They quickly walked past me, inside. I followed behind them down the long hallway and into the formal living room.

"We were talking, and he rushed out of the room," I explained quietly.

Thomas sat on the piano bench with the cello between his knees and his body moved as he drove the bow across the strings. There was a small recorder on the bench next to him. His eyes were closed as he hummed with the cello. His hair became tussled as he tugged the bow forcefully over the strings. His eyebrows raised when he began to play higher and quieter notes, but fell into a passionate frown with louder and deeper notes. It was beautiful the way he played—as much as *what* he was playing. I'd never heard a song quite like it. Everyone smiled and watched as he continued to play with a passion that was rarely seen in person. I imagined it's what Beethoven would have looked like as he composed his music.

"You didn't break him," Noah whispered. "You inspired him."

I looked up at Noah as he watched his father with a smile. I looked back at Thomas and watched him play. When he stopped, there was a joy and pride-filled smile on his face.

His eyes flashed open. "I've finally done it," he said quickly with the same smile held in place. "Pleiades has been written."

I frowned a little, trying to understand his meaning.

"Congratulations, Dear," Linna said kindly with a loving smile.

"I'm sorry. I don't remember your name." Thomas looked at me, snapping his fingers as he tried to recall.

"Holly."

"Yes. Thank you, Holly," he said with a sincere gratitude. "I have composed thirty pieces for thirty different constellations, and this makes thirty-one. Pleiades, more commonly known as the seven sisters, has been eluding me. I've been trying to explain Pleiades in music, but it's foreign, it's unexplainable. That's what you said, right?"

I still felt confused, but nodded in agreement.

"Way to go, Holly. We don't have to put dad in a straitjacket." Moses elbowed me playfully.

I looked at him with a frown. That wasn't funny. I'd honestly worried that I had caused some kind of a mental break.

"Relax, it's just a joke." Moses put his hands up.

"Get better material," Noah smirked. "Come on." Noah tugged at my arm and walked out into the entryway and back out to the backyard. When we were outside, Noah walked with me over the stony path that wound through the gardens. "Have you ever heard of Acquired Savant's Syndrome?"

I nodded and looked at Noah. "A result of the stroke?" I asked.

"Seven years ago. How'd you know?"

"The muscles on the left side of his face have slight deterioration. Also, he has a twitch in his pinkie and a subtle tremor in his voice."

Acquired Savant's Syndrome was caused by a form of trauma to the brain. It allowed for an ordinary person to suddenly become a prodigy at any one task. I had studied a case of a man in college who was electrocuted while working on an electrical line, and was suddenly one of the world's best mathematicians. The curious part was that he'd never learned anything above basic math before the accident.

"What was he like before?" I looked at Noah to gauge his reaction. My question was more of medical curiosity rather than personal.

"Average. I mean, he was still really smart, but he knew how to be around people. When he had his stroke he came home from the hospital and sat down at the piano. He'd never played a day in his life. And the more he played, the more we didn't exist." I could hear the heartache that Thomas's sudden brilliance had caused.

I looked at Noah. "The adjustment must have been hard for all of you."

"Yeah. He spends more time with his books and his music than us... I'm sure you noticed we're not exactly on speaking terms." Noah looked out at the path in front of us. "When Kate died, he gave me every mathematical explanation of how the accident didn't make sense from a physics standpoint. If we were going forty-five miles an hour, and the semi was going twenty, and you were perpendicular... blah blah blah, Kate shouldn't be dead... He was so enraged over the laws of physics not adding up, he refused to come to the funeral. I said a bunch of things I shouldn't have, and he's not as forgiving as he used to be. The smarter he gets, the more his social skills decline."

I didn't know what to say to him.

Chapter 7

We didn't stay at Noah's parents' for very long after our talk in the backyard. We did some sight-seeing while it was still light outside, then went walking around downtown after the sun had set. It was beautiful outside and everyone was active. Noah started talking about building houses again and asked me what I wanted to do going forward.

"Do you want to go back to being a doctor?"

I shrugged. "Of course I do. That's been my dream since before I knew what a dream was…"

"Well, the Mayo Clinic in Rochester is about forty minutes from the house. You have the cities with an abundance of hospitals to choose from. Tell them the truth about what happened in Portland, I'm sure somebody will take you. You graduated Berkeley with honors, they're not gonna just slam the door in your face."

I shook my head. "I don't have what I need to get started... I don't even have my social security card in order to take my boards here."

"So, we'll go down to the social security office and get you a new one. Or call your brother and ask him to send what you need. You're letting a pebble in the road keep you from crossing. I'm gonna run out of things for you to do eventually..." Noah stepped aside so someone could walk between us.

"I know," I said quietly.

Noah looked forward as we walked down the sidewalk together.

"You make me feel like a child sometimes."

Noah laughed. "Why?"

"Because, you always have these 'life lessons'. It kinda makes me want to hit you or something." I put my hands in my pockets to hide my nervousness.

Noah laughed. "Sorry."

I tried to suppress my smile as I looked at the ground in front of me.

He let out a small huff with a smile. "Let me guess, you're used to being the smartest person in the room?"

I nodded simplistically, looking at him. "That's exactly right."

He laughed. "You're smart in your ways, I'm smart in mine. You can take the reins if someone needs medical attention."

I shoved Noah's arm. "I know more than medical stuff."

He laughed and kept walking forward without a word.

We walked back to the truck and got in. We were going to find a late bite to eat and drive back home. When Noah tried to start the truck, it turned on, but died right away. He tried again, but the same thing happened.

"Come on, Baby." He rubbed the dashboard and pumped the clutch before trying again.

"I think she wants us to stay here," I said when the truck didn't start.

Noah got out of the truck and lifted the hood. After a string of cuss words, he dropped the hood down.

"Well, I guess we're stuck here," he laughed as he walked around the side of the truck.

I smiled. "There was a hotel back that way." I pointed in the direction we'd come from.

Noah sighed and wrapped his arm around my shoulders as we walked back up the hill.

"We need two rooms, please," Noah said to the lady at the front desk.

The hotel was old, but nice inside.

"I'm sorry. All we have available is a single king room." The lady gave Noah a sympathetic look. "We have the Late Nights festival going on. There's a pull-out bed in the couch though."

Noah looked at me. "I can stay with my parents."

"Uh," I gave a hesitant look, "staying by myself didn't work out so great in Stillwater. I'm fine with sharing a room or we can call around." I shrugged.

I could see that he was frustrated.

"Yeah. I guess." Noah handed her his card.

"I'm sorry, our credit card machine is broken. There's an ATM at the bar just down on the corner." She pointed behind us.

Noah turned around with a forced smile that made

him look like an evil vampire. The same face that Moses had made earlier. I cracked up with laughter. The lady behind the counter must have thought we were crazy.

I laughed and pulled my wallet out of my purse. "How much is it?"

"It's three-o-four," the lady said nervously. "And I need your ID."

"Don't mind him, he's just grumpy," I laughed as I handed her the cash and my driver's license.

"Grumpy. That's what I am." Noah chided quietly with a crazy look on his face.

"He's hypoglycemic." I rubbed Noah's arm as I spoke to the girl behind the counter. "Do you have any food here?"

"There are vending machines near the elevator, and some take-out menus in the room. There's a lot of places that deliver." She handed me the change, my license, and the cards to the room.

"Thank you," I smiled and took Noah's arm to pull him toward the elevator. "Come on. Let's find you a snack and a puppy to kick." I rubbed his arm and pulled him down the hallway.

We went up to our room and I looked out the window at the lake while Noah looked at the take-out menus.

"I'm gonna go raid the vending machines, do you want anything?" Noah asked quietly.

"No thanks." I walked away from the window to the couch, pulled off the cushions, and pulled out the bed while Noah went to the vending machines. It was already made up with sheets and a blanket. I stole a couple of pillows from the bed and sat with a magazine from the coffee table. The routine felt normal to me. It's what I did in every town that I stayed in.

"What are you doing?" Noah asked when he came back in the room.

"Reading, because I don't like watching TV."

"You're sitting on my bed."

"No, I'm sitting on *my* bed. Your bed is over there." I pointed to the king-sized bed in the room without looking up from the magazine.

"No. I'm taking the pull-out bed."

I looked up from the magazine. "You won't fit. *I* barely fit. You'd have to sleep diagonally on this thing."

"Get off my bed." Noah sat his stash of junk food on the desk.

"I'm not *on* your bed." I looked back at my magazine. "Did you know that this town used to be home to more millionaires, per capita, than any other city in the world?"

"I'm gonna sleep on that bed whether you're in it or not," Noah threatened.

"Three million cows live in Minnesota."

Noah flopped on the bed next to me and stole the pillows from behind me. I pretended not to notice.

"Hey." His voice was quiet as he touched the scar on my arm.

I let the magazine down against my chest and looked at him.

"I'm serious. Take the bed." He looked at me as he kept tracing the scar.

I pulled down my sleeve and picked the magazine back up. "I've slept on worse. And this bed is way too small for you."

Noah took my arm and pulled up my sleeve to show the scar that he'd been tracing. I moved the magazine to my lap as I watched him turn my arm to look at the scar.

"Did you have stitches?" He traced the scar again.

I nodded. "I did it myself. I couldn't stand the pain, so I drank *a lot* of alcohol. It looked nice when I did it, but the next morning I realized I'd botched it pretty badly." I laughed a little.

Noah looked up at me with serious eyes. He didn't think it was funny.

My smile fell. "Don't look at me like that," I shook my head.

"Like what?"

"'Poor, stupid girl. Must've been hard.'" I pulled my arm away and pulled my sleeve down. "I did it to myself. I knew where the door was." I stood up from the bed and tossed the magazine on the table.

"Where are you going?" Noah asked from behind me.

"For a walk." I grabbed the key card off the dresser and walked out the door.

I stood at the elevator, waiting, when Noah came out of the room.

"I just need some air," I said as I looked up at the screen that displayed what floor the elevator was currently on—with my arms crossed. Elevators didn't provide fast exits.

"Then I'll come with you."

I looked at Noah and thought for a moment. I knew I was being unreasonable, but looked back at the elevator doors as they opened. "I'm gonna call a taxi and go to the store for a few things." My voice was quiet as I stepped into the elevator and leaned against the wall.

Noah nodded. I could feel him staring at me. The muscles in my neck tightened as I fought my emotions. I was overly aware of how pathetic I'd sounded.

"I didn't mean to upset you."

I shook my head. "It's not you." My voice was gone.

"Come here." He reached over to take my arm and pulled me closer. He wrapped his arm around my shoulders and rested his head on top of mine as he rubbed the top of my arm. "I'm sorry," he whispered.

We took a taxi to the store to get a few necessities. Noah convinced me to buy a swimsuit for the pool because he wanted to go swimming. He threatened to walk around the store with a bra on his head if I didn't. When we got back to the hotel, he had me in stitches as he wore a fedora and sunglasses he'd bought when I wasn't looking. He wrapped an arm around me while we walked into the hotel proclaiming to be my "sugar daddy."

"I take care of you real good, Baby," he said as we walked past the front desk.

I cracked up and pushed the button to the elevator, hoping that no one else would see or hear us. Once we were inside the elevator, he took off the hat and glasses.

"I'm not as uptight as you think I am." Noah smiled lightly and set the hat on my head.

"I never said that." I tried to keep myself from laughing. "I said you were crazy."

Noah pulled me in front of him and kissed me as he leaned against the wall behind him. My knees felt like they were going to buckle under me.

When the elevator doors opened, he let go of me and smiled. "You'd miss me if I joined my friends on the funny farm."

I smirked and walked to our room.

Noah gently tossed my swimsuit at me with a light smile.

"I only agreed to buy it, not wear it. You're not in the store anymore, so you can't threaten me with public humiliation." I shook my head and walked to the bed to pull the tags off the pajamas I'd bought.

"You don't have to do anything you don't want to. I just wanted to see you smile." Noah sat on the edge of the bed and looked at me with a light smile.

The smile on his face gave me a feeling I didn't quite understand. I wanted to keep it there. I grabbed the swimsuit, staring at him with fake agitation before going to the bathroom to change. I kept my denim shirt on over the swimsuit.

We walked down to the pool and all the lights outside, and in the pool, were off.

"Is it closed?" I asked, looking around for a sign.

"No. The sign says twenty-four hours. It's better this way anyway. More privacy, and you can see the stars." Noah stepped down into the water and looked up at the sky.

I sat down on the edge of the pool at the shallower end and stuck my feet in. When I looked up at the sky, I thought about Noah's dad. Little was known about Acquired Savant's Syndrome. Nearly every case was different, the only thing in common was a trauma to the brain. The ways in which the trauma occurred were all different, and in different parts of the brain. There was no medical treatment, and most didn't *want* to treat it. They loved their new-found gifts. I wanted to test Thomas' brain to see if I could even out the effects of his Savant's. As much as I loved the surgical practices of neurology, I loved the research end of it too. My dad had been working on using the pathways in the brain to cure ailments. I wanted to continue that work. I didn't want to take away Thomas' gift—he loved playing his music—but I wanted to help him get some normalcy back in his life.

"What are you thinking about?" Noah asked as he held the sides of my knees. He was waist deep in the water.

"Your dad." I looked down from the sky at Noah, doing my best not be distracted by his touch. "He was so happy when he played the cello." I gave a small smile.

Noah returned my smile. "You inspired him. He's been trying to find the music for that constellation for three years."

I shook my head. "I didn't do anything. He asked me a question and when I answered him, he just shot up out of his chair and started humming all the way down the hall."

"Well, for him, you did something pretty amazing. He won't forget your name again. He'll probably love you more than the rest of us... Can I ask what you were talking about though?" Noah's thumbs rubbed over the tops of my knees.

I couldn't think with him touching me.

"Um... he just asked me a question about you." I looked up at the sky again trying to focus my muddled thoughts.

"I'm foreign and unexplainable?" Noah laughed.

I looked back down. "Yes," I agreed sarcastically. "He asked me what my interest in you was. I told him I didn't know because it was unexplainable." My voice was quiet as the wind moved my hair gently.

"It's not that unexplainable, is it?" Noah's voice had a

hopefulness in it that I didn't recognize.

I held up my shoulders. "I've known you for three months, but sometimes it feels like it's been years... We make certain connections and realize that we're crossing lines we didn't want to. We hold hands like we're comfortable with each other, but stand like opposing magnets. We kiss," I gave a slight shrug, "but we walk away from it like it never happened... Every time I think about what this might be, I worry it *is*, then I worry it isn't. It's not 'unexplainable', it makes my head hurt." I gave an embarrassed smile. "I gave your dad the simpler response."

Noah gave a smile so small it was hardly noticeable. "I don't know either..." He looked down as he rubbed his thumbs over my knees.

I looked down at his hands. "Can we agree that whatever is, or wherever it goes, that it won't affect the arrangement we have?" I looked at him. "I can't go back," I shook my head.

"Of course." Noah gave me a gentle and reassuring smile. "Now, get in the water. I want to show you something." His smile grew.

I sighed and slid myself into the water, still covered in my denim shirt. Noah pulled me out to where I could barely touch the bottom of the pool.

"Float on your back," he said as he wrapped my arm around his shoulder.

I let out a breath and let my weight shift as I floated up to the surface of the water. I was extremely uncomfortable, but arguing had no weight with him. Noah put an arm under my back and one under my legs.

"Now pick a cluster of stars to stare at and keep your eyes on them."

"Okay..." I smiled shyly as I stared at a grouping of stars.

"Don't focus on anything else. Just watch the stars and float." He dropped his arms after a minute.

I took in a deep breath and did as he instructed. After a few minutes, I started to feel like I was part of the sky. Nothing was holding me. I was just floating with the stars. No gravity, no weight. I stared for so long I could see the stars as they moved above me. The music Thomas had played came to mind as I looked at Pleiades. I smiled because it somehow described what words couldn't.

••••••

The next morning, I woke up in the king size bed. We'd had a twenty-minute disagreement the night before about who was going to take the pull-out bed. Noah won. I'd tried to convince him that I was perfectly happy to sleep on the pull-out bed, but he said that he'd wait up and move me to the bed as soon as I fell asleep. I knew it was a losing battle, so I folded.

Noah had already left to find the part to fix his truck. I decided I was going to be brave, put my swimsuit back on and go for a swim down at the pool. If anyone asked about my scars, I'd tell them that I fell through a roof. Thankfully, nobody was at the pool. I smiled to myself and dove in.

While I floated on top of the water, I thought about what I was going to do. Noah was right, I didn't want to hide above his garage the rest of my life. I was too ambitious. I'd worked far too hard to become a doctor to give it up so easily. I needed to find a way to tell my brother enough of the truth to convince him to send me my stuff without telling Greg.

Noah was most likely right about other hospitals accepting me. Then I got to thinking, why would I tell *them* what happened and not my boss in Portland? She would probably be understanding if I just told her the truth. At the very least, I owed it to my friend, Bethany. She'd lost her job for me, the least I could do is try to get it back for her.

"Look at you," Noah smiled above me as I floated on my back near the side of the pool.

I set myself upright in the water. "Can you grab my towel? I need to go make a phone call." I pointed to my towel draped on the chair.

"What are you up to?" He reached over and grabbed the towel.

"I'm gonna call my boss in Portland and tell her everything. She can't report Greg because I'm no longer in that situation. Also, she doesn't know who he is. If she decides to call the police because she heard from me, the trail will dead end in Duluth and not in Red Wing where people know me." I pulled myself out of the pool and took the towel from Noah.

"It's Sunday. Is she gonna be there?" Noah followed me as I walked toward the building.

"Probably. I'd be surprised if she wasn't." I grabbed the door and walked into the hotel.

"Are you sure you've thought this through?" Noah followed me down the hallway.

I turned around. "I've worked too hard to lose everything."

"Does this mean you're going back?" Noah's face was almost sad.

I gave him a light smile, understanding why he was unsure of me making the call. "I'm not going back. I'm happy here... but you were right, I have to move forward. I don't know what that means yet, but I have to start with this call."

Noah nodded. I could see that my words weren't as reassuring as I'd meant.

I walked to the front desk and asked the lady to look up the number for the hospital in Portland. She wrote down the number for me and I went up to the room to call. I sat in my towel, dripping wet, and waited as the phone rang. When the receptionist picked up, I told her who I was and that I wanted to speak with Dr. Wiley.

"This is Dr. Wiley."

"Dr. Wiley, it's Holly Bennett." I took in a deep breath and tried to calm my nerves.

"Dr. Bennett, what can I do for you?" I heard some chatter in the background.

"I need to talk to you about what happened."

"I have a surgery in ten minutes, make it fast." Her tone was short.

I quickly explained to Dr. Wiley what had happened and why, without oversharing. The details of what had happened with Greg were still *my* secrets and I wasn't ready to share them all.

She didn't say anything when I finished talking.

"Are you still there?" I asked after a minute.

"Why didn't you tell me this to start with?" she asked quietly. The shortness was gone from her demeanor.

"I was trying to protect my brother, and I know that's no one's problem but my own, but I wanted to let you know for Bethany's sake."

I could hear Dr. Wiley taking in a deep breath. "Okay... well, I can't bring you back, but if you send me a backdated letter of resignation, I can clean this up for you, and I'll give you a letter of recommendation. You don't need to worry about Bethany. I'll take care of that too. Are you okay otherwise?"

"I am."

"Where are you? There's been a bit of a manhunt for you here. I have a missing person's paper with your face on it downstairs."

"I'm in Minnesota, but please don't tell anyone. I need a little time to figure everything out."

"I won't tell anyone under the condition that you never let something like this happen again. Part of being a doctor is taking care of patients, the other part is making sure that *you're* taken care of first. You have more talent than any resident I've ever encountered, don't put yourself in compromising situations to jeopardize your talent."

"That's why I left."

"Alright, well, I have to run, but take care of yourself and send me that letter with an address I can respond to."

"I will. Thank you for everything."

"Of course." She hung up quickly.

I hung up the phone and took in a deep breath. I was so happy and so relieved I wanted to scream.

"Well?" Noah asked. He was sitting on the end of the bed.

I smiled and slumped back. "It's too bad you don't drink, because I would *really* like to celebrate." I looked up at the ceiling.

"Okay...?"

I sat up and looked at him. "If I send her a backdated letter of resignation, this all goes away. She's even gonna write me a letter of recommendation."

Noah smiled. "See? I told you it was fixable. Put some

clothes on and we'll go celebrate."

Noah and I went out to lunch at a pub, then headed back to Red Wing. I felt about eighty pounds lighter. All I could do was smile the whole way home. I could go to any hospital now and do what I loved. I was almost free again.

•••••••

"Who's that?" Noah asked as the trees opened up about two hundred feet before his house. We were finally home, and a gray car with Minnesota plates sat in the driveway. Nobody ever came out to Noah's house, not even his friends.

Chapter 8

Brad got out of the car as Noah pulled into his normal parking spot next to the house.

"What are you doing here?" I asked as I got out of the truck quickly. I looked around to make sure that Greg wasn't with him walking around somewhere.

"Payphones have reverse directories, Holly. After I thought of it, it took one click online to find where you called from. I showed a picture of your face in town and someone told me I'd find you here. So, the better question is, what are *you* doing here? Please tell me that you didn't go looking for Mom..."

"Brad..." I sighed loudly and pinched the bridge of my nose for a moment. I dropped my hand and looked at him. He looked exactly the same. He was tall with a kind face and dark brown hair that was cut short. He was the male version of me.

Brad shook his head. "You found her... I told you she wasn't worth the time. Dad told you that too. Can't you ever listen? Go pack your stuff and let's go. I have a deposition in the morning." He pointed at the car. His face showed his irritation with me.

"I'm not leaving. I like it here and I'm staying."

"What would dad think of you right now?" Brad looked at me angrily as he crossed his arms. That made three of us. Noah was sitting on the front bumper of his truck with his arms crossed and I was standing about four feet in front of him with my arms crossed. All of us wore angry expressions.

"You got fired, ran away from home, ditched your fiancé, and went looking for a woman who doesn't even care about you. He'd be real proud." Brad held up four fingers as he counted my transgressions out loud.

I shook my head. "You don't know the first thing about what's going on. And Greg's not my fiancé. I did *not* say yes. I walked out of the house and I didn't come back. Also, did you know about Garrett being my biological dad?"

He partially turned with a tired and irritated expression, then looked at me again. "Yeah, I knew, and stay the hell away from him. He's a drug addict. Just—come home... Whatever happened, I'm sure we can fix it. Just come home."

"I'm not coming home. I spoke with Dr. Wiley, and I can't have my job back. I really like it here, I'm happy, and I'm submitting a relocation for my residency. There's a lot of really great hospitals within driving distance." I felt tired trying to explain to him, knowing he wasn't hearing me. "It would be really nice if you would send me all of my diplomas, licenses, and ID's. I'm starting something new, and I need just a little bit of support."

"Why don't you call Greg and ask him for that stuff?" I could hear in Brad's voice that he still didn't understand.

"Because I don't want to talk to Greg... I can't..." I looked at Brad and hoped that he would take some kind of message. I really didn't want to have to tell him about Greg. It would flip his life in all kinds of directions. Brad worked for him, they were best friends, and he loved Greg like family.

Noah stood up and rubbed my arm as he passed me to go into the house. I knew he wanted me to tell Brad the truth.

"Who is *that?*" Brad asked quietly after Noah was in the house.

"His name is Noah."

"How long have you known him? Like a month?"

"You need to go back to Portland and pretend like you never came here and you never saw me. Send me what I need, and go on with your life. You can visit after I get things straightened out."

Brad looked at me and shook his head again. "I don't understand you right now."

"Me either," I shrugged.

Brad looked defeated. "So that's it then...? You're not coming back?"

I shook my head and watched Brad carefully to see if he would accept my answer.

He looked away, shaking his head. "Just tell me what happened. Let me help you." His voice was less irritated and more kind and quiet, like he usually was. "If you just freaked because you don't want to marry Greg, I get it, but you can't just shit on everything you worked for." He gave me his sad, brown puppy-eyes.

"I'm not. The Mayo Clinic is forty-five minutes from

here, and there's some good hospitals in the cities. I'm not throwing my career away... just everything else."

"And you're really not gonna tell me why?"

"You can't tell Greg I'm here. He'll come looking for me and—you have to promise me. I can't—" My voice started to cut out on me as my nerves fed into the fear I already felt. My eyes watered and my panic started to build.

"Don't cry... I won't tell him."

I took in a breath trying to clear my overly emotional state.

"Will you stop acting like I've done something to you?"

I walked over and hugged him tightly.

"I miss you." He wrapped an arm around my shoulders.

"I miss you too..."

I pulled away from Brad and shoved my hands in my pockets. "I don't want you to worry about me. I'm doing really well here."

"You and Noah?" He looked at the house and back at me.

I shrugged. "I don't know... but he's been the best thing to happen to me since med school." I gave a small smile and kicked at the gravel under my foot.

Brad tried to smile. "Well... you look happy..."

I smiled. "I'm getting there."

"What happened with Mom?"

I nodded. "We went to a coffee shop. She put ten bucks on the table and told me it was child support."

He raised an eyebrow. "Not surprised."

Brad was old enough to remember our mother. He didn't remember her well, but he remembered she was mean and that she left.

I shrugged. "I knew better." I looked up at my apartment and back at him. "Do you wanna come inside for a few minutes?"

He nodded. "Just for a few. I have to leave for my flight soon." He held up his wrist and looked at his watch.

I walked up to my apartment and he followed behind me.

"How long have you been here?" Brad asked as he looked around.

"A couple days before I called." I slipped off my sandals and went to the fridge for a couple of waters.

Brad looked around into the living room. "Where'd you get all the money for this? You haven't touched your account since you left."

"I work for Noah." I handed him a bottle of water.

"Doing what?" He looked at me skeptically.

"Fixing up his property. It looks rough now, but it looked a hell of a lot worse before I got here." I walked into the living room and sat down in one of the chairs near the large window.

Brad continued to look around at everything as he walked to the couch and sat. "What happened at the hospital?"

I let out a huff. "I told you. I got fired."

"I know *that*. Why? We're you writing prescriptions you weren't supposed to? Hit a nurse? Did a surgery without consent? What?"

I frowned. "I think you know me better than that."

"No. Right now, I don't know you at all. You lost your job and took off. Greg said you were acting weird before, and that you were taking pills because you were working too many hours."

"I've never taken pills to help me sleep, or help me stay awake. I can do *both* just fine. Nothing happened at the hospital. They let me go, and I'm glad they did. Their residency program was bull and I learned way more from Dad. I wasn't happy with my life—any part of it—so I left. I didn't want to listen to another one of your, 'hang in there,' speeches, or fight with Greg. I just wanted out." I closed my eyes at the tiredness of just thinking about it. "I needed to leave, and I need to stay gone." I rubbed at my face, then looked out the window. Gif was having a sniffing frenzy around Brad's rental car.

"Greg's really busted up, Holl..."

I looked at Brad. "I honestly don't care *what* he is," I said calmly. "If you tell him where I am, you'll never see me again. I will throw away being a doctor, my name, everything. I will run, and you'll never see or hear from me again." I tried not to be overbearing with my words, but I wanted to be clear. Brad had always kept my secrets, even when we were kids. He'd always been my best friend, but I knew his loyalty to Greg was almost as strong.

"I know he was getting a little heavy with drinking, did something happen with *him*?" Brad continued to look at me with his pitiful puppy face.

The door in the kitchen slammed open and Gif came running into the house with a happy trot. He knew how to push down on the levered handle and let himself in.

"You are going to bust that wall, Mister." I reached my hand over the side of the chair to pet Gif's ear. He put his chin up on the arm of the chair and looked up at me. "Go find a squirrel."

Gif perked his ears up excitedly.

"Go." I pointed toward the door.

Gif took off running outside, his nails scraping for traction on the wood floors.

I looked at Brad, who was still waiting for an answer. "I told you, I needed out. It doesn't matter why, or what led to it. It is what it is, and I'm not going to sit here and spin in conversational circles."

Brad rubbed at his forehead and let out a loud breath. "Fine... Whatever... I need to get back."

I nodded and stood up. Normally, I would try to do or say something to ease his frustration, but I wanted him to leave.

Brad stood up and we both walked out to the car. I hated the look on his face. It was putting a pit in my stomach and I had to say something.

"I'm glad I got to see you again. I miss you."

Brad turned and looked at me with a raised eyebrow, implying his words instead of saying them.

"Go be a blood sucker." I smiled at him.

"Go be a body butcher." He gave a halfhearted smile.

It was our private joke. I was a body butcher as a doctor, and he was a blood sucking lawyer.

Brad hugged me, then got in the car and backed out of the driveway. I waved at him and went inside to talk to Noah. He was in the kitchen cleaning things that were already clean.

"Done already?" Noah asked as he set a cup of coffee on the counter for me.

I sat down at the breakfast bar and crossed my arms on the counter so I could rest my head for a moment. It felt like it was going to explode.

"He took it that bad, huh?"

I shook my head. "I didn't tell him." I pulled my head up and rested my chin on my arms.

"Why not?" Noah sat next to me and pushed my bangs away from my face. He brushed his fingers lightly over my cheek.

I let out a huff of air. "I couldn't do it... it would flip his world upside down and it's unnecessary." I sat up and took a sip of my coffee.

"You're eventually gonna have to tell him."

"Yeah... but it doesn't have to be now."

"You didn't tell me Greg proposed."

"Wasn't much of a proposal. 'My dearest Holly, if you marry me, I promise to never smack the crap out of you.'" I imitated Greg's voice sourly. "It was a do or die, and by that standard I was going to die either way." I laughed, but didn't know why I was laughing.

"Little dark there." Noah smiled and looked at me like I was crazy. He looked at his watch. "Do you wanna go into town and find some ice cream?"

"No. I should go to bed. I'm exhausted."

"It's only four-thirty."

I sat up and covered my mouth as I yawned. "Yeah, but we've been up late every night and you're gonna work me like a dog tomorrow."

"Naw... Not me." Noah smiled. "Come on. Let's go. I'll have you home by a reasonable hour." He bumped his shoulder into mine.

......

"What were you talking about with your dad not being your dad?" Noah asked as we walked down the sidewalk in front of the shops downtown.

I looked ahead of us for a moment. "I found out in Stillwater... I met my mom first, then before I called you, a guy came to my door. It scared the hell out of me because he's literally identical to my dad, but he's my dad's brother. I didn't even know my dad *had* a brother... His name is Garrett and he and my mom were having an affair behind my dad's back. I was the resulting product."

"Why didn't you tell me?" I could feel Noah's shocked and disapproving stare on the side of my face.

"I don't know... I'm kind of embarrassed, but I can't really tell you why that is." I looked at him. "My brother is also my cousin." I smiled in an attempt to make light of something I didn't want to talk about.

"And this guy, Garrett, he's a drug addict?"

"He used to be. He said he works at the Mayo Clinic as a cardio surgeon. I don't really know all that much about him or the situation because I didn't listen for very long. All of it kinda shook me up, so... I called you and we left."

Noah had a hard line across his eyebrows, but with slight sympathy. "I wish you would've told me. Have you contacted him since?"

I shook my head. "No... I don't want to hear it. Francis Bennett loved me and raised me, I'm not interested in the man I share closer DNA with."

"Understandable... So, what's your favorite color?" Noah smiled a little.

I looked up at him with a funny grimace.

"I'm serious."

"I don't know... it changes."

"Then, what is it now?"

"Light yellow."

"I like white."

"White? Is that even a color?" I raised an eyebrow.

"It's a reflection of every color in the spectrum. What's your favorite animal?"

"Llamas," I grinned, giving the sky a smile as I thought about their adorable little faces.

He laughed. "Llamas? Who likes llamas? It's like a sheep and a giraffe had a mutant baby."

I looked at Noah with crazed eyes. "Are you poking fun at my llama babies?"

He smirked and tried to repress some of his smile. "Llama babies?"

"Yes."

"Remember that nice funny farm we talked about? I'm sure they have llamas you could talk to."

I laughed and shook my head. "No. But I do love llamas. They have such cute, goofy looking faces." I put my hands up like I was squishing someone's cheeks. "When I was little, my dad would take us to the zoo a lot. Brad always wanted to see the lions, but I loved the llamas. Then for my ninth birthday, I had a llama themed party.."

"Yeah? What'd the other kids think of that?"

"Mm... my brother and my dad thought it was great."

"Oh," he laughed a little out of pity, "no one came?"

I smiled at my ice cream cone as I peeled the paper away. "I was a nerd, I didn't have friends." I smiled up at him.

"Well, *I* would have been your friend. I was friends with everybody."

"Mm-hm. So I've heard." I did my best to hold back a smile as I looked at him from the side with a raised eyebrow.

He raised an eyebrow back. "You're mean."

"It's not my fault Terri has a big mouth." I laughed a little.

"Well, much like you, I grew out of it. So, you can't hold it against me."

I laughed. "I didn't grow out of it. I still have no friends and I'm very much a nerd."

"Fine. *I* grew out of it."

"No, you didn't," I sang with a smile. "You're friends with me and I'm still a nerd."

Noah laughed and went back to asking me simple questions. He must have run out of complicated ones. When our ice cream was gone, we went back home, but he still wouldn't let me go to bed. Instead, he pulled me through the woods behind his property to a clearing of grass that covered the side of a hill. There was one tree standing alone just before the grass started to run down the hill.

"It's a little creepy out here at night," I said as I stood in the tall grass.

He shrugged. "I have a gun. You're safe."

"Guns won't protect me from ghosts."

Noah laughed. "Please don't tell me you're one of those people?"

I nodded and raised my eyebrows. "I am very *much* one of those people. I've seen some crazy stuff." I shivered.

He sighed with a huff. "I've been out here a thousand times. Nothing bad has ever happened."

"What are we doing anyway?" I looked around at the silhouettes of trees past the grass. The moon sat high up in the sky, and with the light color of the grass, everything was well lit.

I heard bark scraping behind me and I whipped around quickly. Noah was climbing up the tree that stood alone.

"What are you doing? You're gonna break your neck." I looked up in the tree.

"Here, catch the rope." He dropped a thick rope with a wood plank attached at the bottom, then dropped to the ground.

"It's a swing." I smiled. "Did you put that up there?"

"Kate did. She used to come out here all the time." Noah brushed off his hands. "Here, stand on the board."

I grabbed the rope and jumped up. Noah caught my waist to keep me from swinging forward.

"You're not afraid of heights, are you?"

I shook my head.

He pushed me forward and I felt like I was flying. The rope was set up high in the tree, and with the hill below me, I was several feet above the ground. The only sound was the rush of wind going past my ears and the soft creek of the rope as it rubbed against the tree limb. I looked at the moon as I fell back. I was reminded again at how good I felt being here. It was another moment that I didn't have to worry. No one would ever find me this deep in the woods.

Noah pushed me again and I glided out over the grass. I closed my eyes and felt the air around me. It was gentle as it touched my skin. I pulled the hair tie from my braid and let my hair whip out in front of me as I swung back. When I was near Noah, I jumped off.

"What? You don't like it?" He asked with a smile.

I looked at Noah as I stood in front of him.

His smile started to fall because I wasn't returning it. I closed the gap between us and wrapped my arms around his neck. I pressed my lips against his and held onto him tightly. He put his hands on either side of my waist at first, but then wrapped his arms around me. He hadn't done that before, and there was a rush of tiny bubbles in my stomach again.

"Are you okay?" he asked quietly.

I pressed my forehead against his chest and nodded with a smile he couldn't see.

"Can I ask you something?" He rubbed my back and stepped back from me a little.

"That already sounds like a loaded question."

"Maybe, but I'm more asking just to know... Why'd you stay with him? Firstly, I don't know how anyone could hurt you, but I don't understand why you let it go on for so long."

I took in a slow breath and felt my cheeks burn. I didn't know what to say to him. All of it sounded pathetic, and like I knew better, because I did. Out of sheer spite, I wanted to ask him why he would drink a bunch of alcohol and drive his pregnant wife home.

I chewed on the inside corner of my lip, keeping my gaze down and off to the left in the grass. "I don't know how you expect me to answer that. Or even why you would ask." My voice was quiet and marred by the press of emotion in my chest and throat.

"So I'd have a better reason to tell you that I'm glad you're here, and that I'll kill him if he comes near you... Seems a little abrasive without something before it." He touched my cheek.

I looked up at him. "You've never had a problem with abrasive before."

He smiled and let out a huff for a laugh. "I wasn't trying to upset you."

I took a deep breath and let it out. "We should head back. You're going to work me dead tomorrow."

Noah took my hand and walked to the front of the tree that overlooked the grassy field. He sat down and pulled on my arm to make me sit next to him. I sat down and looked at him. I felt like I had to answer his question.

I looked out at the grassy field below. "I don't have a good reason for staying as long as I did. I keep asking myself and I come up empty handed... because I knew better."

Noah pulled up a piece of grass. "What did you tell yourself while it was happening?" He split the blade of grass in two and grabbed another.

"At first it was, I knew he didn't mean to. I'd directly told him that he was hurting me the first time he grabbed my arm too tightly... He stepped back like I'd electrocuted him and apologized immediately." I grabbed my own piece of grass to fidget with.

"And later, when it got worse?"

I gave a small shrug. "He was drunk... Then Brad... he's the only family I have, and he's been my best friend my whole life. I have to protect him."

"Are you worried Brad would do something if you told him?"

I nodded. "He'd turn himself in... be convicted of a crime I'm not sure was even his doing."

"Well... I met your brother for about five seconds, but I know if it was me in your situation, I'd do anything to protect my family... And like I said before, I'm glad you're here, so maybe walking away wasn't the worst thing."

"Yeah. It's okay when you're not biting my head off for something." I glanced up at him with a small smile.

"Well, I kept hoping to run you off, but I think I'm over that now." He bumped my arm and laughed a little.

I sighed. "Why didn't you just say so?" I pushed myself up.

"Hey, where are you going?"

"I'm off. Bon voyage." I gave a little wave behind me.

"Hey."

I heard him get up and run after me. I laughed and started running. I was fast, but so was he, and he had longer legs. He caught me around the waist and flipped me up in his arms.

"Oh good. A taxi service," I laughed. "Mush." I pointed down the pathway that led to the house.

He laughed. "Nice try, Charlie. You're walking." He dropped my feet.

I laughed. "So, I answered your questions, now you have to answer one of mine." I smiled up at him.

"Tit-for-tat?"

"Yep."

"I feel like this might be bad." He had a slight cringe on his face.

I shook my head. "I'm nicer than you."

"Quieter, maybe, but I don't know if you're nicer."

"I am." I flashed a smile.

"What's your question?"

"Why'd you stop?" I looked up at him and slowed my pace. If I kept walking too fast, he wouldn't say as much.

He looked at me for a moment and realized what I was talking about. "Because it's twenty miles into town and you looked like you were about to drop from exhaustion."

I raised an eyebrow.

He sighed. "Can I have a different question?"

"No."

"Alright... But I don't think you're gonna believe me."

I shrugged. "Don't lie and I'll believe you."

He let out a quiet chuckle and looked down. "I saw Kate walking next to you on the road." He looked at me like he was nervous. It was strange because he was never timid.

I looked at him. "That's it?"

He shook his head and reached out a hand to stabilize me as I stepped over a dead tree. "I fell off a ladder when I was pulling the gutters off. I hit my head hard enough to pass out or something. I don't really know... but Kate was sitting on the ground next to me when I looked up. She was only there for a second before she walked out to the end of the driveway, and there you were... Kate walked next to you. When you got past the trees and I couldn't see you, I panicked because I couldn't see Kate..."

I wanted to give him a medical explanation for what he'd seen, but it seemed cruel somehow. To take any form of Kate from him wasn't right.

"I got in my truck and raced down the road after you... I didn't know what I was doing. I still considered myself married, with vows that I intended to keep until I died."

"And I'm ruining your plans of being alone and grouchy." I looked at him with another small smile.

"Mostly." He flashed a beautiful and perfect smile, but it faded quickly. "You faked smiles... and I'd find myself thinking of ways to change that, then get angry again because I was spending more of my day thinking about *you* than Kate." His face had an angry set to it and his voice wasn't far off.

"And that's when you would try to run me off, by being

an ass."

Noah shook his head with a small laugh and a smile that didn't touch his eyes. "I stayed up baking you those cupcakes, because the night before, I had a dream that disturbed me. The dream was short, but it felt real."

"Ghosts. I'm telling you. They're real." I smiled at him, hoping that he'd lighten up and smile again.

"No, they're not." His smile still failed to touch his eyes.

"They are. Anyway, dream. Keep going." I rolled out my hand for him to proceed.

"It was the first time I dreamed of Kate since she died..." Noah was quiet for a second and looked up like he was seeing something I couldn't. "In the dream, she didn't speak, she just smiled and walked over to you in the backyard while you were working, and she took your hand. It looked like she said something to you, but I couldn't hear. You both walked toward me as Kate held your hand. You and Kate stood in front of me, and when she grabbed my hand, I swear I could feel her." He looked down at his left hand. "She put your hand in mine and walked away smiling." He looked at me. "That day, I was angry at you for stealing my time with Kate. I barked orders at you and you didn't complain, which pissed me off more. You carried the cinder blocks to the side of the garage, and when you stopped for a moment, I could see I was breaking you... and for a second you had the same sad look on your face that you did in the dream, before Kate walked up to you. I started thinking about the way Kate would have screamed at me for treating *anyone* the way I treated you. And worse, I started thinking about what you might've ran from... That scar on your wrist doesn't look like something cut you by accident..." He stopped walking and turned to face me. "It looks like a suicide attempt, and all I could think was you're too beautiful from the inside out, and there I was being another thing in your life that made it terrible."

"You *were* terrible to me. I almost packed my stuff and left after you went to bed. But... this really *is* from getting knocked through a door." I looked at the scar on my wrist.

Noah pulled me against him and hugged me. "I'm sorry..."

I smiled a little. "You were forgiven when you made me cupcakes."

"Cupcakes aren't an apology."

"They're not," I pulled back just enough to look up at him, "but making sure I didn't have a sucky birthday up in my apartment was nice, and not being an ass through the proceeding days was nicer." I smiled at him.

He smiled a little, rubbing his thumb against my cheek.

"So that's it then?" I dropped my arms and turned to keep walking. "The idea of Kate yelling at you was enough for you to stop being a jerk?"

He shook his head. "I don't want you to leave. I agree with what you said the other night, about not knowing what the hell we're doing, but I don't want you to leave."

I nodded. "I don't *want* to leave. I meant what I told Brad today... I'm happy here." I looked up at him, not sure how he'd respond to my honesty.

He smiled and put a hand against my back to keep me moving forward.

Chapter 9

The next day, I woke up to the sound of a truck and a woodchipper outside. Noah had paid a friend to come remove the stumps from the trees we'd cut down. I got dressed quickly, realizing I'd overslept, and walked outside as I put my hair in a braid. Noah spotted me walking across the backyard toward him and smiled. He held up his finger to the guy he was talking to and jogged toward me.

"Morning," he yelled over the rumble of the woodchipper.

"Sorry. I slept through my alarm." I struggled to make my voice loud enough to be heard after getting up so fast.

Noah shrugged. "Don't worry about it. There's breakfast inside for you. You can go eat, then we're gonna throw all the branches at the front of the house into the woodchipper."

I nodded and gave a shy smile at the ground.

"Are you okay?" He touched my arm.

I looked up and nodded. "Just tired."

"Today will go fast. Go eat breakfast." He kissed the side of my forehead quickly and jogged back to the guy he'd been talking to before.

I walked around the house and went inside to scarf down my breakfast. When I walked in the kitchen, there was a small bundle of wildflowers across my plate. I smiled and picked them up, then walked to the glass door and opened it. When Noah saw me standing in the doorway, he smiled. I laughed quietly and went back in to eat. When I was finished, I walked outside and put my work gloves on. I grabbed a large branch and started hauling it to the backyard to put it in the chipper.

"You can load a bunch of branches in the back of the truck and haul them back here," Noah yelled over the wood-chipper.

I shook my head. "I don't know how to drive a stick shift."

Noah shook his head with a smile and walked toward the garage. He hooked up a trailer to the back of the four-wheeler and pulled it up to the front of the house near the pile of branches. He helped me load branches onto the trailer and haul them back. It took about four hours to feed everything through the chipper. After that, I went and helped the other guys fill the holes in the ground from the stumps. My hands became blistered after a while—even with the gloves—but I pushed through. Everyone else was done around five, but I was still filling holes.

"Holly! Come on!" Noah waved me to the front yard. "Call it a day."

I stuck the shovel in the ground and walked to the front yard.

"We're gonna meet up with those guys in town." Noah pointed with his thumb to his friends that were pulling out of the driveway. "Go take a shower and we'll grab a bite with them."

I nodded and walked up to the garage.

While I was in the shower, I carefully rubbed my hands with soap to try to clean the dirt out of the broken blisters. Once they were clean, I got out of the shower, changed my clothes, grabbed my purse, and ran out the door.

Noah was waiting at the truck. He smiled at me and opened the driver's door and directed his hand to the seat inside. "Time for a driving lesson."

I shook my head. "Another day. Those guys are gonna be waiting on us."

"They can wait. Get in."

I took in a deep breath and sighed as I let it out, getting in the driver's seat. Noah shut the door and walked around to the passenger's side.

"Alright." He rubbed his hands together with a smile. "Now, push the clutch and break in and turn the key." He pulled the stick out of gear.

I started the truck.

"Good, keep the clutch in and put it in reverse. You're gonna push the gas pedal and slowly let out on the clutch. It sounds counter intuitive, but if it starts to get jumpy give it a little more gas."

I put the truck in reverse and followed his instructions. The truck started to back up slowly out of the driveway and onto the country road.

"Look at you." Noah smiled proudly. "Now, do the same thing going forward, but you'll wanna start in second gear in this truck."

I pushed in the clutch and tried to find second gear. I gave it some gas and let the clutch out. The truck rolled forward but jerked a little.

"Give it more gas," Noah said quickly.

I pressed the gas pedal a little harder and the truck started down the road easily.

"Come on, nobody is this good the first time. You've *never* driven a stick shift?"

I shook my head and smiled.

"Push the clutch in and put it in third."

I did as I was instructed, but grabbed the shifter a little differently because my hand stung.

"What's wrong with your hand?" Noah asked.

I flipped my hand over so he could see the sores.

"How'd you do that?"

I showed the other hand. "Shoveling."

He took my right hand and kissed my palm below the broken blisters. "Push in the clutch."

I pushed the clutch in and he shifted into fourth gear.

"When you come up to the stop sign, you'll push the clutch again and start braking. If you don't push the clutch in when you come to a full stop, you'll kill the truck." He kissed my hand again.

My cheeks burned. "You're distracting me," I said when he kissed my hand.

"Yeah?" He kissed my wrist with a smile.

"If I wreck your truck, it'll be your own fault," I warned.

"You're not gonna wreck my truck." He kissed my hand

again.

I drove to the restaurant only stalling once at a stop sign in town, but redeemed myself quickly. We had dinner with the guys that had worked at the house earlier. They all had a couple of beers and I had a few with them. I wasn't going to because of Noah, but he ordered one for me when the rest of the guys got one.

"This must be the hardest workin' girl I ever seen. You were chuckin' those limbs in like they weighed nothin'," Carl said with a full grin of crooked or missing teeth.

Carl used to work for Noah when Noah was still building houses. He was probably in his early fifties, but looked older. His skin was tanned and wrinkled from the sun. There wasn't much left of his hair, but what *was* left was gray. Everything about him was plump and round. I could hardly watch him eat because I could see the plaque building in his arteries.

"She puts shame on all of us," one of the guys said. I couldn't remember his name, but he was fairly nice.

"Ya put shame on *yourselves*." Carl shook his head. "Not that I don't respect a hard workin' woman, but I think Noah's got you workin' *too* hard. I need someone to come 'n run my office if you're interested." Carl looked at me. "We could use a pretty face in the office." He grinned and groaned slightly as he breathed. He'd had a few too many beers.

"Actually, Holly's going back into the medical field soon," Noah said with a relaxed smile.

"Oh yeah? You a nurse or somethin'?" Carl grinned again, showing a few more of his missing teeth.

"She's a neurosurgeon."

I gave Noah a hard look. The way he said *neurosurgeon*

was like he was gloating. I didn't like bragging about what I did.

Carl laughed. "There's no way. You look about twenty-five at best."

I raised my eyebrows and gave a quiet sigh with a reserved smile. "It's true."

"Well, that's pretty impressive." Carl smiled and took a drink of his beer. "So, how'd you two meet?" He pointed his sausage finger between Noah and I.

We looked at each other. It sounded kind of bad when I thought about it.

"Patsy's diner. I saw her looking through the help-wanted ads and offered her a job," Noah answered.

Carl nodded for a second and looked around. I stood up to go to the bathroom. I didn't like being questioned, and the group of guys we were with made me uncomfortable.

The third beer was making my exhaustion worse, so I splashed some water on my face before I left the bathroom. Carl was in the hallway.

"Hey pretty lady," he grinned. "I's wonderin' where you went." Carl's words slurred together.

I gave a polite glancing-smile and tried to walk around him, but he blocked me with his arm. He smelled like bad cheese, beer, and wood chips. He seemed to be grunting a little more as he breathed.

"Where you goin'? I came to say hi to ya." Carl wrapped a hand around waist.

"Let go of me, please." My voice was forceful, but not rude. He was Noah's friend, and I couldn't be rude.

"Don't be like that, Darlin'. I'm just a harmless old man, and you's just a pretty lady." His hand reached around to my butt. "We can have some fun and call it a night."

"Get your damn hand off me," I warned coldly as I tried to push his fat arm away from me.

"Aw. You're cute when you blush." He tightened his arm.

"Get off me!" I pushed myself away from him and slammed my fist into his face. I felt a pop in my hand and cussed. I gripped my wrist tightly in an attempt to cut off the pain, but it didn't help.

"Hey!" Noah yelled and shot up out of his chair toward us when he heard me.

Carl stumbled into the wall and everyone in the restaurant stared as Noah and two other guys ran back toward me.

"What the hell's wrong with you?" Carl asked as he held his nose. "I wasn't doin' nothin'!" He grabbed my arm, trying to stabilize himself. He was bent over and trying not to fall.

Noah pulled him back by the shoulder, throwing him to the ground to get to me. "Come on." Noah reached over for me. Carl was laying on the floor between us, blocking the hallway.

I reached my arms out and Noah lifted me quickly over Carl, then pulled me toward the door by my arm. I looked back and watched as the other two guys helped Carl up from the floor. I held my hand against my body as it throbbed. I knew I'd broken it.

"We're done!" Carl yelled at Noah.

"Come on." Noah grabbed my arm, forcing me to keep walking forward.

We went out the door of the restaurant and turned left toward the truck.

"You're a little slut! You hear me!?" Carl yelled as the other guys pulled him outside to their truck.

I looked back, feeling stunned. The words felt like a knife in my chest.

"Get in the truck," Noah said quickly as he kept pulling me forward.

I got in and tried not to cry. My hand hurt like hell, but those words...

"Are you okay?" Noah asked quietly when he noticed I was holding my hand. He pulled out into the street, but looked at me.

"It's broken," I whispered as a baseball-sized lump choked my voice.

Noah cussed and turned around in the middle of the street toward the hospital.

......

"Well, you're right, typical boxer's fracture. Thankfully, it's nothing to worry about. We'll get it casted and you'll be good to go," the doctor handed me the x-ray so I could look at it. "I *do* need to speak with you in private if that's okay." His eyes flashed to Noah, then back at me.

Noah started to stand, and I pushed down on his shoulder to make him sit. "I know what it's about. I'm perfectly safe at home. No one is hurting me. It's from something else." My words were short and clear.

The doctor looked at me for a moment, then nodded. "I'll have someone in here to cast your hand in just a minute."

I looked at the door after the doctor walked out. My embarrassment was too much.

"Holly... I'm so sorry," Noah said quietly as he slumped back the way he was before.

I shook my head. "It's not your fault," I whispered. I moved the ice pack away from my hand to look at it again.

Noah reached over and put a hand on my knee, but didn't look at me. I didn't understand why he seemed so guilty.

••••••

When we got home, Noah babied me, which drove me crazy. He opened doors and anything else that required my hand.

"I'm not handicapped," I snapped as he took the gallon of milk from me to pour it in a glass.

"Doesn't mean I can't help you." He poured the milk and handed me the glass.

"There's a difference between helping and doing everything for me." I took the glass and walked into the living room. We were in my apartment. I'd planned on going to bed, but Noah followed me up to take care of me.

I sat down on the couch and let out a sigh. It felt good to be home. I was completely exhausted.

"I talked to Carl's wife while you were getting your—"

"He has a *wife*?" I interrupted.

"Yeah. She said that they'd pay for your hand." Noah sat next to me on the couch and grabbed the remote for the TV.

"They don't need to do that. I'm the idiot that can't hit."

"Come here." Noah moved his arm so I could scoot closer. "I'm sorry about tonight."

"For the fifteenth time, it's not your fault." I laid my head on Noah's shoulder. "Please stop apologizing."

"I know, but I feel bad." He wrapped an arm around me.

I closed my eyes. I was so tired and I didn't care about what was on TV.

Chapter 10

The birds outside chirped so loudly it woke me up. *Rotten animals...* I opened my eyes and looked at Noah. I was cramped between him and the back of the couch. Carefully, I pushed myself up and walked into the kitchen. It was five-thirty in the morning and the sun wasn't up yet. I looked out the window and realized it wouldn't matter if the sun *was* up, it was cloudy and about to rain.

I quietly opened the door and sat down at the top of the stairs outside. I rested my elbows on my knees with my hands out in front of me and put my head down. My mind circled around what had happened yesterday. I'd felt so much panic when Carl grabbed me. All I could see was Greg standing in front of me. And when Carl called me a slut... it was exactly the way that Greg had said it before he grabbed the knife.

······

"Are you ready to go Holly? We need to leave," Greg asked as he walked through our bedroom and into the bathroom.

"Yeah." I turned around and smiled.

"I don't like that shirt. Wear a different one." Greg's voice was cold and flat.

My smile fell. "I just bought it. Why don't you like it?" I looked down at my shirt, then at him.

"Because you look disgusting. Take it off."

I could smell the alcohol on his breath and felt a little defeated. I'd been looking forward to the party tonight; and now there would be another disaster while I tried to drag him to the car before he passed out.

"I think we should stay home. You've had too much to drink." I walked past Greg into the closet as I started to take my earrings out. I slipped my heels off and walked out of the bedroom.

"It's my party!" Greg yelled from the bedroom as I walked down the hallway to the stairs. "Hey!" Greg yelled loudly. A glass flew past me, shattering against the wall to my left.

I was going to grab my keys and leave. I couldn't take another night of screaming. "I'm talking to you!"

I walked into the kitchen and grabbed my work bag. Even though I'd just come off a fourteen hour shift, I could put in a few hours until Greg fell asleep and sobered up. At least I'd be safe at the hospital.

I slipped my work shoes on and grabbed my keys.

"I'm sorry, Baby. Please don't leave. Come'ere," he slurred as he gently grabbed my arm to pull me closer. "I'm sorry. I didn't mean to yell. Okay? I'm sorry." He held me in a hug. "Please, come with me." Greg rested his head on my shoulder. "I promise, I won't have another drink the rest of the night... I'm sorry... Will you come with me?"

I took in a deep breath and nodded. He was trying not to be violent which was a step forward. Unfortunately, I had to reward the good behavior.

Greg picked up his head and smiled. "I love you, Baby." He cupped the back of my neck and kissed me. "I'm sorry."

I nodded again, walked into the kitchen and set my bag down before I slipped my shoes back off.

"Go change your shirt though." Greg's voice was still gentle.

"I bought this shirt for tonight, and you liked it when I showed it to you."

"Take the damn shirt off. You look like a slut." His voice got louder as he stamped out each word.

I started to walk past him, but he grabbed my arm and threw me back into the kitchen island.

"Take the shirt off!" He grabbed a knife from the knife rack and bent me back over the kitchen island. The blade of the knife scraped the skin on my stomach as he ran it under the front of my shirt. With one quick yank back, he sliced the thin fabric.

I looked at him with wide eyes, shoved him off me, and ran into the hallway. My mind raced as I scrambled to get away. If I didn't kill him, he was going to kill me. Why hadn't I just walked out of the house like I'd planned?

Something smacked the back of my ankle and I fell to the ground.

●●●●●●

I touched the scar on my heel. Greg had thrown a frying pan to trip me.

A tear slipped down my cheek.

"What are you doing out here?"

I jumped. My memories had consumed me, so I didn't hear Noah come outside. I wiped the tears from my face quickly and smiled.

"My hand was hurting and I couldn't sleep," I said as I stood up.

Noah's smile fell when he saw my face. "What's wrong?" He looked me over quickly. There was a hard frown on his brow while he waited for me to answer.

I forced a gentle smile and shook my head. "Nothing."

"You were crying... it's not nothing."

"Please let it go." My voice pinched as I spoke around the lump in my throat.

He let out a huff and looked at the sky like it had spoken his name. "Come on. It's gonna start pouring soon." Noah wrapped an arm around my shoulder and started down the stairs with me. "I'll make you some breakfast and you can lay down for a while."

I nodded as raindrops started to fall on us. We ran to the house, but it started pouring so hard that we were soaked before we reached the door.

"Good grief." Noah brushed the water from his hair. He looked at me and laughed. "Let me find you something dry to change into." He kissed my forehead and walked back to the bedroom.

He returned with a pair of sweatpants, a white shirt, and a hoodie.

"You can go change in my room and lay down for a while. I'll come get you when breakfast is ready."

I nodded and walked back to Noah's room. Everything was neat and perfect like the rest of the house, but there wasn't much in the room. There was a California king-sized bed that was perfectly made, a single nightstand, and a dresser on the opposite wall. Not much too it.

I pulled my shirt off and looked at the scar on my side until the pink line blurred.

"Holly?" Noah knocked on the door. "I got you a towel."

I stepped over and opened the door. Noah shifted and became uncomfortable as he held out a towel.

"What do you see when you look at me?" I asked quietly.

"I'm not really sure how you want me to answer that. You don't have a shirt on." The corner of his mouth pulled up in a chagrined smile.

I didn't smile back because it was an honest question.

"Do you think I dress inappropriately?" I changed the question hoping he would answer me.

"No. Why would you ask that?" He frowned.

"Do I dress in a way that attracts the wrong kind of attention?"

The corner of his mouth pulled back in a disappointed expression. He stepped past me and grabbed the shirt off the dresser. I took it as he handed it to me.

"Is this about last night?" Noah sat on the end of the bed and looked at me.

I pulled the shirt over my head, followed by the hoodie.

"Come here," Noah held out his hand to me.

I stepped forward and stood in front of him.

Noah took my left hand and rubbed my palm, below the open blisters. "What's wrong?"

I shrugged. "What Carl said last night... it's bugging me."

"Carl's an ass. Whatever he said shouldn't matter." Noah looked at me carefully.

I sat down next to Noah on the bed. "It's about who

said it first." I looked at him, then down at my casted hand. "I'm wondering if I bring these situations to myself..."

"No... You don't control other people and their actions."

"Once is a coincidence, twice... and I have to wonder if I'm doing something wrong." I looked out the window at the pouring rain. "He called me a slut, just like Greg."

......

"Get back here!" Greg screamed with a rage I'd never heard.

I got up to my knees only to have Greg step on my back. I flipped over and grabbed his leg out from under him. He fell back and landed on the frying pan he'd thrown at me. I pushed myself forward quickly to grab the gun Greg had hidden, but he pulled me back by my foot. I just needed a few more inches.

The gun was under the bottom shelf of the table in the hallway. I reached forward and Greg flopped himself on top of me. I kept reaching for the gun, inching myself closer with my foot. As I reached, I felt a sharp pain run down my side. I screamed as loud and as hard as possible, hoping that the neighbors would hear. Greg covered my mouth, and I grabbed the pan and started beating him as hard as I could from behind my back.

I could feel my own blood running down in a puddle on the floor. If I was going to die, so was he. I flipped myself over and swung with all my might, hitting Greg in the head. He fell over and I quickly grabbed the gun, scrambling to get up. I'd knocked him unconscious and had the clear opportunity to shoot him.

A fast trail of blood ran down the side of my pants and my hand shook as I pointed the gun at him. One bullet to the head. He wouldn't know, and wouldn't feel it. No one would deny it was self-defense...

I let out another scream in frustration. I couldn't do it. I couldn't shoot another person, and I knew I couldn't live with

•••••

I touched the long scar on my side, and a tear ran down my cheek. It had been the worst pain of my life, being sliced open like a fish. The memory made me feel sick to my stomach. "I duct-taped my side closed, then drove myself to the hospital. I walked in, pretending nothing was wrong, and had a nurse page my friend Bethany."

"And no one said anything about the blood on your clothes?"

I shook my head. "I changed before I walked in the hospital. Usually, I went to one of the other hospitals so no one would know, but a fourteen-inch cut wasn't something I could explain with a lie... Beth and I got caught, and Dr. Wiley thought we were being surgery junkies."

"What do you mean?"

"Surgeons live for surgery... It's like a drug."

"So, she thought you sliced yourself open for fun?"

I held up my shoulder with a slight shake of my head. "She thought I let Beth cut me open for more practice." I didn't have to look to know the sympathetic frown he wore. "Don't look at me like that." I looked down at my hands in my lap again. "I couldn't kill him... He was kind and loving more than he wasn't... and that's all I could see when I pointed the gun at his head. As for getting fired, that was entirely on me."

"Holly, you should've called the cops..." Noah leaned forward with his elbows on his knees to look at me. "You still can."

I shook my head. "I can't or my brother goes to jail too. He has proof of Brad committing a felony... I did the right thing. I left, my brother stays out of jail, and I stay alive..."

Noah got up and walked out of the room. He came back with a marker and sat next to me again. I looked at him with confusion when he pulled my arm over, and uncapped the marker.

"What are you doing?"

"Writing on your cast." He wore a smile that made the corners of his eyes crinkle.

I watched Noah's face as he wrote on my light-teal colored cast. He grinned and let go of my hand.

He'd written the word "Beautiful" along the inside of the cast. I looked at Noah and raised an eyebrow.

"You asked me what I see." He tapped my cast with the end of the marker. "There you go."

I pressed my lips together as my cheeks started to burn, and I picked at my nails nervously.

"What? You didn't know?" He bumped my shoulder gently, looking at me.

I laughed nervously. "I don't know how I'm supposed to respond to that."

"'Thanks Noah, I didn't know that,' or 'I know I'm beautiful, but thanks for saying it.'"

I smirked. "I look like a wet rat." I looked at him with a nervous smile.

"No." His lips wrapped around the word. "More like a cute otter or something."

I smirked again and laughed.

"And after seeing you with your shirt off, I've realized I'm not feeding you enough." He took my hand. "Come on." He stood up.

"I eat like a horse." I looked up at him as I stood.

"*I* eat like a horse, *you* eat like a gerbil."

"A gerbil?"

"Yes, another animal cuter than a rat."

I laughed.

• • • • • •

Noah made me breakfast and we stayed inside watching horror movies while it rained. I would cover my eyes every time a scary scene came up and Noah would pull my arms away to force me to watch it. After two horror movies and endless cups of coffee, I made him watch a chick-flick. He would cover his eyes during mushy scenes and laugh as I tried and failed to pry his arms away because he was stronger than me.

"I give up," I said as I flipped the TV off.

Noah laughed and dropped his hands from his face.

"You're impossible." I got up from the couch and grabbed our coffee cups.

He kept laughing as I walked toward the kitchen for a coffee refill. There was a knock at the door and Noah stood up to answer it.

"I don't want any trouble. I just want to apologize to you and Miss Holly."

I turned around in the hallway when I heard Carl's voice.

"You need to leave." Noah's voice was instantly threatening. There was no inkling that he'd been laughing just a second before.

"I drank too much last night, and that ain't no excuse—I know—but I'm very sorry to you and Miss Holly." Carl looked past Noah at me.

"If you don't get out of here, I'll knock you on your fat

163

ass," Noah warned. Gif started growling, responding to Noah's anger.

I touched Noah's arm and made him step aside.

Carl looked at me with fearful eyes like he was being threatened by *me*. "I'm real sorry. I don't remember everythin' that happened, but what I do remember is pretty awful, and I'm real sorry. You're a sweet girl and ya don't deserve bein' treated like that. I know my wife called ya and said we'd pay for your hand. I gone down to the hospital and talked to 'em already. I know ya won't be able to work with your hand the way it is, so I wanted to bring you a check to help ya out until your hand gets better." Carl handed a check to me.

I shook my head. "That's very kind of you, but I have all I need. Thank you for taking care of the medical bills, and coming out here to apologize."

"Really, I'd feel better if ya took the check. I can't tell ya how sorry I am."

"No. Just find yourself some help. Your friends looked like they've done this a few times. There's no hard feelings as long as you try to get some help." My voice wasn't friendly, but it wasn't rude.

Carl nodded. "I'm very sorry to both of ya's." Carl looked at Noah, and I almost felt sorry for him.

Noah wouldn't look at him. Carl nodded at me and walked back out into the rain from the porch.

Noah slammed the door shut and I jumped. His knuckles cracked as he balled his fists and walked to the kitchen. I followed him and watched as his anger boiled. I felt unsure of him which made Gif stay at my side, instead of Noah's.

"'No hard feelings'?" Noah looked at me.

"Sometimes forgiveness goes further than anger." I

took a small step back.

Noah gave me a look, like he couldn't believe the words that were coming from my mouth. "Your hand is broken!" He gestured toward my cast.

"And he's paying for it. My hand will heal." I shrugged, feeling uncomfortable and nervous.

Noah shook his head and leaned against the counter behind him. "Is this what you did with Greg? You just kept forgiving him? He'd smack you around, and you'd just shrug and say, 'it's okay, wounds heal'?"

I paused for a moment, then nodded at the verbal stab as I looked down. "Yep. You're right," I whispered.

I should have known better. He'd judge me no less than anyone else. I turned and walked away.

"Holly, I'm sorry," Noah said quickly.

I stood in the living room for a second and looked around. I felt confused. I didn't know if I was leaving to go up to my apartment, or just leaving.

I walked out the door and hurried through the rain into my apartment. After standing there for a few minutes just to reel, I changed into a pair of shorts and a tank top, pushed the table in the kitchen to the living room, and pulled out a can of paint. The kitchen was already painted, except for the trim at the top. I stood on the counter and used my left hand to paint. The more I thought about what Noah said, the angrier I became.

The door behind me opened and Noah came in. I didn't turn around to acknowledge him. I just kept painting.

"I shouldn't have said that... It must have been hard... I don't understand what went on with you and Greg, but I know you wouldn't have stayed as long as you did, if you didn't have to protect your brother. I'm sorry."

I kept painting.

"Will you please come down and talk to me?"

I stepped over the stove to the other section of counter space and kept painting.

"Holly?" He rubbed his hand down the side of my calf. "Please... Come down and talk to me. Let me have the chance to apologize."

"You already did," I said quietly.

"Then come down here so I can convince you to forgive me." He kissed the side of my leg.

A shot of adrenalin hit my stomach and made my mind feel momentarily dead.

"Please." He kissed my leg again and his hand ran up the side of my other leg, stopping just above my knee. I could hardly focus on what I was doing. If I didn't get down, I was going to have more than a broken hand.

I turned around. "You have to let go of me if you want me to get down."

Noah reached his hands up to my hips and lifted me down. I turned to the sink and started washing out the paint brush I'd been using. He brushed my hair to the side and kissed the side of my neck making my mind feel even more muddled. My hands went weak, and I dropped the paint brush when Noah's hands ran up my sides. He reached forward and rinsed the wet paint off my hand and shut the sink off before turning me around. His hands were still wet as he held my face and kissed my lips. Another hit of adrenalin made air catch in my chest, but I had something to say.

"Don't ever rub my face in my past. You don't understand it because you've never been the underdog. Out of sheer size and strength, you could win a fight against someone. You're not so light that someone can pick you up and throw you through a window like a ragdoll." Tears stung my eyes and my throat felt dry. "I am *physically* incapable of fighting off someone who is twice my size and in a *true* blinded rage. Think about what you could do to someone my size if you were mad enough. Then imagine yourself on the other side of it—" My voice snapped and cut off the last of my words.

Noah wiped the tears off my cheeks with his thumbs. "I know. Don't cry." He pulled me into his chest and wrapped his arms around me.

"You don't know, Noah." I pushed myself back against the counter behind me, away from him. "It's easy for you to stand there and judge me, but you weren't there and you don't know Greg. Things are *rarely* black and white. And you can think I'm a scared bitch for running, but it's the *only* thing keeping me alive and Brad out of jail."

Noah put his hands on the edge of the counter, on either side of me, and leaned down until his face was level with mine. "I have plenty that people can judge me for, and probably do. What I said earlier was screwed up and *shouldn't* have been said." His beautiful green eyes held mine in a straight lock. "It pisses me off, Holly... There are people out there like Greg, or Carl... they hurt beautiful people like you, and get away with it. I'm not twisting what I said to make myself sound better, but understand where it came from." He pulled a hand from the counter and wiped my cheek of another stray tear before putting his forehead against mine. "I'm sorry for what brought you, but I'm glad you're here." He pulled his head away from mine enough to kiss my cheek and down the side of my neck. "Will you stop being mad at me now?"

I swallowed and nodded. My cheeks burned and my heart started pounding significantly harder while he kissed along my collar bone.

"Am I making you nervous?" he asked quietly as he kissed along the other side of my collarbone.

"No." My voice didn't make a sound.

"Are you sure?" He held one side of my neck as he kissed the other.

I nodded because I couldn't focus enough to speak. My brain was in a fog.

"Your heart is pounding," he whispered below my ear.

I nodded and wrapped my arms around his neck so I wouldn't fall. He kissed my lips and reached down to lift me up. I wrapped my legs around his waist as he walked through to the bedroom.

......

Noah and I laid on the bed with just a sheet pulled up over us. I was tucked up against his side with my head on his shoulder. He was watching me as I traced my fingers over his. He had long, perfect fingers that were rough from always working with his hands. His gold wedding band still hugged his ring finger, nicked, scratched, and worn.

"What was she like?" I asked quietly as I turned his ring a little to hide one of the deeper scratches.

Noah took in a deep breath and laced his fingers through mine. "A pain in the ass."

I looked up at Noah. That was definitely something I didn't expect him to say.

He laughed a little. "She *was*... Imagine putting Bridgett and Terri together. Kate was smart and she knew it, and also had a big mouth."

I frowned a little. "They said she was quiet."

Noah smiled down at me. "Isn't anyone compared to them?"

I raised an eyebrow and nodded. "True."

He took in another breath; his smile stayed but turned nostalgic. "I don't know. She was quiet around other people, I guess." He shrugged and looked at me again. "I got a different side of her though. She also had commonalities with Gif, always excited when I came home, even if I was gone for five minutes."

"That's horrible," I laughed. "You're comparing her to a dog."

He laughed lightly. "Lovingly." He pulled my hand and kissed the back of my fingers. "I don't know. She was a *one-of-a-kind* person. She did and said whatever she wanted. She'd order a pizza, then decide she wanted Chinese too."

I laughed. "You let her order take-out?"

"Okay, you basically admitted that you've spent the last ten years eating take-out. I cook better than anything you're gonna find in town, and it's not good for you to eat out."

I laughed again. "You act like all I ate were greasy burgers and fries. I like salads, sushi, light sandwiches with fresh meat. And Brad cooked for me a lot."

"Still, I'm a better cook than anyone in town."

"Mm. I don't know. Janine made that couscous thing and it was better than yours." I raised an eyebrow with a disagreeing smile.

Noah's face fell and his eyes turned crazed. "Take it back."

I laughed. "She used regular black olives instead of those Greek ones, and it was better."

Noah rolled over, pinning me down. "Take. It. Back."

I smiled and shook my head. "Janine's was better."

Noah kissed my lips gently. "You'll regret that." He kissed me again. "Gif is gonna love switching menus with you." He kissed down the side of my neck.

I giggled quietly. "It'll taste better than those horrible olives."

Noah's teeth pinched an inch of my flesh.

"Ow. I was kidding," I laughed as I pushed on his shoulder.

He didn't stop.

"I take it back. Yours is better."

Noah released his teeth and pushed himself up to flash a smile at me. "Thank you."

"If you can live with a lie, so can I."

"Dog food. You get dog food for dinner."

"Naw. I'll just order take-out." I bit the side of my lip.

He laughed in a slightly threatening way. "I'll hide my phone from you."

I shrugged and shook my head. "Towns not that far of a walk. I can get there before the diner closes."

Noah looked my face over with a small smile and brushed my hair back. I'd only seen someone look at another person like that in a movie, but no one had ever looked at me the way he was.

"No more walking." He looked at my eyes, and his smile started to fade.

"You won't say that tomorrow when it's done raining and there's work to do."

"You have a busted hand. What work?"

I looked at him and blinked. Was he serious?

Noah put his forehead against mine with a smile. "I'll help you with whatever you need. No one wants a surgeon with a broken hand cutting up their brain."

"There's plenty I can do." I pulled my head back to look at him. He was breaking our deal. I still needed to stick to the arrangement.

"I know." He kissed my lips, then a straight line down, toward my belly button, but stopped when my stomach growled loudly. Noah laughed and moved back up to kiss my lips again before he sat on the edge of the bed and pulled his clothes back on.

"My stomach growls and you decide to ditch me?" I touched his back with the tips of my fingers.

"Your stomach growls and I make you food." He turned his head and looked at me with a smile.

I smiled at him, but my mind was too distracted. It seemed so easy for him to be happy, like he didn't have to think about it.

Chapter 11

I walked into the house and there was a clatter of nails scraping the floor as Gif ran from the kitchen to greet me. I bent down and scrubbed his soft fur for a second before I followed the smell of bacon back to the kitchen. Noah flipped an omelet over in the pan and turned the burner down.

"Good morning," I said quietly.

Noah smiled and opened his arm to me. "Did you scratch my truck?"

"No. I'm not that nice. I smashed it to bits and sold it for scrap metal." I tucked myself into Noah's side.

I'd taken his truck to my appointment to have my hand x-rayed again. The joke last night was, it was going to come back with a new dent.

"How'd it go?" He kissed the top of my head and poked at the omelet in the pan.

"I traded in my cast for a fancy brace," I sighed, "I have

nothing else nice to say."

He laughed and dropped his arm from around me. "Why's that?"

"Nope. I have nothing nice to say."

Noah laughed again and slid the omelet onto a plate. "Are you claiming to be a better doctor than someone?"

"Maybe I read more, maybe I had the advantage of better professors and a brilliant dad. I don't know their situation." I picked up a piece of bacon and took a bite. "Whatever it was, I was clearly more qualified to read my x-rays than the doctor I met with."

He burst out with a loud laugh and handed me the plate with the omelet. I smiled a little. I'd heard him laugh, but never quite the way he did now.

"I knew you had an ego in there somewhere." Noah kissed the side of my forehead. "Go eat. I have to check the forms before they pour the concrete."

"You're not making me sit out today. I mean it, I will have a fit like you've never seen."

Noah had been putting me on the sidelines too many times over the last few weeks and it'd driven me up a wall. Mostly because he was insisting on paying me, even when I wasn't working.

"Nope. I need your help today." He walked down the hallway. "Keep Gif in the house. I don't want him in the way." Noah opened the door to the basement and grabbed his boots off the top step. "And can you make sure to lock up the house and your apartment? I don't know these guys that are coming out today."

"Can do." I took a bite of my omelet and pulled over my book from the spot next to me to read while I ate.

A barking gray streak ran through my vision for the door before the doorbell had a chance to ring. Noah snapped his fingers once and Gif ran back to sit beside me. I looked through the hall at the front door from where I was when Noah opened the door.

"Good Morning," a skinny guy greeted easily. He had on black pants and a bright yellow shirt. It was interesting because he sort-of looked like a more gangly version of Moses. He had the same curly mop of hair and nerdy red-rimmed glasses.

"Can I help you with something?" Noah's voice was low and grouchy. He clearly didn't know whomever it was, or he wouldn't have sounded like he was about to throw a fist.

"I'm looking for Dr. Holly Bennett? Is she here?"

"Who are you?" Noah's voice was threatening and even more unkind.

"Uh—Tim. I work for Snap Courier Service. I have a package for a Dr. Holly Bennett, from a Bradley Bennett. Do I have the wrong address?"

"Mm. No. You have the right address." Noah turned and looked at me.

I got up and walked to the door with a polite smile. "I'm Holly," I said kindly. The kid seemed unaffected by Noah's threatening demeanor, but I still felt bad for him.

"Good morning, Ma'am. If you could sign for me here." He handed me a clipboard.

"Are you sure it's from your brother?" Noah asked quietly from beside me.

"If it's not, there's nothing I can do about it now."

"There's also a security question," the delivery guy said, looking at me, then Noah. "Besides DNA, what did you and your brother have in common with your dad?" The guy raised an eyebrow.

I smirked. The package was definitely from Brad. "Blood lust."

"That's a new one." He handed me the box. "Have a good day."

"You too." I pushed the door shut.

"Do I want to know?" Noah smiled at the corner of his mouth with an almost mocking look.

"It's a long-winded answer."

Noah stepped back to look out of the living room windows. "Concrete is here. I gotta go. I need you outside in twenty minutes."

I gave him a salute as I walked toward the kitchen.

"Wrong hand, and you're supposed to hold it until it's returned," Noah laughed.

"My hand is broken, Mr. Marine."

He was out the door before I finished my sentence. I grabbed a pair of scissors from the kitchen and cut the box open before I shoved a mouthful of omelet down the hatch. My brother had carefully packed all my certificates and papers in a large envelope, a large cashier's check written in my name, my dad's stethoscope, and a letter. I sat down and read it quickly while I shoveled down the last of my food.

....

"Hey beautiful, are you ready to call it a day?" Noah asked, stomping his boots off on the mat in front of the basement door.

"Almost." I flattened a piece of tape on top of one of the boxes I'd finished packing.

"Looks good down here, but you were supposed to let

me know when it was time to start moving boxes."

I shook my head. "I got it. Besides, it looked like you had your hands full." I picked up the box and walked it over to the shelves I'd set up.

"Ugh. I should have waited the two weeks for my guys to do it. Then those crack-heads welding the gates..." He let out a huff, shaking his head, and stepping out of his boots.

"I heard you." I looked at him and smiled.

Noah smiled and walked toward me. "The state of Minnesota heard me."

I laughed quietly. "I started dinner already, and fed Gif."

Noah raised his eyebrows. "*You* started dinner?"

"Yeah. It's still in the oven, but I followed your recipe, so if it doesn't taste good, it's your fault." I flashed a smile and looked up at him as he stood directly in front of me for a kiss.

"Nope. You put it together, it'll be your fault." He smiled, touching my cheek and looking my face over.

"You gotta stairin' problem, buddy?"

He let out a short laugh. "Nope." He bent his head down and kissed me, keeping his hand against the side of my chin. "You wanna take a shower with me?"

Kiss ruiner. "Definitely not."

He frowned a little, but his smile didn't leave. "Don't be a baby."

"I'm not. I don't wanna take a shower with you."

Noah took in a deep breath and looked over at the shelves behind me. "How'd that get down here?" He frowned at whatever he was looking at.

I turned and looked in the same direction he was, and as I was about to ask, he grabbed my legs and flipped me over his shoulder.

"No!" I swatted his butt. "Put me down."

"Uh-uh."

"You can carry me like a sack of potatoes, but I'm not getting in that shower with you." I smacked his butt again.

He laughed. "We'll see about that." He started up the stairs and I hugged his waist tightly.

"You're a dead man walking, Sir. One scream and Gif will take you out."

"Good luck with that."

"Gif! Help!" I yelled.

The sound of scattering claws on the hardwood started, along with a snarling bark.

"Stop that." Noah swatted my butt. "Gif, go lay down," Noah called loudly before he opened the door.

Gif growled and snorted as he danced. A combination of happy to see Noah and ready to kill.

"Gif, help." I reached out for him.

Gif danced closer to Noah like he was considering a nip, but backed up and barked.

Noah laughed. "He knows he'll be a dead dog."

"Bite him in the ass, Gif. Sick 'im!"

Gif barked more confidently, but that was it.

I grabbed the edge of the bathroom doorway. "No."

"Stop that." Noah pinched the back of my leg with a laugh as he continued forward into the bathroom.

"Noah, I don't want to take a shower with you."

He set me down and smiled at me. "Aren't doctors supposed to be desensitized to naked bodies?" He started to unbutton his flannel shirt.

"Most people just have sex in the bedroom." I raised my

eyebrows.

He laughed a little and pulled his shirt off. "Who said anything about sex? I said *shower*."

I rolled my eyes and stepped toward the door.

"Hold on there." Noah pulled me back by my belt loop and wrapped his arms around me from behind. "Do you have a better reason than being embarrassed about your scars?" He kissed the back of my jaw and watched my face.

"I don't need one."

"I've seen them a couple of times already. You remember that, right?"

"Noah." I was becoming thoroughly irritated by his persistence.

He let out a huff and opened the door. "Stay here."

Noah walked out of the bathroom—still shirtless— then came back. I looked at him skeptically when he came back in. He held up a black marker with a smile.

"I think you might have a little trouble writing on my *black* brace," I laughed.

He smiled. "We'll see." He turned his back to me, pinning me between himself and the wall, then pulled my hand around in front of him.

"I get it. You think I'm beautiful. You don't care about my scars. Blah, blah. But I care, and—That's not my brace. Why are you writing on my arm?"

"I'll let you go in a second. Hold still."

I stood there for a few seconds, but the marker was moving over more of my arm than I wanted. "Okay. Whatever you're doing, that's enough." I pulled my arm back and Noah stepped forward and turned around to face me.

Over five scars, he'd written different words. Beautiful,

funny, brilliant, kind, and loved.

"Some people leave bad marks, some of us wanna leave good ones."

I looked at Noah. "All this because you want me to take a shower with you?"

The corners of his mouth twitched back in a smile, but didn't stay. "No. All of this because you're stubborn and refuse to see past something that doesn't matter anymore." He gestured at my marked-up arm. "If you're going to put so much attention on them, then I'm gonna attack you with a Sharpie so you see something better."

I took in a breath and held up my arm to look at the words before I looked at him again. I smiled. "You're a sap."

He shrugged. "I'm fine with that."

I let out another huff, pushed the door shut, and pulled off my shirt. "Make it good." I turned to the side. "Draw a tree or something."

He laughed and got down on his knees. "Or something. Hold up your arm."

I crossed my arm over my chest and looked at my side as he drew a long line down my side.

"No looking."

I looked at him and watched his face as he continued to draw on my skin. He looked intent on what he was doing. His beautiful green eyes followed whatever he was drawing instead of staring at the long scar. I let out a breath to release the tension in my back and waited. Usually, he stared at my scars, traced his fingers over them, or kissed them like they might heal themselves away. It made me uncomfortable. I had a bunch of reminders that I was the idiot who stayed and kept making up excuses not to leave.

Noah put a hand on my stomach and one on my back, pulling my side closer to kiss me. "Okay. I'm done, but don't look yet." He stood up and put the marker on the counter. "Step up on the side of the tub and look in the mirror." He held out his hand.

"Should I be worried?"

He shook his head. "No."

I stood up on the edge of the tub and turned to the side. He'd turned my scar into an arrow going through a heart. I didn't know why, but I found it hysterical.

Noah smirked, then laughed. "I didn't know what else to do. That was the best I could come up with."

"I'm gonna have a corny heart and arrow on my side for a week?"

Noah laughed and helped me down. "At least you can cover it. I had 'I'm hungry' written on my hand."

"You had it off by the end of the day." I stretched up and wrapped my arms around his neck.

"Yeah, minus three layers of skin." He tipped my chin up and kissed my lips. "Stop being a pain in the ass about your scars. If I can see them, then you're still here, he's not adding to them, and you're not dead."

I pulled back the corner of my mouth and hugged him.

"I love you," he said quietly as he held the back of my head.

I smiled. It was the first time he'd said it and I'd been waiting. "I love you too."

Chapter 12

Thanksgiving

Over the next few months, I took the Minnesota board, got everything in place to start applying for residency programs at different hospitals, and helped Noah with his house the rest of the time. I went in for an interview at the hospital in Red Wing and came out with an offer from the Mayo Clinic. One of the surgeons there, Dr. Callaway, had worked for my dad years before, and the doctor I'd interviewed with was good friends with him. The forty-five-minute drive to and from sucked, but to me, it was more than worth it. I was working with the best of the best and performing dream surgeries. I'd come home in the middle of the day, from a fifteen-hour shift, and continue helping Noah with his house. He had been pushing for a damn miracle to get the house done by the first of November; we were hell bent and determined on making it happen, and we did.

......

I dug around in the back seat of Noah's new truck, looking for my parking pass for work. His old light blue Ford died and went to Ford heaven after the neighbor's kid accidently ran it into the ditch while hauling stuff from the garage under my apartment to the new shop to the northeast, away from both houses. Noah wanted to save the old truck, but I convinced him to buy a new one. We'd gone out on the same day to buy our vehicles, but at different dealerships. Noah could have his Ford, but I'd wanted my Volvo back. I'd sold mine in Oregon simply because I didn't want Brad to drive it here. I usually got a new one every couple of years anyway.

I gasped and whipped around quickly when a pair of tight arms constricted around me unexpectedly. The body behind me moved with mine and I clasped my hands together and threw my arms up to break his grasp, whipping around, ready to fight.

Noah.

"What the hell, man!" I snapped, putting my hand over my heart.

He laughed with an adorable smile. "Just checking to see if I actually taught you something."

"That's not funny. You almost got nailed in the balls," I panted. My body wasn't taking well to the sudden hit of fear and adrenaline. "God, you're always complaining I'm too jumpy."

Noah had been teaching me self-defense maneuvers on top of everything else.

He continued to laugh lightly and stepped toward me. "I'm sorry. Come here."

I let out a breath and hugged him. I hadn't seen him for more than a minute in the last couple of days. The house was completely finished, and Callaway had over booked us on surgeries so we could have a few days off.

"You smell like iodine and latex."

"Mm. Imagine that. I didn't get a shower before I left the hospital. I lost my damn parking pass, so I had to park about three blocks from the hospital in metered parking because of the giant conference going on. I had to go to the bank for four rolls of quarters to buy myself enough time. Maybe I should have just taken the ticket. I don't know." I rolled my eyes, stepping back.

"I was wondering what you were digging for. Why would your pass be in my truck though?"

"Well, it was in my purse because I rode with Dr. Roth in the ambulance from Red Wing yesterday, then you picked me up to take me back to get my car. I didn't know if maybe it fell out of my purse, or what, but I can't find it anywhere."

"Have you checked your apartment yet?"

"No," I sighed and rubbed at my head.

Noah pulled me against him. "Relax. You have a few days to look for it." He kissed the top of my head. "I made you some soup because I know you said you didn't feel good this morning. Why don't you go take a bath up in my room and I'll see if I can hunt down your parking pass."

I released a breath, letting my head rest against the front of his shoulder. "I'm too tired for either one of those things. My surgery was panic after panic. It was supposed to be four hours and went ten."

"Take a shower then. I want to talk to you before you pass out on me and everyone else shows up later." Noah rubbed my neck.

"Then stop making it so comfortable to stand here."

Noah kissed the top of my head again. "Go inside."

I took in a deep breath and stepped back. I looked under the truck on the garage floor for good measure. My pass wasn't anywhere in the truck.

"I'll look for it. Go."

"I'm going." I straightened up, dragged myself up the steps to the door, and went inside.

The house still smelled like new paint, wood, and drywall. For some reason, I loved the smell. Noah's old house had been sold and moved off the property, and this house smelled like something new. It didn't make a lot of sense, but it was like a new life. I had my new job, Noah had his new house. Anything else before didn't matter. It wasn't even my house, but the change felt so significant that it made life feel different. Maybe it was because Noah felt different in this house. The old one was filled with Kate and the memories he had with her. Walking in, I'd always felt it, and I imagined he did too. This house was just him.

The garage door opened to a hallway that extended to the massive openness of the dining room, living room, and kitchen. The ceiling was a thirty-foot T vault, with short, but wide windows at the top of the T. The dining room had glass doors all along the two walls and a set of twenty-foot-tall windows above them that looked out into the trees behind the house. It had been incredibly beautiful when the fall colors had come in, but now the trees were bare. Above the cupboards in the kitchen, there were more windows like the ones in the dining area. About ten or twelve feet up, there were two long and narrow windows on either side of the fireplace. There couldn't be any below it because that wall was shared with the garage.

I put my shoes and coat in the closet, just before the entrance to the dining room and walked straight ahead to the stairs that led up to Noah's room. There was a small open loft at the top of the stairs with a couple of two-seater couches and a fireplace. To the right of the fireplace was a set of French doors, behind it was the master suite, which was about sixteen hundred square feet without including the two massive walk-in closets and master bath. The back wall of the house, in the bedroom, was made up of floor to ceiling windows and another massive, vaulted ceiling. I couldn't wait for the first big snow because it was going to make for an incredible view.

The well pump for my apartment was busted so I'd been having to come up to the house for showers or water over the last week. Noah's bathroom was another incredible room all on its own, so I wasn't too inconvenienced.

I went into Noah's bathroom, took a bath, stole something to wear from his closet, and went downstairs to the kitchen.

"I don't know how you look even more tired, but you do." Noah frowned and set a bowl of soup in front of me after I sat at the kitchen island.

"Because I took a bath and closed my eyes for too long." I picked up the spoon and pushed the chunks of vegetables inside the bowl. "No meat?"

"You usually fish it out. I can put some in if you want."

"No. I was going to fish it out." I looked at him and gave a tired smile.

He smiled and leaned over on his elbows on the side of the island, facing me, with his own bowl of soup. "I don't know what your problem is with meat in soup."

"My problem is mostly with soup in general, but my

stomach is too upset for anything else." I took a sip of broth. "Do you want some of my vegetables? I'm not sure I can keep them down."

He took a bite, then pushed his bowl toward me. I scooped out most of the vegetables, leaving myself with a few slices of celery and a potato chunk. I pushed his bowl back and we ate quietly for a few minutes.

"You've got me paranoid, what did you want to talk about?"

"Nothing for you to be paranoid about, hoodie thief." He tugged gently at the seam between the cuff and sleeve.

I gave him a cheesy smile, proud of my five-finger discount from his closet.

He laughed a little.

I dipped my spoon in the bowl and allowed one celery sliver onto my spoon. "So, what is it?"

Noah took in a deep breath. "I wanted to ask you if you wanted to move into the house. The downstairs suite was mostly done with you in mind. You're up here a lot when you *are* home, and I'd feel better if you weren't so far down the hill. I'm worried something might happen, and I won't know. Especially with the hours that you come and go. Plus, you helped me build this house and you deserve to reap some of the benefits." He smiled and reached over to move a lock of my hair behind my ear. "And I love you."

...*What?* "I reap plenty. I get free rent—not that I need it. And free food—*that*, I do need—but I'm fine down there. Gif runs down every night when I pull in, I have the gun in my purse, and I keep the door locked. I don't really see how being up here is going to make any difference."

"Safety isn't my only reason for asking." He raised his

eyebrows slightly, looking hopeful.

I itched at the side of my head like it was going to help me come up with a good excuse. Then the tired and irritable side of me decided I didn't need one. "No," I said plainly, shaking my head. I looked at him from my soup bowl. "I'm sorry. I'm not okay with it, and I'm really too tired to talk about it right now." I picked up my soup bowl and walked it over to the sink.

What was he thinking? Moving in together? I'd been here just short of seven months! Granted, it felt like a lot longer, but it wasn't. Three of those months he'd spent basically hating me and being a huge ass.

"Leave the dishes. I got it," Noah said quietly as he set his bowl down on the counter and wrapped one arm around me. "Go sleep. Everyone will be here around six." He kissed the top of my head.

I held onto his arm around the top of my shoulders and rested my head against his upper arm. "I'm sorry. I didn't mean to be a jerk."

"You're okay." He wrapped his other arm around me for a minute and let go. "Take Gif with you. I'll come down and wake you up in a few hours."

I nodded and turned around for a quick kiss.

......

Gif jumped up on top of me and shoved his face into mine, trying to wake me up.

"Knock it off," I groaned, pushing him back. "Lay down." I rolled over on my side and pulled my blankets up more. It was colder than hell in my room, but I was too tired to get up, walk down to the garage below, and stuff more wood in the stove.

There was a knock on the door and Gif jumped down from the bed barking. I let my face pinch up in a pout and got up. If I'd felt like shit before, I *really* felt like it now.

"Stop barking. Go lay down," I said to Gif as I unlocked the door.

He backed up a few paces and laid down. I pulled the door open, expecting Noah—because I was too out of it to look through the window on the door—but it wasn't him.

"Brad, what are you doing here?" I looked around behind him.

"Hi to you too. Jeez, you look like shit. Are you sick or something?" He looked me over.

"Or something." My teeth chattered with a deep shiver. "Get in here. It's cold." I walked away from the door and pulled Gif back when he lurched forward to either bite or greet Brad. "Go lay down." I pulled his collar toward the living room. The simple action drained me of energy and air.

"I think you better go lay down before you drop." Brad grabbed my arm as I staggered.

"Yeah. Come with me." I rubbed at my forehead and walked back to my room. "Greg doesn't know where you are, does he?" I crawled onto my bed and got under the covers to warm up.

"He's in Arizona with his mom for Thanksgiving. She moved down there a couple months ago." Brad looked around my room.

"Then I'm happy to see you." I smiled a little. "Sit down."

Brad moved one of the pillows on top of the others and sat down with his back to them. "You did a lot of work on this place."

"Yeah," I yawned.

"Are you working at a hospital again?" Brad looked at me.

"Yeah. At the Mayo Clinic. Do you remember Dr. Callaway? He worked with dad forever ago."

"Yeah, what about him?"

"I work with him now." I smiled. "It's pretty cool. We've done a bunch of surgeries that he did with dad. He's an incredible teacher."

Brad laughed a little. "Really? Callaway? The guy who gave you a suture kit for your fifth birthday?"

I nodded. "That's the one."

"That's cool. How is he?"

"Still a loudmouth."

Brad laughed. "Yeah. I'm surprised he and dad didn't get in more arguments."

I smirked. "Yeah, me too."

"What about Garrett? I thought he worked at the Mayo Clinic."

I sighed. "He does, but I really haven't seen him. He got called for a consult a couple times, and I found a reason not to be in the room."

He looked at me. "And he's just left you alone?"

I nodded. "Yeah. I've seen him a couple times, he's probably seen me too, but neither of us have said or done anything. People ask me if we're related, and I don't lie, but I'm not fully honest. I just tell them he's an estranged uncle."

"And Clara?"

"Not a peep." I shrugged. I wasn't telling him I'd invited Clara to Thanksgiving dinner at our house today. I'd sent Clara a letter a couple weeks ago.

"So, I take it you're sick because you're working too much?" He looked at me with a patronizing expression.

"Probably. What about you? How's the practice?"

He shrugged and looked away. "I don't know. Kind of getting sick of it, but..." He shrugged again and looked at me. "How are you on money? I tried to send you as much as I could without getting dad's lawyer involved."

"I'm not out to buy a fancy mansion, so I'm good." I smiled at him tiredly.

Brad and I had a joint trust fund that was enough to last us for a few generations and keep our dad's estate in California fully staffed.

"And you and what's-his-face?"

"Noah... We're good. Are you and what's-her-nose, still together?"

He took in a breath, looking like he didn't know what to say. "No... There's someone new."

"I told you she was evil. What happened?"

"She found somebody to buy her a condo in Seattle." Brad sank down on the bed. "Holl... I have to tell you something." He rubbed his forehead.

"Oh no. Did you knock someone up?" The look on his face was stressed and him getting a girl pregnant was my only assumption.

"No..." He shook his head, keeping his eyes across the room.

I watched him carefully. If he was that worried about telling me, then I was preparing for the worst. We were buddies, and if he thought I was going to freak out, then it was probably bad.

"I'm not seeing a girl." He looked at me, searching my

face and waiting.

I raised my eyebrows, for a second I was trying to figure out if he was kidding, but then I realized it just kind of made sense. Brad didn't really fit in in a lot of ways. He'd had girlfriends, and he was always sweet to them, but his heart never seemed in it.

"You're not saying anything." His worried frown turned a little deeper.

"I don't know. I don't know what to say. I still love you the same..." I shrugged and turned my dad's watch on his wrist so it was facing up right. "After briefly thinking about it, I think it kinda makes sense. You've never seemed to pursue anyone. All the girls you dated were people who pursued *you*."

Brad shook his head. "I know... I've never been sure what I wanted, and... Dad would have killed me."

"Mm, he probably would have been a jerk at first, but he would have gotten over it. Big Christmas presents would have been involved, lots of head scratching, and pacing." I smiled at the very thought of how our dad would have tortured himself trying to figure out how to apologize without actually saying he was sorry.

"I have to tell you the rest though. There's more." Brad let out a breath.

"*He's* pregnant?" I teased.

Gif got up and ran out of the room before the door opened.

Brad wacked me lightly with a pillow. "No one is pregnant."

"Holly?" Noah called.

"We're in here," I called back with a laugh.

Brad sat up a little bit before Noah walked in. Noah looked like he was ready to beat someone until he saw it was Brad.

"Brad, it's good to see you again." Noah nodded with a tight smile.

Brad nodded once. "You too."

"I just finished telling him that I'm gonna inflict different forms of torture if he doesn't spend Thanksgiving with us. Do you still have that zappy-stick thing for when the neighbor's cows wander over?" I smiled at Noah. He wouldn't care that Brad was staying without an invitation, but Brad's ego would.

Noah laughed with a quiet huff. "For your brother's sake, no." He looked at Brad. "We're glad to have you. My family and friends make a big deal about the holidays, so it's usually pretty interesting."

"Are Gabe and Moses here?" I asked.

He nodded. "A couple of minutes ago."

"We'll be up in a few minutes then. I need to change and get in an argument about where Brad's staying."

Noah looked at Brad. "Good luck."

Brad laughed. "Too late for luck. I already lost."

Noah laughed. "I'll see you guys up at the house." He turned and left.

I got up from the bed. "Go bring in your stuff—assuming you brought more than one change of clothes—and I'm gonna change."

I walked to the closet and grabbed my red sweater, skinny jeans, and brown boots. I went into the bathroom to change while Brad brought his small suitcase in. I was glad he was here. I knew he wouldn't have anyone to spend Thanksgiving with if I wasn't there. We usually went down to my dad's estate or Greg and I held it at my house. Thanksgiving was a tough holiday for us because the day after was when we got the phone call about our dad.

Chapter 13

"**O**h my gosh. I got married too soon. He is *delicious*," Bridgett said as she stood next to me.

"He's like model pretty." Terri tilted her head like a confused puppy. "It's just wrong to look that good."

"He's off limits. And you still have a boyfriend." I opened the bottle of water I'd grabbed from the fridge and popped a couple of aspirin in my mouth. I could have told them of what I'd just been informed of, but I didn't know if Brad was okay with anyone knowing.

She sighed. "I could reconsider. Is he nice?" She looked at me.

"He's quiet."

"Boo." She pouted, looking in my brother's direction again.

"He's fun to look at though." Carrie rested her arm on Bridgett's shoulder.

"I wouldn't know. He's my brother."

"You're rotten, you know that?" Terri looked at me jealously. "You're surrounded by pretty people and they like you. Noah's hot as hell, Gabe is gorgeous, your brother's gorgeous, even Moses—who's a nerdy, cynical, ass-hat—loves you."

"Might be because I'm not looking at them like a hungry dog in front of raw meat. And what are you talking about? Moses is crazy nice." I looked at her like she'd lost her mind. Had she meant Gabe?

"Only to you and his family, Honey. He's kind of a dick to us." Bridgett raised her eyebrow.

"Really?" I couldn't picture it. I'd never seen Moses be anything but nice, though I hadn't really seen him around the girls much.

"Yeah. He was even a douche to Kate," Carrie answered. "They pretty much got into it everytime we got together."

"And Gabe?" I *had* to ask. If they thought that about Moses, they must have thought Gabe was the next generation Stalin or something.

"Gabe is nicer than Moses, but he's still an ass. Noah's the only nice one out of those three." Bridgett took a drink from her beer.

Noah looked over at me from the kitchen and nodded for me to come over.

"I'm being summoned. I'll be back."

I was thankful for the break from the girls. Their mindless prattle was funnier when I didn't feel like I was dying from the inside out.

"What's up?" I asked as I walked up to Noah.

"You looked bored with the three bobbleheads." Moses handed me a beer.

I shook my head to the beer and stood with my back against Noah, in front of him.

Noah wrapped an arm around the front of my shoulders and put his other hand over my forehead. "You look like hell and you're burning up."

"I feel like it." I rested my head back against his chest.

"I say ditch the party and have a siesta. The bobble heads won't know you're gone, and Brad's getting along with the grim reaper over there." Moses lifted a finger from his bottle to point at Brad and Gabe.

"Who pooped in your cereal?" I frowned at Moses.

He laughed. "Is that what those things are in my cereal? I always thought they were marshmallows."

I smiled and shook my head. "You're absurd."

He bared his teeth in a cheesy grin.

I looked over at Brad and Gabe talking, making sure nothing appeared to be heated. Brad usually got along with others, but every now and then, he'd come across one of those over opinionated people and he'd turn into a vicious predator. Brad was extremely smart and well witted, keeping it under wraps until someone ticked him off.

"Don't worry. He'll be nice. He likes you enough not to be a dick." Noah rubbed my shoulders.

"I'm not worried about it."

"Yeah, Gabe knows she's meaner than him. It's cool." Moses laughed a little.

"Watch who you're calling mean." I looked at Moses with a raised eyebrow. "I'm not the one calling people bobble heads and grim reapers."

Noah chuckled. "Or standing here so you don't have to be nice."

"Need I remind you of the endless ways you and those chumps used to bully me?" Moses looked at Noah. "Hm? What about Bridgett yanking my pants down at the pep-rally?" Moses looked at me. "Have you ever tried to balance a tuba and try to pull your pants up from your ankles?"

I laughed. "Weren't you older than them?"

"Why do you think it was so insulting? They were picking on gangly nerds bigger than themselves. Everybody called me a weeny."

I covered my mouth, letting out a laugh I couldn't hold back. My stomach hurt and didn't like the disruption, but the mental image of an even nerdier and scrawnier Moses, fighting a tuba and yanking his pants up, was too much.

Noah laughed. "And that time we put a bat in your locker. Your history book should have been registered as a lethal weapon. And *scream*."

"Oh," I laughed. "That's terrible." I held my stomach. "I can't stop laughing."

"Yeah, neither could the teachers. I'm over there getting attacked by a rabid flying-rat while they're all pissing themselves with laughter."

"It looked like he was having a seizure," Noah laughed. "Really, you should have heard him scream. It was like a caught rabbit."

I'd never heard Noah laugh so hard and it made my giggle fit worse.

"You shouldn't encourage his jokes with laughter," Gabe grumbled as he walked over with Brad.

Noah calmed himself from laughing. "We were telling her about the bat in Moses' locker."

Gabe let out a hardy chuckle and looked at Brad. "Ever

seen a giraffe have a spaz attack?"

Brad laughed a little. "No, but put Holly in the same room as a kitten, and I imagine it's about the same."

"What?" Noah laughed, looking at me.

"Okay. That thing was evil," I laughed, wiping under my eyes. "And I'm not afraid of kittens, I just hate them."

"Keep telling yourself that." Brad smiled and looked at Noah. "Our dad got her a kitten to replace her dead fish." He looked at me. "I think you were—what—five?"

"Something like that."

"Too young to be *that* depressed over a fish. Anyway," he laughed a little, "our dad puts this gold fur-ball in her hands. I don't know who screamed first, her or the cat, but that thing went flying across the room. She just lobbed it and ran to her room screaming."

Everyone laughed.

"Okay." I pointed at Brad. "The thing hissed at me, and Nana's cat always hissed and attacked me. At five years old, I knew that thing was going to grow up to be a furry asshole with razorblade feet, and I was right."

"Probably because you threw it across the room," Noah laughed.

I looked up at him and raised an eyebrow. "Do we need to tell a story about Noah and a certain furry creature this summer? Remember whose side you're on."

He laughed a little and looked at me sweetly. "I'm on your side, and you promised to take that to the grave."

"And I will," I smiled gleamingly, "as soon as I'm done using it as leverage."

A squirrel had fallen out of a tree onto the back of No-ah's shirt collar, and he'd screamed and swatted frantically to get it off him. Its back foot had gotten stuck in the tag of his shirt, so it couldn't just jump away from him like a squirrel normally would have.

"Noah, how do you work this damn thing?" Dallas called from the living room, holding a remote.

"Did you try the power button? It's the one at the top. There's a circle with a line going through at the bottom." Gabe's voice was flat.

"Ask your wife. She's good with power buttons," Moses laughed.

Both Noah and I backhanded Moses in the gut, but it didn't stop him from laughing. Noah dropped his hand from my waist and walked into the living room.

"Noah. Furry creature. Summer. Go. Hurry." Moses elbowed me playfully. "Let's hear it."

The doorbell rang and I looked to see if anyone would get it. "He'd kill me."

"I can still take him." Gabe took a drink from his beer.

I gave a disapproving look. "I believe I heard something about you on a hunting trip with Noah and getting too close to a raccoon nest."

Moses barked with laughter, and I walked away with a smile to get the door. I looked around for who might be missed from the group we'd invited, and thought maybe Janine and her husband had decided to come after all. Or, it could have been my mom, but I wasn't really holding hope. I'd sent a letter to explain some things and invited her to Thanksgiving dinner.

When I opened the door, I froze and every inch of me prickled with fear.

"Hey..." Greg smiled like he wasn't quite sure. "I didn't

think you'd be the one to answer the door. Um..." His eyes lit with a better smile. "You look good."

"What are you doing here? You said you were going to your mom's."

I turned and looked at Brad, wondering why he only seemed mildly surprised, and didn't really sound upset.

"I know we agreed, but I couldn't let you come by yourself." Greg held up a shoulder, looking slightly guilty, but apologetic.

"Oh, Holly!" Linna crooned cheerfully as she came up from behind Greg. "I told Noah you better be here this time." She walked up the steps and went straight for a hug.

I forced a smile and hugged her. "Yeah. I'm here." My voice was weak.

She pulled back and squished my face in her hands. "Good. I was beginning to think you were avoiding us."

"Of course not." I held as much of a smile as I could.

Linna looked at Brad. "And I haven't seen you before, but you look just like Holly, so you must be her brother." She reached out a hand.

"Brad." He nodded with a smile shaking her hand.

"Nice to meet you, Honey." Linna turned. "And I'm sorry. I rushed right by you, making sure Holly didn't run away on me. Are you part of Holly's family too?" She smiled at Greg.

My blood boiled as I glared at Greg.

He looked at Linna, flashing a quick and dazzling smile. "Sort of. I'm Brad's fiancé, Greg." He held out a hand.

My neck felt like it was going to break as I looked beside me at Brad. He looked at me guiltily.

"Oh," Linna held a bright smile, "well, it's so nice to meet you. I'm glad we get to finally meet Holly's family. We just love her to itty bits and pieces." She wrapped an arm around my waist and squeezed my side.

"Us too." Greg smiled at me gently.

"Where's T-Thomas?" My mouth struggled to form words, but I was hoping I could make her realize she was missing a person and go find him so I could try to deal with my mess.

"Oh, he's out in the car. He's stuck on a classical station, so I just left him." She waved dismissively, unwrapping her scarf.

"Hey, Ma. Who's this?" Noah took the step up on the platform from the living room.

I looked at him and felt like the blood in my body was slowly flowing out onto the floor.

Linna's quick smile reappeared as she looked at Greg. "This is Brad's fiancé, Greg."

Noah looked at Brad, then me, no longer acknowledging that Greg was a body standing there.

"I, um..." Words weren't there. I had no words or explanation.

"Sorry. I came unannounced," Greg said quickly to fill the gap I was leaving. "I was supposed to be in Arizona but my plans were canceled, so I came to spend the holiday with Brad and Holly."

Noah gave the hardest glare I'd ever seen on him in Greg's direction. "Ma," Noah cleared some of the anger off his face and looked at Linna, "will you check on the turkey for me?"

She knew something was off but smiled anyway. "Of course, Honey." She gave him a quick hug and went toward the kitchen. Bridgett and Carrie stopped her along the way to greet her.

"Holl, I was gonna tell you, but we got interrupted and I chickened out," Brad spoke quietly.

"Oh shit, Holl." Greg glanced at Brad, then looked at me again. "I'm sorry. I should have waited to say anything and made sure you knew."

I stared at Brad and tried to figure out which part I was more betrayed over. That he'd led Greg straight to my door, or that he was *engaged* to the person who'd beat the hell out of me. Brad looked as sorry as he could, and ready to take whatever I was about to lash at him. The problem was, I couldn't lash out. He wouldn't know why, and there were far too many people in the house, which was likely what Greg had counted on.

I took the beer from Brad's hand. "There's water in the fridge for both of you. Anything else is for guests." I looked at Greg.

He nodded, appearing legitimately guilty. "Understood. I don't drink anymore."

I nodded as I turned, but wasn't sure that it wasn't from the quiver throughout my body. Noah followed behind me to his office, then shut and locked the door once we were in. I set Brad's beer on the desk and pulled my hand over my mouth.

"How do you wanna handle this?" Noah asked quietly.

I shook my head, keeping my hand over my mouth. There still weren't words and I genuinely didn't know what to do.

"I have zero problem telling him to leave, but that probably means Brad'll go with him."

My lungs pulled in a jagged breath behind my hand.

"Come here." Noah pulled me against him and hugged

me tightly.

A short bursting cry came out into the front of his shoulder, sounding almost like a loud cough because I stopped it dead in its tracks.

Noah rubbed my back with heavy pressure. "You're safe. No one here is going to let anything happen, especially not me."

I turned my face away from his shoulder so I could breathe. "I know…"

Noah moved my hair away from my face and kissed the top of my head. "Tell me how you wanna handle this, and that's it. No questions asked… Running isn't an option. I'll tie your cute butt to a chair."

"Can I hide under the bed with a plate of cookies and live in a state of denial?" I took in a breath and stepped back. My cheeks were burning, so I held my cold hands against them.

"You could, but Gif gets territorial about his spot." Noah moved to sit on the edge of the desk and turned me to face him. "What do you wanna do?"

"I don't know." I shook my head. "If I make him leave, Brad's gonna be pissed, and hurt because he'll think I'm being unsupportive and petty. I can't say anything to him because there's too many people here." I shoved my hand through my hair. "And there's just too many people here." I looked at Noah. "I don't wanna make a mess in front of your friends and family."

Noah shook his head. "Don't worry about them. One short explanation and they'll all be picking up their pitchforks." He ran his hand up my arm to get my hand out of my hair. "I just need to know what *you* want. As much as I want to take that asshole out back and turn him into a tree ornament by the neck, this isn't my fight. Which isn't to say there won't be one if he so much as looks at you wrong, but…"

"No, I'm not asking you to do anything." I shook my head out of exhaustion. "It isn't fair to you." I let out a breath. "I don't know what to do. Going out there and just leaving them be isn't fair to you, and neither is causing a scene and making them leave. I know you and everyone else will understand, but it's still not fair to ruin anyone else's holiday because of me and my shit." I shoved my hand through my hair again, wanting to scream from the frustration building up in my body.

"Stop." Noah pulled my hand out of my hair again. "Look at me."

I took in a breath and looked at him.

"Don't worry about anyone else. You've dealt with plenty of their shit. Bridgett and Dallas howling at each other like dogs, Carrie and Chris' psycho kids, Terri and her laundry list of guy drama, me and the pissed off mood swings. Hell, the last time you saw my parents, my dad trapped you for four hours and made you play the piano for him. Why do you think my mom thinks you're afraid to be here when they show up?" He smiled a little and rubbed his hands against my sides. "Everybody's got shit, Love. Stop thinking about how to be pleasing, and decide what you want to happen when we walk back out that door."

I shook my head, looking away to rub the heat out of my cheeks. "I really don't know… Any suggestions?" I looked at him.

He took in a breath. "I think for the sake of sanity and getting through the day, just get through the day." He shook his head with a slight shrug. "If the pot is going to get stirred, let *him* be the first one to do it. You have a room full of people who'll rip his goddamn throat out before either one of us has to. Think about Bridgett." He raised his eyebrows with a smile.

I let out a huff. "Thinking about it means I'd have to clean the blood off the walls of my brain."

He chuckled and rubbed my sides again. "Exactly."

"Are you sure you're okay with that though?"

"As long as no one's hurting you, I'm good." He pulled me forward to hug me and kissed my neck, then pretended to cry. "I've never wanted a drink so bad in my entire life."

I laughed a little. "You and me both," I sighed. I turned my cheek down to the top of his shoulder and held onto him.

Noah moved to the chair in front of his desk, taking me with him, and squishing me against him so my boobs were in his face. "That's better."

I laughed. "You're pathetic. Stop." I pushed against his shoulders.

"No. You can drink if you want to, I can't. This is all I have." He moved his face like he was trying to get more comfortable.

"If I drink, I'll start throwing up. So, no, I can't either." I continued to pull myself back.

Noah loosened his arms just enough to put six inches between us and looked up at me with a smile. "But you could puke on Greg. Maybe he'll leave of his own accord."

I rolled my eyes. "I don't need a drink for that."

"Are you gonna be okay?"

I nodded.

Noah patted my hip. "Okay. Get up. I need to make sure

my mom's not ruining my bird."

I stood up and tugged on his hand to pull him out of the chair. Once he was standing, he kissed me.

"I need a minute before I go back out there."

Noah rubbed his fingers over my cheeks. "Don't take too long. My mom'll think you're hiding from *her*."

I nodded. He kissed me again and went out the door. I let out a breath, sitting back on the desk.

"Is Holly in there?" Brad asked from outside the door.

"Yeah, but she needs a few minutes," Noah answered. "Look, I'm not gonna beat around the bush here. I don't have a problem with *you* being here, but your guest is *your* responsibility. Holly already doesn't feel good, she's been working her ass off the last couple weeks, and watching her be as upset as she is isn't going to sit well with me. She didn't come here in a good place, but she's busted her ass to be in one, so if your friend does anything to change that, he should know the amount of hell that'll rain down will make war look like child's play. Are we clear?"

There was the Noah I'd been expecting.

"Yeah." Brad's voice was quiet. I could imagine the look on his face just from his voice. Brad didn't have a backbone in most situations. I was the only one he'd bother to bicker with. For that, I blamed our dad. He'd always been hard on Brad, to the point of taking the fight out of him. I'd always thought that was the reason he chose to be a lawyer, it was the one place he could fight back.

"Good. If you don't mind, I need to talk to you about something else, and I need help bringing some wood in. The girls are getting ready to complain about the cold. I can feel it." Noah's voice was slightly less harsh.

I listened to their steps as they turned around the half wall to go to the basement, and let out another breath. Noah probably didn't think about it, but he was taking away my buffer against Greg. If I went out there now, Greg would feel compelled to talk to me. At this point though, it was all unavoidable. People would think it was weird if I didn't say anything to Brad's "fiancé". And *fiancé?* Brad I could believe, it made sense, but *Greg?*

I stepped out of Noah's office, shutting the door behind me, went down to one of the bathrooms in the hall to check my makeup, then went out to see Linna in the kitchen.

"There you are." She smiled at me as she scraped a pot of mashed potatoes into a large bowl.

I gave her a gentle smile. "Sorry. Family drama. What can I help with?"

"You scrape, and I'll hold this darn thing. It's heavy." She held out the scraper.

I walked around the corner of the island and helped. "We made up the big room downstairs for you and Thomas. Noah said you weren't sure if you guys were staying or not." I didn't really know what else to say to start the conversation.

"Well, I think we'll just about have to. It looks like our nasty weather followed us down." Linna nodded toward the window above the sink.

I looked and saw the large cotton ball snowflakes that were falling. "Yuck. It's only the start of winter and I'm already tired of snow."

She laughed. "Didn't I tell you? It's hell in the winter here."

"We don't get a lot of snow in Portland, and it pretty much melts off the next day," Greg said as he walked up with a water bottle in hand.

"I tell ya, if Thomas wasn't so hell bent on being close to the boys, you'd find me down south in the sunshine." Linna smiled as she shook her head.

"Dad, or *you?*" Gabe approached with a slight mocking look on his face.

"Go ask him, smarty pants." She nodded toward the living room where Thomas sat with headphones on.

"That's it," I said as I took the handle of the pot from Linna.

Moses stole the scraper out of my hand and put it in his mouth. "Not frosting." He scrunched his nose.

"Why'd you think it *was?*" I laughed.

He smiled quickly. "I didn't. You guys need help?"

I raised an eyebrow. "And you think I forgot about three weeks ago?" He'd made a disaster of the kitchen making cinnamon rolls. Thomas' cousins had come from Nebraska and I'd been dumb enough to let Moses help me in the kitchen the day before they showed up. I couldn't be there to meet them because I was on call and had been paged just as soon as I pulled out of the parking garage. Last week, Linna and Thomas had come down for a friend's birthday. I was absent because an intern called in sick, which was why Linna thought I was avoiding them. I never minded spending time with Thomas, no matter how many hours he made me play the piano. I adored him.

"I can't help it. I'm passionate." Moses bared a dopey grin.

"So is Noah, about his kitchen not having flour and dough stuck underneath every counter and cupboard. Go watch the game or something." I turned the faucet on and started filling the pot partially to wash it.

"I'd rather be mindless enough to watch the snow fly." Moses grabbed the soap and dumped a little in. "I can find someone else to bug," he whispered, "but I'm trying to keep him away from you."

I looked at Moses, wondering what the hell he knew, but he crossed his eyes at me. I shook my head and looked back down into the pot to watch what I was doing. "He shouldn't have told you. Who else knows?"

"Gabe, Dallas, and I don't like anyone else enough to find out. Pretty sure it's just us." Moses took the spatula and swished it in the pot obnoxiously. "Dammit lady. I told you not to make a mess of my kitchen," he teased in a deep voice.

"Your obnoxious level is bordering my temper," I warned with a raised eyebrow.

He laughed. "I don't know what you're talking about. I don't know *what* Noah's getting you for Christmas," he announced loudly.

I widened my eyes. "Linna, your son is bugging me."

"Moses Eugene, get out of this kitchen, or so help me god," she chided quickly.

He looked at her with a pouting face. "But Mom, she's being mean."

Linna reached over to grab him by the ear, the normal trick when he was being a pain.

Moses covered his ears instantly. "No, okay. I'm being good. I'm sorry."

She pinched his stomach. "Go be good somewhere else."

I laughed a little and Moses winked at me before he walked over to open the back door for Brad and Noah. I shook my head and dumped the soapy water out of the pot before rinsing it.

"Sweetie, where's the measuring cups?" Linna put a hand on my back as she passed behind me.

"In the drawer next to the stove, right there." I nodded in front of her.

"Thank you. I need that pot again when you're done, I put the gravy in the smaller one, and I shouldn't have." She opened the drawer and got the measuring cups.

"There should be more pots in the cupboard on the other side of the stove. We just keep the bigger stuff in the island because we don't use them much." I grabbed a towel and dried my hands so I could look for her. "Are you making the hollandaise?" I got down to look at what pans were left and grabbed one.

"Yes ma'am. Just for you."

I set the pan on the stove top and opened the fridge to get the butter. "Here. Noah got this butter from the neighbor down the road." I set the bucket on the counter.

"Honey, don't take this the wrong way, but you look like you're dying. Go sit and rest. I got this."

I looked over to find where Greg was, and he was in the dining room talking to Gabe.

"Don't worry. The boys will keep him occupied. Go have a glass of wine with the girls." She rubbed my arm.

"You too?" I looked at Linna. Something about her knowing made everything even worse.

"Me too, what? My boys were off in the corner plotting something while you were with Noah. They don't get along enough for something like that unless there's a problem. And since Noah looked like he was about to strangle your brother's friend, and you look like you saw a ghost, I'm assuming *he's* the problem."

I let out a breath and looked over at Gabe and Greg again. Gabe looked at me briefly, then nodded at whatever Greg was saying to him.

"They've got it handled, whatever *it* is," Linna pushed on my arm. "Go sit and rest."

I turned around and went to the living room. One look at Thomas and I didn't feel so lost. He was probably as happy as could be, reading his book and listening to his music, but I felt badly that he was so isolated.

"Love, where's the lighter?" Noah asked as he stepped back to look around the mantle.

"You put it up, remember?"

The last time Carrie and Chris brought their kids, the oldest boy took it upon himself to burn whatever he could in the fireplace. I'd spent a good hour laying rags on the floor of the fireplace with an iron to get up the candle wax.

I sat down next to Thomas and put a hand on his arm.

He looked up with a frown at first, but then smiled. "Oh, Holly." He pulled off his headphones, then seemed con- founded as to how to turn them off. "I didn't know you were here."

"It's this button," I pointed.

"Thank you." He pushed the button, set them in the case beside him, before he turned to hug me. "How are you, Sweet-pea?"

"I'm good. How are *you*? I heard you had a little scare a couple days ago." They thought he'd had another stroke, but it turned out to be fatigue. The boys had demanded that his test results were sent to me just to be sure.

"Oh, I'm old. That's nothing new." He patted my hand. "How are things at the hospital?"

I smiled. "They're good." The couch sank next to me and I looked over to see Brad. "Have you met my brother yet? This is Brad."

"If we did, I can't remember. I'm Thomas." He reached a hand over.

"This is Noah's dad," I explained as Brad reached to shake Thomas' hand.

"Nice to meet you."

"Are you a doctor too?" Thomas closed the book on his lap.

"Holly, where's the wine? I know you have more," Carrie called from the kitchen.

"I'll be back." I got up and let Brad and Thomas converse. They'd find they had plenty in common, and Thomas would probably end up liking Brad as much as he liked me. I wasn't the only well read and knowledgeable one in my family.

Noah was already grabbing the wine from above the fridge for the girls, but they were still waving for me to hurry up and come over. Noah wasn't paying attention because Linna was basting his precious bird.

"What gives? What's the story?" Terri whispered anxiously.

I shook my head. "About what?"

"Your brother and that guy!"

"Also very handsome, by the way." Carrie stole a glance.

"You wouldn't think so if you knew him. Be nice, but just stay away from him."

"You didn't tell me your brother was gay." Terri turned

her lips in a pout.

I held up a shoulder. "He only told me before we came up to the house, and I didn't think he was ready to drop the banner."

Carrie dropped her jaw. "Are you serious?"

Terri's eyes were wide. "Tell us. What happened? What'd you say? That's like a super sticker shocker."

"Ugh," Bridgett rolled her eyes and stepped through the center of them, "you guys are annoying. Go down another bottle until you're too tired to gossip." Bridgett put an arm around my shoulders and walked away with me. "Are you okay?" she asked, stopping at the start of the hallway.

I nodded and gave her a look like she was crazy for asking. "Yeah. Brad's orientation doesn't bother me any."

She held out her wine glass to me. "Not asking about your brother. I'm asking about you."

I shook my head to the offered wine. "I'm fine. Just trying to get through the day. I'm internally burning to death and I'm exhausted."

She raised an eyebrow. "Well, Noah's worried enough to say something to *me*, so are you sure?"

"He's being paranoid. And yeah, I'm sure. Just a rough day."

She nodded. "Okay. You know where to find me if you need to talk. I'm way better at my job drunk."

I smirked and rolled my eyes, but it was probably true.

"Okay, let's eat," Noah called loudly over the chatter and TV.

Chapter 14

The doorbell rang again. I cringed a little and looked at Noah. He looked at me and I realized there couldn't be anyone worse at the door than Greg. It was probably someone we actually invited, so I walked over and got it.

"Who's behind door number two?" Moses teased as he walked up beside me and rubbed his hands together.

"Stop. It's not funny." I wiped my hand over my forehead because I felt like I should be sweating from how badly my body was burning. All the activity and stress had probably raised my fever.

"Hey man, I'm just trying to lighten things up." Moses looked at me apologetically, reaching for the door.

I instantly regretted the snap because it was the first time I'd ever seen Moses be serious about anything. "I know, I'm sorry." I looked outside, then smiled. "You got my letter."

Clara raised her eyebrows. "Yeah. I'm sure we're late,

but the roads were bad."

I shook my head, holding my smile. "Everyone's just getting ready to sit for dinner, so you're not late." I looked at Garrett nervously. The invitation hadn't been extended to him, but I'd known there was a possibility he'd come with Clara.

"Uh," Clara looked at him, then at me, "you remember Garrett. Another god-complex, but more tolerable."

Garrett looked at me like he was in awe somehow. "Hi, Holly." His voice was a little gentler than my dad's, but he sounded just as similar as he looked.

I blinked because I realized I was standing there staring like an idiot. "Sorry. Um," I reached to take the basket he was holding so he could take his coat off. "I forgot just how much you look like my dad." I reminded myself to smile.

"He is your dad, Girly." Clara rolled her eyes at me as she pulled her coat off.

Garrett wore a kind-eyed smile. "People thought Fran and I were twins growing up."

"Awe jeez, you didn't say your brother was going to be here." Clara looked past me.

"Yeah, he and that person I mentioned in my letter showed up unannounced." I took her coat from her and held out my hand for Garrett's coat.

Garrett traded the basket for his coat as Clara raised an eyebrow at me.

"You won the damn lottery, Girly."

I gave an unamused nod and opened the closet to hang their coats.

"And what the hell are *you* doing here, you gangly lunk-head?" Clara looked at Moses with a smile.

Moses laughed. "That was my question. How the hell are ya?" He bent over to hug her.

"Clara! Oh my gosh!" Linna pretended to jog Clara's way from the kitchen.

What? I looked back at Noah for an answer. He shrugged, wiping his hands on a towel as he followed behind his mom.

"What on earth are you doing here?" Linna hugged Clara.

"Somehow, I knew my laundry was going to get aired if I showed up." Clara hugged Linna like she was relieved, but also regretful of something.

Linna laughed and stepped back. "What are you talking about?"

Clara directed a hand toward me. "Anorexic daughter that appeared out of thin air six months ago."

Linna looked me up and down in shock.

"Less anorexic this time though." Clara pulled back on the side of my sweater. She looked at Noah. "And this would be the tall ass that yelled at me in my store."

Linna looked at Noah. "What—Well, this is my youngest, Noah." She looked at me, confused. "A small world, but how come you told us your dad was dead?" Linna gave me a confused smile as she stepped to Garrett's side to give him a small hug.

"Because the man named on my birth certificate *is*." I rubbed my forehead. Clara wasn't the only one getting her dirty laundry aired.

"It's a complicated situation. Holly only learned about me a few months ago," Garrett said kindly.

"I told you both to stay away from her."

I looked over my shoulder quickly, thinking only Noah

was behind me, but Brad was there too. He wore an angry glare directed at Clara after his heated words.

"Yeah. Just like your father, sweep it under the rug. It doesn't exist."

I rubbed at the side of my head thinking it might actually explode. Noah wrapped an arm around the front of my shoulders and pulled me back against him.

"I birthed you, meaning I don't take orders from you." Clara looked at me again. "You okay there? You look ill."

Brad took my hand. "Holl..."

I pulled my hand away in a jerk, and felt so hatefully angry at him that I nearly exploded in a verbal uproar.

"I think maybe we better go." Garrett's voice was quiet.

"No," I responded automatically. "Everyone's going to sit and have dinner and be kind. I asked you to join us and you *should*."

"Of course. There's no need for anyone to leave. And I'm sure Holly will have questions after she gets some food in her." Linna's voice was kind. "Garrett, come say hi to Thomas. He asks about you all the time."

I gripped Noah's hand. "Go get started. I need to talk to Clara."

Noah kissed the top of my head and let me go.

"Holly, can—"

"No," I cut Brad off. "You need to go too. Go sit with Greg, be nice to my guests, and I'll talk to you when I don't want to sever your head from your body."

He raised an eyebrow at me, pointing at Clara. "You didn't tell me she was coming."

"I'm not doing this with you right now. Go sit and eat." I looked at Clara. "Come with me, please. I don't feel good and I need to sit." I tried to make my voice less bossy, but it didn't work.

Clara nodded, then followed me over to the hallway. Noah wouldn't have cared if I'd chosen to go into his office, but I didn't feel like I should, so I went into the spare room just down the hall and across.

"Linna's sister and I were good friends. She passed about a year and a half ago and she and I became close. That's how we know each other," Clara explained as she sat down on the bed next to me.

"That's not really what I want to know right now." I held my hands to my cheeks, begging my body not to crap out on me.

"I know. I was starting somewhere." She picked at her long almond-shaped nails and took in a deep breath. "You were never supposed to know, I wasn't going to tell you, but he obviously ruined that. Francis never let him see you past the day you were born. It's a long and complicated story, but the gist of it is, I hated your father, had an affair with Garrett, you were a product of that affair, and Fran was hell bent on making sure no one ever knew it. We agreed you were better off with him, that no one was going to tell you the truth, and I left."

"And it just worked out for you that you didn't have to raise your children." I pushed my hair back.

"Like I said, it's long and complicated, but at the end of it, you were *much* better off with Fran. I wasn't fit to be a mother, I hated it, and Garrett was too unstable at the time. I don't need to badmouth him, I'm sure he'll do it himself as soon as he has the chance to talk to you, but right now, you're just gonna have to take my word for it."

I bit the insides of my lips together, just trying to process.

"Listen, I'm terrible at this shit. I don't do the touchy feely crap—that's Garrett and your dad—but I'll take whatever heat you have to dish out. Whether we like it or not, I made you, so it makes me responsible."

I shook my head. "It's hard to be mad at one of the few people who's being honest..."

"Then you need to dig deeper. You're still half me, so it's in there." She patted my knee.

I massaged my forehead.

"So, what's the deal with the abusive dip-shit sitting at your table?"

I shook my head. "He's here as Brad's fiancé."

Clara let out a hardy chuckle, then stopped it abruptly. "Sorry. I'm just going to keep that comment to myself."

"Please do." I stood up. "Let's just go out there and get through dinner."

Clara nodded and stood up. "I can do that. Are you sure you're gonna be okay? It doesn't happen often, but I feel bad."

I shook my head. "Don't. I appreciate you being honest."

"I'm not Fran, Girly." She gave my arm a few gentle squeezes. "You're welcome to ask me whatever you want, all I ask is you give Garrett a chance. He's a fragile little puss and I'll have to listen to his butt hurt all the way home." She rolled her eyes and dropped her hand from my arm.

I would have laughed at her crassness, but my energy was put into standing and not falling to pieces. Who knew what else I'd have to deal with before I could pull the covers over my head tonight.

There was loud laughter from the dining room as Clara and I walked out. Carrie's daughter, Elsie, got up from the kids table and walked over to me. She was four years old and incredibly cute, unlike her older brothers.

"Ant Holly, can I sit with you?" she asked quietly as she held my hand and squirmed nervously. Despite the several times I'd previously corrected her, she continued to call me "Ant Holly," instead of "Aunt".

I bent over because if she said anything else, it'd be hard to hear her. "I'm sorry, there's not a lot of room at the adult table. Can you sit with your brothers during dinner and I'll sit with you after?"

She nodded innocently.

"Yeah? Come on." I kept her hand and walked her over to the kids' table. Just as I pulled her chair out, the lights flickered, then went out completely. Elsie clung to my leg.

"Anyone got a lighter?" Noah asked among the chatter.

"Mine's in my purse," Bridgett answered.

"I got one." Greg lit his lighter. "Can someone pass one of the candles?"

"Me too." Clara reached into her pocket and pulled out a lighter.

"Can I borrow that?" Noah held out his hand.

"Sit down," I told Elsie quietly so I could follow Noah.

She sat down and I pushed her chair in before I went down to the basement.

"The candles are in the laundry room behind the Christmas boxes." He didn't know where I hid them.

"I'm just flipping the breakers to start the generator. We'll run them until people get ready to go to bed." He reached his hand back to me, turning to the laundry room where the breaker box was.

I took his hand. "Do they have enough fuel? We used a lot last time."

"Yeah. I thought the storm might roll this way, so I had the tank filled up. Forty gallons should last a couple days as long as we don't run the furnace and stick to burning wood." Noah let go of my hand to open the fuse box and flipped the bottom breaker.

The generator kicked on outside and the lights came back on in the TV room in the basement. Noah walked over and flipped on the lights in the laundry room and shut the door.

"I really don't want to talk about it." I shook my head.

He reached forward and pulled me toward him. "That's not what I was going for." He wrapped his arms around me. "Good god, you're burning." He put a hand on the back of my neck.

"I know."

"Can I do anything for you?"

"Don't ever let me answer the door again?"

He chuckled, rubbing my neck. "I know. I thought you were safe the second time."

"So did I... Stupid us."

"You can go up to my room and sleep if you want. Everyone pretty much knows you don't feel good."

I shook my head. "No. That's not fair to Clara. I invited her."

"She's fine. She and Garrett have my parents to talk to. It's crazy that they know each other."

"No, I need to go up there and be a buffer. Brad won't hold back on Clara." I stepped back and pulled my hair away from my neck. "And I'm not happy with *you* either."

"Why?" Noah sounded honestly shocked.

"Because you told Dallas and your brothers about Greg." I looked up at him and shook my head. "Why would you do that?"

He shook his head like he was shaking a feeling away. "I talked to them a long time ago. I told Dallas because he's a cop and it's better to know someone if something happens. Gabe's a lawyer in case shit really goes wrong, and Moses is all smiles, but you heard him, he got his ass kicked in school. He knows how to fight." Noah smiled a little.

"You think you're being cute, but it's embarrassing and you didn't ask me."

Noah cleared his smile. "I didn't tell them to embarrass you, I told them because I didn't know if Greg would show up here and under what terms." He directed a hand upstairs. "We still don't know what the hell he's doing here, or what shit he might start. You can't blame me for being worried after seeing the scars and what you've told me."

I couldn't, and I knew it, so I nodded. "We need to go back up."

"I can handle everything up there, you should go to bed. You look like you're barely standing."

I shook my head. "I know my limits. I'm okay."

Noah brushed the back of his fingers over my cheek. "You also like to push those limits." He reached back and opened the door.

I went out first and he followed behind.

The dinner conversation was light between everyone. It was relieving, but also made me feel slightly isolated in my own misery. Certain people sat there oblivious that anything was wrong at all, others only knew pieces. Noah may have been aware of all situations, but I was the only one who really held all of it.

Chapter 15

"Can I sit with you?" Garrett's eyes were light, but he looked a little worried.

I gave him a kind smile and nodded. "Yeah." If I was going to give Clara a chance, it only seemed fair to give Garrett one. "Did you get any pie?"

"Eh, unlike Fran, I don't have much of a sweet tooth." He sat down on the ledge in front of the fireplace next to me.

"Me neither." I scratched my nail over the rim of my water glass.

"I'm not really sure where I stand with you right now, but I wanted to apologize for the ambush a few months ago. I've felt terrible about it, and that's why I've left you alone at the hospital."

I shook my head. "Don't worry about it. As much as I wish I was still living in my world of ignorance, it doesn't change the fact that the man who raised me was an incredible dad... No offense."

"None taken. Fran was a good man..." Garrett rubbed his hands together in a nervous fidget. "I had a lot wrong with me back then, and I didn't pull out of it easily, so I'm really glad to hear he gave you what I wouldn't have been able to. I had a bad drug problem, and while it's never *fully* kicked, I didn't clean up until about five years after your mom and I left. Then, it was a matter of struggling my way through becoming a respectable person without the drugs."

I nodded, but didn't really know why. Acknowledgement, maybe?

"I tried to see you when you were about eleven, but Fran wouldn't allow it." He chuckled a little. "Brad tried to shoot me with his BB gun. I think he was about sixteen."

I looked at Garrett, then over at Brad who was talking with Thomas and Gabe. "Sounds like something he'd do... Jerk."

"Naw. He was doing what big brothers do. The day you were born, he wouldn't let you out of his sight. It drove your mother up a wall." He looked down and rubbed his hands together again.

"He never changed... We've always been super close."

"I'm not trying to smear anyone's name or image, but I know what toxic relationships can do to people, and I read the letter you sent Clara... I know it's not my business, but why is that guy here and still breathing?" Garrett looked at me.

I couldn't look at him, but I wasn't bothered by him asking. "Great question. I'd feel better if I had an answer... I don't know if he's playing at something, or if he's really here just to be with Brad."

"You don't know me from Adam, I know, but if there's anything I can do to help, I'd like to. I didn't raise you, but I still have the innate parental instinct to protect you... Fran would have slashed him with a scalpel by now."

My dad would have gone after Greg with more than a scalpel. There would have been bone saws, beds with leather straps, and sheets of plastic. His Hippocratic oath would have been a pile of words among Greg's blood.

"Are you safe here?"

I nodded. "Yeah... probably more so than anywhere else. Noah's not far off from Dad in personality." Was I still allowed to call my dad "Dad" in front of Garrett? I didn't think about it before I said anything.

"He seems like a pretty good guy. Linna and Thomas are great people."

I smiled. "Yeah. They are," I agreed easily. "Noah is too." I looked across the room at Noah, watching him smile as he talked to Linna and Clara.

Garrett laughed quietly. "Mm. I know that look."

My cheeks burned a little, but not from the fever, and I looked back down at my water glass. "It's odd when you think you know what it's like to love someone, then meet the right person and really find out."

"Yep... It's pretty incredible when you come across it."

I took in a deep breath. "Sorry, I'm sitting here in kind of a funk and making you do all the talking. And I'm sorry Brad's been so rude this evening. Though, I'm not entirely certain why he's so hostile toward *you*. Clara, I understand."

"Embarrassingly, he's the one who discovered Clara and I together. I think the animosity comes from the thought that I took his mom away."

"That would do it, I guess." I watched Noah talk to Elsie and point in my direction.

"Is that Noah's little girl? She's pretty attached to the two of you."

"No. We're just unofficial Auntie and Uncle." I set my glass down and opened my hands to Elsie. "Uncle Noah's your God-father, huh?" I smiled at her.

She nodded and tucked herself back into my arm, unsure of Garrett. "Uncle Noah said it's time for the Santa hat."

"The Santa hat. It's not Christmas." I poked her side lightly and she snickered into my shirt. "Go tell him it's in his office."

Elsie walked back over with her golden curls bobbing behind her.

"Are you being a carrier pigeon again?" Carrie ran her fingers through Elsie's hair as she passed by.

She nodded simply and Garrett and I both laughed.

"What's the Santa hat about?"

"Noah and his friends all draw names for Christmas. Apparently, this is a normal holiday group."

"You're terrible at taking a hint," Noah said to me from across the room. "Come with me."

I sighed and looked at Garrett. "I'll be back, I guess."

He smiled and nodded. It was so uncanny how much he really looked like my dad. He had different glasses, and his hair wasn't a silvery white yet.

I went into Noah's office and pushed the door closed partially. "Yes?"

Noah pulled me against him in a fast movement and bent me over while kissing my cheek.

"Uh." I partially groaned and laughed at the same time.

"What's the matter with you?"

"I love you." He kissed all over the side of my face.

"I love you too, but you're too much right now." I gently pushed on his shoulder.

Noah tipped me back up, but kept me squished against him. "Is it enough?"

"Me loving you, or you being too much?" I looked up at him.

"Yes." He smiled at me and brushed my hair back.

"I hope so, and yes." I appreciated his cheerfulness. He was picking up my mood just a little more, and I needed it.

"I love you a lot." He tugged on a lock of my hair.

"I love you too. What'd you do?"

"Nothing yet." He grabbed the Santa hat and walked around me with another smile.

I rolled my eyes and followed him out.

"Okay, before we start, Holly and I want to thank all of you for coming. It's been a few years since I've had everyone here for the holidays. We all lost Kate, someone pretty important to the group, and it wasn't quite the same without her today. She's definitely not forgotten, and she'd be really happy to see that we're all together for the holidays again, and that Terri's finally in a committed relationship."

Everyone laughed, including Terri. She looked up at Jess and squeezed him from the side.

Noah laughed a little. "I also want to thank Garrett, Clara, and Brad, Holly's family, for being here. It means a lot to *her*, and she means the *world* to all of *us*."

"Yeah, baby!" Terri yelled, then laughed.

Bridgett held up her champagne glass with a grin, and my cheeks turned red. I noticed that Noah left Greg out, a subtle blow, and I appreciated it more than I should've.

"Holly, I beg of you, choose me. I'm better looking, and funny." Moses pleaded with his hands folded.

Linna smacked him in the gut. "Stop that."

Noah rolled his eyes and sighed. "*Anyway*, anyone who isn't family is doing secret Santa. Draw a piece of paper, no switching, and be fast because it's past my bedtime." Noah walked over to Carrie first because she was the closest.

Carrie reached in and her eyes widened for a second.

"Take a piece of paper and zip it," Noah grumbled.

She smiled and pulled out a paper. She looked at it and laughed. Everyone pulled one out and Noah came around to me.

"Not last, because I didn't draw one yet." Noah smiled as he held the hat out.

"Because I have a problem with last?" I reached into the hat with a smile, but my fingers touched something that wasn't paper.

I felt a little shocked at the realization of what it was, then raised my eyebrows. "Really?"

Everyone laughed including Noah, who took the hat and handed it to Linna as he got down on one knee.

"Why not end the day with something good?" He took the ring from my fingers and held my hand. "I was planning on doing this for Christmas, but I didn't wanna wait. A couple days ago, you said you didn't know where I stood, and I want you to know, I stand wherever you are." He swallowed hard, but still smiled at me gently. "From the second I lost Kate, I couldn't understand why I had to be married to someone just to lose them... then I met you and realized you have to appreciate who you *have*, *or* you lose them. As much as you think I helped you, you were right there reaching back, teaching me things I already knew but didn't bother to put into practice... Both of us get to have our lives back, and I want the rest of mine with you. I love you beyond what I'm capable of saying, so, *Doctor*," he paused for a smile, "Holly Bennett, will you marry me?"

"Do you promise not to smash cake on my face?"

He laughed. "I promise."

"And you'll keep the freezer stocked with unhealthy items if you're not here to cook?"

He laughed again and shook his head. "No, but I'll compromise and promise to have something ready for you to stick in the microwave."

I winced with a nod, shrugging my shoulders, while I tried to appear as though I were contemplating it. "Eh, okay. I can live with that."

"Will you marry me now?"

"Yes, but you have to promise to fix and or replace the water heater in my apartment after you put in the new well pump."

"Oh my gosh," he breathed, slipping the ring on my finger. "I'll replace the water heater."

I laughed. "Jokes on you, I would have married you for nothin'." I nodded once.

"By the time I smash a big piece of cake in your face, it'll be too late. We'll already be married." He got up and picked me up in a hug. "Pain in my knee," he whispered against my cheek while everyone clapped, yelled, or what-the-heck-ever they were being loud about. "I love you... so, so much. I don't care who your dad is, or what sewer rat got dragged into the house, no one gets to steal that beautiful smile. I'm here with you, you're safe, and I love you more than I have words for." His voice remained quiet in my ear as he spoke, then he kissed my cheek. "Got it?"

I nodded. "Yeah." I buried my face in his shoulder.

Noah took in a breath and squished me tighter. My arms were already wrapped around him as tightly as I could get them, but I wished it was more. My heart was so full after feeling completely drained. I was exactly where I belonged, and it felt whole-heartedly right.

"Well, good heavens you two, stop hugging each other so everyone else can hug you," Linna laughed.

Noah lifted his head up from my shoulder and kissed my cheek before he let me down. I smiled up at Noah, then gave him another short hug.

Linna smiled brightly and held her hands up to hold my face. "I'm so happy I don't know what to say."

I laughed a little. "Say you'll make me more cookies or teach me how to make them."

She laughed and hugged me. "I don't share my recipes, but I will gladly share them with you. It's every mom's dream for her children to find someone who loves them nearly as much as she does... I'm so glad it's you."

"You've raised some good ones. They're hard not to love." I pulled back and smiled at her.

"See? You hear that?" Moses nudged Linna's arm. "She loves me. She just said it."

She shook her head and rolled her eyes. "You're too much today."

"She said 'some good ones.' She didn't specifically mention you." Gabe looked at Moses with his normally flat expression before he hugged me.

I laughed a little.

"You were family before, but now it's more official. Welcome to the family." He patted the back of my shoulder.

I smiled. "Thank you."

"I'm next. Line is behind me. He just cut, and it's not fair. I was behind Mom." Moses spoke and almost sounded like a parrot.

"You're not allowed to hug her. You have the side-effect of causing headaches." Thomas wore a frown and stepped in to hug me.

"Dude! Did you forget I get to decide what nursing home you get stuffed in?" Moses looked at Thomas incredulously.

"I hope your love will *always* feel foreign and unexplainable. It's the best kind." Thomas said quietly with a gentle hug.

I smiled and thought about it. The day I told him that I didn't know what Noah and I were, he knew right then and there. "Thank you." I let go of him and smiled.

"Well, I'll hug you, but I'm not congratulating you because the ass behind you never apologized for yelling at me." Clara stepped forward and wrapped her arms around me.

"And I'm not going to. You deserved it," Noah said simply.

"Linna, you didn't teach your son not to make an enemy of his future mother-in-law." Clara rubbed my back. "And I'm not babysitting kids if you decide to procreate." She pulled back and tapped my nose.

"Because you think I'd ask?" I raised an eyebrow and laughed.

"I'm covering my bases. Hug Garrett before he gets all

weepy." She nodded behind me with disgust.

I turned and smiled at Garrett. He had the same crinkly-eyed smile as my dad.

"Congratulations."

"Thanks." I stepped forward and gave him a short hug. It didn't feel wrong, just awkward because I hardly knew him.

"I'm telling you. You're picking the wrong guy. I'm a stud muffin." Moses pulled his glasses off. "Superman." And put them back on. "Clark Kent."

"Move it, nerd." Terri pushed Moses to the side and all three girls stepped toward me.

I held out my hand knowing they weren't after hugs or congratulatory words.

"Noah, good boy." Bridgett flashed a smile at him and looked back at the ring. "That's one hell of a rock."

"You're spoiled and I don't want to be your friend anymore." Terri pouted and looked back at Jess. "Jess, you're a loser and I'm done with you."

"Didn't Jess just buy you a new car? I think that goes if he goes," I reminded.

"Just kidding. I love you, babe." She blew a kiss over her shoulder.

"Okay guys," Noah put his hands on my shoulder. "I'm tired. Bridgett, you guys are downstairs in the room to the left of the master room my parents are in. Carrie, you guys are in the TV room down there because I'm out of room. Terri, you and Jess are up here in the back room on the right. Clara and Garrett, you're across the hall from *them*. Moses and Gabe, you're in your usual rooms."

Bridgett shriveled her lip at Noah. "You're such an old man."

"Mm-hm."

She raised an eyebrow at me. "You're marrying an old person."

I smiled. "I know." I tipped my head back to look up at Noah with a smile.

He kissed my forehead. "You wanna go tell your brother and Greg they're in your apartment?"

"Yeah," I sighed.

Greg and Brad were by the fireplace talking to Gabe again. Thank god he was there because I didn't want to approach either one by myself.

Greg gave me a light smile. "Congratulations."

I pulled back the corner of my mouth and nodded once. I wasn't going to thank him, even if the circumstances he put me through brought me here.

"The county road is closed down, so you guys are snowed in for the night. You both can stay in my apartment." I didn't bother to hide my bitterness or the fact that the extended hospitality was nothing more than having no choice. If there wasn't a foot of snow on the ground, I would have told them to get lost and find a motel.

"Holly, can we talk, please?" Brad's voice was quiet, but not timid.

"As long as it's an appropriate topic in front of company."

He nodded behind me. "Company's going to bed."

I clenched my jaw and looked at Gabe.

He pursed his lips to the side. "'Night." He gripped my elbow lightly as he turned.

"Goodnight," I said quietly, then looked at Greg with a glare. "He doesn't need a bodyguard to talk."

"Holly…" Brad shook his head and let out a breath.

"No. My turf, my rules. I'm allowed to have unsupervised conversations." I looked at Greg with another glare.

"We just wanted to explain." Greg shook his head, looking upset. "I told him everything, Holl."

I narrowed my eyes. "Really? Everything?"

He nodded. "Everything. The back door, the faked car accident… everything."

I looked at Brad. It was worse. Brad was standing there, not oblivious, but apparently fully aware.

"The fourteen-inch scar on my side?" I lifted part of my sweater just to show it.

"Holly, he was sick, and I made sure he got help. I know what this looks like, and believe me, I was furious." Brad looked at me with fear, and it was real because his eyes were dilated.

I smiled because tears were filling my eyes and the amount of anger I had was insurmountable. "You were furious," I repeated. "So furious that you fell in love with him? And when did that happen exactly?" I looked between him and Greg, but my eyes landed on Greg. "Late nights at the office, phone calls I couldn't listen to… Exactly how long?" I shook my head. "Don't answer that. I don't care. I have this." I pointed at the floor. "Here. I don't need your explanations and *bullshit*."

"Holly, you don't understand." Greg tipped his head down and parted his curls to show a scar. "I had a tumor." He looked at me again. "It was pressing on my brain and causing me to do things I wouldn't normally do."

It was completely possible. I'd recently operated on a man who'd been filled with hate and anger. When he woke from surgery, he was extremely kind. That didn't mean anything to me, though.

"I know you're mad, and you're hurt—not even just about this—but I came here to talk to you." Brad stepped toward me slightly. "I didn't know what was happening because you didn't tell me, but the second I found out, Greg ended up in the hospital because I lost it, and that's when they found the tumor." He glanced behind me and took a step back.

I heard Gif tearing at the carpet, coming to greet me, so I put my hand down. He whined and danced around me, snorting and acting crazy. Noah had shut him upstairs because Carrie's boys loved to torment the poor thing.

"Gif, outside," Noah commanded.

"I had those headaches, and you kept telling me to go get them checked," Greg said quietly. "I didn't mean to hurt you."

"No. You meant to *kill* me," I snapped. "Do you somehow think this gives you a pardon for everything? Breaking my bones, throwing me into walls, smacking me around—it's forgotten?" I shook my head and turned around.

"No. That's not what I'm saying. What I did is unforgivable, and I'm sorry. Holly, please stop and just listen to me." Greg caught my arm.

The pop of anger felt like my spine snapping clean in half. "LET GO OF ME!" The words came out in a hateful shriek as I whipped around and slammed my free hand down on his wrist.

Greg let out a yelp of pain.

"Hey!" Noah's voice was sharp and angry before Greg had even made a sound.

"Holly!" Brad grabbed me from behind as I was mid elbow toward Greg's face, and he dragged me back.

"Get off me!" My voice broke as I dropped my weight to make Brad lose his grip, but he didn't and ended up just holding me. If I really tried to get away, I'd seriously hurt him, and I almost wanted to. "Get off!"

"Brad, let her go," Greg said through a strained voice, holding his wrist.

"Goddamnit. Let her go!" Noah jumped the couch and looked like he was out to kill.

Gif came in from the doggy door barking his head off and scrambling over the tile.

"She's *my* sister." Brad took another step back. "This is bullshit, Holly." He let go of me immediately because Gif was in a fast dive to attack.

I bent down and snagged Gif by the collar to stop him. "Upstairs." My voice didn't work enough to make a sound, but Gif stopped his fight and lowered himself, thinking he was in trouble.

"I don't think it was just Greg, I think you were part of the problem too," Brad spoke angrily from behind me.

Noah put a hand behind my shoulder as I walked forward but didn't follow me. "You know what. You've got about one second to shut your damn mouth and go down the hill before I put you both into a wall."

"She's my sister and I'll talk to her if I want to."

"Not like that, and sure as hell not in my house!" Noah yelled despite Brad not having raised his voice. "Leave! Go down to her apartment or take your chances out in the snow—I don't give a shit—just get the hell out of my house."

Gabe, Moses, Garrett and Clara were standing at the

end of the hallway as I went for the stairs, and all of them followed me up. I didn't want them to because I was in the process of a breakdown I couldn't stop. Gif stayed beside me and snapped at me with a whiny bark. He licked my fingers once I got up to the loft.

"Go lay down." I opened the door.

He whimpered and trotted toward the bed. Normally, he would go straight under, but he only put himself partially under.

"Is your wrist okay? Let me see." Garrett gently took my elbow and ran his other hand over my arm to my wrist.

"I'm okay. I just need to—" My stomach lurched, and I covered my mouth and ran for the bathroom. Gif bolted with me, and I barely made it to the toilet fast enough. It was a struggle to get my hair out of the way, then try to swat away the overly concerned dog that was trying to lick my face while I puked.

"Come on, buddy. Get out of here." Garrett pulled Gif back by the collar. "Clara, get a washcloth wet, would ya?" He gathered my hair back and held it behind my neck. "Rough day, Kiddo." He rubbed my back.

Maybe my stomach decided to be shy, but nothing else was coming up, and I felt like I was done. It was probably only the third time I'd ever thrown up. Even as a kid, I'd only get a fever and feel like hell, but I didn't throw up. That was usually Brad.

"Here. I can't stay in here or I'll start too." Clara's voice was raspy.

Garrett gave a breathy, but otherwise silent laugh. "She should work in the hospital for a day, huh?" He held the wet cloth next to my face.

He was right—after a certain point, you got used to people's bodily fluids, no matter how gross.

I took the washcloth and flushed the toilet before I sat back on my feet and put the cloth over my mouth.

Garrett dropped my hair and put the back of his fingers to the side of my forehead. "Do you have some Tylenol up here? She's got a good fever going."

I thought he was talking to me at first.

"I think I only have ibuprofen." Noah's voice was quiet.

"Are you sure that wrist is okay?" Garrett's voice sounded identical to my dad's. It made me remember one time when I was little and sitting on the ground with a scraped knee from my rollerblades.

I nodded and wiped the washcloth under my eyes. "Yeah. It just pulled my skin."

"Okay. I think Noah's got you taken care of. I'll see you in the morning." He rubbed the back of my shoulder.

I nodded. "Thank you."

"Don't mention it." He stood up from his squatted position next to me. "You guys have a good night."

"You too," Noah said quietly before he bent over to hand me a cup of water and two pills.

"Thanks." I took them and popped the pills in my mouth, followed by the water.

Noah took the cup back when I was done and helped me up. "Do you wanna take another bath and try to cool off a little bit?"

I shook my head and grabbed my toothbrush. "No. I just wanna go to bed."

He took my hand and looked at my wrist. "Did he grab you that hard?"

I shook my head. "No. It was just an automatic response to clench when I flipped around on him, so he was gripping when I slammed my hand down."

"You got *him* pretty good."

I shook my head and put toothpaste on the brush. "I shouldn't have. I could have yanked my hand back and gotten away, but I *really* wanted to hurt him."

Noah shrugged. "He shouldn't be grabbing you, and that's the least of what he deserved."

I shook my head. "It's not okay to want to hurt someone."

He put a hand on my shoulder, massaging it lightly. "I'm sorry, Love... I really thought you'd be okay because you were in the house and I was across the room."

"I shouldn't have engaged. I was too angry, and they really were just trying to talk."

Noah turned me to face him. "Mm-mm." He shook his head with an angry expression. "You're not putting blame anywhere other than where it belongs. If you were mad and actually talking—*good*. It's about damn time. You weren't grabbing anyone, you weren't raising your voice, and you weren't the one showing up and causing problems. It was fine for Brad to show up, Greg *knew* he wasn't welcome here, and Brad did too. A *lot* of shit got put on you today, but don't sit here and play 'victim'. You know better."

I frowned. "I'm not playing victim, and don't talk to me like I'm three."

He raised his eyebrows, shaking his head. "Then don't act like it." He pushed off the counter and walked out of the bathroom.

Great...

Chapter 16

I was up before anyone else. The power was back on, but the white from the snow reflected the dim morning light into the house, so I left the lights off and started breakfast for everyone. I finished the French toast and put it in the oven to stay warm when I heard the first bedroom door open. I expected it to be Gabe, because he was usually the first up, but it was Garrett.

"Good morning." I managed a kind smile.

"Good morning. I heard movement out here so I figured I'd come out and see if I could help with anything."

"Um, I'm just starting the eggs, then I was going to cut up some fruit. But there's coffee or tea if you want some."

"Oh, I think I'll take some coffee if you have it." He pulled out a chair at the island.

"Sure." I turned the burner down on the pan of scrambled eggs and stepped to the left to get a coffee cup. "Anything in it?"

"No, I take it black... How's that fever?"

"Low. I think it's on its way out." I turned with his coffee and set it in front of him. "Thanks again for helping me last night." *Even though it was awkward as hell.*

"That dog of yours is a pretty protective fellow." Garrett leaned over to look at Gif on the floor. He was laying down against the side of the island.

"Yeah, it's as menacing as it is sweet." I rubbed my foot over Gif's side and turned back to the stovetop. "Did you guys sleep okay? I don't think anyone's slept in that room yet." I shoved the eggs around in the pan and turned the burner back up.

"Everything was fine. Clara's still passed out, and she's the finicky one."

"So, are you guys in a relationship? You kind of make it sound like you are, and she makes it sound different." I turned my body so I could see him, but also keep an eye on the food.

"Yes..." He took in a breath, seeming like the thought hurt him a little. "It's complicated, but Clara's the kind of person who needs her space. She has her house, and I have mine, but we're usually together in one place or another."

"Were you and my dad close before the whole thing with me?" I continued to scrape slowly at the bottom of the pan.

"Yes, but you weren't the reason we fell apart. It wasn't even my affair with Clara. My addiction started with accepting pills to help me study in college; and it got out of control. Fran continuously tried to help me. He'd pay my rent, try to get me into rehab... I just kept taking. When he and your mom had Brad, he made one final attempt to get me into rehab. It was never the same after that. I was invited over for holidays, but that was about the extent of our relationship."

I nodded. "I don't mean this in a derogatory way, but he must have loved you a lot. He was a very intolerant person. Brad came home stoned once, and I thought our dad was going to kill him."

Garrett gave a low chuckle. "Yeah, I can imagine. He wasn't so tolerant of me either, I think he more felt guilty because I didn't exist to your Nana and Pops. They played favorites pretty hard when we were growing up, and the day I turned eighteen and said I was going to Peru for six months instead of starting college, it was over with them."

I looked at him. "Did you go?"

Garrett smiled. "One of the best experiences of my life. No regrets there."

I smiled. "Dad took us for a week when I was thirteen. It was a culture shock, but an amazing trip... And I understand about Nana and Pops with their favorites. Bradly could do no wrong. He was the perfect grandchild, while I may as well have belonged to the mailman." I laughed to myself as the realization sank in. "I think my relationship with them just explained itself. They *must've* known."

Garrett sighed. "They did... I'm sorry if they were un-kind."

I looked at him and shook my head. "I didn't spend a lot of time with them. Brad would go for sleepovers, then it was just dad and I to watch videos of his surgeries and eat pounds of ice cream."

He laughed. "You two were pretty close then?"

"Oh yeah." I smiled and turned the burner off on the eggs. "He was my best friend, and that doesn't even seem like an adequate description. He worked a lot, but when he didn't, we were attached at the hip. Then by default, because Brad and I were close, we were our own twisted version of the three musketeers." I carried the pan to the island and dumped the eggs into a bowl.

Garrett let out a breath. "I feel like I should be jealous, but I'm honestly just relieved. I always worried about you."

I looked at him, feeling like that was a peculiar statement. "I know he was a brute, but he had a giant heart for people, and especially kids."

He shrugged. "I know he did. And he really did love you the second you were born, but it's still unnerving to hope that someone will love your kid the way you want them to, then never know."

That made more sense. "I was *very* well loved." I gave a small smile before I turned and put the bowl of eggs into the oven with the toast.

Gif got up quickly and made a bee-line for the front door, while gruffing all the way. I looked over at the windows and saw Greg trudging through the snow in front of the house. Garrett looked back.

"Would you mind getting the door, and then *not* leaving me alone with him?" I looked at Garrett and hoped he understood.

He nodded with a gentle smile and got up. I continued with what I was doing, pulling fruit out of the fridge, getting a cutting board, another bowl, and a knife. I was scraping the inside of a cantaloupe when Greg approached the island with Garrett.

"Holly, can I please talk to you?"

I pointed at the chair he was standing behind with the

knife in my hand. "As long as your ass stays in the chair."

Greg pulled it out and sat down with a slight sigh. He looked at Garrett. I was going to tell Greg that Garrett wasn't leaving, but he beat me to it.

"You put a hand on my kid last night, so you don't get the privilege of private conversation." Garrett reached forward for a paring knife I'd set out. "Do you have another cutting board?"

I nodded and stepped back to grab one from the skinny cabinet to the right of me.

"Thank you." Garrett reached for the carton of strawberries when I set the cutting board in front of him.

"I'm sorry about last night. I wasn't trying to hurt you when I grabbed your wrist. I wanted you to hear the rest of what I was trying to say, and you walked away—I should have let you." Greg paused, probably waiting for me to say something. "Can you look at me for a second...? Please."

I set my knife down, put my hands on the counter, and looked at him. Greg appeared calm, but also afraid, not a way he usually looked. Not even before, when he thought he was in the doghouse.

"Last night, I couldn't understand why you were still so upset after I told you about the tumor. I didn't expect you to instantly forgive, but I expected you to forgive just enough to listen." He shook his head. "That wasn't right either, but it didn't occur to me until about two in the morning. That first night after the award you received for Fran, I should have known something was wrong and gotten help. I can't say that the cause would have been found right away—it probably wouldn't have—but I should have done something more... Three years of us never having any kind of problem, and then out of nowhere like that..." He pressed his lips together and raised his shoulders. "I should have done something, and I'm sorry I didn't."

I shrugged. "Hindsight is twenty-twenty. I should have dropped you like a rock. Obviously, Brad was safer than you ever implied." I shrugged again. "Maybe if I would have left, you two would be three or four years into a marriage by now."

Noah came down the stairs and kissed the top of my head as he passed behind me.

Greg shook his head. "I shouldn't have ever threatened Brad either."

"'*Shouldn't have*,'" I quoted bitterly as I picked up the knife and started cutting the cantaloupe again. "You have three quarters of a million of those. Exactly what is it you're expecting here? You've apologized, and apologized again. All along the way, at the end, here we are now. I believe you *are* sorry. I've believed it every time. I know *you're* 'sorry' better than cutting a skull plate, but I don't know what you want. Do you want me to tell you it's okay? Do you want to hear you're forgiven?" I dropped my knife and looked at him. "Everything worked out. I'm here, happier than I've ever been, so everything's okay." I picked up the knife again. I needed to release my anger into something. "And I don't give a shit enough to forgive you. They're hollow words, and I never took you for the kind of person who needed them, but if it's really that important to you, I forgive you because I no longer care to *give a shit*."

"I'm not asking you to forgive me."

I dropped the knife again. "Then *what?* Why are you here?" The words came out in a hard snap.

He bit the inside of his cheek for a second, something

I'd always hated. "I love Brad, but you know as well as I do, I have no future with him if you and I can't find some kind of ground to stand on. Anyone is on the second burner with you two, you guys don't let anyone else take first."

I shook my head and directed my hand to the front of the house. "You didn't get shot at the door. What more do you want? I didn't go around shooting my mouth off at either of you yesterday. I said I didn't want to talk to him because I got a nice blow at the door, and I'm *still* trying to wrap my head around *that*. But, what? The two of you think I'm a petty bitch and I won't show up to a wedding, support whatever twisted mess you two have with each other? We're never going to be the laughing friends we were, but Brad's a big boy. He doesn't need my approval, he's got my acceptance—even if it *kills* me—because he's my brother. I don't know what the hell twisted shit you have going on with each other, but as long as he's happy and he's good, then I'm just fine. But pray to your *god* if you think for half a second I won't snap your fricken neck if you *dare* hurt him. Beat the shit out of me and I'm pissed, but look at Brad wrong and I'll *gut* your sorry ass."

Noah touched my arm.

I stood there in a shaking rage with a dead glare set on Greg. He sat there continuing to look wounded, but I had no sympathy because I'd seen it too many times.

"I can't say anything here," Greg said quietly, glancing down. "Time has to be proof."

"Are we done then? Did you get what you needed?"

He pressed his lips together, looking down as he nodded.

I looked at Noah and moved my arm away from his hand. "Was that victimless enough for you?" I grabbed the hand towel from the counter by the stove and turned to leave. "Sorry, Garrett. I need some air." I touched his arm before walking around him. "Take a plate of food down to Brad. I'm assuming he's too chicken shit to come up and I won't be ready to talk to *him* for a while." I reached into my back pocket and put Greg's ring in front of him on the counter. "And I'm selling my house, so get your shit out."

I grabbed my work coat and boots out of the closet by the garage door and went out to the garage. The sooner I could get the driveway plowed, the sooner Greg could leave. I jammed my feet into my boots, yanked my coat on, and smacked the button to open the garage door. Thankfully, there wasn't a snow drift up against the door like the October snowstorm. There was a foot and a half of white fluff on the ground, but Noah's truck backed out without a problem. I put the blade down, pushed through the first line, and across the county road to move the county plow's work.

After the driveway was clear, I shoveled the sidewalk in front of the house. It wasn't enough to burn my anger out, so I went behind the house and started feeding logs through the wood splitter. There was a second round to the storm we had, and the power would likely get knocked out again. We wouldn't use as much tonight, because it would only be Noah's family left, but I kept stacking like it was going to last a month. What I really wanted to be doing was poking around in someone's brain. Just to stimulate my thoughts, I recalled a procedure Dr. Calloway and I had done.

"You're gonna make Noah insane if you stay out here all day splitting wood," Bridgett called from behind me. "He's too afraid of you to come out here and stop you."

"Probably because he knows he was an ass." I shoved two split logs onto the pile and pulled my gloves off. "Did he used to patronize Kate too?"

Bridgett sipped at her mimosa, then smiled. "He patronizes everyone, Sweetie. He's Noah."

"He's irritating." I bent down to turn the wood splitter off.

"Oh yeah, but he's not usually far off with whatever he's saying." She leaned against one of the posts that held up the back deck. "Mind you, I don't know what he said."

"Last night, I was talking to Brad and Greg. The thought being, the sooner I could get it over with the sooner they could leave. Anyway, I went to walk away because I was pissed, and Greg grabbed my wrist. Instead of just pulling my hand away, I went for a full slam on his wrist, tried to elbow him in the face and Brad grabbed me before I could. I told Noah I didn't need to do that. I could have just pulled my hand away—and to begin with, I shouldn't have been standing there arguing with them. I didn't feel good, it was probably one of the worst days I've had since my dad died—happy anniversary to that today—and it was just blow after blow. Better sense says that you don't try to have a civilized conversation when you're pissed, you wait, chill out, and think about it."

Bridgett bit the side of her bottom lip as she nodded in understanding. It was her tell that she didn't agree.

"What? You clearly don't agree." I directed a hand at her bitten lip.

She shrugged. "I agree with you. I *also* know that you don't talk after you've had that time to wait and chill. You internalize things, reason situations into these neat little boxes, and put them away. It's not a bad thing to avoid confrontation, but it's not bad to embrace it either. Tell me you don't feel better after throwing words at Greg this morning."

"You heard that?"

"We literally had our ears pressed to the door. Not the point. Do you feel better?"

I shook my head and shrugged. "I don't know. There's still too many things rolling around."

"If you hit the redo button on that conversation, what would happen? No consequences or negative side-effects, you can say or do freely like it's something just to exercise with. Would that conversation roll out the same way?"

I shook my head. "Probably not."

"What would be different?"

"There'd be fewer words."

She held up her shoulders. "Elaborate, Hun. Why fewer words?"

"Because I was slashing unnecessarily. I could have cut it into a tenth, been done, and walked away less frustrated."

She raised her eyebrows and shook her head. "I didn't hear a single word that wasn't necessary. Maybe you got a little aggressive about protecting your brother, but I also see that as necessary, given the fact that you know what Greg is capable of. You have the right to protect your family and let people know where they stand. Wouldn't you agree?"

I shrugged. "Of course."

"It's completely understandable if you don't feel great about this morning—you might not feel better about it tomorrow even, but everything you said was necessary. If it wasn't, you wouldn't have said it, Hun. You are the most level-headed person, to the point of being detrimental to *yourself*. So, if you had something to say, it *really* needed to be said, and you're not wrong for doing it."

I shoved my hand through my hair and let out a breath. "It was just such a 'Francis Bennett' thing to do. My dad used to just rip into people, and I hated it. I used to look at him and think he could have resolved things so much easier and with less hostility. This is the same thing."

"No, it's not," she said quickly and almost laughed humorlessly. "Unless someone beat the crap out of him, or was really, truly hurting him, it's not even remotely the same. There's a continent's worth of distance between blowing off at people for stupid petty shit and expressing to someone that they *hurt* you. The conversation this morning was, 'hey, I hurt you,' and 'yeah, buddy, you actually hurt my *life*.' Sweetie, you lost everything. Your family, your job, your daily routines, friends, mental sanity, your right of safety, personal belongings... He didn't physically kill you, but you *died*. He brought you to the point where you committed suicide on every part of your life you knew, except for the body you're standing in..."

Her words felt like they packed the punch of an earthquake.

She pulled back the corner of her mouth in a sympathetic look. "Zero people have the right to do that to another person. It is *equal* to pushing someone into committing *real* suicide... You have the right to be mad, or hurt, and you have the right to express it to the person who caused you to feel those things. Greg committed a horrific crime against you, you're allowed your feelings without judgment from yourself for whatever comes out."

I nodded and wiped the tear under my eye.

"I hope you don't feel like I just lectured you, Honey."

She set her glass on a log, walked over, and hugged me.

"No." I hugged her and wiped another tear.

"I just watched you go from a hundred to like negative seventy yesterday, and I can't help it." She patted the back of my shoulder.

"I know... You kind of hit me in the gut with the 'life suicide' thing."

She giggled menacingly. "We both make people's heads hurt after we're done. Weeks, sometimes months of recovery time."

I laughed. "At least it pays well."

She laughed and stepped back from the hug. "Yours probably better than mine."

I shook my head and wiped under my eyes to check my makeup. "No, we're probably pretty closely matched. Give me ten years though."

"Psh. You're already loaded. Anything else you wanna get out before I drag you in against your will?"

I shook my head. "No. I'm good."

"Well, I have something. What the hell is your dumbass cute brother doing with that asshole? I mean, he obviously knows shit, right?" She bent over to get her glass.

"Apparently it's all explained away by a tumor. He showed me the scar on his head, but I don't know."

"Wait. What? How's that even—what a cop-out." She looked at me with disgust.

"Yeah, I think I'm equally as mad about *that* as the rest of it. Three years of shit over a goddamn tumor I could have cut out one handed and blindfolded." I started up the steps and held out a hand to help Bridgett. She was wearing a new pair of Uggs in foot and a half snow. I'd only shoveled where

I worked, not the steps to get there.

Bridgett took my hand. "That's bullshit." She stepped into the hole from my boot.

"I assume Dallas is the one who told you about Greg." I continued forward slowly.

"Psh. He doesn't tell me shit. I'm trained to know the signs of domestic abuse, you looked like you were going to shit your pants yesterday when he showed up, I've seen a few of your scars, and he also looks like an asshole. Handsome, but an asshole." She followed me up the steps and let go of my hand as soon as we were on the plowed driveway.

"Do the other two know?"

"Oh god. Are you kidding? Do you have any idea how bad yesterday would have been? Terri would have ran up and kicked him in the nuts. Carrie probably would have boiled a pot of water and dumped it on him, then let her demon kids play piñata with the body."

I laughed and opened the garage door.

We walked into the house and Bridgett went ahead to her place with the girls. The house was a little louder than it had been the day before, and when I walked in, I saw that we had more people. Janine, her husband, Linna's oldest sister and two of her sons had been added. Dr. Roth from the Red Wing hospital was also new. He was the one who'd gotten me the job at the Mayo Clinic with Calloway, and he was friends with Linna from when she'd worked at the hospital. It was really crazy how my life in California connected to Noah's life here. There was something to be said about fate.

"Hey Girly, where've you been?" Clara pinched the back of my arm, stepping away from her conversation with Linna and her sister, Mary.

I stopped. "Outside blowing off steam."

"Well now, you just sound like Garrett. That's sad." She reached up and pulled something out of my hair. "What's the prognosis? Are you gonna live?"

"Yep."

"Good..." She looked me over. "Thank you for being nice to him."

I held up a shoulder. "I don't think I have a reason not to."

"He's a gushing bag of feels. *That's* reason."

I laughed a little. "I'm gonna go take a shower real quick. Are you okay?"

"I don't know, did you clear a place for me to smoke outside?" Her eyebrow arched.

I pointed to the garage door. "You can go out the back door. Bridgett put a can out there."

"Good. I'm gonna do that, then come back and laugh at these two old bags." Clara walked past me.

I had to smile at her crassness.

"Holly."

I looked over into the living room. Garrett was standing in front of Dr. Brimmer and Thomas, waving me over. I pulled the hair tie from my hair, hoping it would make me look a little more presentable, and walked over.

"There's the prodigy surgeon." Dr. Brimmer smiled as I approached. He was a stout man with dark hair and black rimmed glasses. "I was just telling Garrett and Thomas about you finding that tumor the size of a fingernail clipping the other day."

"Oh," I laughed nervously. "I think that's mostly attributed to a high-quality CT."

"They take pictures, but it's up to the doctor to analyze." Dr. Brimmer looked at Garrett. "Seven different specialists looked at those scans, this gal gives one look-over and points it out like it's the state of Texas. And did you tell him the surgery you practically led yesterday in the wee hours?"

My cheeks burned a little.

"What would *you* have to talk about?" Thomas asked with a raised eyebrow.

The three of us laughed, while Thomas held a straight face against his question.

"I have plenty," Dr. Brimmer laughed. "Go on, tell him." He lifted a finger from the glass in his hand to tap my arm.

I sighed and looked at Garrett. "I *assisted* on a sphenoid meningioma."

Garrett's eyebrows raised.

I looked at Thomas to explain, "It's a tumor behind the eye, pressing on the cranial nerve. They're nearly impossible to fully remove."

"Yeah, nearly impossible, and she did it *unassisted*. Dr. Calloway choked, and *she* with her brilliant little fingers and skills, asks if she can give it a whirl. Calloway agrees, steps aside, she gets in there and removes every last bit of the tumor, like she'd done it a hundred times. No big deal. Cool as a cucumber. Even better, the chief of staff and chief of surgery are in the gallery watching, and she acts like there isn't a soul up there. They came down to the scrub room to shake her hand and congratulate her, and she gives every cent of credit to Calloway. You should have seen the flabbergasted looks on their faces as she stepped over to the sink to scrub." He laughed, shaking his head.

Dr. Brimmer only meant his words as a good thing, but

I felt like he was listing out my transgressions.

"That's pretty impressive, Kid." Garrett bumped my arm gently.

I looked at him and forced a smile.

"I'm not surprised though. Holly comes from two generations of surgeons," Garrett said smoothly. "Her dad was someone to be reckoned with."

I looked at Thomas. "Can I get you some water?" I really hoped from the bottom of my stomach that he'd say yes.

A slow smile formed and he pinched the side of my chin. "Ask Linna for a cup of tea?" He winked.

I gave him a returning smile and nodded before I turned out of the conversation. Before I went up the step out of the living room, Brad came in through the front door. It was interesting how someone's appearance changed when you were upset with them.

I took the step up. "Are you guys leaving?"

He nodded.

"Text me when you're home."

"I will, but just give me a second." He wiped his shoes off on the rug.

I stepped closer so I could speak quietly. "I'm not gonna talk to you with Greg hanging around, and we have a house full of guests. It's not the time."

"I know. I just came up to say goodbye and let you know I left something on top of your dresser for you."

"Okay. I'll check later." I shrugged.

He reached into his coat pocket, then held out a butterscotch candy with a sullen look. My heart split for a second, and I took the candy, then hugged him. It was a melancholy day for us, and normally we'd go to our Dad's house, suck on butterscotch candies, binge on the snacks our nanny made us, and watch the old western movies our dad forced us to watch as kids.

"I'm sorry, Holl," he whispered.

"I know... I just need time."

"I didn't tell you about Greg because I don't wanna hurt you. And I didn't mean for him to come here."

"Well, you did, and *he* did. A lot. So, give me a few days to chill out."

He nodded, rubbing my back, then let go of me.

"Are you leaving?" Noah asked from behind me.

I turned to look at him because I couldn't tell his demeanor by his voice. I still couldn't tell by looking at him. His face was too sober.

"Yeah. We gotta catch a flight out before the next part of the storm rolls in."

"Well, fly safe." Noah reached out a hand.

"Thanks." Brad shook his hand. "I'm sorry again."

"As long as it doesn't happen again, it's forgotten."

Brad nodded and looked at me. "Call me, okay?"

"I will," I nodded.

He put a hand on top of my head. "Love you, Butch."

"Love you too."

He dropped his hand and turned out the door.

I turned around to face Noah. "Can you go ask your mom to make Thomas some tea, then meet me upstairs? I need a shower and I'm trying not to get pulled into another conversation."

"Yeah."

I gripped his arm as I passed and went straight upstairs. Gif poked his head out from under the bed, then ran to me.

"Hey buddy." I scrubbed his fur. "Hopefully those rotten kids leave so you can socialize again. Come on."

Gif backed himself up to my side, then followed me to the bed. I flopped down and he jumped up to snuggle up against my side. I wrapped my arm around so I could twist his ear around my finger. For a moment, I wished he was my dog, then I realized he pretty much was. In all the chaos, I forgot there was a ring around my finger. Soon enough I wouldn't live in my apartment anymore. It was both overwhelming and relieving that I was staying here with Noah. The permanence had never been felt before. In the back of my mind, I was ready to pack up and run, but Greg had already found me, and here was still the only place I wanted to be.

"Why's the dog on the bed?" Noah asked out of irritation when he came in.

"Because he's fluffy and I like him..."

"I don't like fur on the bed." Noah sat down, but turned on his side to face me and held his head up with his hand.

"He's on my side."

Noah put a hand on my forehead for a second, then brushed my hair back. "You're still warm."

"I know. It's almost burned out though..." I continued to stare up at the ceiling.

"Are you gonna talk to me and end the stand-off?" He pulled my hair off the front of my shoulder.

"You were an ass."

"And you know I wasn't trying to be." He brushed his fingers over my chest above the scooped neckline of my shirt.

I turned my head to look at him. "*That's* exactly what I'm talking about." I shook my head. "Stop talking to me like I'm an adolescent, because I'm not. You don't have to approve of how I choose to handle situations, *I* do. Last night, I didn't like how I handled the situation, but *I* have that right, not you. I was standing there feeling like an emotional idiot, just talking to you, and you had to jump in and give me your two cents I didn't ask for. I know you were going for the opposite, but you made me feel small. Telling me not to act like a victim? I *was*. Bridgett said it this morning and it knocked the air out of my chest—I lost my *life*. I had to give up everything I've ever known, cared about, or loved and—regardless of some stupid words this morning—I didn't have a choice. You lost your life once," I shook my head, "it couldn't have felt good. You were a victim of a tragedy, but how would you have felt if I told you 'don't be a victim'? You *were,* and it hurt worse than anything else in your life. You'll never get over it, and it'll never stop pulling you down, no matter how brief the feeling lasts."

Noah leaned forward as he put a hand on my cheek and kissed the other. "You're right. I'm sorry," he whispered against my cheek. "I wanted to make you feel justified, not small."

"I don't handle things the way you do, and yesterday, I was trying to handle anything at *all*." My voice broke and I swallowed to push down the lump lodged in my throat.

"Don't cry. Come here." He moved his hand from my face and scooped my side off the bed, pushing me against him.

I slid forward and hugged him. He took a breath and let it out like he was relieved as he hugged me.

"I have a bad feeling about Brad and Greg," I said quietly after a minute.

"How so?" He moved his hand under my shirt to rub

my back.

"I don't think it's real. Greg can lie so convincingly that no one would ever know, but Brad... I don't know. Something's wrong and I feel it in my bones."

"Yeah. They seem like they're both having to really work at it, but I don't know. It could just be jitters, you know? They were around strange people with no idea who's accepting of them being gay."

"Maybe." I reached up and rubbed the side of my forehead and let out a breath. "I need to get up before I lose all energy."

"Mm, I'm not ready to let you up yet." He snapped his fingers behind my back. I thought he was making Gif get off the bed until there was a furry lump plopping against my back.

I laughed a little. "A Holly sandwich."

"Mm-hm." He pulled my chin up and kissed the side of my neck.

I smiled. "Holly berries aren't edible."

He moved me up and started kissing around on my chest. "This one is."

I laughed. "I need a shower. I was outside trying to sweat out my fever."

Noah rolled me on my back, making Gif jump off the bed, and pulled my shirt off. "I don't care." He kissed down my stomach while unbuttoning my jeans.

Chapter 17

Christmas passed and I still didn't really talk to Brad. I honestly didn't know what to say to him. Whatever Brad had going on with Greg, I didn't want to know. Every time I thought about it, it put a pit in my stomach. When he called, I either lied and said I was working, or kept the conversation on a focused point. He sold my house for me, so there had to be some form of communication.

Clara and Garrett made themselves semi-permanent people in my life after Thanksgiving. It was mostly Garrett's doing. He'd invited Noah and I to Rochester for a weekend. He had a guest house, so it wasn't too terribly awkward staying with him. Watching him and Clara was interesting and gave a lot of insight to their twisty form of a relationship. It also gave me a lot of perspective into why her relationship with my dad would have never survived. She was probably as bullheaded as he was, and I could imagine the arguments it would have led to. When I asked her more about what happened with my dad, I appreciated her brutal honesty, but it was hard to hear. He'd never laid a hand on her, but he'd made her feel as small and battered as Greg had made me feel.

After the weekend at Garrett's, he texted me every few days. I was sure he would have done it everyday, but was likely trying not to seem overbearing. He'd ask about my surgeries, send articles he found interesting, or simply ask how my day was going.

In the middle of January, I was given the opportunity to assist on a surgery Dr. Calloway had been preparing for since before I began working with him. It was the kind that came with publicity, medical conferences, and a great deal of preparation. Garrett had come to the day long conference and sat like a proud father the whole time. Dr. Calloway, myself, and the team he'd put together were given twenty-four hours at home to sleep and mentally prepare. The next morning, it was show time, and the gallery was so full that most people were standing. Garrett, Noah, and unfortunately, Brad and Greg, were at the after party. Fifteen hours of surgery wasn't enough torture; Calloway had to have a party.

"Gosh, what are you doing here," I asked Brad as I hugged him.

"We saw Dr. Calloway's article with your name mentioned, so we thought we should come show support," Greg answered for Brad.

"Oh." I held a polite smile, but didn't know what to say.

"It's a big day for your career." Brad gripped my shoulder lightly. "I wanted to be here."

I gave him a better smile. "You realize I was just an assist, right?"

"What in the hell bullshit are you spreading?" Dr. Calloway tugged the end of my braid from behind. "Bradly, I haven't seen you since you had braces and pimples on your face. How the hell are ya?" Dr. Calloway held out his large hand to Brad. He was a six-foot-five giant, and equally as loud.

"I'm good," Brad laughed, shaking Calloway's hand. "Congratulations on today."

"Why, thank you," Calloway gleamed with a smile and looked at me. "See? That's how you take a compliment, then you say something like, 'I couldn't have done it without my prodigy.'" He looked at Brad again. "This girl's a chip off the old man's block, isn't she?"

Brad smiled. "Good luck getting her to agree."

Dr. Calloway laughed loudly. "Ain't that the truth." He looked over at Garrett and Noah as they approached. "Goddamn. Every time I see ya, I think I'm staring at a ghost. Did you get a spot in the gallery today?" Dr. Calloway held his hand out to Garrett.

"Front and center for the whole thing." Garrett smiled gently at me.

"She was magnificent, wasn't she?"

I cringed and looked at Noah, wishing he had a reason to get me the hell out of there. Instead of an understanding expression, he laughed a little. He'd been taunting me for days about my inability to accept the attention. I narrowed my eyes at him.

"Wake up, Penny." Calloway snapped his fingers in front of my face. From the time I was a little girl, Calloway had always called me his shiny penny.

I raised an eyebrow and looked up at him.

"I just announced to your posse that you've been promoted to my new chief resident."

I frowned. "What? Why?"

Dr. Calloway looked at me incredulously. "Because you're better than everyone else." He popped the back of my shoulder. "Congrats, Penny."

"What about Yin?" I continued to stare at him like he was feeding me horrible news.

"He's a flying monkey now."

Calloway called people he didn't like monkeys. Interns were scrub monkeys, residents were regular monkeys, and attendings were flying monkeys.

"He's leaving for some piss-bucket hospital in No-one-cares, Kansas. He's out of neuro and into general. He can't hang. Take the damn victory lap, you're irritating me." Calloway gripped my shoulder, turning behind me. "Hause, wait up!"

I took in a breath and let it out. Being the chief resident at any normal hospital wasn't the same as somewhere like the Mayo Clinic. I was competing against the best in medicine on a daily basis.

Brad raised his eyebrows, looking at me like he was watching an unexpected mental breakdown. "You okay there?"

I covered my mouth and let out a stifled squeal before I jumped at Brad.

He caught me in a hug and laughed. "Nerd."

"Two years before Dad, I win. Ha ha!" I danced even though I was off my feet.

Brad laughed again and dropped me on my feet. "Congrats on your desk job."

"Oh no, friend. I get to keep every badass surgery for myself." I rubbed my hands and turned on my heel to face Garrett and Noah. "You have no idea what the hell is going on," I waved dismissively at Noah and hugged Garrett. "Ha ha, I beat you too."

Garrett laughed. "That's not hard. By the time I was a resident, I was too old to be dazzled by shiny titles."

"Buh, you sound like my dad." I let go of him and went to Noah, looking up at him with a smile. "I think the equivalent in your world would be getting that big house-fish."

"You mean the Huntsman bid I got the call on today?" He smiled, brushing his fingers over my cheek.

"Really?" I raised my eyebrows with a smile.

"Yeah," he laughed.

I shook my head, holding my smile. "We're never gonna see each other again," I laughed.

He bent his head and kissed me. "Congratulations."

"You too." I smiled at him.

"We should go celebrate somewhere, and get out of here," Garrett suggested.

I looked over at the group of people near the food table shaking a bottle of Champagne and making a mess, turning up my lip in disgust. "Um." I looked up at Noah.

"Don't look at me. You're the one who's been on your feet all day."

I shrugged. "I'm on my tenth wind."

"Our hotel has a really nice restaurant inside," Greg suggested.

I looked at him and forced a smile, but internally wished Greg didn't exist. "Okay." I looked at Brad. "Drop a pin and we'll meet you there. I just have to change out of my scrubs first." I looked at Garrett. "I'll text you the address as soon as Brad sends it."

He nodded. "I'll meet you there."

"Did you want to stay at the house so you don't have to drive all the way to Stillwater tonight? I'm sure Holly will let you have her apartment," Noah offered to Garrett. He'd hired Noah's company to put new windows in his house, but there was a mistake with the window company. They were supposed to be sent in the spring, but arrived four days ago. Noah and Garrett didn't want to take the chance of them getting broken, so Noah's guys started putting them in this morning. The house was open to the freezing temps in the process, so Garrett was going to stay with Clara.

"Actually, that'd be great." Garrett looked at me.

I smiled. "You got the place to yourself, and I wanna pick your brain on the surgery tomorrow." I squeezed Noah's hand. "I'm gonna go change. Are you in the garage?"

"Yep." He ran his hand down the end of my braid and pulled the hair tie off.

I rolled my eyes and left for the locker room.

•••••••

Brad, Greg, and Garrett already had a table at the restaurant when we got there. I felt badly for Garrett because of the lack of conversation going on. Brad didn't like Garrett, and Garrett obviously wasn't going to strike up a conversation with Greg. Brad and Greg were on their phones, scrolling, and Garrett was just sitting contently, people watching. I sat between him and Noah, and there was an open chair between Noah and Greg. I tried to get a conversation picked up, but it seemed to fail. Garrett and Noah got talking, so I was left with Brad and Greg, but apparently failed at including Greg, because Brad cornered me when I excused myself to the bathroom.

"Can you at least *pretend* to get along with Greg?" Brad snapped quietly in the hallway.

"I am." I frowned, feeling a little attacked out of nowhere.

"No, you're acting like he's the monster under your bed. Every time he takes a drink, you look like you're going to shed a layer of skin." Brad stared at me angrily.

"If I did, I didn't mean to. Force of habit, he's been known to have a problem." I kept my voice calm, hoping he'd stop being so over the top.

"*Had,* Holly. *Had* a problem. He has one drink at dinner and that's it. And besides that, every time he tries to talk to you, you give the shortest answer you've got and go back to *anyone* else. He's trying, and you're being rude." The corner of his mouth twitched, showing that he was holding back more than he was saying.

"I'm sorry." I put a hand on his arm. "I'm nervous and I don't know how to be around him. I'm not intentionally trying to be a jerk. I'll go back and do better. Okay?" I looked at him with sincerity. I wasn't looking to bring more problems forward.

Brad let out a breath. "Can you tell Noah to back off too? The second you left, it's been daggers across the table."

I nodded. "I will."

"Thank you." He turned and went into the men's room.

I let out a breath, shoving my hand through my hair and went back to the table. Noah had a hard look on his face and Garrett looked slightly concerned.

"Avoid the bathroom if you can. They have people standing inside to hand you towels. It's super awkward," I said in an attempt to break whatever tension there was at the table.

"Can you imagine having that job? I'm sure it's equally as terrible for them." Greg picked up his glass which was fuller than when I'd left.

"Probably worse." Garrett cut a sliver off his steak.

"I hope you don't mind, Holly. I ordered you a glass of wine. They had your favorite, and I know it's hard to find." Greg set down his glass.

I raised my eyebrows. "Wow. I'm surprised they had it. Noah and I were in the cities and no one carries it."

He shrugged casually with a smile. "Lucky night, I guess."

"Yeah." I forced a smile. "So, how's the firm? Any crazy divorces?" I had no idea what else to ask, and Brad was coming back from the bathroom.

•••••••

The rest of dinner was thankfully short, and must've gone okay, because I didn't get any more harsh words from Brad. On the way home, the exhaustion finally set in, and it was all I could do to walk in the house.

"Ugh," I sat down at the island, "why did you build a house with so many stairs? I'm wiped out at the thought of trudging up." My breaths were tired and heavy from the walk from the truck to the kitchen.

"I don't think a house that takes as long to cross is any easier. Do you want some water?"

"Yeah." I rubbed my chest, wondering why my heart was pounding so hard. I definitely wasn't out of shape, and

272

I'd had far longer days than today. "My heart is going crazy right now."

"Go upstairs and lay down. I'm gonna make sure everything's locked up, and I'll be up." Noah pushed the glass into the button for the water.

"Yeah." I put my hand against my cheek because it was burning, like I was blushing over something. "I'm still resenting you for making me go up the stairs." I got up from the chair and pushed it in, feeling even more off, but not in a way I could describe.

"Here. I'll be up in a second."

I reached for the glass, and I had it, but everything drained in my body and the glass dropped on the tile.

"Shit!" Noah cussed quickly.

"Holly, wake up. Look at me." Noah's voice was urgent.

Something cold was being pressed against my face. My heart was pounding, and it was difficult to breathe, but I forced myself to open my eyes. I felt like someone was sitting directly on top of me, and I knew something was wrong.

"Keep your eyes open. Look at me." Noah patted my cheek.

I didn't know they'd closed again. "Something's... wrong." Words were just as hard as breathing.

"Keep your eyes open. Do you wanna go in?" He brushed my hair back.

I looked up at the light on the ceiling, trying to focus my lazy vision. "Garrett."

"Okay. Hold on." He turned me and reached into my back pocket for my phone.

I tried to reach my hand up to my chest, but it felt like

there were weights on my arms, and I didn't have the energy to fight it.

"Holly, keep your eyes open," Noah said again, shaking me. "Hey, can you come up here? Holly passed out and I can barely keep her awake... Okay, thanks."

"Noah... help." I didn't know what I wanted him to do, but I felt so much worse.

"Please. Wake up. Come on." Noah sounded almost dismayed, but also winded.

I pulled to take a breath in, feeling like my throat was closed. A door opened and shut.

"Get the truck door. We have to take her in, she's not breathing right, and I can't get her to wake up again."

"Let me see her first. We might need to keep her here and call an ambulance." Garrett sounded exactly like my dad when he was in doctor mode. Short and direct.

"Open the door. Let me set her down."

Poor Noah. He sounded scared. I tried like hell to open my eyes as I struggled for another breath.

"Lean her forward, it'll make it easier for her to breathe. Just hold her up."

The second I was set forward, I could breathe easier. I managed to open my eyes just enough to see two sets of blurry legs.

"Her heart rate's high. Do you know if she's allergic to anything?" Garrett prodded around on my neck.

"No. She's never mentioned anything."

Garrett picked up my head. "Hey, Kid. What's going on with you?"

I could breathe, and struggle to keep my eyes open,

but I couldn't tell him I felt like my muscles didn't work. He pulled my eyelid open wider and looked at my eye. His face was blurry.

"Her eyes are dilated. Let's go. We'll call an ambulance on the way if we have to." Garrett pulled me forward and got in the truck with me. "I'm gonna listen to your heart, Kid." He pulled me up and put his ear to my chest.

My head was tipped back again and it made me gasp for a breath, but it almost sounded like a snore. He corrected the problem, setting me forward again. My body tingled, and I tried to fight the feeling of passing out again, but I couldn't.

......

When I was little, I used to beg my dad to take me to work with him, and on certain and very special days, he did. Sometimes the day was spent in his office, digging through old medical records that I read like books, and sometimes I got to be in the scrub room with my face pressed to the glass. I loved the smell, I embraced the feeling, and I knew without a single doubt that it was where I was meant to be. As soon as I was old enough, I was a volunteer at my dad's practice. Every Friday, after the last morning surgery, my dad would take me into the practice room and teach me something new on Ed the dummy. I'd spent enough time in hospitals to know where I was... and I was on the wrong side of it.

My fingers moved first until I felt a hand under mine, and I opened my eyes. I felt tired, but not like before. Noah had his arm on the bed and his head down on his arm, holding my hand. I squeezed his hand and pulled the oxygen mask off with the other. His head picked up and he looked at me tiredly.

"Oh, jeez," he breathed as he sat up and slid his chair

closer. "How are you feeling?" He traded hands and reached up to put a hand on my cheek.

"Better than I *did*." I put my other hand over his, on my cheek. "Did they figure out what happened?"

He shook his head. "They did a bunch of tests and nothing came back. Garrett made them do more, and we're waiting. He'd probably be better at explaining, but they said your muscles weren't responding. It put your heart out of rhythm, and you were barely breathing."

The scared look on his face made my heart break for him. I let go of his hand and touched his cheek. He must've felt like he was close to losing another person he loved.

Noah put his hand over mine and turned his head to kiss my palm.

"Where's Garrett?" I looked over, already knowing he wasn't there, but confirming that I hadn't missed him.

"I don't know. Probably going around telling everyone they're incompetent." Noah shook his head. "For someone normally so quiet, he sure can turn into a dick the second someone slips up."

I smiled. "You've never seen a Bennett at work. It's like building a house with a grouchy Jackson."

Noah smiled like he was relieved and rubbed his thumb over the back of my hand. I turned my head and looked at the heart monitor. My heart rate didn't appear abnormal, but it didn't feel quite right in my chest.

"God, I felt like I was dying." I looked at Noah again. "I was trying to stay awake and talk to you, but I couldn't."

He shook his head. "I'm glad Garrett was just down the hill. There wasn't a lot he could do, but at least he was there to help."

"I'm glad he had the sense to set me forward in the truck. I really couldn't breathe, but I couldn't say it." I took a breath just because the memory made me feel like I needed the air. "Do you know what they gave me to straighten me out?"

He shook his head. "No. I was too preoccupied praying you wouldn't die."

I gave him a gentle smile. "I'm still here."

There was a quiet knock on the door and we both looked. Brad came in, followed by Greg.

"Hey, what are you doing here?" I held a kind smile, forcing myself to not be irritated that Greg seemed to follow Brad like a dog.

"I got a call, so we drove over." He walked toward me. "What happened?"

I pulled back the corner of my mouth. "I don't know. I just woke up a few minutes ago."

Greg crossed his arms, looking at me like I was broken. "Have they done any tests?"

I nodded. "Waiting on them to come back."

Brad took my hand. "It's weird seeing you in a hospital bed."

I laughed a little. "Feels wrong too."

He smiled a little, but just like everyone else, he looked scared.

"I'll be fine," I reassured, squeezing his hand.

"Do you think it was something you ate at the restaurant?" Greg continued to stand there with his hands on his elbows with the same look. "Maybe the fish?"

"I don't think it was. They said it wasn't anaphylaxis," Noah said quietly.

"What exactly happened? I kinda stopped listening after you said she was in the hospital." Brad sat on the edge of the bed.

I shook my head. "I lost muscle control. My heart went crazy, and I could only breathe if my head was propped correctly."

"And they don't know what's wrong?" Greg looked back at the door with a disgusted frown and back at me. "What kind of podunk hospital is this?"

"We would have taken her to Mayo if we thought she could make it, but we barely got her *here* in time." Noah stroked my fingers out to the ends.

Greg let out a huff and turned to the door.

"Greg, don't," I said quickly. "This isn't a bad hospital, it's just complicated symptoms."

He turned around. "They should take you somewhere else if they can't handle it."

I shook my head. "It's fine. Really. I'm awake now, so if I think they're doing something stupid, I'll be the first to say something." My heart clenched tightly and I reached up to hold my chest with a wince. The monitor dinged. "Get someone," I breathed out of pain.

"Get Garrett," Brad said quickly.

"Put the bed back." I tried to hold my voice steady, but my chest hurt too badly.

Brad got up and pushed the button. It was irritating that the dumb bed was too slow to respond. They weren't as comfortable, but I wished I was in an ER gurney.

"Stop," I told him when I felt like the bed was back far enough. I looked up at the light on the ceiling, feeling like someone was crushing my heart in their hand while it tried to beat.

The door whipped open.

"What happened?" Garrett demanded. "Give me your scope."

I kept my eyes on the ceiling and let Brad answer. "She was fine, then her heart rate spiked and it's down now."

Garrett stood next to the bed, putting the stethoscope on. Another doctor I'd never met, and two nurses, walked around the other side of the bed. I grabbed Garrett's sleeve on the hand he wasn't using.

"I know, Kid." His voice was a whisper as he listened around on my chest.

"She's in v-fib. Get a crash cart," the other doctor said looking at the monitor.

"Hold on. She's coming out of it." Garrett stared at the screen while keeping the stethoscope on my chest. "Still get a cart to keep in here." He looked at the doctor across from him. "I think we should put her on a temporary pacemaker."

The doctor nodded in agreement and looked at the nurse. "And page Dr. Copper again."

My chest still hurt, but it was better than before, and I let out a breath. "Do *not* call Dr. Copper, he's an idiot. Call Schroeder. Has anyone done an ultrasound?"

"We did, but we can do another one." The doctor grabbed the oxygen mask from behind my head.

I took it from him because I didn't want to continuously wear it. "And why isn't the second round of labs back? I'm clearly not stable, so there should have been a rush put on them. I wanna see the first round, and the results for everything else you've done."

The doctor looked a little taken aback. "The lab is short

staffed and backed up." He looked at the nurse. "Get her chart, call for a portable ultrasound, and call the lab again." He looked at me. "I'm Dr. Jay Zimmer, I'm—"

"You're leaving to get a pacemaker because my heart is still not in full rhythm," I snapped and put the mask over my face to breathe for a second.

"I guess I am. It's nice to meet you. Your reputation precedes you."

I gave him an unamused glare and he turned.

The second he was gone, Garrett smirked and laughed. "I thought *I* was giving them hell."

I picked up my hands and looked at them closely, surveying every inch of skin up to my elbows.

"What's wrong?" Noah asked quietly.

"I'm making sure I don't have any cuts. There's nothing to really contract from my surgery, but my dad died because of a cut on his hand and a glove that got nicked." I felt my face and lymph nodes. Everything was normal. "My gloves weren't broken. I always check." I tried to think about the environment I'd been in, and anything that might have caused this kind of a reaction. "Can you text Calloway? He's probably passed out drunk, but just ask him if there's anyone presenting with muscle weakness and abnormal heart rhythms." I looked at Noah.

He nodded and reached into his pocket, pulling out my phone.

"Have you been around any questionable patients?" Garrett asked.

I shook my head. "I can't think of any."

"Maybe we should call over to the hospital and see if anyone else has had something similar."

"Let's wait until I see the labs." I rubbed my forehead. It was overly irritating for me to be in the hospital as a patient.

......

I was right to have them do another ultrasound. My heart was enlarged from the stress. I was also right to demand to see my lab results, because I found things that were missed on the first set. The second set included a new set of tests that shed some light. I had an extreme amount of hospital grade caffeine and beta blockers in my system which explained the symptoms. The unexplained part was how they ended up in my system.

Garrett called the restaurant in the morning to ask them if any of their staff was on beta-blockers. They refused to be any kind of help and gave him the number of a lawyer to contact. Brad called that lawyer, a complete asshole of a lady, and without drawing up formal complaints and charges against the restaurant, we wouldn't get any kind of information back.

I remained at the hospital for a week before I was allowed to go home and be on bed rest. Brad, Greg, and Garrett all had jobs to go back to, so they didn't hang around. Linna came down for a couple days to keep an eye on me because Noah had meetings I refused to let him miss. On the weekend, Garrett and Clara both came to the house.

"I've been thinking. Do you think Greg might've done something?" Garrett asked as he removed the blood pressure cuff from my arm.

I shook my head. "I definitely thought of it, but he never left the table, and he wasn't close enough to me to get something onto my plate without anyone noticing. Two, I don't know why he'd do something like that. He has problems, but that's a whole different kind of issue. I really do think it was just something at the restaurant. They were overly defensive, so it just makes sense. Most places would cooperate and look for some type of employee misconduct."

He let out a breath. "It's making me crazy. I don't think it was the restaurant, just because of the caffeine."

I held up a shoulder. "I don't think we're gonna get an answer."

Garrett nodded. "How are you feeling otherwise?"

"Bored out of my skull, and over pampered. No one lets me out of their sight and I'm hardly allowed to lift a finger." I shook my head. "I'm not good at sitting around doing nothing. I made an intern FaceTime me during a surgery just so I could be stimulated for an amount of time."

"You're probably fine to move around a little bit, but nothing excessive."

"I know. It's just not worth the fight with everyone else." I reached down and pet Gif's ear. "Huh, buddy?"

Gif opened his mouth, panting happily as he absorbed his attention.

"Alright, Girly. Time to make some decisions," Clara sighed.

I looked over the side of the couch as Clara walked around.

"Your wedding is gonna come up fast and this is the only time your ass is gonna be pinned to one place."

Chapter 18

I got in my car, thankful to be leaving the house and driving *myself* for a change. My poor car had been sitting since the day before the big surgery with Calloway. Today, I was supposed to be cleared to go back to work. All that stood in the way was one stupid appointment. Three weeks of sitting on my ass had driven me up a wall, and all I wanted to do was work.

I pulled out onto the county road and got up to speed. Snow came down at a fair rate, but it wasn't terrible. One thing Minnesota did for a person was force them to learn how to drive in snow like a pro. I did it so much I hardly cared anymore. Instead of panicking like I used to, I enjoyed the winter scene. Even if I was tired of the snow, I was so damn happy to be out of the house that I didn't care.

Three things seem to happen almost simultaneously. My dashboard flashed at me, forcing me to glance down and take notice; when I looked back up there was a truck pulling out in front of me, and I smashed my brakes. The car didn't stop. It didn't even slow. The light on my dash was telling me my brake fluid was low, and I had two options: I could hit the truck at fifty miles an hour, or push the e-brake, spin out of control, and hope. I pushed the e-brake, forced my body to relax back into my seat as much as I could, and took what was coming. My car didn't slide out of control until I collided with the truck, and the back end of my car slid into the other lane and was clipped by another oncoming vehicle there'd been no way for me to see. I was shoved off the side of the road into the steep bank of trees just before the creek. It was a slow form of torture to watch my car tip down nose first and go completely upside down. Just as my car was fully stopped, and I thought it was over, there was a hard jolt as the weight of my car crushed the ice in the creek.

I didn't know if I was hurt. My windshield was broken, and water was coming in slowly. It would be at the top of my head by the time it filled to the level of the creek. I pulled on my seatbelt, but it was locked out from my weight. I jabbed at the button while also trying to wiggle myself free. The button finally released, dropping me on my head into freezing water.

"Shit!" I cussed, trying to get my feet under me. Thankfully, I managed to quickly, but the cold was over my feet now instead of my head and back. "Phone." I dug through the spilled contents of my purse on the ceiling. I put only the important stuff back in my purse, and as soon as I found my phone, I stuffed it in the front of my shirt and pulled the head rest completely out from the seat. I'd watched a video once, and really hoped that the trick would work and that I could break the glass.

"She's alive! Get something to break the window!" A guy yelled from outside the car.

I smacked the window, and not only did my hand slip on the leather from being wet, but I didn't have enough room to have the force. It made me look around to think of something else, and my thought was to grab the jack from the spare, but then I saw that I didn't need to. The back of my car was unobstructed.

I crawled back and banged on the window. "Open the door!" I yelled to whomever was out there. "The back door! Open the back door!"

"Hank! She's at the back!" a lady screamed from the top of the bank. She grabbed onto a tree, trying to make her way down.

"Push the button and open the door!" I yelled when I saw a pair of boots in front of the window.

The button was pushed and there was a click as the door unlatched. I stood as much as I could and pushed the door while the man tried to pull it back. There was a stupid lip that had a taillight that prevented it from opening easily.

"I got it. Can you fit out the side?" The man strained to keep the door open.

I wedged myself up between the door and the woman who'd come down the bank reached to help me. I took her arms and let her pull me out.

"Oh my god. Are you okay?" The lady's voice was panicked, and she was about to cry.

"Yeah."

"Your head's bleeding." She reached up to put the sleeve of her coat against my forehead.

I looked around, trying to remember exactly what I

should do.

"Let's get you up to the car to get warm." The man put his coat over my shoulders.

Phone. That's what I was supposed to do. I reached into my shirt and pulled out my phone. My hands shook, but it was just two taps to call Noah.

"We called nine-one-one already. Let's just get you up the bank." The man tried to carefully push against my shoulder to get me to move.

"No." I moved to avoid his arm. "I can walk." I looked around, then back at my car. It was unreasonable, but I felt like I shouldn't leave it there, but what choice did I have?

"Are you on your way to your appointment?" Noah asked without a normal greeting.

"Where are you?" I asked shakily.

"Just coming up on the last four way stop before the house. Are you okay? You sound rattled."

"No. Go past the house. I'm across the road from Jenson's farm."

"What?"

"My car's flipped upside down in the creek." I looked back at it.

"What!?"

"My car's upside down." My voice broke. "I have to go."

"No. Holly, stay on the phone with me. What happened? Are you still in your car?"

"No. I'm out. I have to go." I put my phone back in my shirt and reached for the nearest tree to grab onto before I threw up.

"Do you guys need help up?" someone called from the road.

"No. We're just waiting for her to walk up with us," the other man behind me yelled.

My stomach retched a few times and I felt dizzy, but I started grabbing trees to pull my way up to the road. The guy that was already at the top of the road slid down the bank a couple feet to help me over the steep ridge.

"I got ya." He wrapped an arm around my waist and dug his foot into the dirt and snow before he stepped and partially lifted me. My foot slipped and it was only at that point I realized I was missing a shoe.

"Oops. I got ya." He caught me around the waist and got me up to the road. "Can one of you help her? I think I might have a tarp or something in the truck."

I looked down the road, feeling like Noah should have been coming toward me, but time probably wasn't moving like I thought it was.

"What's your name, Hun?" the woman asked carefully as she approached me.

My foot was so cold it hurt. I put my foot on top of the one that still had a shoe and chewed on my lip as I watched down the road.

"Hey, it's okay. Help is coming. Why don't you come to the car with me and sit."

I shook my head.

"You're all wet, you'll freeze out here just waiting. Come with me. My name's Juliann. What's yours?"

I continued to stand there like an idiot, madder than hell because I didn't want to sit at home anymore. I wanted to go back to work. Today was supposed to be easy. I was going to go to my appointment, get cleared for work, go up to the neuro floor, see Dr. Calloway, and worm my way into doing something. I'd even brought scrubs with me. What good was a chief resident that was never at work?

"All I've got is an extra shirt," one of the men said.

"Do you care if it gets dirty? She's missing a shoe, and I can't get her to go to the car with me." The lady, Juliann, kept her hand on my back.

"She's probably in shock. As long as she's standing, she's probably alright."

Shock. Why hadn't I thought of that? It was my job to think of that.

"Here, Hun." Juliann bent down. "Stand on this."

A blue truck. It was moving fast, but it seemed like it was crawling. Maybe it was. Maybe he was driving like an old man the way he usually did. It was almost infuriating being driven around by Noah. He never broke the speed limit, and waited the respectable three seconds before starting out from a stop sign.

Noah put his flashers on before he was at a full stop, and ran toward me the second he was out of the truck. I didn't move because my foot hurt from the cold. Other parts of me were starting to hurt too.

"Is everyone okay?" Noah asked as he slowed from his run, noticing the back of the truck and front of the SUV.

"The rest of us are just fine. It's just this poor thing," Juliann responded.

He reached his hands out to me before he was actually looking, and didn't actually touch me once he looked at me. "Jeez, you're banged up good." He pushed my hair back, looking at my forehead.

I stepped forward and hugged him.

"You're alright." He rubbed my back.

"I assume you know her?"

"Yeah." Noah squeezed me gently.

"We tried to get her to wait in the car, but she wouldn't budge. She's missing a shoe and she's all wet under that coat. Her car broke the ice in the creek and it was coming in on her."

Noah rubbed my back again. "Can I move you to the truck?"

I nodded, letting go of him. The shock was starting to wear off, though I wished it wouldn't because it came with more pain. I pulled the coat off me.

"No, Hun, you keep it."

"It's okay. She can take mine." Noah unzipped his tan work coat and pulled it off. "Are you okay to let me carry you?" He put his coat around me.

I nodded and lifted my good arm. My other shoulder hurt from the seatbelt.

Noah bent under my arm and scooped me up. "Has anyone called this in yet?" he asked Juliann.

"Yeah. They should be getting here soon, I hope."

"Alright. I'm gonna get her in the truck. See if that truck driver has any cones or flares we can put out."

"That's a good idea."

Noah turned with me and kissed my forehead. "You're just one mess after another, aren't you?" He went to the truck and set me in the driver's seat before he opened the back and grabbed a blanket.

I started to take off his coat so he could have it back.

"No. Keep it on. I'm just getting this around your lap." He tucked the blanket under my hips.

I winced. "Ow. Be careful."

"Sorry." He looked at me. "What happened?"

"My brakes went out. That truck driver pulled out in front of me from Jenson's farm, and I couldn't stop."

"What do you mean your brakes went out? You slid on ice?" He pulled the handkerchief from his pocket and shook it out before he wiped under my nose.

"No. My dash light came on, saying I had low brake fluid. And right when I looked up, that truck pulled out in front of me. I pushed the brakes and they didn't work. I had to push the e-brake, but I still hit him. The other people were coming the opposite way and they clipped my back end." I wiped the tear off my cheek.

"Your car is brand new, how the hell was it out of fluid? Did you run over something the last time you drove it?" He held a frown.

I shook my head and regretted the movement. "No. I don't know. I just couldn't stop."

"Don't cry. Everyone's okay, and we can get you a new car." He wiped the tear off my cheek.

"I don't care about the car. I'm just in a lot of pain."

"Okay. Do you want me to call Dallas, and I'll just take you to the hospital now?"

"No. The ambulance will be here sooner." I pulled the neck of my sweater to the side to look.

......

"You have shit for luck, girl," Dallas said as he walked over, turning down the police radio on his hip.

"Did you see anything?" Noah asked. I'd already told Dallas what happened, and Noah had asked him to see if he could find anything wrong with my brakes or brake lines, not wanting to leave me.

"It looks like there's some fluid on the road. There's a

small spray line just before the point of impact. I looked at the car and can't see much, but they'll take the car in to be inspected." Dallas looked at me. "When's the last time you drove your car?"

"The day before I was in the hospital."

He nodded, pursed his lips slightly, and looked over toward the excavator they were chaining my car to, to pull it up the bank.

"Please tell me that guy is getting cited. I've told Jenson a hundred times to cut those damn trees back so his guys can see, and people *driving* can see." Noah looked like an angry rock as he glared over at Mr. Jenson and his truck driver.

"Yeah. The chief is tired of us coming out here for this shit, so I imagine."

"Well, I'm calling Gabe, and I'm gonna *make* him."

"It was an accident, Noah." I appreciated that he was upset because I was hurt, but he was extremely angry and I hated it.

Noah continued glaring in Jenson's direction. "And it shouldn't have happened. You would have been fine, if he hadn't pulled out. You said yourself, you would have downshifted to a stop if you could have seen him."

Dallas smiled a little. "God rest his soul then." He looked back at Noah and I. "You guys can head to the hospital now if you want. We got everything we needed, and they're just gonna pull the car up on a wrecker as soon as it gets here."

Noah nodded and looked at me. "You ready?"

I nodded. "Yeah. Can we stop at the house though? I wanna change and get shoes."

"Yeah." Noah turned to Dallas. "Thanks, man. I appreciate it."

"Of course." Dallas shook Noah's hand. "Just don't be pissed when Bridgett comes pounding on your door like a mad woman. Cuffs, a badge, and a gun aren't gonna stop her."

Noah chuckled. "We'll see you guys later then."

"Thanks Dallas," I said as I slowly tried to move myself over so Noah could get in the truck. The medics from the ambulance had already checked me out, and without their recommendation, I already knew I needed to go in.

"You got it. Do us a favor and invest in some bubble wrap."

I rolled my eyes, the only movement that didn't hurt. Noah got in and Dallas walked out to stop the one-way traffic so we could turn the truck and go back toward the house.

When we got to the house, Noah pulled up near my apartment. He was going to carry me up, but my body was so sore that I told him I'd take a cold foot. I went upstairs and he started swiping the snow back where my car had been parked.

"Your car was definitely leaking," Noah said as he walked around the corner to the bathroom. He showed the greasy dirt on his fingers, then put them under the already running faucet. I was cleaning some of the small cuts on my knees from crawling on the glass. They were minor.

I shook my head. "I don't know why the light didn't turn on when I got in the car. I wouldn't have driven it."

"Because there's a reserve, that's gotta drop, then the lines bleed." He gripped the towel hanging on the wall. "Did you want me to grab anything for you before we go?"

"No. Just help me change real quick." I turned the faucet off and tossed the washcloth in the hamper.

Noah went to my room and sat on the bed. I followed and went to my dresser. When I opened the drawer, I frowned because things weren't like I remembered. I hadn't been in my apartment since before the big surgery with Calloway, so maybe I was remembering wrong.

"What's up?"

"Nothing." I pulled out a shirt and opened my pants drawer. My scrub bottoms were on the right side of the drawer and looked like they'd been rifled through.

I let out a breath and turned to face Noah. He carefully pulled my shirt up and got it off my arm without hurting my shoulder.

"Jeez. I hope your collar bone isn't broken." Noah frowned.

"Sh. I don't need any more bad ju-ju out there. I wanna go back to work."

He smiled a little and grabbed the clean shirt. "I want you to go back to work too. You've been grumpy."

"We'll make *you* sit for three weeks and see how grumpy you get."

"No. You'll leave me." The smallest bit of a smile held as he slid my arm into the sleeve of my shirt.

......

My collar bone had a minor hairline fracture. It likely would have been fine if it hadn't been the same spot that Greg had broken. The rest of me was fine, I was just insanely sore, but cleared to work as soon as I could handle it. Dr. Calloway gave a barking laugh when I called him and told him what happened. He thought it was hysterical that I wanted to go back to work so badly, only to be stopped by something else.

It was irritating enough that I contemplated hanging up on him.

Bridgett and Dallas came over later in the evening, which was fine, except for the fact that I didn't want company. It felt like ever since we'd built the new house, there was constantly someone there. It wasn't true, but it bugged me nonetheless. I was used to it being Noah and I all the time, and us working on something. The house was done and anything that was left to do was outside, so it had to wait. The only thing left for me to do was clean. So, when the rest of our friend's showed up, I stayed upstairs for a few minutes, then went downstairs to the basement to go through boxes of my stuff that Brad had shipped from my house. They'd been sitting in the storage room in the basement since the day the shipping container came.

It was amazing how many meaningless things a person could accumulate. There were several boxes I went through and pulled nothing to keep. The words that Bridgett said the day after Thanksgiving just kept ringing in my head. *Life suicide.* All the simple things that'd been important to me before, decorations, certain articles of clothing, jewelry I'd bought for myself as a treat... I might as well have been going through someone else's stuff. Certain sentimental items that'd been given to me I kept, but after twelve boxes, I only had half of a small paper box of things.

"I know you don't feel good, but everyone was here to see *you*," Noah said when he came into the storage room.

I sighed. "I know." I put a large seashell in my box to keep and looked up at him. "Sorry. It was loud and I couldn't take much more of it."

Noah picked up a jewelry box from one of the boxes I'd put aside. "You can find places for your stuff around the house if you want. I don't think your apartment has much room left."

I shook my head. "That's all going. I figured I'd let the girls go through and pick out whatever they want, and donate the rest."

He opened the jewelry box, then looked at me like I was crazy.

I held up my good shoulder. "I don't want any of it. A bunch of those were gifts, or stuff I bought to make myself feel better about my life."

He raised an eyebrow. "There's a lot of money in here." There was a slight humorless laugh to his voice.

"Because I need more?" I pulled out a picture of my dad, Brad, and I to put in my keep box.

"True..." He walked over and dropped a crate behind me. "I forget you have limitless resources." He sat down and picked up the picture I'd put in the box. "How old are you in this?"

"Ten. My dad lost a patient, and he had a rule about not performing any more surgeries after someone died. He'd come home and spend the day with us." I picked through a folder of papers.

"You always make yourself sound like this gangly nerd with glasses. You were cute... And wow, Garrett looks *exactly* like your dad. That's weird."

"I told you." I pulled out a few books and set them with the other stuff I wasn't keeping.

"Okay, now I know there's something up. You're strongly against getting rid of books." He put the picture back.

"They're not mine."

"You're strongly against getting rid of books. What's up with you? You're basically tossing everything you have." He gently started massaging my neck.

"Be careful," I cautioned.

"I am. Why are you throwing your stuff out?"

I moved back by the crate and rested my head against Noah's chest. "I don't know..." I closed my eyes, accepting the relief from the pain in my neck. "I didn't miss anything when I left. Going through it now, I feel the same way. Whatever's in my apartment is more mine than this stuff. Greg dictated so much... Even my house. It was beautiful, but it wasn't the one I wanted. The same goes for pretty much everything else." I directed my hand to a box with clothes piled in it. "All my clothes, they were all things *he* liked. When have you *ever* seen me wear something with print on it?" I pushed the box away with my foot. "It pisses me off... It went so far beyond him hitting me, and if I was ever looking at any part, that was it. I didn't notice that everything I bought was to please *him*... I don't do that here... I bought a robe that has stupid llamas on it because it's fun and I like it."

Noah chuckled. "I don't think I've ever seen you wear it."

"No, but I bought it, and I didn't hide it in the back of my closet from you... This isn't even my house and you let me pick out like half the stuff in it." I pointed at the washer and dryer. "You would have bought a washer that was cheap and worked, not some fancy thing that has cute little chimes and a drawer to wash one or two items. You spent an extra three thousand dollars on the kitchen cabinets because I liked the cream-colored ones with the windows and the lights inside.

And that's not including the counter tops."

Noah leaned me to the side so he could put his lips against the side of my forehead. "I built a house because I wanted you in it... And in the morning, when the sun comes in, and you're standing at the island with your medical magazine and your coffee, you look beautiful in that kitchen. I don't care about the extra three thousand because you look content and happy." He kissed my cheek. "And you like houses with lots of windows and glass doors," he smiled against my forehead, "and look what happened."

"Ya lost your damn mind over a girl. Getting my name tattooed on your arm would have been cheaper."

He chuckled lightly. "Maybe."

I reached my hand up to his arm, placed around the front of my shoulders. "I love this house."

"Go through this stuff another day. Go soak in some epsom salt before you go to bed. It'll help."

"Will you take this box for me? I wanna bring it down to the apartment in the morning." I put my hand on the half-full box.

"Or you could just find a place in *this* house, the house that I built for *you*."

I sighed and tipped my head back as much as I could without severe pain to look at Noah. "This conversation again?"

"Why not?" He brushed the back of his fingers over my cheek. "You've pretty much been living up here. Wouldn't it be nice to not have to freeze your ass off just to go change your clothes?"

I looked in front of me. "I don't know... I'm attached to my apartment."

"It's not going anywhere. And if it's a matter of having your own space, you have a whole spread down here."

"Can we wait on it? I don't know why the thought makes me squirm, but it does. I need my space just a little longer." I moved my hand over his, hoping he'd understand and not be hurt, but not brave enough to look at him.

"I'm not asking to be a jerk, but do you feel like the wedding is coming too soon?"

I tipped my head back to look at him, not knowing how he really meant that question, but his face was honest and slightly concerned.

"I'd be ready to marry you tomorrow, but that doesn't mean *you're* there yet." His eyebrows raised with a sympathetic expression.

I felt a little guilty and taken aback. "No. That's not what I meant *at all*. I wouldn't have said yes if I wasn't ready or had cold feet. I just..." How did I say it without sounding like a jerk? "I can't wait to be married. Honestly. But this is the only time I've had to be in a place by myself. I went from having roommates to buying a house I didn't really want, and Greg just moving in without there even being so much as a conversation about it. And I know it's you and me, and not me and him. I'm not trying to compare. There's just something nice about you coming down to my apartment and watching a movie with me, or me running up here to give you a quick kiss before I go to work. I want to be married after we get married, not right now, because then what's the point or the special part about getting married? I know you don't like how I squeeze the toothpaste tube instead of rolling it. I want five more months of squeezing the toothpaste."

He smiled. "You're worried about toothpaste?"

"No. I'm worried that's all you heard in that conversation."

He laughed. "No. I heard you, and I get it." He rubbed my arm. "As long as we don't end up like Garrett and Clara, I can live with five months."

I smirked. "Yeah, I'm not *that* neurotic."

Noah wrapped his arms around my ribs and stood up, bringing me with him. "Bedtime. I'm tired and you need to take your pills."

"I'm gonna need an anti-gravity chamber to sleep," I sighed.

"Too bad. You have a bunch of pillows and a dog. Come on, Mutt. Go to bed."

Gif got up from behind the stack of boxes I hadn't gone through, darting out of the room, and I laughed. "I didn't even know he was down here."

Noah bent down and grabbed the box. "Nobody else exists as long as you're around."

"Jealous?" I smiled at Noah.

"Nope. He's a hairy pain in the ass, and he's not under my feet anymore."

I rolled my eyes and walked out of the room. "You love that dog."

"Didn't say I didn't." Noah shut the light off.

Chapter 19

A Month And A Half Later

Work. I loved my job; I loved working so many hours that the drive home was tedious. It meant I had a good day of patients needing things, or surgeries that went long. My days at work were certainly different with the new position, but I liked it. Calloway was overly happy having someone he deemed competent make things run more smoothly. He was also happy his involvement with the "monkeys" was lessened. Thankfully, the interns and other residents liked me, so they were all extremely cooperative with the changes.

"Holly?" Noah called after letting himself into the apartment.

"In my room," I called back as I pulled on a pair of pajama bottoms. My brain was out of it, so I had to look around for where I'd put my shirt and found it on the end of the bed.

"Are you just getting home?"

"Yeah. Sorry, I was gonna text you, but I didn't have a chance." I pulled my shirt on, then a hoodie. "It was alarm after alarm with my patient; and on the way home Brad called me and I didn't want to text and drive." I was supposed to be home around the time Noah left for work, but it was three in the afternoon.

"That's okay. I was just coming up to wake you. Mom and Dad are in town and wanna spend the night."

I stepped forward to hug him. "I'd come up for a few hours, but it was a *really* long day, and I'm dying right now."

"That's fine. Did your patient pull through?"

"No." I held onto him and was grateful he was standing there.

"I'm sorry... Are you okay?" He rubbed my back.

"Yeah." I let go of him, walked to the bed, and got in. Gif jumped up and dropped in a tight ball in his rightful spot. "It was probably the worst one I've ever had though. She was twenty-seven, with a three-year-old daughter and a husband. It was hard enough telling *him*, then he asked to see her, so I took him in the room..." I shook my head as the lump in my throat swelled again. "That poor little girl knew the second she saw her mom. She reached out her hand and just started wailing..."

Noah sat down beside me and took my hand. "I'm sorry, Sweetheart... Can I do anything for you?"

I shook my head, pulling back the corner of my mouth. "No. I just need to sleep it off."

"Okay... Did you want me to come back down and wake you up, or did you want to sleep through?"

"Come get me up around eight or so, but if I'm dead to the world, just leave me."

"Okay." He leaned forward, giving me a quick kiss. I pulled him back by the shirt for a better one. He put his hand on my side and butterflies started shooting around kamikaze-style in my stomach. Just as I started to slide down, there was a friendly double honk from outside.

I scrunched my nose at Noah as he pulled away.

"Why are *you* shriveling your nose? You have an excuse to not deal with them." He kissed my lips again.

"Because they ruined the only thing I was looking forward to more than sleep."

Noah smiled. "I'll be back later, and I'll make up for it."

I gave him a small smile. "Okay. Tell them I said hi."

He raised an eyebrow. "I'll tell them you're dead asleep, or my dad's gonna walk down here and harass you."

"Good idea."

"Goodnight." He kissed me one more time, then sat up and pulled the blankets over me. "Love you."

"I love you too." I rolled over, facing Gif. "Come here, you. I need somebody to snuggle me."

Gif got up, moved five inches, and plopped down against the front of me, letting out a huff as he put his head on my pillow. I hugged him and kissed the top of his soft head.

......

Gif barked loudly.

"No. Shut up," I groaned as I rolled over, covering my head with a pillow.

He dug at the covers on my back, then my back.

"Ow! What the hell, dog!?" I rolled over, opening my eyes, and they widened at the thick smoke hanging over my head. "Shit!" I flipped the blankets back and covered my face with the sleeve of my hoodie over my hand. The second I put my feet down, the floor was hot. Not hot enough to burn me, but enough to be concerning. Smoke billowed up from the bottom of my bedroom door. I stepped into my Uggs, staying bent below the smoke.

Gif gave a whining bark from my bed.

"I know, buddy. Stay there." I went to the door and felt it. It was hotter than the floor, and not a chance I was willing to take.

"HOLLY!" Noah's voice was stifled from outside.

I went to the window and pulled hard to get it open. They were old and a pain in the ass to slide up.

"Holly! Hurry up and get out!" Noah yelled.

"Hang on. I have to get, Gif," I yelled back and turned.

Flames licked at the bottom of the bedroom door and were doing their damndest to climb up.

"Okay. Think." I looked at Gif and my bed. Immediately, I yanked at the bedsheet. "Lay down buddy."

Gif whined, but listened.

"I know. I'm getting you out." I tied the bedsheet around him. He'd be easier for Noah to catch if he wasn't flailing in a free fall.

"HOLLY!" Noah yelled.

"Hold on!" I picked Gif up and turned to the window. "Here. Catch him."

"Drop him. Come on."

"Sorry, Gif," I said before I let go. The poor thing panicked and let out a fearful cry, but Noah caught him.

Noah put Gif down, but didn't untie him. "Okay. Your turn. Come on."

"Hold on." I looked back at the door. The flames weren't traveling that far, so I grabbed my purse, keys, hospital badges, and the box with my certificates in it. "Look out," I called down before I dropped the purse and box.

"Damn, it! Just get out of there!" Noah yelled angrily.

"I am!" I turned myself to feed my legs through the window first, until I was hanging from the windowsill by my hands.

"Let go. I've got you."

I released my grip and dropped down. Noah caught me around the waist, then let me down to my feet. I grabbed my purse and the box before I backed away.

"Honey, are you okay?" Linna jogged to me.

"Yeah." I looked at the blaze, completely stunned at how badly it was burning. It was amazing I hadn't died of inhalation already.

"Come on. Get back." Noah pulled on Linna and I. "I'm gonna move your car, before you need *another* one. Keep Gif away."

I looked down and Gif was beside me, freed from the sheet. "Good boy. Come on."

Linna and I walked over toward where the old house used to be. There was a difference between leaving your stuff behind and watching it burn.

"My gosh..." Linna whispered.

"Are you alright, Sweet-pea?" Thomas walked up with a blanket from the back of Noah's couch.

I nodded and took the blanket. "Yeah. Thank you."

"Good thing I looked out the window." He put a hand on Linna's shoulder as he watched the flames. They were in my bedroom now, and smoke poured out the open window.

Gif leaned against my leg, sitting beside me, and let out a choking cough.

I crouched down and rubbed his side. "Poor boy." If he hadn't been there to wake me up, I probably wouldn't have. The cloud of smoke had only been a foot or so above my head.

There was a crash from the apartment and more smoke and flames rose from the open window. I didn't want to watch, but it was like a train wreck, I couldn't look away. Noah came back over and I stood up, looking at him.

"Did you have a candle burning or something?" He looked me up and down.

I shook my head. "I don't have any I don't use for decoration." I had no reason for never burning candles, I just didn't.

"Did you leave anything on?"

I shook my head again. "No. Nothing."

He looked at the blaze and scratched the back of his head. "I cleaned the chimney on the wood stove last month. That's about the only other thing I can think of."

"I didn't start a fire in the stove. It wasn't that cold when I came home." Mucus caught in my throat and I started coughing.

Noah pulled me over in front of him and rubbed my back. "Did you breathe in a lot of smoke?"

Of course I'd breathed in some, but probably not enough to be damaging, so I shook my head.

"Go drive my parents back up to the house. There's no sense in everyone standing out here. The fire department's on their way." He kissed the top of my head and hugged me a little tighter. "The world's got it out for you. I'm glad you're okay."

I nodded, feeling completely exhausted.

"Come on, Sweetie. Let's go get warm." Linna put a

hand on my back.

I pulled the blanket tighter. "Come on, Gif."

We walked to the car and I made Gif wait for me to get in before I let him get up on my lap. He knew he wasn't allowed in my car otherwise.

"That dog sure loves you." Thomas shut his door.

"He's what woke me up." I pushed the button to start my car and drove up the hill to the house.

When we went inside, I could smell the smoke on my clothes, so I went upstairs, and rinsed off in the shower with Gif. He smelled worse than I did. After I got him semi-dry and myself dressed, I went back downstairs. There were three fire trucks below, and my apartment was still glowing with flames in the dusk. It was gone... all my things, the hours of labor to make my apartment a home, and the security I'd felt there.

"Can I heat you up some dinner, Sweetie?" Linna asked setting a cup of tea in front of Thomas.

I shook my head. "No. I'm gonna go down with Noah."

"You should stay up here and take it easy. There's nothing to do down there, and Noah said you had a long and hard day at work." Linna looked at me gently.

I looked out the front windows. She was probably right. If I walked outside, I'd probably be struck by a lightning bolt.

"Come on. Sit down with us. I'll heat you up some food."

I sighed a little and sat down next to Thomas. "What have you been working on lately?"

"Oh, I'm getting some of my work published, I suppose."

I smiled. "Your constellation symphonies?"

"Those would be the ones."

"That's great."

"And that's not all. The Minnesota Orchestra is going to play them every night for a week next month."

I raised my eyebrows and smiled. "I hope you're taking me."

Thomas held a gentle smile with little wrinkles in the corners of his eyes, and patted my hand. "I wouldn't let you miss it."

"That's really incredible. Make sure to give me the dates so I can make sure I'm off."

......

"Holly." Noah's voice was quiet as he rubbed my arm.

I opened my eyes tiredly, and only then realized I'd fallen asleep. I'd sat on the couch with Thomas while he played his cello, and apparently knocked right out.

"Sorry." I pushed myself back to sit. "I'm up."

"No. I was just waking you to get you to come to bed."

I looked out the window of the living room and it was dark outside. There was no fire and no lights from fire trucks or police cars.

"What time is it?" I gathered my hair back.

"It's after ten."

I rubbed my face. "Did everyone just leave?"

"Yeah. I just came in."

I shook my head, still in disbelief of the fire. "Do they know what started it yet?"

"Fire Marshall said it started on the back wall of my shop, but there's nothing to show what really started it. Another investigator is gonna come out either tomorrow or Monday and take a look, because he said it's like a flame was just held against the wall until it caught on."

I frowned. "That's weird... You pretty much had nothing down there. We moved everything out to the other shop already."

He nodded. "I know..."

"Do you think it was that kid, Brandon, or whatever his name is? The one that rolled your truck?"

Noah shook his head. "Brenton. I really don't know..." He scratched the back of his head, looking tired and stressed. "I suppose I can talk to his parents tomorrow, see if he was home or not, but there's not a lot I can do."

Brenton was an angry kid who cared about nothing and no one. He was only sixteen and had the criminal record of an LA gang member. Drugs, vandalism, you name it.

"I'm sorry if you thought I was blaming or attacking you earlier." He rubbed my arm.

I shook my head. "What are you talking about?"

"I asked if you had a candle lit or left your curling iron on, and you looked at me like I kicked you."

I shook my head again. "No. I was honestly just disoriented. Gif had a hell of a time waking me up. He scratched the crap out of my back, and I rolled over, saw the smoke and shot straight up. I only got my shoes on and touched the door before you yelled at me from outside."

He sighed and rubbed his eyes with his thumb and middle finger. "Your kitchen was too thick with flames for me to get in. I thought I was already too late."

"I'm still here." I took his other hand and squeezed it lightly.

He pulled on my hand to make me sit up. "You better be."

I sat forward and let him pull me into a hug.

"Are you okay? I know how much you loved your apartment." He kissed the side of my forehead.

"It's real, but it hasn't sunk in yet."

"It will tomorrow when you see the place caved in."

I shook my head. "Don't make me think about it. I'm tired enough that I'll start bawling like a three-year-old."

He patted my hip. "Let's go to bed. I'm sure you're gonna break a credit card and my patience tomorrow."

I laughed. "That's what you're worried about now?" I smiled at him.

Finally, he smiled back. "No. I'm thinking I made a promise earlier, and it's time to make good." He picked me up off the couch and kissed me.

I laughed again. "Put me down."

He kissed me quickly and let my feet down. "Go call your dog. I'm gonna pull your car in the garage."

I rolled my eyes. "He's not *my* dog."

"He's not *mine* anymore. My dog wouldn't sleep on the bed."

"He likes to snuggle and he has an adorable face." I opened one of the glass doors in the dining room. "Gif! Bedtime."

I looked around the back deck and out at the tree line. It wasn't a usual sensation, but I felt like I was being watched. I'd felt that way for a while. Ever since Greg had showed up at Thanksgiving, I felt like there was a target on my back, or like I was waiting for the other shoe to drop. The seemingly "random" disasters that kept happening didn't help. None of the things that happened were things that Greg would do. The guys who'd looked at my car's brake line said it looked like it'd just been nicked, not cut. There was nothing to suggest someone tampered with my car. The restaurant was still a mystery, and I felt like nothing was going to come of the fire investigation.

••••••

The next morning, the inspector said he found cigarette butts on the dirt floor, but they were too burnt up to do anything with and not the cause. Noah called Brenton's parents, because he smoked, but he couldn't have done it because he was in town getting busted for public drinking an hour before the fire. There was also the possibility that the cigarette butts were there from Chris when he was hiding his new snowmobile from Carrie, so we still had no explanation.

After the investigator left, Noah and I went to Rochester. I got new clothes, new scrubs—and took them in to be monogrammed—new shoes, and a few other necessities. There was a difference between shopping for an item or two because you wanted to and replacing an entire wardrobe. It was irritating and I wanted it over with more than Noah.

Chapter 20

"Tell me I can get out of here," Cindy, one of my patients, said with a worried, hopeful, and tired look.

I smiled and handed her a clipboard. "I brought you the discharge papers myself."

She dropped her head back, looking up. "Thank the lord. I love ya, but I can't take it anymore. I wanna go home and love on my grandbabies."

"As long as you're not running around or trying to keep up with them, and they're not sick, love away. I *do* want to see you again in a week and we'll decide from there. You *have* to make sure you keep up with your physical therapy. Unfortunately, playing with the grandkids isn't good enough." I looked at Cindy's husband Mike. "Make sure she goes."

"I'll dangle an ice cream cone in front of her," he teased with a laugh.

I smiled. "Do you guys have any questions for me before

you go?"

"No!" Cindy held up a finger to her husband. "So help me god, you are not slowing up the process of me getting out of here."

I laughed. "You can always call me from home if you need something later."

Cindy looked at me fondly. "Thank you so much. Really."

I smiled. "It's what I do. You're welcome."

She reached out her hand to me with a teary-eyed smile and I took it. "No one believed me. Only you."

I pulled back the corner of my mouth. "My dad used to tell me, 'if someone tells you they don't feel good, believe them. There *is* a reason.' He's never been wrong."

"Smart guy." She squeezed my hand and let go.

I nodded. "Incredibly. I'll see you guys in a week. Enjoy your walks again."

"I will," she smiled.

I turned around and let out a breath of relief and satisfaction. Cindy had been going to different doctors for five years, telling them her left leg hurt. It would become so severe she couldn't walk some days. She'd had many tests and everything came back fine. She went to a nerve specialist and they told her everything was normal. A few doctors had even labeled her as a hypochondriac. Calloway thought so too. He'd talked to me about Cindy right after the consultation, and I asked for her case. If there was something there, I'd find it, and I did. It was a very small linear tumor, easily missed, but I didn't miss it. Dr. Calloway didn't even notice when he first looked at the scans. It was extremely difficult to remove, but I did it with only supervision from Calloway.

Garrett smiled at me as I approached the front desk. "You look like you're having a good day."

"I am. I just got to send a proud grandma back to her grandkids." I gave him a hug from the side as I handed the nurse the clipboard and my tablet.

"Are you ready for lunch, or do you need a few more minutes?"

"Nope. I'm all set, and my stuff is out in the car." I dropped my arm.

"Dr. Bennett?" one of the other nurses said from the other side of the counter.

I smiled at her and glanced at the person standing at the counter out of normal instinct. My smile fell and my immediate response was to grab onto Garrett's arm. Greg gave the nurse one of his charming smiles, thanking her.

Garrett rubbed my hand, which was squeezing his forearm. I let go, realizing that my grip was probably too tight. I also didn't need to make myself look like a coward. Greg was walking around the counter and I didn't want him to see any sign of weakness.

"What are you doing here?"

"I need to talk to you. Just a few minutes." He glanced at Garrett, keeping a light appearance.

"No." My answer was clear and direct.

"Greg, this is Holly's place of work. This isn't appropriate." Garrett maintained an even tone.

"I thought it'd be better than me showing up at the house. I really need to talk to you. Brad's upset with me and I need your help." Greg continued to look and only speak to me.

"Whatever it is, I'm not helping you. I don't want any

further contact with you, direct or indirect. You are not welcome at my house, or this hospital unless you have a medical emergency. You need to leave and don't contact me again. I *will* file a restraining order against you." I knew exactly what Greg was trying to pull and it wasn't going to work. If Brad couldn't understand, then he didn't belong in my life either. I had the right to be free of Greg.

"Is that really how you want to play this right now?" His eyes flashed with anger, and the top corners of his lips turned in.

I looked to my right. "Ann, will you please call security?"

"Of course." She gave me a kind look, picked up the phone and glanced at Greg before she dialed.

"Goddammit, Holly. Are you kidding? I just wanna talk to you. We're in a public place. What am I gonna do?" Greg looked at me incredulously. "I came because Brad's really upset. He just took off. No one has seen or heard from him."

"How sad for you, but it sounds like he got some sense." I pointed back to the security guard's office as Tony, the guard, came out. "This is your last chance to leave."

Greg looked back at me. "You're not getting it, Holl. Brad's not right. I think he's gonna hurt himself. Please, you have to hear me out. Neither of us wants to lose him."

"Dr. B, what's up?" Tony looked at me with raised eyebrows.

"Mr. Bradshaw needs to be escorted off the grounds. I asked him to leave, and here we stand." I crossed my arms, feeling like my heart pounding was visible from the outside.

"You're incredible. He's your brother. You have to do something." Greg looked at me with anger and disbelief.

"Let's take a walk, Mr. Bradshaw. Where're you

parked?" Tony's voice was chipper but forceful.

"Holly." Greg's was quiet and demanding.

"She doesn't wanna talk, man. Let's go." Tony pushed against Greg's arm.

Greg jerked his arm forward and walked to the elevators.

"You need to make sure he leaves the premises. He's a legitimate threat to my daughter," Garrett said to Tony when he didn't follow Greg.

Tony looked at me and I nodded. "Please."

He walked over toward the elevator and Greg was instantly pissed that he was being followed. I swallowed hard and remembered that I needed to move and not stand there frozen.

I looked at Ann and Jen, the two nurses. "If either of you see that man again, or he comes asking for me, please call security and have them call the cops."

They both nodded.

A loud chortle sounded in the open room. I rolled my eyes so hard it hurt.

"Look at you two. The little family duo."

I turned to see Dr. Calloway reaching out to shake Garrett's hand.

"You have an incredibly big mouth. Can you try to contain it?" I snapped at Calloway.

He laughed again. "Oh, who cares. He's your uncle and we both helped you get matched here." He popped Garrett in the arm. "I'm on my way to the OR or I'd chat." Calloway looked at me again and started down the hall.

Garrett sighed. "How did Fran get along with him?"

"Million dollar question." I shook my head. My cheeks

were burning, my stomach was on the verge, and my spine felt like it had an electrical pulse to match a city transformer.

"Let's go." Garrett put a hand on my shoulder.

I nodded and walked with him to the elevator. I pulled my phone out to text Noah and warn him that Greg had showed up. He was home because he was doing payroll for his crew. I didn't know that Greg wouldn't drive straight out there and wait for me to come home, so I told him to text Dallas too.

"Do you think there might be any validity about Brad?" Garrett asked as we walked onto the elevator.

"I don't know. I'm gonna check." I opened my contacts and clicked on the house number for my dad's house. If Brad had gone anywhere, that would have been the place. Our dad may not have been there, but it was still home.

"Hola?" Lupita answered cheerfully.

"Hola, Lupita. ¿Está Brad en casa?"

"Holly! Oh, I miss you! Si. You wanna talk to him?"

I smiled a little. "I miss you too. No. ¿Él está bien? Greg dijo que Brad podría estar en problemas."

"No. I think maybe he's sad when he come here, but I cook for him, and he's better now."

"Okay. Keep an eye on him and call me if you think something's wrong, okay?" I rubbed at my forehead, walking off the elevator with Garrett.

"He's fine. I take care of him, Baby. Yesterday, I buy tickets for your wedding. Martin coming with me."

I smiled a little more. "I know. Martin texted me. I'm excited for you to come. I have to go though. I'll talk to you later. Te amo."

"Te amo, mi bebé."

I ended the call and put my phone back in my pocket. "Brad's okay."

"Good. I didn't know you spoke Spanish."

I nodded. "Lupita taught me, then I took French, German, and Sign Language in elementary, middle school, and high school, and Latin in college."

"I don't know if I'm ashamed or proud," he chuckled.

"I didn't have a choice with French and German. Dad was insistent. Latin was necessary, and Sign Language was practical."

"I'd have to agree. Did you text Noah to warn him about Greg?"

"Yeah. He's putting the fortress on lockdown and calling in reinforcements." I felt entirely too awkward that I had to address what I didn't want to. Garrett and I didn't want other employees of the hospital knowing we were related. "I'm sorry Calloway has a big mouth." I swiped my key card to open the door to the employee parking garage. "You helped me get matched here?"

"I did. Fran was none too shy about your abilities."

"And you wanted me here where you could keep an eye on me?" I looked at him and smiled a little.

He chuckled quietly. "Even if you weren't talking to me, I wanted to know you were alright."

"Did I ever apologize for my initial reaction? If not, I'm sorry. Things weren't great right at that moment, and I could've been kinder." I looked at him as we approached my car.

"You didn't react as badly as you think you did, and it was much better than I expected. Part of me wondered if Fran had maybe told you when you were older, so I was expecting you to tell me to get lost the moment you opened the door."

"I still could have been kinder." I went to the door and opened it so the car would unlock, then bent down to look under the car to make sure it was clear before I got in. The employee garage required a hospital badge, but I was still paranoid.

Chapter 21

Two Days Before The Wedding

The doorbell chimed and Gif got up to run for the door.

"Are you getting that?" Noah called from his office.

"I can but the door hates me and I'm trying to finish this article." I was submitting a medical piece on a case Dr. Calloway and I had.

Noah and I had both taken the day off before the wedding hoopla started tomorrow. We'd have people in and out of the house to move stuff to Lars' house and the set up would begin. My article was the only thing standing in the way of me being a lazy sack of crap on the couch.

"Thank you," I said sweetly when I heard Noah come out of his office.

"Mm-hm."

I continued to read through what I'd already written, checking for clarity of language and potential mistakes.

"You better be alone, or I have the right to shoot you both for being on my property."

I looked behind me with a shocked frown at Noah's words and demeanor.

"No. I'm alone. I promise." Brad's voice was quiet like he normally was, but he didn't sound quite right. Noah's body was blocking me from being able to see him.

Noah kept his hand against the doorway and didn't open the door as he looked back at me. I got off the chair and nodded. If Greg wasn't with Brad, I was willing to talk to him. We'd had some words a few weeks back because I didn't want Greg in my life, and I especially didn't want him at my wedding. I'd also told Brad I thought Greg's brain tumor thing was faked. Brad flew off the handle at me and we hadn't spoken since, which was why I didn't want to talk to him when Lupita offered.

Noah looked at Brad and pushed the door open. "If you start shit, I'll kick your ass straight out the door and you won't be welcome back." He turned away and started walking toward me, looking like an angry bear.

I stopped, watching Noah walk toward me, because maybe I shouldn't have said it was okay to let Brad in. He'd been fired up about Greg showing up at the hospital, and there were now guns out of the safe and strategically hidden around the house.

Noah's angry expression softened when he got to me, and he kissed my forehead. "I'll be in my office with the door open."

I nodded. "We'll be okay."

He rubbed my cheek with his thumb and turned down the hallway. I looked at Brad. He was in a t-shirt, jeans, and sneakers looking drained and sorry.

"Does Greg know you're here?" I asked as I slowly started forward again.

Brad swallowed, then shook his head. He looked like he was about to cry.

I nodded toward the living room. "Come sit down." I took the step down, looking back to make sure he'd follow me. His entire appearance was worrying me.

Brad stepped out of his shoes and went to the big chair next to the end of the couch where I sat. He sat forward with his elbows on his thighs and stared at his hands as he fidgeted.

"Are you okay?" I asked quietly after he remained silent.

He pressed his lips together for a second before he shook his head. "Not really. No..."

I waited. He and I were the same, we had to think before we spoke when we were too upset, or things wouldn't come out right.

"You were right..." He sniffed and opened the clasp on his watch, pulling it off to look at the engraving on the inside. "There was no tumor... He faked the whole thing. I lied to you on Thanksgiving. I made it sound like I was there when he was in the hospital, and I wasn't. He *told* me he was. I believed him, and I wanted *you* to believe him, so I lied. He's been my best friend for so long, and he knew about me being—" He reached up and pinched at his eyes, shaking his head.

"I messed up bad, Holl." The corners of his mouth pulled down for a half second before he took in a deep breath and looked at me. "We weren't together when you were still dating." He shook his head. "But I knew he was cheating on you. I didn't want to hurt you, but I was afraid he'd out me

323

to everyone if I told you what he was doing." Tears hung in Brad's eyes, and they were bloodshot. His voice had only been above a whisper, which for him meant he was about as devastated as he could be.

I sat there, just breathing. Honestly, I didn't know what I felt. If I'd cared about Greg at all, I would have been furious and hurt, but I didn't, so I wasn't. I truly despised him as a person, so it was hard to feel like anything had ever been taken. On the other hand, my own brother had betrayed me and lied for Greg.

"Please say something. Call me an asshole—something."

I reached back and rubbed at the back of my neck. "Um... I don't really know what to say." I looked at him. "I'm processing."

Brad shook his head. "I know it doesn't mean shit, but I'm sorry... You didn't deserve it, and I don't know what to do, and I didn't know he was hurting you... I..." He took in a fast breath and let it out just as fast. "I'm sorry."

I nodded, but it was only to give him some kind of acknowledgement. I still didn't know what I felt.

He put his head down to the butt of his hand and closed his eyes. "When you called me a few weeks ago, Greg was in my office..." His voice was less wavering. "Nothing I said was what I wanted to say. He was there, I already knew the tumor was bullshit, but I was still trying to figure out what to do. I fought with you on purpose to buy me more time without raising suspicion. If I agreed with anything you said, or told you I understood, he would have started in on me. I needed time, and I was an asshole for that too."

"I understand at least that much... I don't have enough

fingers and toes to count how many times I had to lie to you or say something opposite to you because he was nearby."

"You shouldn't have. I shouldn't have either... I should've walked out of my office, not answered the phone and called you later. I had options and I picked the stupidest one."

"I understand that too."

He shook his head. "I still don't know what to do. I've been hiding out at Dad's. Every time he calls or shows up, Lupita and everyone else just lies and tells him I'm not there and they haven't seen me. I haven't left the house because I don't know if he's waiting down the street to corner me... I sat on the floor of Dad's Bentley while Martin drove me to the airport, and I took a private jet here just to double up."

If I hadn't been worried about Brad finding me, I would have done the same thing.

"How'd you find out he lied about the tumor?" I looked over at the hallway, Noah was coming out of his office and going to the fridge.

"Bethany... I told her I was trying to help you. I'm not even supposed to tell you, but I highly doubt you're gonna run and turn her in... Anyway, I talked to his aunt—the one that hates him—and she said that scar is from when he had to have a plate put in his head after his dad beat him. He's had it since he was nine...

"And I can't prove it, but I think he's why you ended up in the hospital when we were here last. He brought a bottle of wine when we came, and I didn't think anything of it. Anyway," he shook his head, "when we went back to the hotel after seeing you in the hospital, I checked his suitcase the second he went to take a shower, and there was one there. Unopened, not the same one you like, but similar in label and color. I think he replaced it, and I think he poisoned you. He doesn't like dessert wines... He went up to the room for a minute while Garrett and I got a table, then when you went to the bathroom, he went to the bar to order the drinks, *he* paid the bill... I tried to find the receipt, and I couldn't. I assume he left it at the table so there wouldn't be a chance of anyone finding it if they suspected him of something... I think he spliced your brakes before we left last time too... He went for a jog before I got up, and he was gone over an hour and a half from the point I woke up... With your apartment burning down, that could've been him too. He was on a business trip. He has receipts, but I've seen him forge papers before. I can't prove anything though."

My lip was sore from chewing on it while I listened. "I don't know what reason he'd have. He's more of an in the moment rage kind of person, not a methodical killer type."

Brad shook his head and looked at me. "No. You're wrong. He's obsessed with you. I didn't even know about your big surgery, that was him. He never took your pictures out of his office. They're still there. I didn't think about it until I overheard a couple of secretaries talking in the break room. There's a new girl you haven't met, Erica, she's going to school for psychology, and she made the comment that Greg had signs of being a sociopath. Deb, who you know, said it was creepy that he still had your pictures all over his office and continued to tell clients you were his fiancé. This, of course, being right after he convinced me that we should fly out here for your big surgery." He let out a huff. "I think he's dangerous, and I honestly don't know what to do about it. Calling the cops does nothing without proof."

"That's why I didn't want him knowing where I was." I turned my ring on my finger, trying to think of what I should do, if anything.

"I know that *now*. I'm sorry..."

"Do you think anything would stick if I made a report against him?" I looked at Brad.

He looked at me again, with his chin resting on his hand as he shook his head. "No... It'd be your word against his, and the second he points out your faked car accident, it's over... I wouldn't even be able to argue it in court without getting you in trouble because you committed fraud. You would've had to call the cops when something actually happened."

"I never used insurance to fix the car or made a police report, I can't actually be charged with fraud. What about *you* though? He could go after you for that forgery."

He shook his head again. "I'm not worried about it. Even if he tried to turn me in, I've got so much shit on him that I could plea my way out of it. I'd get a slap on the wrist and be disbarred." He frowned instantly. "Is that why you didn't say anything?"

I nodded.

He let out a huff and shook his head. "Shit, Holl."

"Well, I didn't know. He's a frickin crazy person and I didn't know *what* he'd do to you if I said anything or left. He constantly threatened you, and I didn't want you to go to jail." My voice broke.

Brad leaned over and took my hand. "I didn't mean it like that. Don't cry."

I shoved my other hand over my cheek to get rid of the traitor tear. "I'll cry if I feel like it. I'm sick of this shit. I *left*. I moved halfway across the country to be done with this shit, and I'm sick of dealing with it."

Brad squeezed my hand. "I'll find a way out, Holl... I owe you more than that, but... I'll figure something out." He let go of my hand and grabbed the box of tissues on the small table that sat between the couch and chair. "I'm staying at a motel in town until after your wedding. I'm worried he's gonna try to show up, and I wanna be here to handle it if he does. I never let him see the invite, but that doesn't mean shit with him."

"No. Stay here." I dabbed the tissue under my eye and checked it for makeup.

"It's okay. I'm pretty sure Noah hates my guts, and I don't blame him. I'm fine in town... I just needed to come here, own up to my shit, and tell you I'm sorry."

"He doesn't hate you, he's mad about Greg. I'll talk to him. As long as he knows you're not here to start anything, it's fine." I stood up from the couch and put the tissue box back. "I'm gonna go see if he's planning something for dinner, if not, we need Chinese."

"No, I'm gonna go. I've been up since three this morning." Brad stood up.

"I heard that you're gonna go get your stuff from the motel and take a room downstairs. I also heard that I own your ass for the rest of your life because you're a huge asshole and you owe me for not throat punching you. You're *also* going to serve your debt as my best man, or I'm gonna grab a knife and cut your balls off, hang them to dry, and make you a necklace with them."

Brad let out a sigh and pulled me forward by the shoulder. "I got it. I'm your bitch." He hugged me and put his face down on my shoulder.

"You're my bitch, and you're an asshole…" I pulled up the shoulder of his shirt and wiped another tear. "And my snot rag."

"Gross."

"You're a dirtbag." My voice broke.

"I know…"

Too many thoughts and emotions hit me at once, and I just started crying. Brad was the only person I'd wanted to go crying to when something happened with Greg, so it was coming out now that I finally could. He crushed me tightly, moving his chin to my shoulder, and tipped his head against mine. Normally, he was completely repulsed by tears. He would have rather someone spit on him than cry on his shoulder, but he stood there, made no crappy remarks, and took it. As soon as I let go of him, though, it was over. He was reaching for the tissues, pulling several out of the box, then pressing them against both my cheeks with both hands.

I laughed. "Stop. I'm done." I reached up to take over my own tissue control.

Brad shook his hands out and shivered with repulsion. He'd always done it, even as a kid.

"Go get your stuff from the motel, I'm gonna talk to Noah and figure out our food situation."

"Please don't make me stay here," he pleaded in a fast whisper, folding his hands. "I agree to be your bitch and be in your wedding, but he's huge and wants to crush me like a bug. I'm a scumbag, but I want to live." He put his folded hands to my shoulder and his head to his hands. "Please, please, please. I love you, and you love me enough to just have a tiny bit of mercy."

I laughed a little. "You're such a baby."

"Yes. A scum-sucking baby. Asshole. Dirtbag. Please don't make me stay here."

"Fine. I still have to go talk to Noah and convince him that Chinese food is happening. Go get Chinese food."

"Thank you." Brad let out a breath of relief and stood up straight. "The usual?"

I nodded. "Get some cashew chicken for Noah."

Brad's nose scrunched, then he shook his head as he pretended like he was tasting something awful.

"I know." I laughed quietly.

"Gross." Brad put his hands in his pockets and looked toward the hallway for just a second.

"Go. I'm hungry."

He looked at me. "Are we at least sort of okay?"

I held up my shoulders. "I reserve the right to bitch or vent later, otherwise I'm glad you're here and away from him."

Brad put a hand on top of my head, then the other, and pulled my face into his arm and shoulder, wrapping his arm around my head. "Love you, Butch. I'm really sorry."

"Air." I poked between his ribs.

Brad kissed my head, mussed my hair, and let go of me.

I started pushing him toward the door. "Go. Food. Please. Before I start to feel sick from not eating." My stomach had been off lately, but I hadn't been eating regularly.

"I can handle puke, as long as you don't cry on me again."

"I reserve the right to that too."

"That's not fair. That actually makes me gag." He stepped into his shoes.

"Shush. Food."

"I'm going." He pulled the backs of his shoes up, one at a time.

"Call me if you can't find it."

"Yeah." He opened the door.

"Hey, wait," I said quickly before he walked out. "Did Greg... Did he hit you?"

Brad bit the inside of his cheek for a second before shaking his head. "No... I think he controlled it because he wanted me to believe the narrative he was creating." He shrugged his shoulders. "That, or he knew I'd hit him back. I don't know."

"Okay. Text me when you're on your way back."

He nodded and went out the door.

I took in a breath and let it out. It didn't feel entirely right to just let go of the fact that Brad had done something really shitty, but I knew he was sorry. He also didn't have a long list of transgressions like Greg. Brad had always been a good brother and my best friend.

I walked into Noah's office and he was sitting behind his desk on his computer. He was focused on what he was doing, but opened an arm to me when I walked around to him.

"Two seconds." He put a hand on my back as I straddled his lap and sat down.

"One one-thousand, two one-thousand." I wrapped my arms around him and kissed the side of his neck.

"I'm just finishing up."

"We've been ignoring each other all day, and we were supposed to be lazy couch potatoes," I whispered against his neck, then went back to kissing just to distract him.

"We have responsibilities before we take off for a week."

"Be responsible later, be irresponsible with me now." I laid my cheek down on his shoulder.

"Nope. Still responsible, because I'm done, and I *know* you're not." He reclined back in the chair and wrapped his other arm around me. "Everything okay out there?"

"It's complicated, but he's here on peaceable terms." I wanted to tell Noah about Brad keeping Greg's affairs from me, but I also didn't need to throw more poison on Brad with Noah. "He left Greg, and I was right about the tumor being a lie. *And* he thinks Greg spiked my wine, cut my brake line, and burned down my apartment."

"How'd that come about?"

I sat up and shook my head. "I don't want to talk about it right now. It stresses me out, and it'll stress you out." I smiled and kissed him.

"Is he still out there?" he asked between kisses.

"No." I unbuttoned the first button of his shirt. "He went to go get Chinese food."

"You don't need junk food, your heart is still healing." He rolled the chair to the side and pushed the shutters closed on both windows.

"Sh," I demanded against his lips.

"Don't shush me." He pulled my shirt off and put a hand between my shoulder blades to push me closer.

••••••

The next day was organized chaos. Everyone showed up early in the morning and started hauling all the decorations out of the basement and into different vehicles. When we got out to Lars' beautiful Norwegian home, Clara and Linna directed the production. The guys worked on setting up the wood flooring over the grass, then the tables and tent. The girls started decorating, and the guys helped when that was all that was left. The overprotective Noah kept making sure I took breaks and was drinking enough water. I reminded him that working at a hospital was more work than setting up for a wedding, but he continued to be pig-headed.

After everything was set up—aside from flowers which Clara would take care of in the morning—the pastor came out to do the rehearsal. Clara and Linna continued to pick to death on details, but I didn't disagree with them. The pastor was kind of a flighty man and had a few things backwards. He wanted Garrett and I to walk with me on the left and Garrett on the right, but then have Noah and the boys on the left and me and my girls on the right. Clara fixed it so the girls were on the left, as was the usual tradition.

When we were done with the ceremony rehearsal, everyone went to wherever their home base was and got dressed for the dinner that Lars was putting on. It was my family, Noah's, and our three sets of friends. Lars had told me to invite more people because he had the room and caterers ready, but he was already being incredibly generous. He'd been the one to insist on having the wedding at his house the second he heard we were getting married.

I walked up to Noah, Gabe, Dallas, Moses, and Brad. The five of them all had serious looks on their faces, and Brad, the shortest among them, looked slightly intimidated.

"What are we talking about?" I asked as I walked up.

All five seemed to have an exchange of a half second glance.

"We're plotting for your big day. Change of plans, you're marrying me." Moses flashed a quick grin.

"Not on your life." I looped my arm through Noah's, then smiled up at him. "Are you ready? Lars has ants in his pants to get started."

"Yep." He turned with me and we started walking to the table.

"What was that about?" I whispered.

"Nothing. We were just talking."

"Brad's face is a tell all. It didn't look like nothing. It looked like a serious conversation."

"It was nothing," Noah whispered as he leaned over to kiss my head.

"We're beginning?" Lars asked.

I smiled and nodded.

"Wonderful. Excuse me, all. Please take your seat. We'd like to begin now." There was a slight inflection at the end of every sentence as Lars spoke over the rumble of conversations. Something about his Norwegian accent was charming.

Noah and I stood in front of our seats as everyone gathered around and took theirs. I didn't know why, but I almost felt embarrassed. If I was speaking at a convention in the hospital, or even to a group of interns, I was fine, but something about the attention of so many friends and family members made me nervous.

Noah took in a deep breath after everyone was seated and quiet. "Well, we've spent all day with you guys, but we still want to thank you for coming out, helping set up, and being here with Holly and I. You guys have shown a lot of support and we're grateful to have you. And a special thanks to Lars for letting us impose on his house and backyard today and tomorrow. You're saving us the headache of too many people running through *our* house and driving Holly to viciously scrub every inch of flooring."

Everyone laughed and I bumped Noah's arm, giving

him a disapproving look.

"It's my pleasure," Lars laughed.

Noah pulled out my chair for me and laughed a little.

"Yeah, you better show some chivalry," I said with narrowed eyes and a smile.

"I'm gonna take an opportunity to make a toast," Thomas said as he pushed his chair back and stood. "I'd pick up my water glass, but I'm old and I have a shake..." He took in a breath and looked at Noah. "Son, we've certainly had our words, but I have to tell you I couldn't be prouder. You've persevered through tragedy and hardship, and while I may not have conveyed it enough, I'm humbled to have raised a man who could endure such hardship and rise to the moment of loving greater the second time around. I, myself, don't believe I'd have the strength—even with such an incredible young woman like Holly. You bring me hope for the world, and great joy." He nodded once at Noah.

Thomas' words were so powerful and unexpected that the entire room could feel them.

"Thanks, Pops," Noah said quietly.

Thomas nodded again and looked at me with a growing smile. "My dear Sweet-pea... we're so blessed to have you in our family. From the very first day we met you, you brought kindness, humility, and profound joy into our home. You adapted to the individuals of our family to forge unique relationships with each of us. Linna could love just about anyone, but not my sons, and not me. We're rather skeptical and careful of the company we keep... It takes an innately strong person to adjust to those around them—put them and their needs first—while remaining yourself in the process. You are a rarity of your own making, and if we'd ever had a daughter of our own, we would have wanted her to be as gracious and whole-heartedly good like you." He smiled again. "I wish you both love and happiness with each other and in your lives as individuals." He picked up his glass and held it up. "To Holly and Noah."

"To Holly and Noah," everyone else toasted.

My cheeks burned again from the amount of attention.

"No. Sit your scrawny butt down," Clara chided at Brad as they both went to stand. "You're a windbag like your father and I'm hungry."

Brad looked at me and rolled his eyes. I smiled and tried not to laugh.

"Okay, so I'll cut to the chase here." Clara held her glass and looked at me. "Girly, you haven't known me long, but know me well enough to know I don't apologize for much. I'm not sorry for stepping out as a mother, because you wouldn't be who and where you are now, and that's a pretty incredible person with a beautiful life. The regret I have is, I *couldn't* be your mother, because dammit girl, you make me regret it every time I watch you." She lifted a finger from her glass to point at Noah. "You can love stubborn," her finger moved in Garrett's direction, "mush-balls," she looked at Brad, "mouthy little shits," and looked at me again, "and you can love people like me. I treated you like shit when you came to me, but you forgave me anyway." She shook her head. "Maybe it's backwards, but I look up to you, Girly... And I love you."

I pulled back the corner of my mouth with a small smile. "I love you too."

"And you," Clara gave Noah a hard expression, "thank you for stepping in and taking care of Little Miss there. Life's hard when you get a reality check on what love isn't, and it's made a lot easier by good men like you. Keep up the good work."

Everyone laughed a little and Clara finally smiled.

"Are you done, or is there more wind left?" Brad asked as Clara looked at her chair before she went to sit.

"*Mouthy shit*," she responded with a wide-eyed glare.

"Then we know who I take after." Brad stood up with a small smile of amusement.

Garrett laughed.

Brad took in a breath and let it out in a huff. "I think I'm gonna forgo all the embellishments with you. You already know I love ya and I'm a proud blood-sucking parasite."

I laughed a little.

Brad smiled at me, then looked at Noah. "I have to thank you. I know I'm not on your list of favorite people— and that's probably a good thing because I haven't done anything worth being on it—but I really appreciate everything you've done for Holly. I should have been looking out for her, I wasn't, but it means a lot to me and the people who love her that *you* did, and continue to. Also, I know you didn't do it for me, but thank you for kicking me in the ass to do the right thing." He pulled back the corner of his mouth. "You already are, but keep being good to my sister. She needs it, and deserves it more than anyone I know."

Noah nodded, continuing to rub small circles on the back of my neck. "Always. And you're welcome."

"Last thing, a word of advice, don't leave the toilet seat up around her. She'll find new ways to initiate torture, and it gets ugly. She'll put rotten molasses in your shoes, or you'll wake up to her duct taping a moldy washcloth to your face."

Brad sat as he spoke the last words.

Noah laughed, with everyone else half a second behind.

I raised my eyebrows. "Dude, I was the only girl in a house of boys. It's common courtesy."

Noah kissed the side of my forehead. "You put anything in my shoes and you'll meet your match."

"Then don't leave the toilet seat up."

He smiled. "I love you."

"I love you too." I reached over and put my hand just above his knee.

"Okay, who's going next. Chop. Chop." Clara rolled her finger in the air.

Moses slid his chair back, and Gabe shoved it forward.

"What?" He looked at Gabe.

"Nobody cares that you're in love," Gabe grumbled.

Moses looked at Noah and I with a look of stunned hurt.

"You'll live. Anyone else, or can it wait until after we eat? I'm starving." Noah looked around the table.

"Bring out the food. We're hungry," Terri said with a mouthful of bread.

Noah laughed. "I think we're at a consensus."

Chapter 22

I stared in the mirror at the illusion neckline of my dress. Thin tulle with patches of floral lace covered my skin. Some of my scars were visible, but I didn't care; they were a part of what led me to stand where I was.

"Okay, Girly. Time to get the show on the road. I got your brother and the girls wrangled and ready to go, and mush-ball is waiting for you." Clara walked in the room with my bouquet of peonies.

I turned around and picked up the bottom of my dress but stopped when Clara seemed to pause.

I looked down at myself because I didn't know what she was staring at. "What?"

"Nothing."

"You're looking at me weird," I pointed out.

"It's nothing. You'll tell me when you want to tell me." She sighed, "I need booze and a cigarette. Let's go."

Garrett and the wedding party all stood in the open living room of Lars' house. He'd moved all the furniture out so it looked like an open cathedral with no bench seats.

"Oh my gosh," Terri gushed as soon as she noticed me.

"Killer dress, Honey." Bridgett shook her head with a raised eyebrow.

"I literally want your face, your body, and your life." Carrie let out a breath of defeat. "Wanna trade?"

I laughed. "No."

Moses shook his head and shoved his hand through his curls. "I think my heart's breaking. Seriously, will you marry me? I'll push him in the lake and we can just go for it."

I sighed. "Will you stop? Please?" His relentlessness was becoming irritating.

"I'm kidding. I'd make a terrible husband. I can't ever find my socks." He pulled up a pant leg to show his bare foot in his shoe.

"No one's ever been able to find your brain either. Go put your damn socks on." Gabe shoved Moses toward the door to the kitchen.

"It's one sock." Moses pulled a sock out of his jacket and dangled it with a smile as he walked backwards into the door.

I laughed a little and looked at Gabe. "Do I even want to know what his original plan was?"

Gabe frowned over at the door. "I don't know. He's a girl and he cries at weddings?"

I smiled a little. "Is Noah holding up okay? He's too 'Noah' to say anything, but I think he's missing Kate a little."

Gabe shook his head. "I talked to him, he's fine. The second he sees you, he'll forget."

"I know, but it has to be hard."

Gabe shrugged and tugged a hand down his trimmed beard. "Yeah."

"Moses, hurry up!" Clara snapped loudly. "We're moving!" She looped her arm through Brad's to stop him from walking toward me. "Come on, Mouth."

Brad pulled his arm up. "Hold on a second." He gave her a dirty look then continued toward me shaking his head.

I smiled and brought my arms up to hug him. "Be patient."

"She's still alive. What more do you want?" He put his chin on my shoulder for a second and let go of me. "Okay. Something old." He pulled out a string of pearls my dad had given me and put it on me. "Borrowed." He took off his watch. "Seriously borrowed." He pointed at my face.

"I can't wear that," I frowned.

"You're not." He took my bouquet and stuffed his watch below the flowers. "Seriously, I want it back as soon as you guys go back down the aisle."

"I'll give it back."

"Blue." He flipped up one of his guitar picks with a smile.

I smiled and shook my head as he put the pick in my flowers too. "You're a nerd."

"I'm the best man and no one else was gonna think of it." He shrugged with a smile. "You look beautiful, Butch."

I scrunched my nose, and he scrunched his back.

"Love you." He stepped forward again and hugged me.

"I love you too."

"I'll see you up there." He reached quickly to muss my hair, but I ducked and hit him in the side.

"Dirt bag."

He laughed and turned to hold out his arm to Clara.

"You're looking pretty sharp there, Kid." Garrett touched the back of my shoulder.

I turned partially to reach an arm up to hug him. "You too. How many times did Clara jab you with a pin to get your boutonniere on?"

He chuckled. "Just one good one." He sighed and watched as the procession started. "Thank you for asking me to walk you down the aisle."

I looked up at him, a little taken aback that he'd ever thought different. "You're my dad too."

He looked at me, seeming heartbroken. "I owed you better... The second I found out your mother was pregnant, I should have cleaned myself up."

I shook my head, recognizing the words I'd once said to him. "You came into my life when I needed you."

He held the side of my chin and rubbed his thumb over my cheek, then hugged me. "I love you a lot, Kid... I really hope you know that."

"I do... I love you too. I don't care where or who you were before, now is more important to me. You don't know how much I need you in this chapter of my life."

He kissed the top of my head. "Let's get you married and make me feel even older."

I stepped back from the hug and smiled at him before I took his arm. Clara was right about him being a softy, but I loved that he was my tender place to fall.

We walked out the doors and it felt like a long stretch to get to the first row of people in the back. There was a clash of my friends from San Francisco, Portland, and Rochester along with Noah's friends and family. We ended up with over two-hundred people. In my head, I'd only expected the people we'd had at the rehearsal dinner, so it was a little overwhelming.

Noah looked at me with a tightened jaw, soft eyes, and the corner of his mouth pulled back with the smallest smile. Everyone was looking at me, but they should have been looking at him, because it was cute to watch him fight for his composure. He stepped down from the platform as soon as Garrett and I were close enough and waited for Garrett to hug me one more time.

Garrett reached out a hand to Noah. "Take care of my girl."

Noah nodded with a kind-eyed smile. "I will."

They hugged briefly before Garrett gave my hand to Noah and pinched the side of my chin lightly before he went to stand with Clara.

"You're beautiful," Noah said quietly before he put my hand on his arm to step up on the platform.

"You're not in a flannel shirt, I don't know what to do with myself."

He laughed soundlessly and we turned to face each other and tried not to act like giggly kids.

"Please be seated," the pastor began.

······

"And now, Noah and Holly have an exchange of words for each other," the pastor announced after several words of his own. He gave me a nod to proceed.

I looked at Noah and smiled. "I'm not so good at this, so you'll have to forgive me in advance."

He chuckled a little.

I took a short breath to calm myself. "You give me

peace... It started when we danced in the park on my birthday last year. As soon as you told me to breathe, I realized I was standing in a place where I was safe and the world was a little less heavy. Then in the same night, behind the house, you brought me to another place of peace. You showed me that I had a choice in letting go of feelings that were hurting me, while also showing me I was capable of defending myself against others who might threaten to hurt me... Every time things spin out of control, you stand right there and bring me peace. I've wished a thousand times that I'd known you before, and I would have loved you, but I wouldn't be able to appreciate everything you do. You once said you needed me," I shook my head. "I've needed you so much more. I promise you... There's nothing I can do to repay you, but I can love you."

Noah rubbed the back of my hand with his thumb. "That's plenty..."

I smiled. "I'm not allowed to kiss you yet, and that feels wrong, so hurry up."

Noah laughed and shook his head, taking a second before he spoke. "Your mom said something last night that struck a chord, about life being hard when you realize what love isn't. It ties into what I was already planning to say... You have this notion that I've always been the way I am now. That's not true... You appreciate everything around you, you forgive people who don't deserve it, you accept people for who they are and the changes they make, and when you're broken-hearted or don't feel good, you still find something to smile about—even just the smallest thing. I know you think I've taught you a lot or done something for you, but you have no idea how much you've changed who I am. You can ask anyone here. I've never been able to overlook people that I don't see as worthy, but now I let people into my house that I wouldn't normally let on my property. I do that because *you* do... You give people chances I don't think they deserve, then you end up with these amazing people in your life. They see who you are, and they step up to the plate to match you." He smiled and chuckled a little. "Sort of like me. I wasn't nice to you, I punished you for things you didn't do, and the second I changed my behavior, you were right there—no thought behind the forgiveness... I knew what love *wasn't*, what you helped me overcome was practicing what it *is*." Noah held another beautiful smile, and his green eyes seemed to have an extra sparkle. "You get to be my test subject the rest of your life."

We both laughed.

"I love you, Holly... more than I have words for. I'll do everything I can to make you feel safe, give you *peace*, and love you without condition." He reached up and touched my cheek. "And you're right, it's weird not kissing you right now." He looked at the pastor. "Hurry up."

The people who were in earshot laughed, including the pastor.

"The rings?" The pastor looked at Gabe and Brad.

I turned to get the ring from Brad and he smiled like he was so proud he didn't know what to do with himself. He pulled Noah's ring out of the box, gave it to me, and I turned to face Noah again.

"Do you, Noah Elias Jackson, take Holly Elizabeth Bennett to be your wife through all grace and time?"

Noah lovingly smiled at me as I slipped his ring on. "I do."

"And do you, Holly Elizabeth Bennett, take Noah Elias Jackson to be your husband through all grace and time?"

I pulled my hand back from Noah with a quick little smile. He looked at me like I was mad.

"Are you gonna fix the garbage disposal?"

Noah's eyebrows raised. "Are you serious, right now?"

"I'm very serious. It's been waiting two months."

His eyes were widened and slightly irritated. "I'll fix it if you stop jamming too much down at one time."

"You'll fix it as soon as we get home?" I continued to smile cheerfully.

"Yes. I promise."

"Okay. Then, I do," I said with a smile and held out my hand.

"I now pronounce you husband and wife, you may now, *finally*, kiss." The pastor chuckled slightly as he spoke.

I laughed as Noah and I stepped closer, and stood on my toes to kiss him.

"You're infuriating," Noah whispered on my lips.

"Things were getting dull. And I'm still gonna jam up the disposal because I like watching you fix it."

The pastor laughed, then Noah did too.

"It's my great pleasure to introduce, Mrs. Holly and Mr. Noah Jackson," the pastor called out.

I smiled at Noah as we turned to face everyone while they stood and clapped. Brad got my flowers back from Terri and gave them to me before we stepped down.

I couldn't say it was surreal being Noah's wife, because it wasn't. It was completely right, as much as me being a doctor.

......

The evening reception was beautiful. The sun fell behind the trees, the sky slowly darkened, and Lars' beautiful house was lined with soft white lights. Noah and I walked around to everyone we knew, sharing laughs and well wishes. For me, it wasn't exhausting like most people described their wedding day to be. I found bliss in having so many people around to celebrate with. And with the exception of the dad who raised me, anyone I wanted to share the day with was there.

"Hey, anti-social. I was wondering where you ran off to." I held up the bottom of my dress as I walked toward Brad. He was sitting on a bench swing in front of the house.

"Hold on." Brad took his jacket off and laid it down on the seat.

"Thanks." I sat down next to him and rested my head on his shoulder. "Everything okay?"

"Yeah… Trying to wrap my head around the fact that you're married. It's crazy."

I laughed a little. "I'm surprised to find I don't feel the same way."

"Naw… you two are good together." He let out a quiet breath. Brad looked content, but also sullen. Normally, I could read him like a book, but not since he'd come back for the wedding. There were moments where he looked so entirely defeated, I worried Greg might've been right to alert me that day at the hospital.

"Yeah… So, what are you doing out here? You know at least half the people here."

"Just thinking."

"About what?"

He took in a breath. "Pulling a Holly. Ditching every-thing... I don't know." He rubbed his arm. "I don't wanna go back to Portland. I moved there to be close to you... I can't go back to my job, and I hate what I do anyway..."

"Move here," I suggested lightly. "The twin cities isn't that far. Gabe and Moses love it. Or there's Rochester. It's a decent size."

"That's kind of what I was thinking... Gabe told me I could come work with him if I wanted, but I don't know. I feel like that's kind of like working with family."

I shrugged. "I think you'd be fine. You two are pretty like-minded, and behind his completely sober and bearded face, he's a really nice guy."

"Yeah, he is."

"I'd like it if you lived here..." I traced a lace flower on my dress.

There was a soft crunch of gravel to the right of us and I looked over. Noah was walking toward us. It was still so strange to see him in his light tan suit.

"I was wondering where you ran off to." He ducked under a low hanging tree branch.

"Brad was trying to make a break for it. I had to wrangle him back in." I moved the side of my dress over so he could sit next to me.

"I'll distract her with a cupcake, you run and start the car, and I'll make a break for it after." Noah sat next to me.

Brad chuckled. "A cupcake isn't gonna work. You need a tranq gun."

Noah laughed. "Lars might have something in the sta-bles."

"You're both jerks." I shook my head. "It's not that bad."

"Then why are you out here bugging the crap outta *me*?" Brad elbowed my arm lightly.

"Because you're my bitch."

"Holly," Noah reproached with a slight laugh.

"He is. He knows it," I said simply.

"My entire life," Brad agreed with a nod.

Noah shook his head. "I can't imagine what that makes me."

I giggled deviously and hugged his arm.

He looked at me for a second with a small smile and kissed my forehead. "You ready to go soon?"

I pushed out my bottom lip. "Can we do it again tomorrow?"

He laughed humorlessly. "No. I'm done. This is too much work."

"HOLLY!"

My spine tightened for just a second, then I looked at Brad for confirmation because I recognized the voice but didn't know if I was crazy. I had no reason to think I was imagining something, but I still wanted the confirmation. Brad wasn't returning my look because he was getting up as he quietly cussed. The music behind the house paused.

"Let's go." Noah stood immediately and pulled me by the hand.

"No. We can't just leave him to wreak havoc on everyone else." I didn't walk forward with Noah.

"Love, it's *you* he's after, and if you're not here, there's nothing he can do. Let's go."

Loud and familiar blasts rang out in the air along with screams of terror. My heart dropped and I ran toward the back of the house.

"Holly, no!" Noah chased after me.

"Stay back! Stay back!" Greg yelled. "Get down! HOL-LY!" His voice was frantic and crackled as he yelled out my name.

I didn't care if I was going to get shot, as long as no one else did. "Greg! I'm here," I called before I ran around the corner. "I'm here! Put the gun down and come with me. Right now. Let's leave."

Greg's curls were wet with sweat along with the front of his shirt. He had the gun raised at a group of people that were only twenty feet or so in front of him. I looked over and saw Brad on the ground with my dad, Clara, Linna, and Bridgett around him.

"Brad!" His name came from my mouth in a shrill scream as I took toward him.

"NO! STAY THERE! LET HIM DIE!" Greg burst in a crazed anger and shot the gun off. Short screams filled the air again, and I had no choice but to stop and listen.

"Clara! Sweetheart! Look at me!" Garrett cried in a panic.

"Greg, listen to me!" I looked at him and took in a loud and jagged breath. "Don't do this. If you want me to come home with you—"

"I don't want you to come home! You don't love me! You *never* loved me! I want to destroy your life like you destroyed mine! You and Brad! *BOTH OF YOU!*" He screamed his last words so hard it made him double over.

"I *did* love you. I constantly tried."

"No! You ran! You always had a foot out the door! You and Brad were fakes!" Spit flew from his mouth as he yelled at me.

I shook my head and slowly stepped toward him. "I didn't. I was always trying to keep my feet in the door because I felt like I was being pushed out by everything else. Please, come with me. Let's go back to Portland and forget about everything. We can start over."

"No." He shook his head as he looked me over angrily. "You're lying. You'll say anything to get your way then twist everything back on me. I'm *done!*"

It was taking everything in me to think on my toes. In an OR it was the easiest thing for me to keep a sound mind, but this wasn't an OR. My brain was only thinking about the danger everyone was in because of me, my brother and mom bleeding out on the grass, and the gun in Greg's hand.

"I'm sorry I made you feel that way. I didn't mean to. Everything was always my fault, Greg. I made dumb mistakes, then blamed you because I couldn't own up to them. I was too embarrassed. I'm sorry."

"You never gave me a chance," he cried. "I tried so hard to be better, and one little mistake and you *hated* me."

I shook my head. "I've never hated you. I wouldn't have been there for seven *years* if I hated you... My dad drilled perfectionism into my head and you're right, I expected too much from you and I was unforgiving when you made a mistake." Every word felt like poison seeping from my mouth, but sounded convincing as it came out.

"Why!? Why wasn't I good enough for you? We had it all, and you couldn't love me."

I shook my head. "It wasn't you, it was *me*. I don't know how to love *me*, and I took it out on you. My career as a doctor wasn't going the way I wanted, I wasn't where I thought I should be in life and I took it out on you. It was never your fault." I would've said *anything* to talk him down.

"I gave you *everything* I had." The corners of his mouth were quivering as he spoke tearfully. "I always put you first, and you either put your stupid job or Brad first. Anyone but me! I just wanted you to love me!" He started working himself back up to anger again.

"Then let's go. Let's change it," I said carefully. "We'll go back, I can work for you, or find something different, and Brad will stay here. We can change and make things different."

Greg shook his head quickly, glancing around but still holding the gun on me. "No... You won't. You don't know how, and you don't want to. I'll never be good enough for you." Even though I was scared as hell, in that moment, I saw the true hurt behind the mania in his eyes. Despite every horrible thing he'd ever done, I felt sympathetic to him. Greg stood in this world feeling so unloved that it had *literally* drove him insane. No person in the world deserved to feel *that* unloved.

"You don't know that unless you give me the chance. I can't show you that things will be different if you don't let me." My eye spotted something in the trees to the left of me but I forced myself not to look. Greg would automatically shoot. "Greg, despite everything, I love you, and I'm sorry I didn't do enough to let you know that."

"You don't get another chance. I'm done with you," Greg seethed, then pulled the trigger.

Two blasts, but I only felt one hot splatter in my leg. I was looking at Greg when it happened, though. Blood had sprayed from the side of his head. My only thought was to get to him, and I ran. Greg's eyes were open and looking around as he stared up toward the sky. There was no exit wound.

"The gun," I said out loud to myself as I got down to my knees and looked for it. "Somebody get the gun! Find the gun!" I pulled the bottom of my dress out from under my knees and started tearing pieces of it off. "Help me! Someone help me control the bleeding!"

"I didn't mean it. I didn't want to be like my dad." Greg's voice was weak like a child's as he spoke. "I don't want to be like my dad."

"You're not like your dad, Greg." I quickly started packing the pieces of my dress in the wound on the side of his head.

"I can't see anything. I think I need—" his lungs took a jerking breath, "new contacts. Did you order my contacts, Holly?"

"Yes. They're here. I need you to keep your eyes open so I can put them in." I forced his eyelids open wider to look at his eyes. They weren't responding to anything, not even the touch.

"Holly!" Gabe yanked me back. "Go help Clara, Bridgett, and Brad!"

"No. Someone has to help him too!" I tried to drop down again, but Gabe stopped me by grabbing me around the waist. The wound in my leg pinched as I tried to get my footing to fight him, but I ignored it.

"No! I'll do it! Go!" He pushed me toward my family.

I ran over to the crowd and pushed my way through. "Move! Get out of the way!"

"Holly! Help me!" Bethany yelled quickly. "Someone give me a shirt! Something!"

I yanked wads of lace off my dress as fast as I could. "Here! Here!"

"Oh god, Brad," Bethany cried as she quickly took the fabric from me.

"Holly! Bridge needs help," Carrie cried. "Bridge, wake up!"

I dropped to my knees next to Carrie and Bridgett. "Look out. Let me in," I said quickly as I pulled Carrie's arm back.

"She got hit in the shoulder. I don't know what to do but hold this," Moses said as he kept his hands down on Bridgett's upper right shoulder. He looked absolutely terrified.

"Just keep putting pressure. Has anyone called nine-one-one? Tell them we need every ambulance we can get!" I put my ear down to Bridgett's chest to listen to her airway, breathing, her heart, checked her eyes, then started compressions. "Does anyone know how to do CPR!?" I called out. As much as I wanted to help Bridgett, I needed to help Brad and my mom. "Dad, where was Mom hit?" I tried to lean back to look but couldn't see.

"Just keep helping your friend. We've got it over here." Garrett's voice sounded harsher than normal.

"Bridgett!" Dallas yelled. "MOVE! IF YOU'RE NOT HURT, STOP CROWDING AROUND!"

I stopped to push a breath in through Bridgett's mouth.

"Son of a bitch!" Dallas dropped down on the other side of Bridgett. "You toxic shit-pit!" Dallas pushed me back so hard I fell over. "Get away from her! This is your fault!"

"Goddammit, man. She's trying to save her!" Moses yelled after bashing his elbow into Dallas' upper arm. "Help out, or back off!"

"Holly, are you okay?" Noah's voice was winded as he

helped me sit up.

"I'm fine. I have to help Bridgett. Make sure Brad and my mom are okay." I got to my knees again and leaned over to listen to Bridgett's lungs again. Her right lung still had nothing so I tapped my fingers over her chest and listened. "Someone get me a clean knife and a straw! Hurry!"

"What are you going to do!?" Dallas sounded like he was almost in disbelief somehow.

"Her lung is filled with fluid. I have to drain it," I said quickly, continuing to do compressions.

"Bridge, wake up. Please wake up." Dallas leaned over her head and kissed her forehead.

"Plug her nose and breathe into her mouth," I told him.

"Now?"

"Yes, now!" I stopped compressions, let him blow in a breath, then resumed them. He gave three more breaths before Dr. Roth—a colleague from the hospital—ran over with a knife, a bottle of vodka, and a straw. I cut the side of Bridgett's dress before I dumped vodka on the knife, then switched sides to get in a good position. As soon as I had the knife through, Bridgett gave a choking gasp. Blood came out from the straw but tapered off, which was good.

"There's so much blood. She's going to bleed out before help even gets here." Dallas' voice was broken.

"No, she won't. She's not losing a fatal amount." I secured the straw and moved my hands. "Someone hold this, don't let it move or come out. Tell me if it stops or gets worse." I got up and went to the other side of Bridgett to continue compressions.

"Holly, the first ambulance is three more minutes out. What do you want me to do?" Noah asked quickly but calmly.

"Just help my dad with my mom and Brad." I closed my eyes to focus. This wasn't as nerve-racking as standing in front of Greg with a gun on me. "Greg! Who's helping Greg?" I turned my head to look back.

"No one better be helping that piece of shit!" Dallas got up to his knees to look. "I hope he's rotting in hell!"

"He's a person, Dallas. He's a sick person and he deserves help too. Who's helping him? Is Gabe still over there?" I tried to look through the legs of the people still standing around but couldn't see.

"Gabe's over there with some of your friends from work," Noah answered quietly. "Holl, is she going to be okay?" His voice sounded more devastated and scared than I'd ever heard before.

"As long as the damn ambulance gets here." I tried to focus on my breathing, and not the fact that Noah's very best friend was under my pounding hands or my bleeding leg. I'd never been unaware that I was also shot, but I had to take care of everyone else first.

"Can I take over?" he asked.

"No. I've got it." I wiped my cheek against the side of my arm to get my hair out of my face. The compressions and stress already had me in a sweat, making my hair stick to my face.

Chapter 23

"They're coming in! The police and ambulances are coming in!" someone yelled.

I let out a breath of relief but didn't stop what I was doing. Someone must have called just before everything started because I had no idea how they could've gotten there so fast. I was only thankful they *were*.

"We need four stretchers!" I yelled back. "Hurry!"

"What do you need, Holly?" Garrett asked as he got on the other side of me.

"Nothing! What are you doing? Go help Brad and my mom."

"They're fine. Bethany and Calloway have them taken care of. Let me take over and you pack the wound." Garrett moved in, then took over compressions.

I got out of the way, tore some more fabric off the underlining of my dress, then got down again. There was no exit wound, which wasn't good, so I was careful about how I packed it. After about four minutes, the EMT's were rolling stretchers through. Garrett and I started giving directions, but after an EMT took over, he got up and went over to Brad and Clara. I tried to see what was going on but couldn't because I was getting Bridgett intubated. My leg was starting to hurt more and more, but I couldn't stop until Bridgett was on her way to the ambulance, and I didn't.

"Holly." Noah put a hand on my arm. His voice was quiet.

I looked at him. "I have to go with Brad. I know you hate him, you have every right, but will you go with Greg?"

He shook his head. "They didn't make it, Love."

"Who? Greg?" I turned and looked back in the direction where Greg had been and saw the white sheet over a body on the ground.

"Brad too. He didn't make it. I'm sorry."

I looked up at Noah, feeling like my stomach hit my feet, then immediately went off to the right to where Brad was.

"Move. Move." I pushed people out of the way, only to find a sheet was being unfolded over Brad's body. "No!" I threw myself down so fast I almost fell. "Brad, no." My voice broke as I leaned over to listen to his chest. There was nothing, not a breath sound, not a heartbeat, nothing. I picked my head up and pulled his eyelid back. His pupil was mid-dilated. A short cry started to burst out of me, but I stopped it, and it made the sound of a held sneeze. I put a hand on his chest where the open wound was and could already feel that there was a temperature change in his skin.

"I did everything I could, Holly. He just bled out too fast. I'm so sorry," Bethany sobbed.

I grabbed my chest with one hand as I leaned myself over to rest my head on Brad's shoulder. It felt like my heart was very literally breaking. I would've rather been shot a thousand more times. The pain was so immense, I couldn't breathe enough to let out a cry. The reality was, even if I'd stopped to help Brad before Bridgett, or even Greg, I wouldn't have been able to save them. Even in a hospital, there would have been no help for Greg, and Brad would have been a miracle...

"Mom." My brain wasn't working. I couldn't sit there and cry over who was already gone, I had to get up and check on my mom, make sure Bridgett was okay, and make sure no one else was hurt.

"Holly, can we help you out of your dress? Jess went to start the car so you guys can go." Terri tried to stop me as I headed around to the front of the house.

"No. I don't have time." I wanted to run, but I couldn't. My leg was really hurting, and I had to make sure my mom was okay. She and Garrett were all I had left for family.

Clara was awake in the ambulance.

"Nope. Sorry, we have to go and only one extra person is allowed. We're full," the EMT said as he closed the back doors.

"She's my mom. I just want two seconds to see her," I told him childishly. Every second counted, I knew that, but I just wanted to see her because I didn't know how bad her wounds were. If she didn't make it, I just wanted to have that last minute with her because I *didn't* get it with Brad.

"You can drive to the hospital. Everyone is going to Regions." He walked around the side of the rig and got in.

I rubbed my forehead, unable to process hardly anything around me. Carrie was getting in the back of the ambulance with Bridgett, and Dallas was standing over by a group of cops, showing his badge and telling them something as he pointed to me. When I looked over to the right of me, I saw that guests were trying to leave, but there were officers telling them they couldn't until they gave a statement.

"Ma'am, are you okay? Are you hurt?"

I looked at the woman who was asking. It was another medic. She was looking at the blood on what was left of my dress.

"I can't leave. All this happened because of me. He was here for me," I told her quietly as I continued to look at the chaos I'd caused. All the scared people, friends, family, relatives I barely knew or didn't know at all, the faces of their terrified children... they were put in danger because I'd chosen to do nothing. My lack of fight, my ignorance... *this* was the cost. "I did this."

"Let's go sit down, okay?" The medic pulled on my arm lightly. "Is there someone we can find for you? Where's your husband?"

I heard her, but I wasn't really paying attention. My sights were focused on all the tear-filled eyes, blood-stained clothes, and frightened faces. Some of them were looking back, but some of them just looked lost.

"Are you the groom?" the medic asked.

I looked at her with confusion, then looked behind me because that's where she was looking.

"No," Moses answered. "Her brother-in-law. You need to look at her leg. She was shot."

The pain in my leg came to the forefront of my mind because I'd been reminded of it.

"You were shot?" the medic asked in disbelief before she turned. "We need another stretcher over here! We have another GSW." She looked at me. "Which leg, Honey?"

I shook my head. "Left. I don't need to go in. Give me some supplies and I can take care of it. I can't leave."

"We'll take care of it. You need to get to the hospital. You said it was your left leg, can I have a look?"

"No. I have to stay here." I pulled my arm away from her. "Please, don't touch me. Just get me some stuff to take care of it. I'm a surgeon and I can do it myself. It's just a graze wound."

"Okay, if you're a doctor, you know I can't just let you go. We have to take you in." She grabbed the end of the stretcher as two guys wheeled it toward me. "Sir, can you help us out here?" She looked at Moses.

"You go with them and I'll get Noah," Moses said, holding my arm.

I shook my head again. "No. I have to stay here. I can't leave Brad. I have to go back." I pulled my arm out of his grip and turned to go back to the backyard.

"No, Holly." Moses' tone was short and serious, something I'd never heard out of him. He caught my arm, turned me to face him, and pushed me back onto the edge of the stretcher. "He lost Kate, he won't survive losing *you*. I will get Noah, then I'll stay with Brad. I promise. You have to go. Do you hear me?"

My chin quivered as I looked up at Moses. Everything felt overwhelming.

"Okay?" he asked when I didn't respond.

I blinked and nodded.

"Okay." He hooked me under the arms and slid me

back on the stretcher. "Stay here. I'll send Noah out." Moses glanced at the medics then took off in a jog toward the backyard.

"I'm going to lift your dress to find the wound," the female medic said.

"What's your name, Ma'am?" another male medic asked.

"Holl—Holly Bennett." I watched as Dallas and two officers walked toward me.

"We need to talk to her before you take her in, if possible," an officer said.

"She's awake—unlike my *wife*—so it's possible," Dallas said as he glared at me with hatred. "I already told them your failure to report *anything* he did. Do you get it now? It was never just about you? You brought him here and people got hurt because you were too much of a scared bitch to do the right thing. How stupid do your excuses seem now? Huh?"

"Sir, go wait over there," one of the officers snapped angrily as he pointed toward one of the police cars.

"I will in a minute. I want her to know how unbelievably stupid and unnecessary this all is. You wanted to keep your brother from losing his license, keep him from the slap on the wrist of going to jail for a couple months, but you were willing to risk his death and everyone else's? I told Noah to dump your ass. The second he told me, I told him to get rid of you."

"Sir! Back off! We're trying to assess her and you're in the way!" the female medic yelled. "Get him out of here."

The second officer forced Dallas forward.

I wasn't mad at Dallas for being angry with me. Anyone who held me responsible was right to.

"Any questions you guys have for her are going to have to happen at the hospital. She needs medical attention *now*." The female medic pushed the stretcher back toward the ambulance. As much as I wanted to fight her and insist on staying, I knew better. My body was starting to feel tired and my mind was slipping. I'd been in a cold sweat for a while, but it was getting worse and my ears were ringing.

"My blood type is O positive. I'm going to lose consciousness soon," I told her. "I'm allergic to penicillin and latex adhesives." My tongue felt thick as I spoke. "I'm also pregnant. About eight or nine weeks. I found out this morning." I could hear myself talking, but wasn't really processing the words as they came out of my mouth.

"Okay. That's good to know. How old are you, ma'am?" one of the male medics asked as he ripped open a package of something.

"Thirty-three," I answered as I looked up at the bright lights, trying to stay conscious as long as I could.

"Good. When's your birthday?"

"July fourth... My leg is starting to hurt *really* bad now. I think my adrenaline is wearing off."

"Yep. We'll get you taken care of. I'm just going to get this IV line in and we'll get you set up." He worked as he spoke.

"Hold on! I'm riding with you." Calloway's voice was loud, as it usually was.

I looked at him as he got in the back. "Is Noah mad at me? Is that why he's not coming?"

"No. He's staying with his little cop friend to make sure he doesn't get arrested. And who else is he going to trust to take care of you? One of you get me some gloves. You're already doing this wrong, and why isn't there a damn bag hanging already?" Calloway partially stood and reached over the top of me.

"Sir, who are you, and please stay out of our stuff. We have this handled." The female medic was instantly irritated and I didn't blame her.

"I'm a neurosurgeon at the Mayo clinic. My name is Dr. Richard Calloway, and I've got more experience and training in my little toenail than you've ever dreamed of in your life. This girl is my prodigy resident, and I will *not* allow you to mess up her prodigy leg." He pulled gloves on as he spoke.

"Don't be an ass. Just help them," I told him as I continued to take even breaths and focused on staying awake. "I really need someone to get me a bag of O positive."

"I'm working on it," the male medic next to Calloway said calmly.

"Penny, you've got a through and through. Location is top of the VL and base of the TFL, exiting the BFL. No serious active bleeds. One of you get me saline for debridement." Calloway held out a hand without looking up. "Push twenty-five micrograms of fentanyl and one gram of cefazolin, after you get that blood bag going."

"We can't give her fentanyl. She's pregnant," the male medic said quietly, like he was focused on something.

Calloway raised an eyebrow at me.

"You should just wait until we get to... um..." I couldn't think of the word.

"You're not the doctor, you're the patient. Just sit there and let me do what I'm doing." His voice was quiet and calm like it was during surgery. That was the only time he would be quiet, but only when he was actually focused or thinking.

Otherwise, he was loud and obnoxious.

......

Calloway had me ready to go straight in for imaging, then sewed everything up after the scans showed I didn't need any muscles reattached. By some miracle, there were only partial separations in the affected muscles. Even though Calloway was a pain to deal with, I was thankful he was there to take care of my leg because he would do things the same as or better than I would. As soon as he was done—which wasn't terribly long—he went to scrub in to assist with my Mom. Bridgett was already almost out of surgery, but my mom had been hit in the abdomen with no exit wound.

I sat there for about an hour before a nurse came with my discharge papers, a brace, a pair of hospital sweats, and a pair of crutches. She took me to a waiting room, and I sat there until Calloway came another hour later with Garrett, Noah, Gabe, and Moses.

"I told the nurse the wrong waiting room. I'm sorry," Calloway said with a straight face. "Your mom is in post-op. She'll be fine."

I nodded. "Any update on Bridgett?"

"She's awake and doing just fine," Garrett said as he sat beside me. "I didn't know you were here, so I was sitting with her." He took my hand and gave it a light squeeze.

"It's okay. I thought you were either with Mom or just needed time. I'm so sorry." I pulled back the corner of my mouth.

He shook his head but didn't say anything.

Noah took my other hand after sitting on the other side of me. "Is your leg okay? You didn't tell me you were hit."

I nodded. "I'm fine. I didn't say anything because I

needed to help everyone else. I'm sorry." I leaned toward him and let him hug me.

He took in a deep breath and let it out after wrapping his arms around me. I closed my eyes and just sat there because I genuinely didn't know what else to do or say.

"Did one of the officers find you? They're still waiting to talk to you about Greg," Gabe muttered quietly from across from me.

I shook my head and pulled away from Noah's hug. "No…" I looked at Noah. "Who shot Greg? I didn't see."

"Dallas did. He's not going to be charged with anything, but he's on an observation hold for a few hours and he's being put on administrative leave," Noah answered quietly.

"Then we should go sit with Bridgett. She shouldn't be alone." I pointed to my crutches. "I want to see her."

Noah took my hand instead of handing me the crutches. "She's resting and she doesn't want visitors right now." He rubbed the top of my hand. He was being kind, but I could read between the lines, Bridgett was probably upset with me like Dallas was. I didn't blame her or anyone else.

"And you need to talk to the police before anyone else." Gabe got up and walked out of the waiting room.

"Kid, you didn't send Greg an invitation to your wedding, did you?" Garrett asked quietly.

I looked at him and shook my head. "Of course not. I didn't even send one to Brad because I didn't want Greg there."

"Gabe found one in his pocket." Noah's voice was quiet.

I shook my head again. "I didn't send him one."

"There was also a letter with him." Noah reached into his pocket and pulled out a piece of paper. "It's your handwriting. Gabe had the sense to pull it out, but I want to know why the hell you'd send him this."

My heart began to pound unreasonably hard because I didn't know what he was talking about and I'd never send *anything* to Greg after leaving Oregon.

I recognized the style of lines on the paper immediately. "This is from my journal." I took the paper, unfolded it, and looked at it. "I never sent this to him. This was just me journaling a letter to—this wasn't *for* him." I looked at Noah. "This was for me, trying to forgive because I just wanted to let go. He obviously went through my things."

He took the letter back and folded it again. "I hope that's true..." Noah put the paper back in his pocket.

"*Of course it's true.* I have no reason to lie. I wanted him out of my life, sending anything is the opposite of that. I was journaling, trying to work stuff out with myself. You can ask Bridgett, she's the one who told me to do it." I couldn't believe he didn't believe me, and was *afraid* because he didn't. Also, there were things in that letter Noah wouldn't understand, and I didn't know if he'd let me explain.

Noah pointed toward the hallway. Gabe was coming back with the two officers that'd come up to me with Dallas when I was on the stretcher.

"That letter was something I did to let go. It was a therapy thing, not an actual letter for *him*," I said quietly. He needed to know it wasn't anything meant for anyone to see.

"We'll talk about it later. Gabe is sitting in as your lawyer, I need to go check on people." Noah got up and walked out of the waiting room.

"Are you okay? I really need to see your mom." Garrett's voice was quiet, but he sounded exasperated.

I looked at him and nodded. "Yeah, go. I'll be there as soon as I can."

He put a hand over mine as he got up. Moses shoved his hand through his hair and just left without a word. My guts felt like they were being pulverized by the invisible hits. I deserved their anger, but it still hurt like hell. Especially Noah, I thought he'd be the one who'd still stand by me, but... he couldn't. And while I understood why, it still hurt worse than I could've ever imagined.

"Miss Bennett, I'm Detective Barrett and this is my partner Detective Lancer," the older of the two officers said as they walked around the row of chairs in front of me.

I nodded once.

"We have a pretty good picture of what happened tonight, but we still need to get a statement from you. Is your leg alright?" He pointed at the brace on my leg.

I nodded again then looked at Gabe as he sat next to me.

"Can you tell us what happened tonight?" Both detectives sat, but it was Barrett who was asking.

I told him what I could recall, but anything I'd said to Greg wasn't there. It was like the exchange of words had been wiped from my memory the moment he was shot. They asked me if I'd invited him, I told them the truth, that I hadn't. After that, they started asking about my past history with Greg, then why I didn't report it. After a brief lecture about how I should have reported regardless of what or who he threatened, they started asking for information on Greg so they could contact his next of kin. I gave them Scarlett's—his mother—number and address, but asked them if I could be the one to tell her. Gabe advised me not to and so did the officers, but I insisted on it. She may have been the one who raised Greg, but she was nothing like him, and the news was going to kill her.

One of the officers gave me his phone to call her, and they listened as I told her, then spoke to her after. She cried in that horrible way a mother does when they lose a child. It wasn't the first time I'd ever heard it, but it felt just as horrible as if it had been. I could hardly breathe as I sat there and listened to the rest of the call. When the officers hung up, there was another lecture about how my lack of action against Greg had affected everyone around me and how I should remember that in the future. I wanted to scream at them, but that didn't mean they were wrong. I *was* that dumb girl who let someone beat them and didn't speak up, and these were the consequences I'd brought.

The two detectives didn't linger long and I went to go find Clara right after. Garrett was the only person in her room. I didn't know where Noah and Moses had gone.

"Get your tiny butt over here, Girly." Clara's voice was scratchier than usual.

I crutched myself over and sat on the bed next to her.

"Come here." She pulled on my arm.

I put my crutches against the empty chair, then moved to lay up against her side. "I'm so sorry."

"It's not your fault, Honey." She put a hand over the side of my head. "People don't understand how hard it is to walk away from a bad relationship... but I do." She hugged me a little tighter.

I reached a hand up to her wrist as a cry snapped out of me with a violent shove. "I just wanted to leave. No one was supposed to get hurt." My voice was as squeaky and busted as it could be because my throat was clenching from the cry.

"I know... It's not your fault. You did the best you could. I'll kick anyone's ass who says different... No one has an ounce of room to say otherwise unless they lived in your shoes. Brad knew you didn't have options. He told me himself."

The mention of Brad made me break even harder. Clara was about the last person I expected to understand or be my soft place to fall, but she was. I just held onto her and bawled into her shoulder while she stroked my hair.

Chapter 24

"Holly?"

I felt the hand on my arm before I heard Noah whisper my name. My eyes opened, and it took me a second to realize where I was and why. The swelling in my face was the first reminder, then the hospital room and Garrett asleep in the chair beside Clara's bed. I'd cried myself to sleep next to her.

"Let's get going. We have a long drive home," he whispered.

I carefully pushed myself up, trying not to disturb my mom. Leaving her made my heart ache because I wanted her with me. She felt like the only person who was truly in my court.

"Be careful. Here." Noah hooked me under the arm to help me turn on the bed and I let my legs over the edge. The pain hadn't been all that terrible until then. I held my thigh just below my hip to sit there and reel for a minute.

"Did they give you anything for pain?" Noah held the crutches in front of me.

I shook my head and slowly slid onto my good foot before taking my crutches under my arms.

"What? Why?"

"I don't want it," I lied. Delivering the news of being pregnant seemed like it would only make things worse. I crutched myself around the bed to Garrett and rubbed his arm. He took in a deep breath and woke immediately. "Hey, we're gonna go. Do you need anything?"

"No. Are you okay?" He reached for my hand.

I shrugged a shoulder.

The corner of his mouth pulled back. "I love you, Kid." His thumb rubbed the back of my hand.

"I love you too. I'll text you as soon as I get my phone back, otherwise, you can call Noah."

He nodded, glanced at Noah, then looked at me again. "You guys can go stay at Clara's house if you don't want to drive all the way back tonight."

"We'll be okay. I'll let you know when we're home," Noah whispered. "Bridgett is asleep right now, but can you check on her in a little bit? Dallas probably won't be here until morning."

Garrett nodded. "Of course. Do you know if Calloway is still here, or did he take off?"

"He got a hotel room just a few blocks away in case he was needed here again. He said to call him if anything changed."

Garrett took in a deep breath, looked at Clara, then let it out. "Good. I'm sure she'll be fine, but..." He shook his head, then looked at me. "If you need me, call me. Okay? I'm here."

I nodded, but didn't want to leave him anymore than I wanted to leave Clara. Garrett seemed to pick up on it because he stood and hugged me.

"I'm sorry I left you earlier," he whispered quietly next to my ear. "I know you never meant for anyone to get hurt… I was scared for your mom. But she's right, it's not your fault. Okay?"

I just held onto him because I couldn't agree with him. Tears were right there at the ready to make their way out again.

"And I'm so thankful you're okay. I need my beautiful daughter *too*." He kissed the side of my forehead. "Go home and rest. I'll be there as soon as I can."

I nodded, swallowed against the knot in my throat, and stepped back.

Garrett reached a hand out to Noah. "Take care of my girl."

"Yep." Noah shook his hand. "Call me if you need something."

"I will." Garett looked at my mom and reached forward to brush her hair back, then pulled the blanket up higher.

I made my way out of the room, then followed Noah out to my car without a word. Gabe was in the driver's seat, Moses was in the back and Noah opened the front door for me.

"I can sit in the back." I opened the back door.

"You won't fit with that brace and it's a long drive. Sit up front."

I wanted to hide in the backseat, but it wasn't worth the argument, so I got in the front. Noah took my crutches from me, then shut the door and got in behind me. The hour and twenty-minute drive was spent in complete silence. No one said a single word and the radio wasn't on, but it felt like the loudest silence I'd ever heard. Guilt and fear continued to eat at me until I was about to puke when we pulled into the garage. It didn't help that my leg was throbbing with pain that radiated up and down my body. Another minute in the car would have made me lose my mind, and I didn't wait for Noah to get out and give me the crutches before I got out. I let the silence continue when I went into the house and straight upstairs.

After a cold shower to scrub off all the blood, I sat on the edge of the tub to re-dress my leg. I stared at the wound on top of my thigh for a moment. It would be the last one Greg ever inflicted. There would be no more looking over my shoulder, staying vigilant of my surroundings to make sure he wasn't there, or a reason for the constant paranoia, but it didn't seem real. I still felt like he could show up at any given second. He was dead, I'd seen his body, I'd watched him get shot in the head... but it still didn't seem real.

"Holly, can I come in?" Noah asked after a light knock on the door.

"Yeah." I picked up the gauze bandage I'd already made for the back of my leg and put it on first. In the morning, I was going to have to go into town to get more. I'd made the bottom bandage first to make sure I'd have enough because the entry wound on top was smaller.

"Do you need help?" Noah asked after walking over to see what I was doing.

"No. I got it." I placed the top bandage on, then grabbed the roll of thin gauze to wrap around my leg. "I'll be out in just a second, then you can have the bathroom."

"I was just bringing you some clothes. My parents are staying down in your room, so I just grabbed you a pair of shorts and a hoodie from my closet. I never grabbed our stuff from Lars' house, so I don't even have *that*." Noah set the clothes next to me.

"I'll stop by there when I go back to see my mom tomorrow. I have to get my phone too." I carefully folded the edge of the gauze strip under a couple pieces that were wrapped around my leg instead of using tape.

"No. You need to stay home and stay off your leg." He sat on the edge of the tub facing away from me. "Also, Dallas will be at the hospital, and I don't need anymore problems. He's fired up right now."

"I'm allowed to go see my mom. I won't go say anything to Dallas or Bridgett." I grabbed the hoodie and pulled it over my head with the towel still around my body.

"Holly, *please*. Just stay home tomorrow. It's not gonna go over well if you go up there right now. There's a ton and a half of other shit we have to deal with, and I don't want to have to knock my best friend out just because he's looking for a fight with you. I *told* you this was all going to come back, that you couldn't run from it. I was right about *that,* and I'm right about the fact that Dallas will be itching to start a fight. So, please, just listen, stay home, rest, and let me handle it."

I looked at Noah, having a hundred different things to say about his choice of words and slights, but looked back down to pick up the shorts and kept my mouth shut. He was tired and stressed, so I had to maintain any semblance of peace. I slipped Noah's basketball shorts over my legs as far as I could get them under the towel before I stood on one foot inside the tub, pulled them up the rest of the way and pulled the towel off. The only way out of the tub was to sit back down on the edge and turn myself around, the same way I'd gotten in. Noah took the towel, hung it, then gave me the brace.

I shook my head. "That's only for when I'm moving around." I grabbed the crutches from the wall and went into the bedroom. My stomach was still churning, and I had to grab the waste basket beside Noah's nightstand because I wasn't sure I'd make it without throwing up. At first, I attributed it to stress, but then I remembered I was pregnant and hadn't eaten for several hours. I knew I needed to tell Noah, but I didn't have the slightest clue as to how...

Noah took a shower, got dressed, then went downstairs for a minute because I'd asked him to get me some crackers. After he came back up and was in bed, he laid there quietly and didn't so much as reach a hand over to me. It made me want to get out of bed and find another place to sleep.

"How did he get that letter if you didn't send it?" Noah asked quietly after several minutes of silence.

I looked at him. "I don't know. I think he tore it out when he sliced my brake line. The day of the car accident, I saw my dresser had been trifled through. And I even told the police the next day, so you can't tell me I'm making it up just to make myself look better."

He kept his gaze on the ceiling. "I wasn't implying, I was asking... but I still don't understand why'd you'd write something like that and keep it. I also don't understand why you'd write *that*."

"It wasn't meant to be read by anyone. It's a diary. I didn't realize people were supposed to shred everything they write in a diary. And what '*that*' are you referring to?"

"All the reminiscing on good times, saying you still loved him, you missed being with him, if you were being 'whole-heartedly honest' you didn't say anything in the beginning because you were too afraid of losing him, that if anything good came of him being violent it was the weeks after, filled with spontaneous vacations, laughter, and fun-bantering texts all day... It's kind of disturbing." His voice was quiet but the bitterness was still there, and the loathing remained in his eyes as he continued staring upward.

I sat up because I didn't feel like I could just sit there and take the hit. "Disturbing? I didn't realize I was supposed to hate a person and every second of the seven years I spent with him. I didn't realize relationships were black and white, that they weren't complicated with no gray areas. I *was* afraid to lose him in the beginning. It was four years before anything ever happened, and I was pretty damn committed to being with him by that point. And why do I have to hate the good times I had with him? Why am I not allowed to try to find the bright spots in a dark time and try to appreciate them? What, you look back on your drinking days, your fights with Kate, and that whole period of your life is just dark and ugly? There was nothing good in between the wrong doings?"

He finally looked at me and I could see the fury in his eyes before anything even came from his mouth. "Don't you dare drag Kate or my past of drinking into this." His voice was seething with anger.

"I'm not dragging anything, I'm asking an honest question, and that's the only example I have. Also, I don't see the difference, you're talking about a period of *my* life you weren't there for, why is there some kind of double standard?"

"It's not a double standard, Kate didn't come back and

kill anybody or shoot up our wedding. Neither did *I*. Yes, I killed her, and that affected everyone around me, but you weren't there for it and you *don't* have a right to say anything, make comments, or ask. Greg was *here*! He was in *my* life, in *my* house, around *my* friends' and family, at *our* wedding, and people *we* love were either hurt or killed."

I sat there for a second, possibly internalizing more of his words than I should have, but I couldn't help it. My mind was full of everything I could fire back with, but I didn't want to shoot them at him just because he was shooting a whole bunch at me. It took me a second to re-evaluate and choose something better to say. "Maybe you think I don't know that this is my fault, but I do. I'm hyper aware that my actions, or lack thereof, led to what happened, and I'll never stop being sorry or regretful. All I can do is apologize to the people who were hurt, regardless of it meaning *nothing* to anyone, and hope to be forgiven. I'm sorry, Noah. I put you and everyone else in danger, I didn't mean to, and I'm sorry." My throat burned and felt like it was about to close completely.

He sat up. "You're right, it doesn't mean anything. How many times did I tell you to report him, to do something, to get him out of here before something happened? You didn't listen, Holly. Don't sit there and act like this poor put-upon victim when you didn't listen or even *try* to do the right thing! You *knew* he was dangerous and you did *nothing!*"

"I knew he was dangerous to *me*!" The words burst out of me in a loud yell because I was tired of being berated. "I never in a million *years* would've thought he'd show up and open fire at anyone!"

"What's the difference!? Whether it was you or some-one else, you knew he was dangerous! Why does that make it any better? What, there aren't people who don't care about you, who don't love you? God, it's sickening how little value you hold for yourself sometimes! Wake up, Holly! Open your eyes! You were playing with fire this *whole* time, too damn scared to call it in, and now you're surprised that everyone around you got burned!? Wake up! You're not dumb!"

I moved the blankets off my legs and turned out of bed slowly.

"Where are you going?"

"I don't know. Out of *your* house, I suppose."

"Oh, grow up. You know what I meant." He let out a huff.

I looked at him for a moment. "What do you want, Noah...? Either you want me to know that I'm worth more than being someone's victim, or you want me to sit here and be your punching bag. Right now, I'd take getting the shit beat out of me by Greg than suffer your words. Somehow, they hurt worse without leaving a mark. You don't want to talk, you don't want to ask questions to try and understand, you want to put me down because you're mad." My voice was calm and quiet.

He chuckled humorlessly. "I'm the abuser for pointing out that *you* messed up? That your actions got people killed?"

"When you're doing it to put me down and to hurt me because *you're* hurt and mad, yes." I faced forward and carefully got myself up on one foot before I reached for the night-stand to balance myself before I reached for my crutches.

"How do you love someone like Greg? How is it he can beat the shit out of you, and you just turn the other cheek, walk away, pretend like nothing happened, and think you can get away from it by simply leaving?"

"I don't know. Hate and anger have never been my strong suits, but no amount of words you throw at me is going to change it because it's a quality I love about myself. I choose to realize that some bad actions don't make a human entirely bad." I turned on my crutches. "It surprises me that you fail to see the benefit of that. If I were to judge someone the way you want me to, I'd have to judge you for being a drunk, for killing your wife, for being a complete asshole to me when I showed up here, and for not even bothering to have a few minutes of compassion over the fact that I lost my brother tonight." I wiped the tears off my cheeks forcefully because they weren't welcome. "Don't think I don't know it wasn't my fault or that I'm not painfully angry at myself or Greg. I have to live the rest of my life knowing I'm responsible for someone's death, the same way *you* do. I truly did not believe Greg would ever do something like that, and the fact that you think I *would,* and that I'd do nothing about it is... I don't know, I don't have words, but I'm pretty sure we're done here because I'm exhausted and in more pain than I've ever been in, so—" I shook my head and turned around. It was hard to even hold onto my crutches because my entire body was weak from fighting off more hysterical cries.

"Holly, come back to bed." Noah's voice was non-combative. "I'll go sleep on the couch if you don't want me in here, but you're going to hurt yourself even trying to get down the stairs."

"I'll be fine." I opened the door and went out to the loft, then to the stairs.

"Will you please come back here? Everyone is sleeping, we're both tired, and I don't want to deal with this right now. You're right, it's not black and white, you made your point, let's just go to bed." Noah's voice came unexpectedly from the doorway to the room. I hadn't realized he'd followed me out.

I shook my head. "I don't care about being right." I let the crutches slide down the stairs to the kitchen floor, then used the railings on both sides to lift myself down a few stairs at a time.

"Love, you're making me crazy. Will you please stop and come back to bed?"

"What's going on up there?" I heard Linna's voice before I saw her turn the corner from the basement stairs. "Oh, Sweetie, be careful you're going to hurt yourself. Noah, help her." She bent down and picked up my crutches.

"No, don't touch me. I've got it," I told Noah. He was only a few stairs behind me.

"What's all the noise for?" Thomas walked over behind Linna, then looked at me as I swung myself down the last three stairs.

"I'm sorry. I didn't mean to wake you." I took the crutches from Linna as she handed them to me.

"They were very *loudly* fighting," Moses grumbled as he rubbed his face, "and now they're bringing it downstairs."

"Moses, don't be rude," Linna snapped. "Sweetie, what's wrong?" she asked as I went between her and Thomas toward the hallway to the garage.

"Fighting about what?" Thomas asked, his voice was oddly dark.

"Nothing. Everyone, just stay out of it." Noah let out a sigh. "Holly, please, can we just go back to bed. You're not supposed to be up and moving around, and I'm too tired to chase you around."

"Fighting about what?" Thomas asked again.

"Thomas, don't get in the middle of it," Linna said quietly.

"No. Fighting about what? You've been married all of eight or nine hours, so what's it about?" He was determined to get an answer.

"What do you think?" Moses sighed. "Noah's pissed because Holly didn't go to the police before something happened. Dallas is being a dick about it, so Noah's being a dick about it."

"I think you're oversimplifying it," Gabe grumbled.

"Are you kidding me!? You're badgering her over what happened!?" Linna's voice was shrill. "Shame on you!"

"Jesus, Mom. Stay out of it." If a person could hear an eye roll, Noah's would've been heard.

"Don't you take Jesus' name in vain to *me*. I remember, not too long-ago, Dad hounding you right after Kate died, and the two of you have barely said a word to each other *since*. Not to mention the countless times before that, of people telling you to lay off the drinking. The only difference *I* see is Holly couldn't control another person, and the only person *you* had to control was *yourself!* How dare you make this out to be—"

I went out the garage door and the conversation was cut off from me. It took me a good half a minute to get down the four stairs to the garage floor, then I got in my car. While I waited for the garage door, I started my car and put my seatbelt on. My stomach was churning again, and I had to take careful breaths so I didn't throw up. I went to call Garrett but remembered my cell phone wasn't with me so I couldn't. He wouldn't care if I stayed at his house anyway, so I backed out of the garage. Noah came running out. It felt like a chore because all I wanted to do was leave, but I stopped and rolled down my window.

"Where are you going?" He opened the door and rested an arm on the top of my car.

"I don't know... I need to be away from you."

He took in a deep breath and let it out. "Bridge got hurt... We've been best friends since kindergarten, and she's been there my entire life."

"Again, not unaware... What do you want from me, Noah? Do you want me to fall at your feet and beg for forgiveness, let you watch me beat myself into nothing, leave and never come back? What?" I kept my eyes forward because I was already trying not to break and looking at him would make it harder. I felt like the scum of the earth, small, and worth nothing. I was afraid of looking into his eyes and seeing that's what he saw me as too.

"No..."

"Do you want me to tell you you're right? I didn't listen to you, and you were right. I didn't make the smaller sacrifice of my brother's freedom for his life, and I should have. I should have stayed in Portland after Greg slit my side. I should've shot Greg when I had the chance and lost my medical license. I thought I'd made the right choice, but I was wrong, and it hurt everyone around me. And even if I didn't do those things, at the very least, I should've left the second he showed up here, but I was selfish and didn't want to give up my life for a second time... No matter how I look at this, I'm responsible. I'm sorry for bringing my problems to your door. You, your family, and friends didn't deserve to suffer the consequences of my cowardice. Please, let Bridgett and Dallas know I'll cover any monetary expense this cost them, now and in the future." I swallowed hard. "Close the door, please." My voice was fading because my throat was closing in on my vocal cords.

"Don't leave. Come back inside and let's go to bed."

I shook my head. "No... I know what you did to yourself after you lost Kate, and I don't want to stay so you can do it to *me*. I can do it myself just fine. I'll have Garrett come get my stuff when he can." I turned the wheel away from Noah and pushed lightly on the gas pedal. He was standing behind the door, so it couldn't clip him, and he'd back up out of instinct. It was slightly dangerous to count on his response, but it worked.

"No! Holly! Don't!" Noah yelled quickly and grabbed onto the door, but he couldn't keep his grip.

I waited until I was at the end of the driveway before I stopped to close my door, then went toward Red Wing instead of Rochester. It'd be the first place Noah went to find me, and I didn't want to be found...

Chapter 25

Two Months Later

"**D**r. Bennett, can I get help with a consult down in the ER? The patient is experiencing a tremor in their speech, but muscle function seems to be fine, blood work is all coming back normal, and I'm not seeing anything on the CT." One of the first-year residents, Dr. Ayad, asked as he sat a tablet down on the charger and picked up another.

"Pull up the scans for me, please." I continued typing my notes from the last patient I'd seen.

"I'm getting them. My tablet was on its last leg."

"Bennett, nine-o-nine is complaining of severe leg pain. She hasn't had the blankets on her legs, so I can't tell if there's any abnormal coldness. Should I send her for a Venography or do an ultrasound?" an intern asked from the other side of me.

"Do the ultrasound first, if you think you see something do the venography." I reached for the tablet Ayad was handing me. "Did you run tests for onset Parkinson's?"

Dr. Ayad nodded. "Everything I can think of. I'm at a loss."

I zoomed in on the CT image to make sure I was seeing correctly, then swiped to another to double check. "Broca's Aphasia. See here?" I turned the tablet and showed what I was seeing.

His black brows furrowed as he looked. "But there's barely anything there, and radiology didn't say anything."

"It's minor and likely to resolve itself with therapy. Do the tests in line with the diagnostic and let me know the results when you have them." I turned back to my tablet on the counter and noticed the intern still standing there. "Did you need something further?"

"Can you assist with the D-ultrasound? I'm afraid I'll miss something. I don't have a lot of experience." She sounded nervous as she spoke, but I didn't know why. Calloway was the hot head, not me. I was just quiet at work.

"I can't. I have to leave in just a minute. Please, find Dr. Ned and ask him to supervise. Do not ask him to do it for you. You need to know this."

"Got it. Thanks." She turned and walked toward the hall.

I let out a breath and finished the last of my notes before logging out, putting my tablet back, and going to the elevator. Supervising the intern would have been better than going to my OB appointment, but I'd already rescheduled twice over patient emergencies. While my doctor understood, I knew it was disrespectful to reschedule just because I didn't feel like going. Garrett texted me when I walked into the room I was supposed to meet Dr. Nell Hannon in. He wanted to know if

I wanted him to sit in on the appointment so I wouldn't be alone, but as I was about to text him no, I saw a figure above my phone.

"What are you doing here?" My heart jump started because I hadn't seen or spoken to Noah in nearly two months.

"I'd ask you the same, but I already know because I got a call at the house about your prenatal visit because the voicemail on your phone was full. Probably from all the unheard messages *I* left." Noah looked the same as before, but somehow not the same either.

I sent the text to Garrett and sat down in the other chair beside the counter in the corner of the room.

"You're not going to say anything?" He sounded more surprised than upset.

I shook my head. "I don't have anything to say," I responded quietly. My heart was still jackhammering so I took a slow breath in and let it out.

"Holly... I shouldn't have said anything or pointed fingers. It wasn't fair... You did what you thought was best for everyone involved, and I'm no more a fortune teller than you are, so there's no telling what might've happened if you *had* reported him. He could've talked his way out of it, turned everything on *you*, still done the same thing... I just... I was hurt by that letter and I shouldn't have been..."

I nodded once, still not looking at him. My eyes were focused on my hands. "I'm sorry the letter hurt you."

"Can you please stop being cold? I'm legitimately sorry and trying to apologize."

I took in another breath to focus on calming myself. "I'm not trying to be cold... I don't know how to face you or accept words that are coming too late." I looked at him. "You were pretty clear about what you thought of me, and I... don't want to be with someone who doesn't try to understand or be on my side when I need them to be. Also, your words are stuck in my head, and I don't know what I'm supposed to do with them. If I stay with you, I'm the push-over, over-forgiving coward you think I am, and clearly falling into another pattern of abuse, and if I don't..." I shook my head, "then I'm just here pregnant with a kid I didn't want, until *you* were part of the picture. I don't know, Noah. I don't know what I'm supposed to do. All I've got is just trying to get through the damn day because I can't stop hearing people's words and feeling the tremendous amounts of guilt because I know it's deserved. I don't have anything for you. Admissions, apologies, they're just words and they'll never be enough. I can't—"

There was a light knock on the door before it opened and I wiped the tears that were falling. My emotions were already out for me because of my hormones, and it was all the worse because of the truly dark pit I was in.

"Oh. There's two in here today." Nell looked at Noah with a smile, then me and her smile fell. "Are you okay, Holly? Do you want me to come back in a little bit?"

I shook my head and stood up. "No. I'm okay." I cleared my throat because my voice was half gone. "This is Noah Jackson, the father."

"Oh, okay. It's nice to meet you. I need to get Holly on the table for a quick exam, would you mind stepping out for a moment?" Nell gave a friendly smile as she spoke to Noah.

"That's not necessary. I appreciate it, but I'm okay, and he's welcome to be here," I told her as I sat on the table.

She gave me an implicative look, like she was wondering if I was really okay.

"Surge of hormones and missing my family." I forced a kind smile.

"Ah. Yeah, the hormones are pesky. Are those antidepressants helping at all?"

I shook my head. "I couldn't handle the side effects, but it's okay. I'm finding alternative ways to handle it." I held out my arm so she could put the blood pressure cuff on.

"How about the nausea?"

"About fifty percent better." I watched what she was doing.

"That's an improvement at least. You're keeping strong on the water intake?"

I nodded.

"Did you weigh yourself before you came back?"

I nodded. "Yeah, but I lost another two pounds. I've upped my intake, but apparently, I need to do more."

"You got it. Tell Calloway you need to cut back on your hours or have him put you on more paperwork duty. Blood pressure is normal. I'll have you lay back and let's see if we can get a heartbeat."

I slid myself back, then grabbed onto my bad leg to lift it so she could pull out the extension on the table. "Did you get my test results back?"

"I *did*. Everything is normal, Baby isn't at risk for anything. Did you want to know the sex?" She pulled out the extension, then held the pillow up as I laid back.

I looked at Noah.

He opened his hands and pulled back the corner of his mouth. "That's up to *you*," he responded quietly.

I looked back at Nell and nodded.

She smiled brightly. "I know you were hoping for a boy, but it's a girl, and I promise once she gets here, you'll love her just as much." She looked at Noah. "The two of you seem like girl parents anyway. I told Holly that was my guess when I met her. I'm very rarely wrong." Nell grabbed a bottle of jelly and squirted some on my abdomen before turning on the heart doppler. "Okay. Let's see if she'll cooperate for us." She put the wand against my stomach and moved it around. "So, there's Mom's heartbeat, and you need to calm down, and..." she continued to move the wand around, "here's baby." Nell looked down at the screen on the doppler. "One-forty-five. Perfect."

I kept my focus on the ceiling because I didn't want to look over and see what might be on Noah's face. If he was happy, it would hurt as badly as if he wasn't. There hadn't been a point in the last two months where I didn't feel like I was very literally dying of heartbreak. As much as I wanted to say it was because Brad was dead, that was less than half of it. Leaving Noah was worse.

"Okay. Here's a towel, hun." She handed me the towel, then helped me sit and pushed the extension back into the table. "Alright, so everything is good so far, but I *really* need you to stop losing weight. Less physical activity. You're burning off the extra calories you're taking in, that with the morning sickness is going to become a very serious problem for you. At this point, I don't care if your diet consists of fast-food, pizza, and candy bars, I *really* need to see you gain a few pounds. I'll write you a note for Calloway—even though he'll probably throw it in the trash—but you need to take it easy outside of work too. Honestly, I'd like to see you take some time off to get rid of some stress, but I understand if you're not able to. Is there anything else you wanted to talk about, or any questions?"

I shook my head.

"How much weight does she need to gain?" Noah asked.

"Overall, I'd like to see thirty-five to forty pounds." Nell looked at me. "You're already pretty small, and counting what you've lost, that's what I'm looking for."

"How much by the next visit?" Noah asked.

"That'd be in a month, so if you could hit the ten to fifteen mark, that'd set us right. Any other questions?"

Noah shook his head. "No. Thank you." He forced a smile, but it didn't look disingenuous.

"No problem. I'll see you back in a month and we'll do your twenty-week ultrasound and get a good look at that cute little tummy monster. You both have a good day." Nell put a hand on my knee briefly with a smile.

"You too. Thanks, Nell." I forced a smile of my own.

"Anytime." She opened the door and went out. I'd worked with her on some OB patients experiencing neurological issues and I loved the way she approached things medically, which was why I'd chosen her.

Noah stood up and stepped in front of me as he held out his hands. I took them because I *did* need the help. I was off the crutches, but it'd only been a week, and if I stepped wrong, I'd get a nice shooting pain up and down my leg.

"Do you have to go back to work?"

I shook my head. "I wish I *could*, but I've hit my max hours already this week. Calloway over booked us, then we had a couple that came in from the ER after a boating accident. I've been here for forty hours." I grabbed my purse from the chair.

"Let me take you home then."

I shook my head and reached for the door. "Garrett will take me."

Noah put a hand on the handle before I could. "Holly, I need a chance here. I heard you, I know I hurt you, but I need a chance... Let me get you some food and take you home, at least give me the chance to talk. *Please.*"

I took in a breath and let it out slowly. His words from two months ago were really just railing me that hard. Normally, I would've given him the chance, but his words had me questioning myself so badly I didn't know what to do anymore.

"Holly, please." There was a desperate hurt in his beautiful green eyes. It felt like it'd been forever since I'd noticed them, and it made things clear out of my mind long enough to manage a nod.

"Okay."

He opened the door for me, and I walked out of the room. Noah followed beside me, but slightly behind. "Does anything sound good for food?"

I shook my head. "Not really. You can stop wherever you want, and I'll find something."

"Do you need to grab anything before we go?"

I shook my head again. We walked in silence to the parking garage, and when we got in sight of Noah's truck, Gif saw me and jumped out of the bed to run to me as fast as he could. I was as happy to see him as he was to see me, even though I didn't express it the way *he* did. The problem was, he was going to push his big butt against my legs and I wouldn't be able to handle it.

"Noah, stop him." I bent over to put my hands out.

"Oh, shit. Gif, sit." Noah snapped his fingers loudly.

Gif sat but danced in his seated position and whined loudly. There was a look of torture in his eyes as he waited to be released from the command.

"I know, buddy, but you have to take it easy on me. Heel." I patted the side of my leg lightly and he got right up against the side of my leg to walk with me and waggled his butt all the way to the truck. I opened the door and let him hop up first. Noah held the bottom of my elbow and lightly placed a hand against my back as I got in. Gif continued to dance on the seat in anticipation. "Okay, come here," I told him as I held his collar to keep him from stepping on my leg, then hugged him. "I've missed you too," I whispered into his silky fur. He whined and nuzzled his head into me.

Noah got in the truck and started it. "I should have had someone out here to record his jump. I think he would have broken a record." He patted Gif's butt. "Sit."

Gif sat, then pulled back so he could look at Noah like he was proud of himself.

"Yeah, I know." Noah pet his head. "This dumb mutt has been relentlessly destroying the house because he misses you. He tore up the carpet in front of the door to your room downstairs."

"Are you an outside doggo now?" I rubbed Gif's ear.

"Mm-hm. Why do you think he misses you so badly?" Noah backed out of the parking spot.

I pulled my badges off my coat and handed them to Noah so he wouldn't have to pay for parking.

"How far along are you?" Noah glanced at me before he took the turn to go down the ramp.

"Seventeen weeks... I found out the morning of the

wedding, but I wanted to wait to tell you once we got to the hotel. That didn't happen, and I didn't want to say anything at the hospital or after because no one wanted to hear what was supposed to be good news."

"I know why you didn't, and as much as I was hurt by finding out the way I did, I understand... Are you doing okay with it though?" He glanced at me again before rolling down his window to scan my badge and hand it back to me. "I know you weren't too sure about having kids."

I held up my shoulders. "Not much I can do about it, and my dad had two—one that wasn't even his own—and still maintained his career, so... That's what I keep telling myself."

"Bridgett said she's been trying to call you, but you won't return her calls, and one of your interns asked her to leave when she came here to see you. She *really* wants to talk to you."

I shook my head. "I contacted the hospital to pay her medical bills, and unless there's something that was missed, I don't want contact." I knew Bridgett was desperately trying to get ahold of me, and it was because Dallas *had* found me and blew up at me.

"She's not mad, Holly. She loves you."

"I love her too, but I won't be the person that stands between her and Dallas. He's made his position clear, and I'm respecting it." I rubbed my stomach because it was hurting. A combination of lack of sleep and food. Gif whined and pawed at my arm, so I wrapped my arm around him and hugged him to my side. It kept him from pawing me, but he continued to whine.

"Has he said something to you?" Noah looked at me,

seeming a little surprised somehow.

"That night, then he caught me outside of Brad's house in Portland about two weeks after." I closed my eyes as I rested my head on top of Gif's. The little furball made me feel better. He just loved unconditionally, and I needed it.

"Shit. I'm sorry. You should've called me, or texted. He's been... I don't know what's wrong with him." Noah let out a long breath.

I kept my arm around Gif, but picked my head up. "It's like you said, Bridgett got hurt. She's the glue between all of you."

Dallas and Bridgett were also extremely close as a couple. They were the air in each other's lungs, the way Noah and I used to be.

"You got hurt too, Love... I think it was seen differently because you were the only one who wasn't unconscious or dead. And you got blamed because the person responsible was too dead to take it... You kept asking me what I wanted from you, and I couldn't answer because I couldn't think enough, but... I just wanted to be mad. I was angry about people being shot, about our reception being taken over by the worst thing that could happen, by Dallas screaming at me that I never should've married you or let you in our lives. I just wanted to be mad, and I took it out on *you*... I'm unbelievably sorry, Holly... And you were right to leave. You didn't deserve to sit there and be verbally abused. You give everyone your heart and soul, and you'd never bring harm to people around you. The proof of that was you walking right up to Greg, ready to be shot and killed just to protect everyone else. You didn't worry about the fact that *you'd* been shot, you just ran to help everyone. You didn't even get mad that we all lied to you and told you Brad was okay even though he was already gone... You didn't deserve any of the blow back from this, Sweetheart... You really didn't."

I sat there quietly. Noah meant every word, I could hear it, but I couldn't feel any less guilty. I'd blamed myself long before people started pointing their fingers at me.

"And I don't know what I have to do to make things right between us again, but I *will*... It's not because of the baby, that was just a good way to find you so I could talk to you. I love you, and I still want to be married to you, and have you *home*. So, whatever it takes... I'll do it, or I'll find a way." Noah's voice was a little strained as he spoke. He pulled into the drive-thru of a little local place we used to frequent when he'd come to get me from long shifts I couldn't drive home from. Noah looked at me when I didn't respond right away.

I nodded because I didn't have words and I was un-trusting of anything. He ordered me a strawberry shake and some tater tots, because that's what I normally got when I wasn't feeling well, and we sat there in silence again as we waited for our food.

"What do you need...?" Noah looked at me, though I still wasn't looking at him. "What puts things on a better path?"

"I don't know right now... I've been trying to figure it out since I left, but I'm stuck..." My emotions were on the rise again and it made Gif start whining and moving his head to my shoulder. I continued to pet the long soft fur on his chest.

"Would you be willing to come home...? We can have separate rooms for a while, have space, but not so much of it..."

The window to the restaurant slid back and the girl handed our food and drinks through. I thought about Noah's suggestion, and it seemed like a good one, but I also felt so *tired*. It wasn't that I wanted the relationship to end, it was that I didn't have the energy it would take to fix it. After everything, my mind was barely coherent. I could still think and do my job, but anything outside of that, trying to maintain relationships, I had no strength left. When I wasn't at work, I was either asleep or in bed all day. The cloud of depression over me was heavy and thick, suffocating me into nothing, but I didn't care enough to move out of it. Going back to Noah would mean I'd have to put forward that effort, and I didn't know if I could.

"I don't know," I breathed quietly after he pulled away from the window.

Noah drove to Garrett's house in silence, then looked at me after the truck was parked in the driveway. "Do you not want to come home or work this out? You're not saying anything, and I don't know if you've already made up your mind here, or there's something I haven't said that you're still waiting to hear." There was no agitation in his voice, just honesty.

I shook my head. "I don't know..." I looked at him, tears getting ready to set in again. "I don't feel good right now. It's all I have to pull myself out of bed for work right now, and if I didn't have *that*, I wouldn't be here." The corners of my mouth started to quiver, so I bit them for a second to make them stop. "I miss you, and I still love you, but I can't tell you I can come home and make things right again when I'm not sure I'll even be able to get myself out of bed." I pushed Gif back a little because he was whining and trying to nuzzle his head against my face.

"Gif, stop it. Come on." Noah opened his door and got

out to make Gif get out. He immediately took off to find Garrett's dog, Burt. Noah closed his door and walked around to my side and opened the door. "Come here. Face me. I don't want to hurt your leg."

I wiped a tear off my cheek and turned myself to face him but couldn't look at him.

"Holly..." he took my hands and held them gently. "I'm going to tell you the truth here, so please don't rat me out or go after Garrett... *He* called me and told me to go to your appointment. He said this wasn't sleep deprivation, or just being upset... You look like you're *dying*. You're even smaller than when you first got here, your eyes have dark circles under them, and you can barely look at me... What is going on? What part of this made you run or is keeping you down? Short of stalking you, I've tried everything I could think of to reach out or apologize. I didn't want you to feel like you had another Greg on your back, so I've tried to respect your boundaries, but I don't know what to *do,* and I'm looking at you and I'm legitimately scared for you." He rubbed his thumbs over the back of my hands. "I really need you to talk to me..."

"I don't know. I don't know what to say." My voice was shaking along with the rest of me.

"At this point, I think you do, but you're afraid to say anything to me because you think I'll go off on you or something, and that's not why I'm here... I was wrong, Holly. If there was a way I could prove to you that I mean my words other than time, I would, but all I can do is be honest the way I always have."

"Fine." I looked at him. "Everyone walked out on me... Everyone I counted on, anyone I had *left,* walked out on me.

The *only* person who even *tried* to understand is my emotionally inept mother. And after *everything* we've been through, after all the 'I love you's' and the promises to be by my side, you couldn't even muster up enough to *fake* caring. I left the house, but *you* left me. You and everyone else abandoned me, and I needed you." I held my breath to starve out the cry and looked away from him.

"I did, but I didn't mean to... Come here." He reached his hands around the back of my hips and pulled me toward him before he hugged me so tightly it almost hurt. "I'm sorry... I made mistakes too... and I need a chance." He kissed the side of my jaw. "It'll never happen again, Love. All I have right now are words, and the actions will follow, but I promise you, it'll never happen again." His voice was just a whisper in my ear.

I reached my arm up around his shoulder to wipe the tear off my cheek.

"I don't know what you did, but if you're here to do it again, I'll cut your scrotum off and make a keychain out of it." Clara's raspy voice sounded from behind Noah, but I couldn't see her. "Are you okay, Girly?"

Noah kissed my cheek, then pulled back to turn and look at Clara. I nodded to answer her and wiped another tear.

"I saw another recognizable mutt in the backyard, so I came out to make sure you were okay." Clara looked me over, then glanced at Noah. "I'd say it's good to see you, but it's *not.*"

Noah's eyebrows twitched upward briefly. "Likewise." He looked at me and offered a hand to help me down. I held onto his hand and arm with both hands because the drop to the ground was too far without help. Noah took my elbow to help me more, then reached behind me to grab my milk-shake, the bag of tater tots, and my purse. "Will you text me after you wake up?"

I looked at him and nodded. "It'll probably be tomorrow morning."

He nodded. "That's fine. Think about what I said too, okay?"

I nodded again and hugged his side. "Thank you for coming, and for lunch." My voice was so quiet I wasn't even sure he heard me.

Noah tipped my chin to the side to kiss my cheek. "Always. I love you."

"I love you too."

He rubbed my back before I stepped away, and he whistled for Gif once I was a few steps from Clara.

I turned. "Would you mind if I kept Gif...? Overnight, I mean."

Noah smiled just a little and shook his head. "Not at all. Get some sleep."

I nodded again, then looked at Gif. "Come on, buddy."

"Pompous asshole," Clara muttered bitterly as we went to the door. "What the *hell* is he doing here?"

"He just came to talk. And why are you mad at him?" I'd never told Clara *or* Garrett what was said between Noah and I.

"Well, you've been mad at him for a reason, and I know you well enough to know it wouldn't be something petty, so I'm mad at him too."

"Don't be. It's been me and him."

"I know, and I pick *you*. Come on, Burt. You dumb mutt."

I looked down to make sure Gif was still with me and he

was. "Is Dad home?"

"He's in the kitchen making more crap to make me fatter." Clara pushed the door closed after Burt was inside. She'd been staying at Garrett's house ever since she came home from the hospital, but I didn't know if it was because she wanted to or because of me. Either way, I was glad she was there. While I didn't spend as much time with her as I should have, she'd been a huge support through everything. She kept Garrett from hovering so much, and she kept me from completely coming undone at Brad's funeral service in San Francisco.

I made my way to the kitchen where Garrett was pouring something from a bowl into a bread pan. He seemed slightly nervous when he looked up at me.

"How'd your appointment go?"

"Same as the others." I walked around the island and hugged him.

"Are you okay?" he asked quietly after a second.

I nodded. "Thank you..."

Garrett let out a breath. "He told you?"

I shook my head. "No. I've never listed his house number on anything, so I assumed it was you." I stepped back from the hug and looked at him.

His eyebrows raised. "You miss nothing, but I'm glad it worked. Were you just coming in to say goodbye?"

I shook my head. "No... I need to sleep and think some..."

"Kid... you're miserable. Read into that. I know you lost Brad, but I don't think this has ever been about him..."

"It's not, but it's not that simple." I set the bag of tater tots on the counter.

"Probably not, but it doesn't have to be that complicated either… You love him, you married him, and you'll both work out whatever this is with time. But if you're *here*, you're not even trying. Call him… get yourself back on track. Stop hiding out in my basement all day and night and go home. I love you, and I love having you here, but not like this." Garrett spoke his words tenderly.

I took in a breath and let it out. Part of my brain was thinking about how I'd clearly overstayed my welcome, and the other part was hyper-focused on the relieving feeling of Noah hugging me in the truck. It was the only brief moment of relief I'd had in months.

"Call him… It's not like you can't come back if it doesn't work out, but I promise you, it *will*. He's been miserable without you too…"

I took in another deep breath and reached into my purse for my phone. Instead of calling Noah, I texted him and asked him to come back.

"See? First step is over. Take it all in small steps and it won't look like such a mountain." Garrett put a hand on my shoulder and walked behind me to the fridge. "I'll see you in a few days for the twins' surgery." We were going to be in a surgery together to separate conjoined twins that were four years old.

"Yeah. I'm gonna go downstairs and grab a few things. Will you keep your phone on? I don't have my car. It's still at the hospital."

"I *will*, but your car is in the garage already. Another part of my plan to make sure you two talked." Garrett looked at me with a smile.

I rolled my eyes and went toward the basement stairs. "How confident of you."

"You're like your mother, you like to run." He laughed a little.

"Bye," I called. There was no need for me to go back upstairs because I'd go out the basement door.

"Bye, Kid. Love you."

"Love you too."

Chapter 26

I went down to my room, threw some stuff in a bag, then went outside and around the back of the house to the driveway. Noah was already in the driveway again. I opened the back door for Gif.

"Is Clara bitching about having him here?" Noah asked.

"No. I wanna go home." I closed the door, then walked around the truck to the passenger door.

Noah reached a hand over to help me up. "You mean home as in our house and not Portland, right?"

"I sold everything in Portland... There's nothing there."

"Brad's house?" He looked at me in a way I didn't understand. Like he was surprised or hurt in some way.

I nodded. "Everything." I pulled my phone out because it was repeatedly chiming with texts. "I kept some of his things from Brad's house and sold everything else. Greg left everything he had to me, so I sold what I could—including the practice—set up a trust for Scarlett—his mother—and got her into an assisted retirement community. She has a niece in the area that's trustworthy, so I set everything up for her to be able to manage everything in the future. I'm sorry, I have to make a call." I put my phone up to my ear and waited for Calloway to answer.

"Why the hell did you tell the scrub monkey to administer blood thinners to nine-o-nine?" His voice was a loud thunderous snap.

"I didn't, and don't yell at me. I told her to do an ultrasound under Ned's supervision. Anything I *did* tell her is in the notes."

"Then she's throwing you under the bus. God dammit!"

"Did the rice implant move? Do I need to come back to scrub in?"

"Oh, it moved, and she's already dead so it's too damn late now. Why the hell didn't you supervise her yourself? Where the hell are you anyway?"

"I had an OB appointment, and I'm already past eighty-two hours this week. I'm done until Monday, but Ayad is there and I rearranged the schedule. Everyone knows if they miss a shift they're done."

He let out a loud huff. "God dammit. I just scheduled another surgery for tomorrow. How are you at eighty-two hours already?" He wasn't yelling, but he was still irritated.

"Because you over booked me Monday and Tuesday, so I was there for thirty-nine hours, got six hours of sleep, and went back for forty-three hours."

"Shit... Can you at least come back and talk to the family?"

"No. I'm already out of town."

"Out of town? Are you back with your boyfriend or something?"

"I have to go, I'll talk to you later." I pulled the phone away and hung up before I sat there for a second.

"Did you need me to take you back?"

I shook my head. "No. We lost the patient already." I dropped my phone into my purse. "He's being unreasonable because he hates talking to families and he has to because one of the interns caused the death."

"Geez... Are you okay?"

I shrugged a shoulder. "Can't change it."

•••••••

On the way to Noah's, I ate the tater tots and drank my shake, then went down to my former room in the basement, took a shower, and crashed. If there was anything to be thankful for, it was the comfort of my mattress. The ones at Garrett's were all hard as rocks. Gif stayed on the bed with me, occasionally curling up against my side or back. Then Noah came in a couple times to have me eat and drink something, but otherwise, I was dead to the world and completely okay with it. Every way there was to be exhausted, I was. When Noah came in to get me out of bed, I was still so tired I could hardly wake up enough to pay attention.

"Holly, come on. You've been asleep for more than twenty-four hours. This isn't any better than being awake for too long." He rubbed my arm.

"I'm just tired," I whispered.

"I know, but let's get up and do stuff. I need to go into town and order some stuff at the lumberyard, then we can go find some lunch and go for a walk or something."

I took in a breath and let it out, forcing my eyes open.

My head was throbbing, and my body ached everywhere. I wasn't the kind of person who got body aches, but it'd been happening more and more.

Noah pulled back the blankets. "I'll turn the shower on for you."

Normally, I would have pulled him into bed with me, so I could keep laying there, but I didn't want him to sit there and hug me and kiss me. I wanted to be alone.

......

I sat complacent and compliant as Noah drove me into town, stopped at the lumber yard, and brought me to the diner for lunch, but that changed the second he pulled up in front of Bridgett's office.

"No," I said before he'd even fully come to a stop. "I'm not doing this, and you didn't ask."

"Because I'm *not* asking." He stopped and put the truck in park. "You need to talk to her, and you need help, Holly." He shut the truck off. "Whatever is going on with you, it's more than being upset with me or being upset over Brad." He took in a deep breath and let it out before he looked at me. "I'm sorry for ambushing you, but I think you need someone who knows you and knows the situation to help."

It wasn't that I was unaware I needed help or that things had gotten worse than "normal" upset, I just didn't care to do anything about it.

"I can't go in there. Dallas will—"

"Dallas won't do anything because for one he's out of town, and two, I'll handle him." Noah opened his door, got out, closed it, and walked around to my side.

He was going to push this, and even if I refused to go in, Bridgett would come out to the house. She'd been trying to hunt me down, it was just that I was vigilant, so she hadn't caught me yet. Noah opened my door and looked down the sidewalk because a couple of teenage boys were being loud.

"Can we make a compromise? I'll go see someone, but not Bridgett." I looked at him, hoping he'd at least concede to *that*.

He shook his head. "She wants to see you, she's your best friend *and* mine, and we need to work stuff out between *us* and I'd rather have Bridgett be the one, because she puts me in check pretty damn fast."

I bit the inside of my cheek and popped my seatbelt. "I'm glad it's about what *you* want, and what *you* need." I didn't let him help me down from the truck, which killed my leg, but I didn't care.

"Is this where we are? Is this what it's going to be between us? This passive aggressive bullshit?" Noah followed behind me.

"I said I didn't want to do this, I didn't want to be here. Did you listen? Did you even try to hear the words out of my mouth? I said no! I love that men think that because they're bigger and louder, they can say and do whatever they want! 'Do *this*, Holly!' '*Don't* do *this*, Holly!' 'You should've done *this* or *that!*' 'You're too fat,' 'you're too skinny,' 'don't think about it this way, think about it that way,' 'feel this but don't feel that!' 'Give them a chance or *you're the* problem, but don't give *that* one the chance or you're a goddamn pushover!' I'm TIRED! I'm unbelievably goddamn tired!" And I was tired of sitting quietly when all I wanted to do was scream.

"Okay, we hear you, along with half the town. Let's take this inside, please," Bridgett said as she guided me by the shoulders toward the door. "Go build something, Handsome.

I'll text you when it's safe."

"Sure, because I'm crazy for being sick of being shoved around by men," I muttered bitterly as I yanked the door open.

"No, because men *make* us crazy, and he *is* one." She followed me in. "Lady, you're done for the day. Lock the door on your way out," she told Adelia as we walked past the front desk.

I walked into Bridgett's office but didn't sit down once we got inside. "Dallas was incredibly clear about me staying away from you."

She snorted. "And you just went on a loud rant about men telling you what to do. Dallas doesn't wear the pants in the relationship, and the threat of not getting in *my* pants is enough to shut that down." She went to her mini fridge and pulled out a wine cooler and a bottle of water. "I'd offer you booze to take off the edge, but Noah told me about the mini Jackson you've been keeping from everyone." She smiled and handed me the bottle. "So, water for you."

I took the water and set it down on the coffee table. "I don't want to be here, and I don't want to do whatever this is."

"I know, but I'm persistent." She cracked open the wine cooler, sat on top of her desk, and chugged a bunch of it. "I waited for this moment all day long. Listening to people's petty problems gets old. Yours on the other hand, *gold*. I need to move to the cities so I can deal with bigger shit."

I rolled my eyes and shook my head. "What do you want? Why have you been so desperate to track me down?"

"Well, number one, I like you because you have a brain in your head unlike my chattier besties. Two, I wanted to thank you for being a super badass doctor and saving my life. Three, I yelled at Noah so bad I almost hit him when he told me not only what he said, but that it was over the letter I told you to write. Four, I'm *crazy* proud you actually *wrote* it. Five, I love your guts. Six, you look like shit. Seven, I'm really sorry about Brad and Greg. Eight, people keep calling me because they think you're suicidal and we should probably deal with that." She took in a deep breath and let it out, like she'd starved herself of air over talking so much.

"I'm not suicidal."

"Do you want to be alive?"

"No, but that doesn't make me suicidal."

She shrugged casually. "You're right... but the lines can get blurry when you're in a place like that, so I ask. I told Noah you committed life suicide again, so *actual* suicide was probably off the table since you didn't just go straight for it."

Bridgett had a way of pointing out the most obvious things that I somehow didn't think of. I *had* ended my "life" a second time.

"I'd try to skip right to the part where I tell you it's not your fault, but I know you won't believe me, so... we'll go at this a different way. Did you kill Greg?"

I frowned. "No."

"Would he have ended up dead if you'd stayed in Portland?"

I shook my head. "I don't know."

"Give it your best guess." She gave a simplistic shrug.

"Probably. Either from drinking and driving or... I don't know, me getting sick of it, or Brad finding out."

"And if he'd gone to jail?"

"Dead in five minutes." I shoved my hand through

my hair. It wasn't the first time I'd thought of it. "He either would've picked a fight with the wrong person or killed himself after sentencing."

She nodded. "And would *that* have been your fault?"

"It would feel like it if I were the one who put him there."

"Just because something feels like it, doesn't mean it is. You're a doctor. The sniffles can look like a cold, but that doesn't mean it is. Could be allergies, could be a sinus infection, could be an abscess in the nasal cavity..."

"Your point?"

"Shit happens. There's a thousand ways you could've dealt with Greg and been right here. You could've left the second he showed up, he still could've killed Brad and the rest of us just to find out where you were. Also..." She turned and picked some papers up off her desk and held them out to me.

I walked forward and took them. "What's this?"

"Your friend, Bethany, she went to the police... They showed up at the house, found Greg passed out on the floor, saw the blood and the mess, cuffed him and stuffed him, and the skeevy weasel talked his way right out of an attempted murder charge. While you'd been seen post slasher-film, his prints were the *only* ones on the knife, and it was only *your* blood on the knife. They found your clothes in the garage, saw where you were cut, deemed that you couldn't have physically done it yourself as he claimed. While trifling through your computer, the police found a locked file where you'd kept record of everything that happened." She laughed humorlessly. "You even had pictures and video footage from your security cameras... but he walked on a technicality... The rookies that brought in your computer had no probable cause to search *your* computer. Then, the judge who was overseeing

Greg's case showed a little favoritism, and it all went away..."

I bit the inside of my cheeks as I held my breath to keep from bursting. I didn't know if I was angry, hurt from everything, or what it was, but I just wanted to throw myself on the floor in a screaming cry.

"You can probably argue that if *you'd* been the one to turn him in, he wouldn't have been let out of the skeevy weasel farm, but I think I'd have to call bullshit on that. This could've happened regardless of who reported him."

I swallowed hard and braved a breath. "Who's seen this?"

"Mm, *me*, Arnie—Dallas' boss—but that's probably it."

I nodded and swallowed against the lump in my throat again.

"Is it still your fault...? After knowing this?" She pointed at the papers in my hand.

I didn't want to admit she was right, it all still felt like my fault, but I couldn't logic my way into a contorted reason that it was still my fault.

Bridgett slid off the end of her desk and walked toward me. "Go make them eat crow, Honey." She hugged me and kissed my cheek. "Hand this to Dallas or any other loud mouthed asshole, and tell them to suck it. Tell Noah he's an ass for what he said and not sticking by you, and when you feel pushed around by men, open your pretty mouth and push back. I know you're not allowed to have claws when you're a doctor, so keep a scalpel in your pocket."

A smirk forced its way out, but quickly turned into something uglier, and I hugged her back.

"See? I'm awesome and this is why you love me. I make you feel better." She kissed my cheek again, then continued hugging me.

••••••

Bridgett had texted Noah to go home and that she'd bring me home after we were done. I wasn't really up for the shopping trip, especially to buy things for the baby, but I felt better having Bridgett back. We went out for dinner and talked a lot more. Everything just came out in a blurt. If it had been in my head at any point in the last two months, it fell right out, and Bridgett cleaned it up the way she did everything else. It didn't make things hurt less, but it felt better to have someone else to help me process the mess.

Around nine o'clock, I finally got home. Noah wasn't in the house, but there was a note on the counter that said he was across the property working in his shop. He would've wanted me to drive out there and let him know, but I texted him instead, then went downstairs for another shower. I frowned a little when all my stuff from Garrett's was piled up in boxes in the basement. It wasn't because I wasn't planning on moving it anyway, just that there seemed to be this big push for me to do it without anyone asking. I wasn't necessarily ready to be in the same bedroom as Noah yet, but I started carrying boxes upstairs to the bedroom. There weren't all that many boxes, maybe six small ones, and four medium ones, but the trips up and down all the stairs had my leg hurting so badly I could barely make it up with the last box, so I stayed upstairs in the closet to put things away. That's where Noah found me when he came in.

"I see Bridgett couldn't contain her credit cards again." Noah stood against the doorway, looking me over.

I nodded. "Yeah... I tried to stop her, but it was like she'd never heard the word 'no' before."

"She's excited... I am too... I was out in the shop working on a crib, so don't go out there. It can't fully be a surprise, but I want it to be a surprise."

I nodded again and closed the shoe box of Brad's things I'd been peeking through.

"Can we talk about this?"

I looked at Noah because I didn't know what he was talking about, then saw he was holding all the papers Bridgett had given me earlier. "Where did you get those?"

"Bridge came out and gave them to me before she left."

I took in a breath and let it out with an eye-roll. "I love how I specifically asked her *not* to share those or tell anyone and she did the opposite of that." I held my hand out for the papers.

Noah stepped forward and gave them to me. "Yeah, it was kind of shitty, but I'm wondering the same thing as her... Why not? Why didn't you want me to know?" There was nothing attacking in his voice. He was still being cautious.

I tossed the papers into the corner so I could burn them later. "Because it'd look like I'm trying to be right and make you eat your words. I never wanted or needed to be right, I need understanding. *Also,* it changes nothing. It *changed* nothing..."

"Even though I'd already come to the conclusion that it probably wasn't as simple as I initially made it out to be, I think it changes a lot... And I guess I don't understand what the problem is with you being right, because you obviously *were.*"

I looked at him. "Was that the point for you? After we came home and you said all the things you said, you only wanted to be *right*...? I don't think that should ever be the point of an argument. It *should* be to express something and find a common ground or a compromise, not to be *right*."

He sat down on the floor across from me but to the side. "I just wanted to be mad and hit you with words because there was nothing else I could do. That wasn't right either, and I know I apologized earlier, but I'm sorry again... I had no right in the world to do that to you, regardless of what happened or how angry I was. And I had no right to badger you over that letter either. I'm not sure why, but I was hurt by it..."

"I don't know what there would be to be hurt by." I opened another box beside me to see what was inside.

"I don't know... I think the idea that you were at some point happy with him made me a little jealous, then... the admission that you still love him. I don't understand it. And that's not to say you're wrong for feeling that way, it just means I don't understand."

I swallowed hard but didn't know what to say, so I kept my focus on sorting things inside the box.

"How do you feel about him being gone...? Honestly." His voice was still quiet and even.

He asked for honesty, but I was afraid to give it because he wouldn't like the answer. "Past the relief that he's not out there waiting for me around the corner... heartbroken."

"The relief was kind of a given, but why heartbroken?"

My chest was filling with pressure, and it made it hard to breathe through it. "Because I never wanted him to die... He wasn't a monster, or this evil person everyone makes him out to be. He was desperate to be loved and accepted... His dad yanked him around as a kid, played cruel mind games, and left him empty. He was always trying to fill it, but he didn't fit in with other people. The drinking started because it was a way to fit in with his clients, to get them to see past his odd quirks and... different ways of doing things. Then it turned into victory drinks, then the victory drinks came home, and went into the office the next day... He lost control and he lost himself in the drinking because he wanted to be accepted, and I watched all of it..." I swallowed hard. "It doesn't excuse what he did, not by any stretch, but..."

"But you saw that there was a man before the monster," Noah finished quietly. "You never really told me how things progressed with him, but I'm sorry for not trying to under-stand... You kind of hit me in the gut when you pointed out the similarities between me and him... It's not that I didn't already know, I was more hoping you never saw it, then feel-ing embarrassed and angry when you did."

"I didn't. I was trying to think of something to get you to understand where I was coming from. There's a massive difference between you and him. You stopped... he didn't." I pushed the box over and pulled over another one. "I wasn't trying to hurt your feelings, and I'm sorry." I looked at him for a moment so he'd know I meant it. My brain had gone over the entirety of everything I'd rubbed in his face, and I still felt sick over it.

"You don't need to apologize. Everything you said, I needed to hear... Things *aren't* black and white, even when it seems like they should be."

I pulled a picture frame out of the box beside me, keep-ing it turned over, and handed it to Noah. "Can you put this in the shoe box beside you, please?"

Noah took it and I went back to sorting. It was a picture of Brad and I sitting on a bench at the back of my dad's property, just before the cliff face. He had his arm along the back of the bench behind me and I had my head on his shoulder. Lupita had come up behind us to take the picture. It was kind of a bad moment for Brad and I. We were upset over a mutual friend we'd lost, so we just went out to our dad's 'thinking' bench to sit quietly. It was one of my favorite pictures, but I couldn't stomach looking at it. Anything of Brad's, anything relating to him, I couldn't handle thinking about it. I didn't know how to be in a world without him, so I tried with every-thing in me to ignore the reality that I *was*.

"You can put this somewhere in the house. You don't have to keep everything in a box." Noah spoke cautiously. "It's your house too. You can fill more than just the closet with your stuff."

I shook my head. "It's okay in the box."

"You had this same picture in the living room in your apartment, so put it downstairs. I didn't mean 'my house' the way you took it that night. I built this house for *you*, for both of us."

I shook my head again. "It's not that... If it's out in the open, I have to keep facing that he's gone, and I can't right now. Please, put it in the box." I held another frame turned upside down. "This one too."

Noah took in a deep breath as he took the second one. "I was thinking about things the wrong way that night... When Brad died... To me, I saw him as this person who caused un-necessary problems and... the person who brought Greg to our door, so I was indifferent to him being gone. I didn't put it in terms of you losing someone you loved your whole life. Gabe is my best friend, and he's done plenty of asshole things, but I can't imagine losing him. Even Moses... he makes me insane because he can't ever take anything seriously, but I'd feel lost without him... I'm sorry I didn't show more empathy or consideration... I should've been more focused on you instead of trying to think of all the reasons that night shouldn't have ended the way it did. I'm sorry I left you alone..." Noah reached out and ran a lock of my hair between his fingers.

It felt hard to find the words to speak. All he wanted from me was for me to talk, but I was struggling to pull any kind of thought together because I felt empty. "You don't have to keep apologizing for things you've already apologized for. I forgive you and I was done being mad a long time ago. Right now..." I took in a breath, staring into the box in front of me, "I just don't have words. It's not because I'm mad, there are no words."

He rubbed my back lightly with the back of a few fingers. "But you're hurt, and even if you've forgiven me, it doesn't mean you're not owed the apology... I know you're upset about Greg and Brad, but I don't think it would've ever been this bad if I hadn't been a complete asshole to you... I feel like that might make me just as bad, or worse than Greg because I've never seen you this bad off."

I shook my head. "Don't make the comparison. You're nothing like Greg. My inability to cope has nothing to do with you or anyone else. And I don't want to talk about it anymore." *Least of all* with Noah. "Can we please just drop it all?"

"Not quite. What you said earlier outside of Bridgett's office, do you really think that? That I'm always trying to control you?"

"Sometimes... I'm sorry I yelled at you." I looked at him for a moment. "Calloway has been riding me hard because he wants me to take my Oral Exams and be done with being a resident. In reality, because of the years of my dad drilling things into my head and presenting opportunities, I'm well above the standard of a seventh-year resident. He's been intentionally rattling my cage to prepare me, but with everything else, I'm out of patience and coping skills right now. No, I don't think that of you all the time, but yes, today, you weren't listening to me, and I didn't appreciate it. I'm hanging onto the last thread of sanity I have. I'm not oblivious to my health situation, my mental health, or that I'm sitting in this really ugly and thick cloud of grief, but I need people to back off of me and let me find my way through. Before I even realized it, I lost everything that was important to me, and that's hard to take."

He nodded. "I understand... I wasn't trying to shove you off a cliff before you were ready, I just... I'm terrified of losing you... and I'm not talking about you running or leaving me... You really look like you're half a step from ending your life all together, and I can't sit and do nothing to help. Can you at least understand my intent and my actions from *my* side?"

I nodded. "I do, and that's why I'm sorry for blowing up at you. I know you meant well... And I know what it looks like, I've lost weight I can't afford to, I can't get out of bed when I'm not at work because when I'm sleeping, I'm not sleeping. It's nightmare after nightmare. I'm exhausted. The morning sickness is killing me because I have a hard time eating. My food aversions are off the charts. I puke if someone opens a bag of chips near me. You need to know, I'm still trying, I'm not giving up, but I need some patience from everyone."

He nodded "I can't speak for anyone else, but you'll get it from me... The only thing I'm asking in return is for you to talk to me. I want you back, and I'm not talking about just physically being here. I want our relationship back, to feel like I'm not enemy number one on your list, and for us to be as close as we were before. I know I had a huge hand in all of it, and not a good one. I have to earn my place again, and that's okay, I'm willing to do that, but I need to know if you'll even let me."

"I'm here…"

"Okay… Can I make you something to eat?" His brow was furrowed slightly, but his expression was kind.

"No, I had dinner with Bridgett earlier and I'm still full."

"Good. I didn't know where you wanted those boxes, so I just left them downstairs, but I would've carried them up for you."

I nodded. "I know. I wish I would have *let* you. My leg is *not* thanking me right now. I'm okay with walking up the occasional set of stairs, but bringing these up was overkill." I pushed another box in the corner.

"I can grab you an ice pack. I haven't locked up the house yet, so I have to go back down anyway."

I shook my head. "I'll grab some on my way down. I just needed to unpack some of this. Would you mind putting these three boxes up on the top shelf behind the door?" I pointed to the ones I was talking about.

"Yeah." He started to get up and so did I. "Let me help you up." He hooked me under the arms from behind and stood up with me.

"Thank you."

"Is there any chance I can convince you to sleep up here with me, or are we not there yet?" He looked at me with a slight smile before picking up the boxes.

I thought for a moment because I didn't know what I

was okay with yet, or how I felt about anything.

"I'll even promise to keep my hands to myself, but I *hate* sleeping by myself." He turned to look at me.

"I know you do..." I took in a breath and let it out because I was still deciding.

"You don't have to if you're not ready, and you also don't have to sleep downstairs either. You can take this room and I can find a bed in one of the six other rooms in the house."

I shook my head. "I'll sleep up here if you go downstairs and get the bag in the chair and anti-nausea pills. They're on my nightstand."

He nodded. "Anything else?"

I shook my head. "I didn't bring much with me yesterday and it's all in the bag except for the pills."

"Okay." He stepped forward, kissed my forehead, then left to go downstairs.

While Noah was downstairs getting my stuff and closing up the house, I changed into some pajamas, brushed out my hair so I could braid it, and checked my phone. Garrett had texted me to make sure I was doing okay, then Clara because I hadn't texted Garrett back. I texted them both, then responded to another message from Dr. Roth.

"What's the frown for?" Noah asked when he came back up and was walking toward the bed.

"Nothing, I'm trying to think. Dr. Roth was asking me about a surgery my dad did to resect a particular kind of tumor, and I can't remember his exact process." I texted Lupita to ask her to find a video for the surgery in my dad's study. If she could find it, she could send it to me.

"Was your dad really that revolutionary? People are always asking how he did things or singing his praises." Noah went to his dresser to take his watch off and put his phone on the charger.

"He was an incredibly successful risk taker if you ask me, but to everyone else, yes." I put my phone down and grabbed the pill bottle off the top of my bag so I could take one. If I didn't keep up on them, there'd be hell to pay. "He developed a lot of the techniques that are used now, so when people find out I'm *that* Bennett, they turn into a bunch of fan girls." I picked up my phone again because Lupita was texting me back.

"It'll be you before too long." Noah walked over and got down on his knees in front of me.

I didn't know what he was doing until he held up my wedding rings. "I think at least four of my internal organs dropped out when Garrett gave these to me when he came to pick up your stuff after you left."

"Hm. Your spleen, gallbladder, tonsils, and olfactory epithelium?"

He laughed and shook his head. "I don't know what the last one is."

I smiled a little. "Your nose."

He chuckled again. "Okay, maybe four more then."

"Any of them include your liver or kidneys?" It was a cautious way of asking if he'd fallen off the wagon and had a drink.

He shook his head. "No... Surprisingly, that wasn't on my radar."

"Good..."

Noah nodded with a more serious look on his face. "Yeah... I need running to not be your first go-to. I know I messed up, and I accept my consequences, but leaving can't be the first thing you resort to. If you need space because you're upset, tell me that. I'll listen next time, let you walk away and have some space, but don't run and hit the destruct button when you go. *Please*."

I felt the need to explain myself, but it was beating a dead horse. He knew what he'd done, he knew why I'd left, and there had to be a point where we both stopped pulling it up, otherwise it would never stop.

I nodded. "I know. It's a bad habit. I'm sorry."

He took my hand. "I'm not after an apology, Love. I don't know what else you were really supposed to do in that situation. I kept going, then my parents got involved..." He let out a breath. "I'll make sure it never reaches a point like that again, okay?" He rubbed his thumb over the back of my hand.

I nodded. "Me too."

"Can I be back in your inner circle again?" He gave a small hopeful smile. I'd missed his beautiful green eyes.

"Did you fix the garbage disposal?"

He laughed. "Yes, *and* I fixed the ice machine."

"Okay."

Noah slid my rings on my finger, and I pulled him forward to hug him. I'd missed being near him, the feel of his arms, and the scent of his cologne mixed with the smell of lumber.

Chapter 27

March

"**O**h my goodness, look at you!" Linna crooned as she walked up to Noah on the back deck. He was holding Lucy, who'd been born yesterday evening. "She's so tiny." Linna looked up at him with tears of happiness in her eyes. "You were that small once, and you grew up on me."

He chuckled a little. "Go wash your hands and you can take her."

"Holly, she's just beautiful. How are you feeling?" Linna came over to give me a gentle hug.

"Good. Little sore and tired, but nothing unmanageable."

"I can't believe you had her at home. You're tougher than I could ever be." Bethany, my friend and now Moses' girlfriend, came in next for a hug. I thought I'd turned him away from her, but after everything at the wedding, they'd stayed in contact, and she moved to the Twin Cities after the new year.

"I don't know. It wasn't terrible, but I have a pretty good pain tolerance. How are you? I haven't seen you in a few weeks."

"I know. I've been working a ton. Where do you want this stuff?" She held up the bags of gifts she was holding in her hands.

"You can set it on the counter in there. I'll take care of it in a minute."

"This isn't your kid." Moses looked from Lucy to Noah. "She doesn't look like you. She's not ugly enough." He looked at me. "We want a paternity test."

"Good lord, Moses. Shut up," Bethany sighed and handed him all the bags. "Go put these on the counter."

"Yes, my lovely."

She rolled her eyes and looked at me. "I swear, he's not like this when it's just us."

I held up a shoulder. "Court jesters usually require a court."

Clara walked up to Noah and looked at Lucy. "Huh…" She looked at me. "I brought you booze."

"You mean you brought *yourself* booze?" I raised an eyebrow at her.

"It's the only way I survived you and your brother for as long as I did." She walked into the house.

"Give me that sweet pea before your mother takes her and none of us see her again." Thomas smiled as he sat down in one of the patio chairs.

Noah put Lucy in Thomas' arms and he smiled at her.

"I never thought I'd live long enough to see one of you give me grandkids." Thomas touched Lucy's cheek. "What's her name again?"

"Lucy," Noah answered.

"Make sure she's not in direct sunlight. I'm going to go inside," I told Noah quietly, then turned to go in the house. Dallas and Gabe were coming around from the garage and I didn't want to see Dallas. Bridgett had been over to the house plenty, but not Dallas. Carrie and Chris had nothing to do with me anymore, but Jess and Terri acted like nothing ever happened. Noah had invited *everyone* because he was over the moon, and I understood he wanted the people who were important to him to see her, but I still wasn't up for whatever fights were about to ensue.

"Sweetie, is there anything you need help with? Washing bottles, laundry, making food, anything?" Linna asked as I was about to go upstairs.

I smiled and shook my head. "No. Everything is taken care of."

"Let me guess, you were doing laundry and cleaning the house the second the contractions set in?" Bethany laughed.

I shrugged. "But I didn't labor long. Six hours, start to finish."

Clara laughed. "Was Noah griping at you the entire time?"

"Mm, I think he knew better."

"Smart boy." She held out a drink to me. "Come on. Pump and dump. Drink with me."

I shook my head. "Drink with Moses. When's Garrett coming?"

"He should be here in a little bit. He was finishing up with a patient."

"Hey! Party time!" Bridgett came through one of the

doors in the dining room from outside. "I brought wine. I want to hear all the gory details."

"Me too. And she's so stinkin cute!" Terri pulled the door closed. "Also, I have a thing I need you to look at. Come here." Terri took my hand and walked toward Noah's office.

"A thing?" I followed her but pulled my hand back because I didn't want to walk at her pace.

"Yes, I did a thing, and now I think it's an infected thing." She walked into Noah's office and turned around. "Close the door."

I pushed the door closed and waited as Terri lifted her shirt, exposing a tattoo of a watermelon slice, and turned around. "Jess said it just looks like it's healing, but it hurts like hell."

"Yeah, it's definitely infected. I'll call in some antibiotics for you. Where did you get this done?"

She looked over her shoulder at me with a cringe. "Mexico."

I raised my eyebrows. "Guess you won't do *that* again."

"I was super drunk. Give me a break."

"Get less drunk next time. Go upstairs in my bathroom, there's a cream in a white and blue tube, put some of that on it for now." I let her shirt down carefully, then opened the door.

"Holly, where's the corkscrew?" Bridgett called. Right as I was about to open my mouth to answer, she yelled, "Never mind, found it!"

"Oh, by the way. I talked to Carrie and she's the one who's mad, not Chris, so be careful," Terri said quietly before she passed me out of the room. "Her kids were there, and they've been having a hard time. Like nightmares and stuff."

I nodded. "Noah talked to Chris. It'll be fine." I forced a small smile. Having everyone involved wasn't going to help anything, so I was more trying to get her to move on than anything.

"Holly, do you still have the tea for Dad?" Gabe called.

"Top left, beside the stove," I called back as I shut the door to Noah's office.

"Hey, how much do you want?" Bridgett held up the wine bottle, looking at me from the island.

I shook my head. "Can't, I'm breastfeeding."

"Boo." She pouted her lip out. Carrie was standing in front of Bridgett, trying extremely hard to ignore me.

"I brought stuff for pina-coladas, I can make a virgin one for you." Bethany smiled at me as she pulled stuff out of a bag.

"I'll take you up on that." I nodded once.

"No matter how you make it, it won't be as good as Lupita's. That lady is magical." Moses stood behind Bethany and rested his chin on top of her head.

"It's Lupita's recipe. She gave it to me like four years ago." Bethany pulled out three pineapples.

"Who's Lupita?" Bridgett looked over with confusion.

"She's the princess' servant," Dallas answered with an eye-roll on his way to the fridge.

"Dallas, stop being a dick or go home." Bridgett frowned at his back.

"She was my nanny growing up. She takes care of my dad's house in California." I walked over and pulled the tea kettle off the stove before it made a hideous scream.

"You'd think with money like that, you would've been able to fight someone off. Or did you have to get permission from your brother back then?" Dallas closed the fridge and cracked open a beer.

"Uhg!" Bridgett folded half her body over the kitchen island. "Please, just let me tell him. I'm sooo tired of listening to this." She looked at me with wide eyes.

I shook my head. "Keep it to yourself."

"She's my wife. She can tell me whatever she wants." Dallas looked at Bridgett. "What?"

"She may be your wife, but I'm her client, which means she can't discuss it." I poured a cup of hot water and dropped the tea diffuser in the cup for Thomas before handing the cup to Moses. "Make sure he gives Lucy to someone else before he takes this."

"Yep."

"Because *anyone* cares what you cry about in therapy. Your brother died because of *your* stupidity. You don't need weekly sessions to figure that out." He walked toward the back door.

"I reported him, asshole!" Bethany leaned over on her hands on the counter as she turned her head to look at him. "There was tons of evidence, literally video footage of him beating her with a rock, and throwing her through the back door, but he still got out of it. Then with his fake brain cancer bullshit, no one *could* charge him even if she *had* reported him. Just because he was a crazy killer didn't mean he wasn't smart!"

"Bethany, don't waste your breath. He wants to be right, not solve a problem. It's not worth the time." I moved the blender out of the cabinet for her.

"Is that true?" Carrie asked, looking at Gabe.

Gabe was looking at me with a hard frown. "If he had

a doctor to sign off that his mental state was affected by a tumor, then yes. You tried to turn him in?"

I shook my head. "No, Bethany did. I was already gone."

"Just give them the police report, clear this up, stop making everything difficult. That's why I gave it to you. Make them eat crow." Bridgett picked herself up from the counter.

"What police report?" Dallas came back over to the island.

I rubbed my forehead, thoroughly irritated with Bridgett and Bethany. Nobody listened. "Bridgett, you do what you want. I'm not dealing with this today." I walked behind Bethany, past Dallas and went outside. Linna had Lucy, and I wanted her back. "I need to feed her real quick."

"Oh, sure. I think she's ready. She was rooting around just a minute ago." Linna held Lucy up so I could take her, then gave me the burp cloth.

"Yeah. She's pretty punctual and it's almost time." I pulled the blanket up over Lucy's head to keep the sunlight from touching her so much. Noah was over by the stairs to get down to the lawn. He was talking to Chris and Jess.

"Hey, congrats. She's cute." Chris smiled at me.

"Thanks. It's good to see you." I gave a smile back.

"Eh, well, it took some convincing. If Carrie gets crazy, don't hold it against me. I have no control over that woman."

The voices inside the house grew loud enough that they could be heard outside. I looked up at Noah and smiled. "That's for you. I'm going downstairs to feed Lucy."

Noah took in a deep breath and let it out in a huff. All three of them walked inside and I went down the stairs *outside* to enter the basement suite. I'd intentionally left the door open for such a reason. While I was downstairs, I could hear the yelling, but couldn't make out anything they were saying. I also didn't care. At some point, it wouldn't be worth it to anyone to fight over it anymore. I was just waiting for that point in time. When Dallas had found me at Brad's house and told me *I* should've been killed because people like me were more dangerous than Greg, I wasn't in any kind of mental state to fight off the verbal attack. Now, it was just kind of moot in my mind. He was a bully, just like any other, and I didn't need to give him the space in my mind.

•••••••

There was a light knock on the door, and I looked back. "Come in." Lucy was asleep on the bed in front of me.

The door opened and Garrett peeked in with a smile. "Noah said you were both down here."

I nodded. "I told him I wasn't dealing with drama today, and I didn't want Lucy around it either."

"Smart girl." He leaned over and kissed the top of my head. "Congratulations, and these are for you." Garrett laid a large bouquet of flowers in front of me.

"You didn't have to bring me anything. Thank you."

"Oh my gosh. She looks so much like you." He rubbed the side of his finger over Lucy's cheek. "Hi, sweet girl."

"You can hold her if you want. I just fed her like thirty minutes ago, so she's out." I moved the flowers to the other side of Lucy, then picked her up and handed her to Garrett.

"How are you feeling?" he asked as he flipped his tie over his shoulder.

"Good. A lot better than being pregnant."

He chuckled lightly. "I know. You looked miserable the other day. Did everything go okay? Easy delivery?"

I nodded. "Yeah. I only labored for like six hours, stayed

as active as I could until I couldn't take it anymore, then it was about an hour after that. I pulled her out, clamped the cord, cleaned her up a little, then had Noah cut the cord. It was pretty straight forward. We brought her to the pediatrician this morning, and they said everything looks good."

Garrett couldn't have wiped the smile from his face if he'd tried. "I'm so proud of you. She's beautiful."

I smiled. "Thank you."

He looked down at Lucy. "I'm going to spoil you senseless. Your mama is going to get mad at me, but I'm gonna do it anyway."

"I don't think you'll be any worse than any of her other grandparents." I laughed a little.

"Try me. I'll buy you ponies, every toy you look at, and make you all kinds of sweet treats. Then when your mom sends you home with me because you've had too much sugar, my plan will have worked. Huh?" He pulled her up a little to kiss her cheek.

"Noah's the hard-ass, not me."

"Why am I a hard-ass?"

I looked over as Noah walked in the room. "Dad is threatening to feed her a bunch of sugar and junk food."

"It's my secret plan to feed her sugar, make her difficult so you send her my way, I'll be forced into an early retirement, and watch this sweet girl while you two are at work." Garrett smiled at Noah. "You did good. She's beautiful."

Noah nodded once as he took a deep breath. "Thanks." He reached forward to rub Lucy's tiny arm. "You're being missed upstairs, little lady."

"You can bring her back up, I'm going to stay down here and finish laying the carpet."

"No."

"No, you're not."

Both Garrett and Noah spoke in unison.

"You need to take it easy and rest." Garrett had his eyebrows raised at me.

"I know my limits, and all I have to do is roll it out and tack it down. It's not—"

"No. I promise it will get done today, but I don't want you doing it. Besides, you need to come back upstairs. My mom is driving Bethany up a wall, Carrie wants to apologize, and my dad keeps asking me to come down and get you every five minutes." He held up a hand as I opened my mouth to speak. "I know. It's my fault for inviting everyone, but I got excited." Noah flashed a smile. "I couldn't help it."

My dad and I both laughed.

"Fine, but anymore drama and you're responsible for kicking everyone but our parents out." I shook my head. "You got this girl? We'll be up in a minute." I touched Lucy's arm, then looked up at Garrett.

"Of course. You'll be lucky if I don't run out the door with her." Garrett smiled lovingly at Lucy and rubbed her cheek with his finger as he left the room.

Noah looked at me after Garrett was out. "If you're going to say 'I told you so,' bite your tongue."

I shook my head and reached my arms up around his neck. "No... Hard day. I just need a hug." I let out a breath as he wrapped his arms around me. "A good day, but a hard one."

Noah kissed the side of my forehead, then kept his lips there as he asked, "What's going on?"

"Brad's not here... Everyone's upstairs, and I just feel

like... there's a hole. Not everyone is here. I know I have you, Garrett, and Clara, but I still feel like I don't have family of my own."

Noah took in a deep breath and let it out slowly. "Mm, well, the rest of us are comparatively new to your life. Brad was all you had left of your childhood, so it makes sense." He rubbed my back. "I wish there was something I could do to help you, but... unfortunately, it just kind of is what it is." He kissed my forehead again.

"I know... I'm just complaining to complain. Things are good, and I'm just trying to focus on that."

"It's not complaining... just how you feel right now."

"Yeah."

"I love you though... and you are somehow even *more* beautiful after bringing that cute little lady into the world," he smiled against the side of my forehead. "I don't know what to do with how happy I am, and I had no idea I could love you this much, *and* I'm so unbelievably thankful to have you in my life."

I smiled a little, closing my eyes and taking a deep breath.

"I also want another kid."

I laughed. "This one has only been out for about fourteen hours. We'll talk in a year or two."

"But we have six rooms to fill and we're old."

I laughed again. "Yeah. You get two max, buddy."

"I'll take it." He kissed the side of my forehead again. "Come on," he rubbed my back, "let's go upstairs."

I leaned back and let him kiss me before we went upstairs. Clara, Linna, and Garrett were in the kitchen talking, and Garrett had Lucy to his shoulder as he swayed with her.

He looked enough like my dad that for a brief moment, I could convince myself my dad was here holding her, but then the thought of taking such a moment from Garrett seemed cruel. It's not that my dad would have deserved it any less than Garrett, and I wouldn't change my childhood, but there would always be part of me that wondered what I'd missed with Garrett. He was a much gentler version of my dad, more outwardly loving and affectionate, and gave more of his time to the people he loved. At first, I didn't understand why Clara would choose Garrett, but after watching them long enough, I understood that she needed his time and attention. It's not something my dad had ever given easily, his career came first, and I could understand that too, but Garrett somehow managed to find a more beautiful balance.

"Hi, Sweetie. Can I make you a snack? The boys are only getting the grill going now." Linna looked at me with a loving smile.

"I'm okay, thank you." I stepped up beside Garrett to see Lucy's sweet face relaxed in her sleeping state.

"You're not taking her back. I haven't had her long enough." Garrett looked at me with a challenging expression.

"She needs to be changed."

He sighed and picked her up from his shoulder. "I want her back."

"I'll make sure you get her back." I took Lucy and held her up to my shoulder the way Garrett had her, in hopes of disturbing her less. She let out a small squeak mid-transfer, then quieted. "I know. It's hard to get any quiet around here, huh?"

I brought Lucy back to her room and opened her diaper.

"Holly, can I come in?" Carrie asked from out in the hall.

"Yeah." I turned my head to look as I pulled out a new diaper from the basket. "If you want to hold her, you'll have to wait until after my dad's done. I promised I'd bring her back to him."

"No. I came to talk to you... Um... I guess I owe you an apology."

I glanced back at her, shaking my head. "You don't. What Bethany did has no bearing on anything. Everyone was put in a dangerous situation that followed me here, and you or your kids could have been seriously hurt. You have every right to be upset."

"To be upset, yes, but not to blame you... With like the fire, and the brakes on your car, and stuff, I didn't know you told the police you thought it was him."

I shook my head. "I don't know why that would matter."

"Cause it kind of seemed like you never cared... like you didn't think about Noah getting hurt. Then when he was here for Thanksgiving and Christmas, you just sat there like it was all okay. I mean, Noah's a good guy, and he shouldn't have had to deal with your ex literally staying here. It's just awkward for everyone. And, you let that guy around my kids and I didn't even *know* he was a threat. Maybe you can understand it now that you're a mom, but we kind of trust our friends to tell us when there's a bad guy in the house, and you didn't say anything."

"I don't need to be a mom to understand. I thought you knew, but I understand I should've told you myself and I'm sorry." Trying to justify to her that I was trying to keep the peace and not upset my brother, or get my brother arrested, would change nothing. Honestly, I *hadn't* thought about her kids while trying to maintain the status quo. I didn't know *what* Greg would have done if I'd reacted badly. "And I'm sorry for putting you and your family in that position."

"Thank you... And I'm sorry too. I said some pretty shitty stuff before."

"Yeah, I heard that." I picked up Lucy from the changing table and turned around. "You told Janine my brother deserved what he got."

Carrie shook her head. "I didn't mean it, I was just mad and running my mouth."

I nodded, tried to think of something to say, but had nothing, so I left the room. Carrie was going to be in my life because Chris was in Noah's, and that was okay, but I didn't see much room left for a friendship. I didn't want friends who said or did things like that, even when they were angry. At least Dallas had the decency to say everything to my face, but that was the only thing I could say of him. If Noah knew what Dallas had said to me at Brad's house, that friendship would be gone. The only reason I didn't do it was because of Bridgett. Noah and I both needed her. She was too good of a friend to lose.

"Everything okay?" Garrett asked quietly as I gave Lucy back.

I smiled and nodded. "Yeah. I'll be outside." I touched his arm as I walked around him to the back door.

Noah and Moses were nowhere to be seen, it was just Bridgett, Terri, Jess, Dallas, Bethany, and Gabe. Bridgett made a pouting face at me.

"Don't worry about it," I told her as I walked up.

"I love you too much. I'm not apologizing." Bethany handed me her piña colada.

I smiled and took it. "You're also not my therapist. Is this virgin?"

"Yep."

"Holly, can we talk to you?" Dallas looked like his tail was slightly between his legs.

"No, I'm good." I clinked glasses with Bridgett.

"I want to apologize. I was being a dick."

I looked at Dallas. "Yeah, the thing is, you didn't come to it on your own. You had to be proven wrong and shown up, so I'm not interested. Like I said before, I don't need to be right. I need people who stick by me even if I make a mistake, and you're not one of those people, so that's okay. You and Noah are friends, and that has nothing to do with me other than I'm married to him. I appreciate the gesture, but I'm good."

He let out a breath. "Okay. I deserve the cold shoulder, especially after what I said at Brad's house, but I *am* sorry."

"Okay." Bridgett held up a finger. "One, you're a badass and I have crazy respect for you right now." She looked at him. "Two, Brad's house? What are you guys talking about? What did you say?" She put her hands on her hips, looking at Dallas like she was about to go off on him again. "And when did you go to Portland?"

I rolled my eyes. "Geez. Just let it go. Everyone."

"No. I want to know what the hell he said."

I handed the drink back to Bethany and held Bridgett's face in my hands. "Let. It. Go. Please. You are stirring a pot that has nothing in it."

She let out a huff. "But I want to know what he said."

"Then you can put a pillow over his face tonight until he tells you. My house is off limits to drama today. I have a cute baby who doesn't need to hear it in any capacity."

She smiled deviously. "That's right. He has to go home with me. You're a dead man walking, Hot Stuff."

"Good girl." I let my hands drop from her face, took the drink back from Bethany, and walked over to sit on the built-in bench along the rail. It was unseasonably warm outside, and I wanted to soak it up.

"What'd he say?" Bethany asked in a whisper as she sat in the corner next to me.

"Hey, is Lucy inside?" Noah called from somewhere outside.

"Yeah!" I called back.

All of a sudden there was a loud eruption of cheering, confetti cannons, and familiar faces coming from the other side of the house. I raised an eyebrow, trying to figure out what the hell was going on, and why? Calloway, Dr. Roth, four of my favorite fellow residents, and my two favorite interns were all shooting off cannon after cannon of confetti. Moses and Garrett were holding a large congratulatory banner. Apparently, Garrett wasn't inside holding Lucy like I'd thought.

"Woo!" Terri shot off yet another confetti cannon while balloons rained down from the roof of the house.

The door to the house whipped open. "Mi hija!" Lupida threw her arms up in the air as she jumped out. Her head tipped back as she yelled, "¡Lo hicisteeee! ¡Felicidadeeees!" to the sky.

I started laughing as I stood and realized exactly what this was a replication of, and *whose* idea it was.

"Hey! Congratulations on passing your orals!" Calloway tossed something at me. "Practice safe!"

I looked at the box of condoms I'd caught and was

slightly stunned, embarrassed, then shocked. "I passed?" I looked at him disbelievingly. During the last part of my orals, I'd had a serious brain freeze. It wasn't out of nerves, just pregnancy brain and I couldn't get my words out.

"What the hell do you think we're celebrating?" he chortled loudly and handed me a paper.

"Oh my gosh." I snatched the paper to look it over. Terri and Bridgett were throwing navy blue and white feather boas around my neck. "Three years before my dad!" I stomped in place excitedly. "YES! Residency can kiss my ass!" I started dancing with the girls, bumping hips with them.

"Lady, you just had a baby, take it easy," Noah laughed.

"Jealous?" I asked flirtatiously. "Because you *should* be!" I threw myself at him and he caught me with ease as he laughed. "Hi. I did it."

He couldn't stop laughing. "I know."

I leaned back a little to yell and throw my hands up, "I FRICKEN DID IT!"

Everyone was laughing as much as they were cheering.

"AND," Calloway bellowed over everyone. "Dr. Bennett, I would like to officially offer you a *new* position as a Neuro Attending at the Mayo Clinic when you return from maternity leave." He handed me an envelope, then pulled it back. "If you don't accept and you leave me, I will be done with you forever."

I bit my lip because I was trying not to outright scream. "I accept. Thank you." I took the envelope.

"You held up your end, I held up mine, Penny." He winked at me. He'd told me if I passed my orals, he'd make sure there was a position available for me in the department.

I hugged the envelope to my chest and dropped forward

into Noah, then wrapped my arms around him. "You didn't have to do all this," I whispered.

"Yes, I did…" He kissed my cheek. "Brad wasn't here to do it, and I know you two were planning a big party. Lupita made sure the details were straight, and everyone was coming for *this*. Lucy happened to be a coincidence."

I hugged him tighter. "Thank you." It meant the world to me. Brad and I always went crazy over milestones. Graduations, intern programs, residency selection, and we were going to have the same one on the day I passed my orals. It was stupid in the scale of things, but it was one of the things I was incredibly disappointed he wouldn't be here for, more than him not being here for Lucy's birth.

"You're welcome." He kissed my cheek again. "Hug your people. I need to get the meat on the grill." Noah was careful as he let me down to my feet.

"Your old man would be a sore loser, but he'd be prouder than hell." Calloway tucked me under his large arm in a partial hug.

"We'd be sending him to the burn unit if he were here," I laughed.

"Congrats, Dr. B," Dr. Roth held out two gift bags to me. "One is for your daughter, and the other is for you."

"Awe, thank you. You didn't have to get me anything." I took the bags then stepped forward to hug him.

"It's nothing. I can't wait to work alongside you as an attending." He stepped back from the hug with a kind smile. He was a short Jewish man with short coiled hair, coke bottle glasses, and the friendliest face that matched his demeanor. Others found him socially awkward, but his brain worked at a much higher level than most. For me, it only happened when I was in the OR, but for him, it was all the time.

"My gift is, I took your attending scrubs in to be embroidered." Dr. Welks, one of my favorite interns, held out another set of gift bags to me. "Calloway checked them to make sure they were done correctly."

"Oh. Thank you. That's so sweet." I hugged her briefly.

"And I'm a practical gifter, so there's a couple boxes of diapers in the house for you. They're different sizes." Dr. Ayad put his hands together and gave a small bow. "Congratulations, Dr. Bennett."

"Thank you." I smiled at him sweetly. He wasn't the hugging kind because he was from the middle east where it wasn't appropriate to hug women.

Chapter 28

While I didn't *love* having a party of people at the house with a new baby, everyone was respectful and stayed outside for the most part. Only the people making food were in the house. I was torn between wanting to entertain my guests and holding Lucy, but I kept telling myself it was temporary. Everyone would leave and I could appreciate her later. Calloway and Dr. Roth stayed, but the interns and residents left before the food was ready. Calloway held Lucy for about two minutes before he was squirming to pass her off. Dr. Roth said a blessing over Lucy in Hebrew as he held her, and it was so sweet I nearly cried.

After everyone had eaten, we all sat outside on the deck to enjoy the beautiful day and the sunshine. People had their little groups and no one was left to sit alone, not even Thomas. He and Dr. Roth found *plenty* to discuss. Clara and Linna had their little conversation. Bridgett, Carrie, Terri, and Bethany were having fun downing drinks and laughing loudly. It was just nice...

"How are you doing, Kid?" Garrett took in a deep breath as he sat down next to me. I was sitting next to Clara because she was holding Lucy and I was waiting for her to throw her at me in repulsion, but she wasn't.

"I'm good. Just waiting for mom to give up the charade." I laughed a little.

"We're scowling at people together and she has my eyes. We're just fine over here." She frowned at Lucy who had her eyes open with a slight frown of her own. "Isn't that right? You like your grumpy grandma."

Garrett and I laughed a little.

"I've got something for you. I didn't want to give it to you earlier because it wasn't appropriate." He handed a book to me, and I recognized it because he'd had it with him the same night he came to the motel to tell me who he was.

"Gray's Anatomy," I sighed lightly as I ran my hand over the cover. "My favorite bedtime story when I was a kid." I smiled at him.

"Your grandpa got your dad and I each a copy for our high school graduation. I know you probably already have *his*, but I wrote something in the back pages of this one for you on your first birthday." Garrett stared at the book as he spoke.

I looked from him to the book with a small smile as I opened to the bookmark in the back.

My dear sweet Holly,

There are so many things I want

to say to you without knowing where to begin. You were born on the Fourth of July in a storm of fireworks. It seemed so fitting for you to have such a welcome, because it matched that sparkle and awe I felt the moment you entered the world, and again when hearing your borning cry. I have never loved someone so instantly or dearly. Looking upon your precious face and seeing those wandering, tired eyes, I immediately regretted every poor decision I had made in life. Even though my choices and actions eventually led to you, I felt inherently guilty because I knew I could never amount to the father you'd need me to be. When your mother begged me to take her away from her life, I knew the best thing I could do for you was to leave you with Fran. He has a heart that could love any child, and I know that because he's loved me my whole life, through the good and bad. He's been my rock, even still, and I know he'll be the same to you, along with Brad.

I have all these dreams and wishes for you on your journey through life, and I fear mentioning them at the risk of setting the bar too high for you to achieve. It was something my parents did to me, causing me to manipulate myself in ways that ultimately caused my failures. With that said, I want you to know, no matter who you become or what you do in life, I will be proud of you. I will love you regardless of fault or flaw, and simply because you are mine. I hope you surround yourself with love. Love your job, love your family, love who you are, and the people all around you. I hope you find joy in everyday moments that would be menial to anyone else but you. I hope you follow in the Bennett tradition of becoming a doctor, but if you don't, I hope you find a career you love. I pray that when challenges come your way, you'll rise to the occasion and see your way through them with a clear mind and fairness. I hope you see that those who are unkind to you are that way because someone, somewhere, was unkind to them and they didn't learn how to cope with their pain. I hope you find that one love in life that is unfailing. I hope he sees you in all his moments and knows how incredibly blessed he is to have you in his life. Should you choose to have children of your own someday, I wish for them to

Know and cherish you as you'll surely cherish them.

I know you'll make mistakes and have shortcomings along the way, and that's alright. To wish for a life without imperfections would be a true death sentence of the soul. Our lives aren't meant to be perfect, they're meant to have beautiful flaws that teach us who we are and what we're capable of surviving. No matter what you face, please remember it's only temporary. Even if you feel you've taken a turn that has flipped your life upside down, always know that your life will have you back. It may not look the same, it may not be filled with the same people, but it will still be the same life you were born to. You will grow, you will change, and you will learn. Those who don't stay in your life were never meant to. It means their purpose and their lessons have run their course on you. Wish them well, say your goodbyes, and find the new ones that have even more to offer. There will be people all around you the rest of your life, and they're all there for a purpose.

I don't know if this letter will ever make it to you, or at what point in your life it'll reach you if it does, but know that you are unconditionally loved. My hopes for you are not a measure of your worth or flaws, they are only wishes from a father to his precious daughter. Should I ever have the chance to meet you again, I will still be in awe of the woman you have become. I will be proud of all your accomplishments and continue to love you as I always have. My darling daughter, you are the breath of my love. You changed my heart, the way I saw the world and everyone in it. You turned a blind boy into a seeing man, and I could not be more grateful for you. So, my hopes for you will be prayers to God, because it is all I can give to you until we meet again.

All my love,
Dad

I sat there for a moment, tears in my eyes, trying not to fall to pieces because all his words were so heartfelt and *needed*. "Thank you. This means... a lot more than I can say." I turned myself into his side to hug him.

Garrett wrapped his arms around me and took in another deep breath. "You can't even imagine how proud you make me... You have all these wonderful friends, a loving husband, a beautiful daughter, you're excelling in your career, everything you've gone through, seeing you persevere your way to this moment *here*... I'm proud." His voice was calm.

There were probably a thousand things I could have said, but I couldn't think of a single one except an idea I'd been holding onto for a while. "I don't know how you feel about it, but I'd like to have my birth certificate changed." I wiped a tear off my cheek and sat up to look at him. "I've been thinking about it for a while now, and I'd like to contest it and have it changed." I held up my shoulders with a weak smile. "I'm proud to be your daughter."

Garrett smiled sweetly and shook his head. "You don't need to do that. You know who you are, and that's all I've ever wanted for you."

Leave it to Garrett to give repeated blows of sweetness.

"Fran raised you, Kid. Let him have that credit." Garrett put a hand over mine and gave it a squeeze. "I'm perfectly happy to be a part of your life."

Clara leaned over. "What he *means* is, he's grateful Fran was stuck changing all the diapers. Here you go." She held Lucy out to me. "She's fully loaded, and grandmas don't change diapers."

"This grandma does," Linna said as she stood up. "Give her here."

I laughed a little. "I can get it. It doesn't bother me."

"No. You sit here and enjoy yourself." Linna carefully took Lucy. "Oh, you sweet thing. I won't ever get enough of you." She kissed Lucy's head, then reached to take the burp cloth from Clara.

"What do you say, Sweetheart?" Garrett reached a hand

behind me to Clara's shoulder. "We've got a long drive up and I'm already beat."

"No. Go home. I'm mad at you."

I looked at Clara with a raised eyebrow. "Did you gain another pound from a slice of pie?"

She looped her arm through mine, then reached over a hand to pinch my arm. "Smartass."

"No," Garrett sighed. "I wouldn't let her steal your thunder today."

I looked at him wryly. "I had a baby and passed my oral exam, I hardly think thunder could be stolen." I looked at Clara again. "What happened?"

"It doesn't matter because your father never said *yes*." There was a sneering quality in her voice.

Garrett took in a deep breath and let it out in a huff, then chuckled. "Woman, I've been asking you for years, if you don't know by now, you're more insane than we thought you were."

I shook my head. "I'm lost here. One of you just spit it out."

"I asked your lunk-head father to marry me, and all he said was, 'just wait, don't steal Holly's day,'" she quoted him sourly.

"AH!" I threw my left arm around to her, partially turning and spinning myself onto her lap as I hugged her. "Yes! I'll say it *for* him! YES!"

"Oh goddammit, Girly! You're going to break my back."

Garrett let out the most honest laugh I'd ever heard from him.

"I'm so proud of you!" I squished her with a hug, then kissed her cheek hard.

"Child! You're too much! This is exactly why I don't like kids. They slobber and hang on you like a jungle gym." She tried to push me away from her.

"I get to be your matron of honor, right? Pretty *please?*" I was intentionally being obnoxious.

"As long as you stop digging your boney, anorexic ass into my leg. Ow!"

I laughed and sat up but kept my arms around her neck loosely. "You're not making him move to Stillwater are you?"

"No," she sighed. "I'm sick of my store and all the ditsy brides demanding their stinky eucalyptus centerpieces. And I told you, I like my grandbaby. It'd be nice to not have to drive two hours to see her."

My smile held. "Free babysitter, I like it."

Clara shriveled her nose with a smile and pinched my cheek. "It's not *for* you. I'm Lucy's Ethel. Now get off my lap."

"No. I'm too happy. You have to suck it up." I hugged her again.

She laughed and hugged me back this time. "You're such a shit."

"Yeah, but you love me."

"Only a little."

"That's a *lot* for *you*," Garrett chuckled.

Clara backhanded his arm. "Shut up, lunk-head." She moved her arm back to hug me again. "I love you, Girly," she whispered. "And I'm proud of you too. Your father doesn't get to be the only one to say it."

I turned my cheek against her shoulder with a smile and just hugged her. Never in a million years did I ever think I'd have my mom in my life, or love her as much as I did. She wasn't perfect, but she came into my life just when I needed her, and that was all that was important to me.

"Everything okay over here?" Noah asked as he walked up.

"Oh, go mind your own business," Clara snapped at him. "We're having a family moment and you're ruining it."

Garrett and I both laughed.

"Which one are we calling the white coats on? They're hugging and Clara's not peeling the paint of the walls with her screams," Moses snickered.

"It *is* concerning." Garrett looked over at us.

"Shut up, all of you, or I'll put thistles in your underwear."

I smirked and sat up to look at Clara skeptically.

"Yeah, she's done it before. It's not that strange." Garrett sighed.

Clara laughed deviously.

I shook my head and got up from her lap. "I love you, but I can't understand you." I looked at Noah. "They're getting married. Mom asked him earlier."

Noah's eyebrows raised as he looked at Garrett. "My truck's got a full tank of gas if you need a runaway vehicle."

"Keep it that way. It's going to be a *long* time until the wedding."

"Oh for hell's sake. Two months. Tops." Clara looked at him with an irritated frown.

"Mm-hm. I've heard that before. A couple of times actually." Garrett sat with a small smile.

"Listen, *I* asked *you*, blockhead. That means I actually *want* to, and your tall ass didn't guilt me into it."

"Uhg. Your mouth," I sighed.

"We'll see." Garrett's demeanor stayed light and casual, but I wondered if he was really questioning her. She'd left him at the altar once, and accepted his proposal two times after, only to back out a week or two before.

"Well, congratulations, best wishes if it happens. I'm grabbing another beer." Moses started to turn.

Noah caught his arm. "No, you're not. You're getting Mom and Dad out of here so I can get everyone else out. Holly didn't get much sleep, and I didn't get *any*."

"But then I will suffer forth with thy brethren who doth detest thee. T'will be a long journey of suffrage." Moses had a cringe on his face.

Noah stared blankly at him. "Keep talking. See which brethren is worse."

Moses looked at me as he started to pout out a whimper. "*Please*. He just wants your forgiveness."

I looked at him skeptically. "For *what?*"

"Just go." Noah pushed Moses away with an irritated frown.

"For what?" I asked Noah.

He took in a breath, letting it out with a sigh. "I don't know, for being a dick. It's Gabe. There's a permanent stick up his ass. Don't worry about it." He looked at Garrett. "I assume you guys are staying, so the suite downstairs is open for you."

Garrett shook his head. "No, we're headed up. Clara's got flowers to get together for a wedding, and I've gotta get some things fixed up around Clara's house so we can put it on the market."

"If you can wait a couple days, I can drive up there and help, or I can send one of my guys up there." Noah tugged at the stubble on his face. The poor guy didn't do as well without sleep as me.

"Or, we can pack Lucy up in the morning. I'll bring her and go help Mom at the store, and you can help Dad," I suggested.

"No." Garrett shook his head. "You guys need to relax and stay home with Lucy, but I'll take you up on sending one of your guys. I'll text you a list of what needs to be done as soon as I get there and have a look around." He stood up and offered a hand to my mom.

"That works. Just let me know."

"Do you need help at the store? I could ask Bethany," I asked my mom.

"No. I've got it. That's what I pay my dimwits for. They just need someone to give them eyeballs and direction." She stepped toward me and hugged me. "Thank you though."

"Yeah. I'm sorry I can't come help, or I would."

"You're fine." She rubbed the back of my shoulder. "Take care of my grandbaby. I'll be back in a few days to hold her while I make you do everything else around here."

I laughed a little. "Deal. Thank you both for being here. It means a lot."

"Of course." Garrett handed me the book. "Wouldn't miss it."

I took the book then hugged him.

"I love you, Kid."

"I love you too... And think about what I said. I really don't mind going through the process of getting it changed."

Garrett stepped back, shaking his head. "No. Keep it the way it is. Fran's a good man, he did a lot for me, and I'm grateful to him." He pinched my chin lightly. "You just take care of yourself and that beautiful baby. No more hopping around."

I nodded.

Garrett reached out a hand to Noah and they shook hands. "Congratulations, again."

"Thank you." Noah gave a kind smile. "And to you too." He nodded once.

"Bye, Girly." Clara swatted my hair before she walked around with Garrett toward the driveway.

Noah took in a deep breath. "Now to get everyone else out. I'm so tired I can barely stand straight."

"I have a stockpile of energy right now, but once I crash, I will super crash. Thank god Lupita is here to give us a break."

"Be sparing with her. I know she has a lot of energy, but she's older than she was when you were a kid. We can't burn her out."

I shook my head. "I still have to get up for feedings, but if I can sleep in between, I'll be okay." I ran my hand through my hair. "I'm bummed though. I'm so excited about work that I don't even want my maternity leave, but I also want to be home with Lucy." I laughed a little. "I've got it all and I want it all at the same time."

Noah chuckled and pulled me in front of him with my back to him, facing everyone else that was still out on the deck. "Take it easy, Turbo... Just take it all in." He rested his chin on top of my head.

"That's all I've been doing today... I was thinking about it earlier, that time you told me to stop fighting the tides... I think I've become a sponge. I won't drown, and I can soak up everything good, then when the tide comes, it can't hurt me. I'll be too full with all the good things." I dropped my head back against his chest and closed my eyes to soak up the feeling of his arms around me.

"This is why I love you... you never stay stuck. It might take you a while to work your way through, but you do it, and it's beautiful to watch... Dallas and Carrie told me what you said to them, wanting me to talk to you, but... all I could think was, 'Good for her... She found her strength.'" Noah dropped an arm from me, reached into his pocket, then held out my old bracelet in front of me. "I think this belongs to you."

I laughed. "You know, I forgot you even took this."

"I didn't. I've been carrying it in my pocket for—what... almost two years now?"

I took the bracelet, looked at the infinity symbol and the word strength. "I can tell, it's all worn down... Funny part is, it doesn't speak to me anymore."

A bracelet with a symbol and a word was just that. There was a difference between reminding yourself of something and actually doing it. Putting in the work was hard. At first, it'd been learning to be okay when I didn't know if I would be. After that, it was small steps toward change. Learning to accept those who had good intentions, knowing the difference between a mistake that was okay to accept and one that wasn't. Then it was learning who was still standing when *I* made a mistake, and seeing who came back to help me pick up the wreckage. Once that was done, it was looking back and finding the value in all of it. Garrett's letter had said it best. My life *did* have me back, but it looked a heck of a lot different. I had the same job, but in a new place, I had new and wonderful people, I had a new and different family... But it was so thoroughly beautiful that I would have never known it was something I would want, let alone be so grateful for. I'd always wish Brad was here to enjoy this life with me, but... I believed in an afterlife, so maybe he was.

Noah took in a deep breath. "What do you say we snag Lucy, go upstairs and ditch everyone, then lay in bed and enjoy the view? These guys don't need supervision."

I smiled a little. "Let them have Lucy for now. Our alone time is going to be limited for a while."

Noah and I went inside, then upstairs to our room. The evening sun was casted on the new leaves of the trees in the backyard, and behind them, in the sky, was a backdrop of dark rain clouds that'd clearly missed us. Both of us sat on the bed, tucked up next to each other, and listened to the laughter and happiness of voices downstairs. Somehow, the sound was calming; it made me appreciate why Noah always enjoyed having a house full of people. I had an incredible and profound feeling as I lay there. For the first time in years, I felt the way I did growing up; I had everything ahead of me. I was no longer being chased by a dark cloud of things from the past... But there was something even *better*; I had everything *around* me... more than I'd ever dreamed of.

Acknowledgements

To my wonderful husband who continues to push me toward my dreams and gives me a love that inspires so many subtle pieces in all my writings. Thank you, and I love you more.

A special thank you goes to my beautiful Godmother, Kc, who has continued to be a leading example of what it means to be a good human. I couldn't be more grateful for you and that wonderful husband of yours, Charlie.

To all my Beta readers, Brittany, Tricia, Teri, Ms. Moschkau, and Kc, a very huge thank you. Another thanks to my editor Leilani. Without all your hard work and special attention to detail, this book wouldn't be what it is. Extra kudos to Brittany for all her help with the publishing process! I would've been lost without you.

My fourth grade teacher, Ms. Moschkau, deserves a most special thanks here. Teachers like her are a rare gem that shape the world. It is because of Ms. Moschkau that I found my love for reading and writing. Eight hugs a day, Ms. Moschkau... I love you, and thank you for being the wonderful educator every child hopes to have.

Finally, I owe a thanks to a couple of friends who gave me the shove I needed to pursue publishing, Stephanie and Nick. Thanks for the push!

ABOUT THE AUTHOR

Growing up between Minnesota and South Dakota, Elly
Magdaluyo kept a pen and paper close—
always ready to write. It all began from a fifth-grade English
project to write a short story
that—let's face it—was never short.
Elly fell in love with storytelling, then found she could
help others with subtle messages of empowerment in the
process. In her stories, she aspires to clear the clouded
window into the mind of a victim and the easy-to-hate
villain.

Elly currently lives in Las Vegas with her husband and two
young children. When she's not wrangling her toddlers or
writing, Elly enjoys playing the piano or finding beautiful
back roads to drive through in her beloved Volvo—with the
music turned up.

In the US, approximately twenty people are abused by their significant other nearly every minute.

If you or someone you know is experiencing domestic abuse, now is the time for help. You don't have to go it alone. Waiting or giving an abuser "one more chance," can be potentially deadly.

For free resources, please visit National Domestic Abuse Hotline:
https://www.thehotline.org/
Call: 800-799-7233 (Available 24/7)
or
Text: START to 88788

Stay safe, stay alive!